GRIMM'S LEGACY

JEFFERY H. HASKELL

aethonbooks.com

GRIMM'S LEGACY
©2025 JEFFERY H. HASKELL

This book is protected under the copyright laws of the United States of America. No part of this publication may be reproduced, stored in a retrieval system, or transmitted, in any form or by any means, without the prior permission in writing of the publisher, nor be otherwise circulated in any form of binding or cover other than that in which it is published and without a similar condition including this condition being imposed on the subsequent purchaser. Any reproduction or unauthorized use of the material or artwork contained herein is prohibited without the express written permission of the authors.

Aethon Books supports the right to free expression and the value of copyright. The purpose of copyright is to encourage writers and artists to produce the creative works that enrich our culture.

The scanning, uploading, and distribution of this book without permission is a theft of the author's intellectual property. If you would like to use material from the book (other than for review purposes), please contact editor@aethonbooks.com. Thank you for your support of the author's rights.

Aethon Books
www.aethonbooks.com

Print and eBook formatting by Kevin G. Summers. Artwork provided by Vivid Covers.

Published by Aethon Books LLC.

Aethon Books is not responsible for websites (or their content) that are not owned by the publisher.

This book is a work of fiction. Names, characters, places, and incidents are the product of the author's imagination or are used fictitiously. Any resemblance to actual events, locales, or persons, living or dead is coincidental.

All rights reserved.

Also in Series

AGAINST ALL ODDS
WITH GRIMM RESOLVE
ONE DECISIVE VICTORY
A GRIMM SACRIFICE
KNOW THY ENEMY
A GRIMM DECISION
TRADITIONS OF COURAGE
GRIMM'S LEGACY
THE LONGEST BATTLE

Calling all SciFi fans: be the first to discover groundbreaking new releases, access incredible deals, and participate in thrilling giveaways by subscribing to our exclusive SciFi Newsletter.
https://aethonbooks.com/scifi-newsletter/

Want to discuss our books with other readers and even the authors?

JOIN THE AETHON DISCORD!

For Papaito. We miss you every day.

CHARACTERS

Captain Jacob T. Grimm

Commander Kimiko Yuki (XO)

Lieutenant Commander Mark West (Ops)

Lieutenant SG Mariposa Marino (Medical)

Lieutenant SG Owusu (Nav)

Lieutenant Fionna Brennan (Nav)

Lieutenant JG Misha Gabriel (Weapons officer)

Lieutenant SG Vivienne Boudreaux (Deck officer)

Lieutenant JG Carlos Sanchez

Lieutenant Beech (Engineering)

Lieutenant Poole – Marines

Chief Suresh

Chief Tefiti

PO Mendez

PO McCall

Spacers Miller and Kolchak (engineering)

Spacer First Class Merrick (engineering)

PO Schrieber (Electronics Expert) Spacer Sebaz

Chief Pierre

Spacer Hillock (Gravity)

Marines

Lieutenant Poole

Gunnery Sergeant Jennings

Staff Sergeant Naki (1st squad)

Sergeant Owens (2nd squad)

Corporal June (1st squad asst. squad leader)

Private John Washington – Brand-new Marine

Private Derrik Samuels – Brand-new Marine

PFC Pascal

Politicians and Civilians
Mia Patel – Presidential candidate from Weber's World

Liam O'Connor – Talmage St. John's chief political advisor

President Johan Sebastion Axwell

Vice President Shuemaker

Senator Talmage St. John

Chief Petty Officer Mike Redelfs – USN, retired (cook)

Fleet Admiral Noele Villanueva

Defense Intelligence Director Charles Gradford

BB-17 – Refurbished Battleship

Greg Connor – Utopia Shipyards civilian head of engineering

Fallschirmjäger Platoon: "Sturmzug Adler" (Eagle Assault Platoon)

Leutnant Hans Weber – Platoon Leader (male)

Unteroffizier Klara Müller – Second-in-Command/

Runner (female)

THE STORY SO FAR...

Against All Odds:

After a disaster that wasn't his fault, Jacob was assigned to the USS *Interceptor*, a Hellcat-class destroyer marooned in the Zuckabar system. While there, the crew discovers a human trafficking ring that leads to the Caliphate and was facilitated by the local governor. After a vicious battle with pirates, the *Interceptor* comes out on top and the whole human trafficking ring is made public.

Notable events: A Caliphate spy base was found and destroyed. Senator St. John leads the fight to annex the four systems of the protectorate. Professor Iker Bellaits discovered the Bella wormhole, the first of its kind.

With Grimm Resolve:

Jacob and the *Interceptor* continue to patrol the Zuckabar system. During a routine customs check, they are attacked. Shortly after, they are sent to investigate a distress signal from a far away mining outpost. Upon reaching it, they discover everyone is missing. They are ambushed by mercenaries and the station was destroyed. After the crew was rescued, the ship went farther outsystem and discovered a secret stealth base and a merchant vessel. Upon contact, the vessel fired a superweapon at them and almost destroys them. From there they discover a secret starlane to a base codenamed Wonderland ran by the Terraforming Guild. *Interceptor* rescues the miners and returns to Zuckabar to defeat the Guild's secret merchant fleet.

Notable events: Nadia stops a saboteur from destroying Kremlin Station. The Guild's spying on every computer system in the galaxy was discovered, and they were kicked out of the Alliance. The Guild provided the Caliphate of Hamid with a stealth ship they then used to nuke Alexandria (The Alliance capital).

One Decisive Victory:

Wishy-washy politicians, along with the media don't want to provoke a war with the Caliphate. Despite the capital bombing they decide not to respond. Wit DeBeck arranges for Jacob to lose command, just so he can set him up to steal the *Interceptor*, go to the slave hub of Medial, raid it, and rescue as many slaves as possible. Meanwhile, he sends Nadia Dagher along to facilitate the rescue of Elsa Faust, the daughter of the Iron Emperor. The *Interceptor* travels through the wormhole for the first time and heads for Medial. Once there, they destroy the infrastructure and rescue slaves. One of Bravo 2-5, Private Cole is killed in action. Elsa is rescued by Nadia, as are all the slaves they can find. A VIP, the head of the ISB, and one of Caliph Hamid's sons are captured. Upon returning to Alliance space, Jacob is arrested and brought before the President of the Alliance, where he's awarded multiple medals and promoted.

Notable Events:

The Caliphate is discovered to have an instantaneous communications device like a space telegraph.

A Grimm Sacrifice:

Jacob and the *Interceptor* are assigned to a destroyer squadron and sent on a long-range patrol toward Caliph space. At first Jacob doesn't get along with his squadron commander. His ship is seen as too old and worthless. After a fire in the galley results in casualties, she has to remain behind to repair the ship. When she discovers a Caliph Navy light cruiser, *Interceptor* goes to war. After a fierce, but short, battle, *Interceptor*'s DAC (Diamond Anvil) is destroyed, and they have to raid the enemy ship to steal theirs.

Catching up with the rest of the squadron they discover an enemy fleet heading for Praetor and the Consortium side of the wormhole. Using clever tactics, the destroyer squadron sneak into their formation and open fire at point-blank range, disabling the enemy battleship. A long, running firefight ensues where *Interceptor* sacrifices herself so that the rest of the destroyers might escape. They buy enough time that the battle group led by USS *Enterprise* is able to intercept the enemy and defeat them.

Notable events:

Nadia discovers a hidden spy ring inside the Alliance. With the help of her onetime enemy, Daisy, she is able to stop them from freeing Hamid's son and putting a puppet in the Palisades. Stopping them costs Daisy her life, and Nadia her freedom.

Know Thy Enemy:

Alliance scientists cannot discover how the Caliph has FTLC comms. Wit DeBeck, the new SECNAV sends Nadia on a secret mission to a hidden planet where the technology came from. A planet that is caught between a dying sun and a blackhole. He sends *Interceptor* to retrieve her and the scientist who invented it.

Along the way they see how the Guild used tech to increase the range of their ships, while providing a back door to the Caliphate. Halfway there, a young ensign named Watanabe, tries to go AWOL and ends up dragging the crew into a fight on a prison planet. While some are killed, they discover one of the Caliph's daughters with a rare, uncurable genetic condition that left her blind. They rescue her and their missing crew. They continue on and find the scientific research outpost, deploy the special forces team led by Master Sergeant Danny Cannon, and end in close combat with an experimental Caliphate ship. Nadia and the SF guys destroy the nerve center of the FTLC. The *Interceptor* uses the newest point defense tech to survive CQB with the Caliphate. They take the crew of the Caliph ship prisoner (rather than leave them to die) and return home.

A Grimm Decision:

Interceptor and the crew are sent on a mission to deliver an ambassador to a planet on the edge of their territory, Cordoba, a Spanish colony that wants military aid from the Alliance and possible membership. The Guild and the Terran Republic conspire to cause a coup on the planet so they can take charge. After one of Jacob's officers is brutally murdered, he seriously considers leaving Cordoba to their fate. However, the President of Cordoba and the Alliance ambassador come to an agreement and Cordoba joins the Alliance. When the Guild sends in a purchased Republic battleship, Jacob ambushes the small fleet and does serious damage before having to depart for the outer system. Meanwhile, the Marine element that came along with them remained on Cordoba, hidden, while they wait for the right time to strike.

Traditions of Courage:

The Alliance has two options, and they can only do one. Send the fleet to Cordoba to assist *Interceptor* or send it to destroy the Guild once and for all. Jacob and the *Interceptor* remain in Cordoba and intercept the Guild's resupply missions. Meanwhile, the Marines on the planet work to find out as much as they can as to why the Guild is there. They discover the ground troops are Terran Republic and they are building an osmium mine. Osmium is used in the construction of gravcoils. The Alliance Marines stage an attack and with the help of Cordoba, manage to overthrow the Terran Republic forces. After weeks of no supplies and no messages, and all his light ships destroyed, the admiral of the Guild fleet decides to surrender to Jacob when he finds out the Guild has sent an auditor to kill him. Using their new battleship, the Alliance forces trick the second battleship and manage to destroy it.

Notable events:

Nadia undergoes genetic therapy to infiltrate the Guild. Using Danny Cannon and his team, they fly to the Guild homeworld under the guise of joining and she takes the leader of the Guild hostage. The Alliance Fleet was waiting just out of range for her to send them the intel they needed to defeat them. Once she did, the fleet came in and destroyed their Dyson Swarm energy collector, causing a chain reaction that turned the Guild homeworld into molten lava. Jacob asked Nadia to marry him at the end of the book, and she said yes.

CHAPTER ONE

Caliph Hamid walked through the vast hall with its towering pillars and gold-lined tiles. Gathered before him were his admirals and his generals, all standing shoulder to shoulder, with their seconds two meters behind them. Anger flared through him, but he wearied of taking it out on his slaves.

"General Kobul, step forward."

"Yes, my Caliph," Kobul said.

The military's complete failure to fend off the Alliance and destroy the Consortium was inexcusable. His highest officers were either attempting to hide their failures or, more likely, planning a coup. That was how he came to power—using his military contacts to corner his father.

Letting officers cement their leadership after failure was a mistake. A mistake Hamid would not make. He walked past Kobul, turned, pulled his sidearm, and shot the general at point-blank range. Plasma burned a smoking hole in the man's head. Hamid sniffed and covered his nose as the acrid smell of burned flesh filled the room.

The doors to the great hall burst open and a platoon of his elite guard marched in, plasma rifles in hand. They lined up opposite the officers and turned as one, stomping their boots to emphasize the movement.

"Raise," Hamid bellowed. The soldiers raised their weapons.

"Great Caliph—" Admiral Omar began.

"Fire," Hamid ordered. Plasma rounds exploded against his officers' corps. In seconds, the smell of burning flesh permeated the room. Massive fans in the ceiling hummed to life, sucking out the smoke and the smell.

All that remained were the secondary officers. None above the rank of captain. They dared not move. Two captains of the Navy, his nephews, caught his eye. Perhaps he could use them for two purposes—both to strike against the Alliance with such force they dare not think of interfering with his Caliphate again, and to rid himself of troublesome family members who might one day attempt to overthrow him.

"Hamza. Aziz. Step forward."

To their credit, both men stepped forward and shouted, "Yes, my Caliph."

Hamid's lips twitched in a sadistic smile. The power he wielded was unlike any other leader in the entire galaxy. Elected politicians could only dream of the force at his fingertips. Men and women lived and died by his word. "You are now my admirals. Come with me."

They followed him as he departed the hall. Just as the door closed behind them, the soldiers fired again, filling the room with the sounds of the dying, clearing out any other officers who might have thoughts of rebellion. His ships were powerful enough that he did not need experienced officers, only loyal ones.

Hamid led the newly promoted admirals to his tactical

room, where he kept his maps and projections. He ordered the two men to sit.

"I tire of this war, and I especially tire of the lack of new slaves. We control almost a hundred planets, but very few of them are sufficiently habitable for our needs. We can only use so many of our own people before we run out. The breeding programs we have under way will take decades to bear fruit. We need an influx of bodies now. This war stops that."

Hamza cleared his throat. "Sire, perhaps if we gathered our forces and attacked Medial, we could reclaim it and resume our previous arrangements."

Hamid dismissed the idea with a wave. "We've tried. Why do you think your predecessor is fertilizer. While our losses there were unfortunate, we have two more fleets we can use. I want to hit the Alliance with everything we have. Everything. This war must end." Hamid's eyes lit with a fervor that bordered on psychotic. "I want to attack them with such a force, the very fabric of space time will shudder at its arrival."

A holographic map sprang to life. Stars glittered in the rotating display. Hamid's hologram showed his regime, highlighting the hundred systems in the Perseus Arm in yellow. Next to them, taking up a much smaller area, were the many systems of the Consortium. The border planets between them were highlighted in red—except for the system known as Praetor, which glowed green, representing the importance of that location.

Across the near-empty space of the Corridor was the United Systems Alliance. While the Consortium had always conflicted with Hamid's desires, only the Alliance had embarrassed him directly. They'd stopped his plan to seize Zuckabar... twice. They killed his favorite son. And worst of all, they crippled his FTLC capability. There were also rumors that his disgraced daughter was publicly speaking against him on the border worlds. The last thing he needed was an internal rebellion.

When he thought about all of it, his blood boiled, and red clouded his vision. A soft hand touched his back, bringing him back to reality. He turned and took the hand of Lurrem, his primary concubine.

"Relax, my Caliph," she whispered.

He hadn't seen her come in but was glad she was there, and he patted her hand. Light from the hologram reflected off her silver collar. Hamid loved her, but he would never allow an uncollared woman near him. They were far too irrational to allow them freedom.

"Aziz. You're to take 7th fleet—all four battleships, and every single light unit—and strike at Praetor with the ferocity of Allah striking Iblis. You will destroy everything. Every ship, every station. When you are done, nothing living can exist in that system. You will then take your fleet into Zuckabar and do the same. No prisoners. Allahu Ackbar."

Aziz stood, raising one fist to the ceiling, eyes gleaming. "Allahu Ackbar!"

Hamid didn't miss his nephews' blanched expressions. The boys felt fear.

A moment of silence passed, and Hamza spoke up. "My Caliph. And what would you like me to do?"

Hamid smiled from ear to ear. "Hamza, while Aziz tackles Shaytan at his head, you will be striking him at his heart. You will take 3rd fleet and prepare them for the final solution. When you are done, you shall return triumphant with many millions of slaves."

―――

Wit DeBeck, President Axwell, and a dozen members of the diplomatic corps waited in the official ambassadorial council room. Axwell sat at the head of the table, Wit to his right. Despite being the SECNAV, Wit had come to be Axwell's chief advisor on military affairs. With his unique understanding of both the Navy *and* the political landscape of the galaxy, there was no one better to confer with.

Especially considering who was about to walk through the door.

Axwell's chief of security leaned down and whispered in his ear. The president looked around his table. "Ladies and gentlemen, please stand." Axwell took the lead, rising to his full height. The assorted group of cabinet members and diplomats rose as well.

Crown Prince Heinrich Faust walked through the wide doorway, two uniformed Kriegsmarines flanking him. While the escorts were unarmed, Wit recognized the two men as Heinrich's security, not advisors. They were followed by half a dozen civilian-attired diplomats and bureaucrats.

Heinrich stopped at the opposite end of the table. His steely eyes examined every face in the room until they rested on Wit. A smile spread across his face.

"Herr DeBeck, it's a pleasure to see you again." Wit had liked the young man since he'd met him years before, and was thrilled something was coming of their continued communications.

"You as well, Henry." The use of his common name shocked the prince's diplomats and even earned him a raised eyebrow from Axwell. "I wasn't sure you would remember me."

"Your modesty does you no favors with me, Herr DeBeck. Once having met, no one could forget you."

Wit gave him a slight bow and a small smile. "Prince Henry, you are too kind. How is your sister?"

"Seeing the sights, as one does in a new place. She has some friends from university she wished to see before more formal duties took her away."

Wit admired the young man's smooth excuse for his sister. He knew exactly who those friends were: the men and women who had rescued young Elsa Faust from slavery on Medial, while at the same time taking out a heavy cruiser and capturing Hamid's son.

"I'm sure she will have a grand time."

Axwell cleared his throat and gave Wit a slight nod. Time to let others in their conversation.

Prince Faust took the hint as well. "President Axwell, I am Prince Heinrich Faust. Henry, to my friends. I hope my presence here conveys my father's commitment to forging a permanent alliance with... uh, the Alliance."

"In hindsight, our founders could have come up with a better name than Alliance," Axwell said. "However, it does succinctly elucidate our nation. Please, Prince Heinrich, have a seat."

To Wit's approval, Axwell waited until the whole of the Iron Empire party sat before he himself took his seat. He had extensively briefed the president on how to handle the Iron Empire delegation.

When everyone was seated, Axwell said, "I would like to open this historic meeting by expressing to Emperor Faust our sincere gratitude for sending his most respected son, Prince Heinrich. The Alliance hopes this is the beginning of something special between our two people."

"Mr. President, I promise you my father would like nothing more than to be a military and commercial partner with the Alliance," the prince answered. "While our own nation has long strived for self-sufficiency, the recent uprising in the Terran Republic—"

Wit didn't move a centimeter at the announcement, but his mind whirled. *What uprising?*

The rest of the meeting was just as cordial, with both sides sharing at length their desire to find a new way forward.

For Wit, it dragged by. Outwardly, he seemed the attentive civil servant. Inwardly, though, his mind raced through a hundred different scenarios.

Had the downfall of the Guild triggered a coup inside the Republic? He'd heard rumors the cradle of mankind wasn't all the Republic would have them believe, but an uprising wasn't in even his most pessimistic predictions. He chafed for this formal meeting to end so he could question Henry one on one—as well as notify his own people to start collecting information about the uprising.

"I think we have achieved as much as two leaders can," Axwell said. "Let's allow our diplomats to do their job. In the meantime, I invite you to a gala we're holding at the Palisades in your honor tomorrow night. Would 1900 hours be agreeable?"

Henry stood, snapped to attention, and gave a sharp, formal bow. "1900 hours would be agreeable. May I make a request, Herr President?"

"Of course. Anything."

"Can you have one of your naval officers present? A man named..." He acted like he searched for an obscure name in his memory, but Wit saw through it. Wit knew exactly who he was talking about. "Jacob T. Grimm?"

Axwell broke into a genuine smile. "I'd be delighted to extend the invitation. *Captain* Grimm happens to be in system at the moment."

With that, the meeting came to an end. Wit couldn't extricate himself from the farewell and expressions of esteem fast enough. Once outside, he triggered his OmniPad—the one from his days as chief spymaster. He typed up a quick message and sent it out to his contacts: *Possible coup in the Terran Republic.*

He only had to wait until one of his agents could confirm. In the meantime, he had a party to attend. Henry would likely have far more information about the uprising than what he shared. It was Wit's job to get it out of him.

CHAPTER TWO

Fleet Admiral Noele Villanueva relentlessly tapped her finger against the faux wooden top of her desk. The last five years of her life were more stressful, more difficult, and certainly far more taxing than the previous sixty. Under her watch, the Navy continued to engage in irregular warfare against a numerically superior foe. Despite their victories in Praetor, Medial, and on the special warfare front, they were still trailing the war.

Since the Alliance had declared war on the Caliphate of Hamid, the Consortium had backed off their operations. She understood they had taken severe and brutal losses. Tens of thousands of their civilians were taken prisoner. They'd lost a massive shipyard and suffered a crippling blow to their economy. It was hard, though, not to feel a little betrayed by their *ally*. On paper, the Consortium Navy would support Alliance operations, but they wouldn't leave their systems to do so.

With the Republic officially severing diplomatic ties with the Alliance over the incident at Cordoba, her list of allies grew thin. Wit was convinced the Iron Empire could be persuaded to join the war on their side, but Noele had seen no evidence of it.

She leaned back, rubbing the constant ache in her neck. Their own shipyard production was going strong, especially with light units. They had proven the usefulness of their two newest battleships in the action against the Guild's home world—a thorn in her side she no longer had to worry about. It was unfortunate the Guild's own technology ended up laying waste to the planet, but she'd looked over Vice Admiral Osler's report and found she'd acted according to her orders. It wasn't quite genocide, but the loss of life was regrettable. Ultimately, though, the Guild started it; the Alliance had just been the ones to finish it.

It left her with "only" the Caliphate and Republic to worry about. She had already decided to leave battleship *Pegasus* and her battle group at Cordoba and make Osler the military commander of the sector. USS *Whirlwind* was on her way to Zuckabar to reinforce the wormhole defense. Task Force 11, including the *Alexander* and *Enterprise* battle groups, were in Praetor. USS *Ticonderoga* and her battle group were heading for Medial to support the Army's ongoing effort to secure the planet, freeing up the Marines for the coming invasion of Caliphate space.

That left her with one battleship to deploy, and a decision of where to deploy it. The planets of *Ohana* and *Seabring* were making noises about defense. If they complained loud enough, President Axwell would be forced to act—which would make her look bad and undermine her authority. She simply didn't have enough ships. If she sent their sole remaining *ready* battleship to Seabring, it would leave Alexandria without a proper defense.

That left the battleship Commander Grimm—*no*, Captain *Grimm*, she reminded herself—had brought back from Cordoba. It was still under refit and would need a crew, trials, and a shakedown before it could be assigned a battle group.

Of course, nothing in the Book says the refit must be done by the shipyard crew. Only a competent crew following established procedure, she thought.

If she could put an experienced navy crew on the ship, and then fill out the holes with whoever was left, she could technically send their sole remaining battleship, USS *Alamo*, to Seabring. She smiled at the idea. With the rivalry between Seabring and New Austin, it would kill them to have the New Austin–built battleship there.

But it was both strategically and politically sound. Timely as well, since *Alamo* had the new giga-pulse laser defense system installed and a crew trained by the man who knew how to use it best: Captain Jacob T. Grimm. She would cut the orders to send the ships where they needed to go.

Without another moment's hesitation, she typed out the orders to send the *Alamo* out within the week. Next, she sent two more orders, one to the new captain of the battleship currently being refitted, and one to Blackrock Naval Academy. Once complete, she made a list of officers and enlisted she wanted assigned to the new battleship and sent those to her assistant to process.

With her work finished, she had one more call to make.

"SECNAV DeBeck," he answered over the comms.

"Wit, I have an idea I want to run by you."

"Noele, I am all ears for you."

"Good. Because, Mon Dieu, is it a doozy."

The more she said, the more she was sure Wit thought her insane.

CHAPTER THREE

BLACKROCK NAVAL ACADEMY – OFFICER CANDIDATE SCHOOL

"For outstanding ship handling, and as the valedictorian of her class, please welcome Lieutenant Senior Grade Vivienne Boudreaux."

Viv winced at the rank—she'd spent the better part of her career as a WO flying Corsairs. She stood from her seat, took three steps forward, executed a right face, and marched to the commandant of the school. Stopping directly in front of him, she snapped to attention and issued the most professional salute she could muster. To an outsider, her movements would have seemed robotic; to her, it was simply precise.

Captain Harrington returned her salute with his own parade ground precision.

"LT Boudreaux, for your exceptional performance as the highest rated officer of your class, I offer you this letter of recommendation. Congratulations."

Her smile stretched from ear to ear, and she could barely

contain her joy. She did her best to maintain her professional demeanor. "Thank you, sir."

Ten minutes later, Boudreaux finished packing up the last of her gear in the quarters that had served as her home for the past three months. All her classmates had received their orders for where they were going next. She still awaited hers. Hefting the blue duffel bag over her shoulder and doing her best not to crinkle her dress uniform, she headed out, stopping only briefly to give her quarters one last look before closing the hatch.

The school had been her home since she'd gotten out of the hospital after Cordoba, and she'd enjoyed her time at school. The only downside was the cafeteria. PO Mendez's food had flavor and never failed to disappoint. Viv was pretty sure wherever the young man ended up, it would become a hotly sought-after assignment—for his cooking alone.

Where would she go? Paul was still on Cordoba, overseeing the rebuilding of their defenses. She'd heard a rumor that the Alliance was ramping up recruiting into the Army to have a ground force independent of the Navy. It made sense to her, since they could fit only so many Marines aboard a ship, and the ships generally needed those Marines.

She used her NavPad to hail an aircar, intending to hit the local bar. As the car landed, her NavPad beeped. The official anthem of the Navy sounded out through the little speakers.

Viv thumbed her clearance and opened the screen. As she read, her eyes grew wider with each line.

"Where to?" the aircar driver asked.

Rain began to drop on her, but she couldn't stop rereading her orders. "Spaceport, and step on it," she said with a massive smile.

Josh Mendez raised his hands, protecting his face from the two-year-old leaping from the couch to land on his head. With reflexes born of battle, he caught the little monster midair and rolled over, pinning him to the ground before mercilessly tickling him.

His nephew howled with laughter, squirming in a desperate attempt to dislodge his uncle.

"You're going to spoil him, José," Josefina admonished.

No matter how old he got, or how accomplished he was, he would always be the youngest. Josh groaned as he stood, sighing inwardly. "That's a tío's job. I spoil them"—he pulled a wrapped *Alegría* from his pocket and handed it to his sobrino, who snatched it and ran before his mama could take it away—"and I leave you with the ramifications."

"Oh, *ramifications*. Such a big word. I guess you navy types are all educated and better than us poor rice people."

Josh sighed. It was an old argument. Everyone else in his family worked at their restaurant. He was the only one who strayed, joining the Navy instead of joining them. He had intended to serve four and out. See the galaxy and then settle down... but then he ended up on the *Interceptor* and with the captain. While he hadn't told Captain Grimm, Josh intended to follow the captain to the end. Chief Redfern had clued him in on how NCOs could *convince* NAVPER to send him where he wanted, as long as their record warranted the treatment. Well, that and a case of Glenanne whiskey arriving at NAVPER on time, as promised.

"Tío, tío." His sobrino ran into the room holding Josh's NavPad.

His sister instantly frowned. "Must you?"

The little device played the official anthem of the Navy, which meant he had orders. "Sorry, Josefina, duty calls."

He excused himself to the guest room and shut the door

behind him. Opening the pad, he scrolled past the hundreds of messages between Fionna and himself, many of which were rather intense. He missed her madly, but she had to go home for her leave. Just like him, she hadn't seen her family in over a year. It wouldn't have been right to ask her to skip them and come with him.

His eyes lit up at the orders. If he hurried, he could make the 1700 shuttle to Navarro City, and from there into orbit. Mission in mind, he grabbed his navy bags, which he never unpacked, and hefted them over his shoulder.

There was one more thing he needed before he departed. Josh went to his closet, knelt, and opened the small safe tucked away in the back. Inside were important documents, extra money for emergencies, and the ring his grandfather had given his grandmother. He snatched the ring and tucked it in his pocket.

Josefina stood outside his door, scowling. "I don't want you to be hungry." She shoved one of her famous black bean burritos wrapped in foil into his hand before turning away.

It was her way, he knew. She couldn't approve of his choice to stay in the Navy, but she still loved him.

"I love you too, sis," he said.

Her steps faltered for a moment. She looked back at him and scooped up her kid and returned to the kitchen.

One day, I'm going to return to the restaurant, and they will all be very glad I stayed in the Navy.

―――

"C'mon Redfern, check or bet. It's an easy choice," Malone said.

Echo Redfern gazed past his cards, holding the steely eyed men he played with at arm's length. They weren't snot-nosed middies or naive kids, but seasoned veterans who played poker with the best of them.

Redfern's expression betrayed nothing. He might as well be made of wood. The river came up 3♣ to go with the 4♣, 6♦, 7♣, 9♦. His hand contained 5♠, 2♠. A straight. Not a straight flush but a middle of the road hand. However, he could do the math. The community cards were garbage. The most likely outcome for such a hand would be a pair, or maybe three of a kind.

Not wanting to scare his opponents from pushing the pot higher in the final round, he checked. It was a passive move, possibly telling them he didn't have confidence in his hand but not wanting to commit to folding.

The next man bet, dropping in a fifty. The third did the same. Malone, grinning like an idiot, pushed his whole pot in. "Call. Eight hundred."

Most of that money wasn't Malone's when the game started, but what he'd won during their two hours of play. The rest of the table followed suit, pushing in their entire stacks. With everyone all-in, the pot grew to well over two thousand. More than enough for Echo.

"Call," Echo said, pushing his pot in as well.

Malone laid down his cards. A pair of 9s. "Three of a kind suckers. Read 'em and weep."

The other players tossed their cards down in disgust. It really was a crappy community hand, just not for Echo.

Malone reached to take the pot, which was exactly when Redfern decided to drop his cards.

"Sorry, Malone, but a straight beats three of a kind any day of the week."

Malone froze, stunned. He was so sure he'd won. The dashed expectations turned to anger in a heartbeat. He jumped up, fists balled at his side, and the chair clattered to the floor, drawing the room's attention.

Echo leaned back, casual as could be. "Now Malone, you really want to go down that route?"

The big man looked dead into Redfern's eyes. "What if I do?"

"Then you're an idiot. It was bad luck, Malone. You've got skill in the game, but lady luck comes for us all. Sometimes you get the bear, and sometimes the bear gets you. Take a breath and move on... before someone does it for you."

Despite Malones bulk, once his anger faded, he realized Redfern wasn't a man to trifle with. No one served as an NCO in the Navy for twenty-five years without knowing how to fight.

"Right. Sorry. It was just... a lot of money." His hands relaxed, and he gingerly picked up his chair.

As Echo reached for his pot, the sound of the Navy anthem played from his NavPad. They all knew what that meant, so there could be no argument.

"Well, gentlemen, normally I'd give you the chance to earn your money back, but duty calls."

Cold rain greeted Echo as he exited the underground poker house. He could go to the casinos, but those games were rigged. He would much rather play against semi-honest low-life dirtbags than slick professionals.

He'd planned to meet Devi Suresh at the rejuve center to give her some much-needed moral support after her procedure. He was surprised she'd decided to go through with it. It was still new enough that not everyone was comfortable having their age adjusted. Checking his NavPad, he saw his orders and whistled. Unusual didn't begin to describe them. If he didn't hurry, he'd miss both Devi *and* the next shuttle.

Devi scowled in the mirror. She hardly recognized the face looking back. While she'd never considered herself beautiful, youth had a beauty all its own.

"This isn't what I wanted," she told the doctor.

"I know, Ms. Suresh, and I'm deeply sorry. The process rarely has any hiccups. We left you in longer because the computer indicated your particular genetic code was more complicated to rebuild. It doesn't happen often, but it does happen... and its part of your briefing package."

"I look fourteen," she said. Even her voice was different.

"Technically your genetic age is eighteen. As you know, the law prohibits going any younger."

She glared at him, a look that would peel paint and send spacers running. Coming from her new face, though, it looked more petulant than serious.

"I'm a chief petty officer, Doc. I can't look like I'm in middle school."

He tried to comfort her, but there wasn't anything he could say.

"In a few years you'll look more like your older self. You've gained sixty to eighty years of life and have all the vigor of the young. They used to say youth was wasted on the young, but now, with rejuve, it isn't. Focus on the positive."

Devi scowled at the doctor's use of the rejuve slogan. Even her scowl looked like a child throwing a tantrum. She'd hesitated to do the procedure, but her age was such that the Navy would move her to a desk job if she didn't turn the dial back. Well, the dial was back—to high school.

"This is some horsepucky."

Devi stormed out of the waiting room. At least she'd had the foresight to order a new, smaller uniform. No matter how well she maintained her conditioning, after almost thirty years of service, she wasn't the same size.

"Devi?"

She spun around, looking for who called her. Echo Redfern stood on the stairs behind her, his mouth agape.

"I thought you weren't going to go that—"

"Stow it, Echo. I'm not in the mood."

He wisely stowed it... mostly. When she turned around, he let out a wolf whistle. She bristled in anger, but it wasn't at him. It was her situation.

"Have you checked your NavPad?" he asked, changing the subject as he sprinted to catch up.

She pulled her NavPad, activating it with her thumb. The familiar tune of the Navy played. Her mood brightened as the new orders rolled in.

"Why, in the hell, is the Navy telling us to report to Utopia?" Devi asked.

"I don't know. My contact at NAVPER had no clue either. These orders didn't go through them."

"You got the same orders?" she asked.

"Yup. Since we both got them, I'm assuming this has something to do with the captain."

"Oh Shiva." She covered her face, pushing down the shame welling in her chest. Her feelings were overwhelming.

"What's wrong?" Echo asked.

"He's going to see me like *this*." She gestured to her young, skinny body. "How is anyone supposed to take me serious when I look like a child."

Echo laughed, long and hard. Each breath he took made her face burn brighter.

"Devi, you're the best coxswain in the fleet. The captain picked you to be the COB based on your hashmarks, not your looks. You've got nothing to worry about."

"That's easy for you to say."

CHAPTER FOUR

Morning light splashed across Pioneer Lake, four thousand meters above sea level in the Koenig mountains. The lake was a little-known spot, difficult to get to, and most of the year too cold for camping.

Little-known—except for the Grimm family who had camped there every fall when Jacob was a kid.

Dressed in warm civilian attire, Jacob cradled his guitar as the sun rose, quietly strumming a tune he only half remembered. Behind him were the two hoverbikes he and his *wife* had used to reach the faraway spot. A fire crackled next to the modest tent where Nadia still slept. He hadn't wanted to wake her. Usually, she was unable to sleep through the night, over the last four days she'd slept like a log.

Camping had that effect.

My wife.

Once he returned from Cordoba, things had moved quickly. With his new training assignment, he couldn't take leave like he wanted, so they decided to have the wedding over a four-day weekend and cajole two days of leave from training command so they could have a honeymoon.

Nadia deserved a luxurious vacation with servants and gourmet food. Unfortunately, he didn't have the time or budget for either. Bringing her to his beloved childhood spot seemed appropriate. She took to camping like a fish to water.

"Good morning, spacer. You play that thing or just use it to impress freighter captains?" she asked. Nadia slipped her hands around his chest as she settled in behind him.

He leaned back and kissed her.

"Morning." He pulled the tab on a self-heating coffee mug and handed it to her.

"You give the best presents," she whispered. Taking the mug in both hands, Nadia cooed with happiness as it heated.

"Mornings can be a bit chilly," he said.

"A bit? There's frost on the ground and steam rising from the lake where the sun's hitting it." She shook her head in amusement.

The last four days were some of the best of his life. Spending time with Nadia made him feel like he could do anything. It was quite the change from where his career was when he met her.

"Want to go swimming?" she asked.

"You were just complaining about the cold."

Nadia stood, gripping the bottom of her jacket top and pulling it over her head, revealing the nothing she wore underneath.

By the time noon rolled around, they'd packed up the campsite. Jacob hated to end it, but he needed to report back to duty. While his job on Alamo was finished, there were countless light ship crews that needed the giga-pulse laser defense system training he'd created.

Nadia tossed one toned leg over her sleek hoverbike, a far newer model than the one Jacob rode.

"Race you back to the house. Loser unpacks and does the cleaning?"

"Sure," he said as he approached his bike. Nadia grinned at him and hit the throttle. Her bike shot off like a bullet. "Cheater," he shouted behind her. He leapt onto his bike, fired up the engine, and shot after her.

The path down the mountain side curved in a hundred switchbacks leading to the valley below. Nadia leaned hard, almost going horizontal as she took each turn like the devil himself chased her.

What has gotten into that girl?

Jacob wasn't nearly as skilled a rider as his wife. A fact that didn't surprise him at all. She had more physical skills than most people he knew. She was even a competent ship's captain, not that he thought she would ever do that again. His hope for her was that she could live the quiet life she wanted. Have their children, raise them in the home his grandfather built.

Could she, though? With every passing second her lead grew as she took, to him, outrageous risks. He had to slow down on multiple corners for fear his hoverbike would careen off the cliff. It wouldn't kill him, but it certainly wouldn't be pleasant. His old bike had barely handled the climb, and he didn't want to have to push it on the way down. Gravity was already doing that.

She missed a corner, whooped in excitement, and pulled her bike hard to the side, using the hovering capability to slide sideways down the steep part of the mountain until she hit the next switchback.

Jacob just shook his head. He couldn't take a risk like that, even if he had the skills to do so. She'd already won. He gave up on competing with her, eased the throttle back, and took the trail one turn at a time.

———

As he pulled past the sign bearing his family name, Nadia was sitting cross-legged on her bike, waiting for him. The absolute joyous smile on her face made the chore he was about to do completely worth it.

"You played it safe," she said.

He parked his bike next to hers. "Always. A man's got to know his limits."

"You should try to exceed them. That's how you grow."

"I landed you, didn't I? I think I exceeded my limits quite a bit."

She laughed, unfolding from her bike with such ease it reminded Jacob how dangerous she could be if the situation called for it. "Thank you for being you." She hugged him.

"I wouldn't know how to be anyone else."

Jacob's dad came out of the house with a cup of coffee for Nadia. He didn't say a word, just handed her the fresh brew and headed for the barn.

"Your dad doesn't say much," Nadia observed.

"He likes you more than he likes me," Jacob said with a half smile.

"No, he doesn't."

Jacob held up his empty hands and pointed at the coffee she held. "You're the only one who drinks coffee."

She took a sip and sighed contently. "It's really good coffee too."

"See."

She was about to retort when the Navy anthem chimed

from Jacob's coat pocket. He looked at her with a raised eyebrow.

"I already have an assignment," he said.

"You going to answer it?"

He thumbed the NavPad open, and his body deflated. The day he'd dreaded had finally arrived.

"What's wrong?" she asked.

"They're decommissioning *Interceptor*."

CHAPTER FIVE

"Stop pulling at it," Nadia whispered to Jacob. She was wearing a long black dress that draped down from her shoulders to her shins. The fabric's deep black color was interspersed with sparkling jewels mimicking stars. Next to Jacob's 193 centimeters in his white mess dress uniform, she almost disappeared. An entire head taller than the next tallest spacer in the room, he commanded attention.

"I hate mess dress," he muttered.

To Nadia, he looked absolutely dashing—especially with all his medals pinned to his jacket. If it weren't for her years of training, she'd swoon. The hall was filled to the brim with officers and NCOs. The decommissioning ceremony for *Interceptor* attracted everyone who wanted to be involved with the ship's grand legacy. Even if they had nothing to do with her.

"Captain Grimm." Admiral Villanueva stepped up next to him.

Nadia leaned forward and glanced at the admiral's medals. She couldn't help but notice that Jacob had almost as many... *Wow, girl. Married less than a month and you're already staking out your territory.* She couldn't help it. Something about Jacob pulled at her. Before she'd met him, the idea of marriage, kids, a family wasn't in the cards. Suddenly she was planning her future, looking at furniture, and deciding she needed to take cooking classes. She shook her head in the strange turn her life had taken since Wit DeBeck asked her to covertly interview a down-on-his-luck, frocked lieutenant commander.

"Ma'am. Always a pleasure to see you," Jacob replied.

A waiter walked by with a silver tray of drinks, holding it out to both officers. Jacob held up his hand, declining the offer. Admiral Villanueva took a long-necked champagne glass and thanked the waiter.

"I'm sorry it's under these circumstances. She's a good ship."

Jacob took a deep breath to keep his nerves calm. From their position near the massive bay window, they could see his former ship, the Hellcat-class destroyer, USS *Interceptor*. The ship floated only a hundred meters from Utopia's observation hall where the ceremony was taking place.

Nadia could sense the pain radiating off her husband—pain in seeing his beloved ship about to be cast aside. Pain that he didn't get to serve one more tour.

Nothing lasted forever. However, he loved his ship, loved it like a family member. Saying goodbye to her wrenched his gut. Almost, she realized, as much as losing his mother had. Jacob had resurrected his career aboard *Interceptor*. He'd reclaimed his name and legacy aboard the ship. Now he was about to say goodbye to her.

She leaned in, slipping an arm around his waist and hugging him from the side. His muscles tensed for a moment before relaxing into her hug.

―――

"I hate to say goodbye to her, Admiral. I understand my new assignment, though, is going to last a while. Training on the new weapon systems takes precedence over command." Jacob had practiced the words countless times, hoping to say them just right to hide the loss he felt in his stomach.

"It's not goodbye, Jacob," Villanueva said. "Only farewell. She's going to Blackrock and joining the Academy fleet as a training vessel. All new cadets will learn the giga-pulse system from her. She will perform a great service."

While it filled his heart with pride, and he stood taller knowing, something in him felt wrong at losing his command. Not losing, per se, just moving on. "I understand, I just..."

Noele Villanueva put a hand on Jacob's arm. "When *Victory* went to someone else, my husband thought I'd lost my mind. Nothing replaces your first command, Jacob. Nothing. Enjoy the party. I look forward to hearing your speech."

The fleet admiral wandered off, finding more guests to speak with. Jacob glanced around the room, his stomach tightening and a bead of sweat forming at his brow.

"Nadia," he whispered.

"No one told you there would be a speech, did they?" she asked.

He shook his head. "I need a minute. Run interference for me, will you?"

Nadia gave him a delightful smile, her eyes twinkling, and he saw the spy he loved so desperately in that look. "You want them distracted, dazzled, or broken?" she asked.

"Distracted will work." Jacob pulled his NavPad and scribbled furiously on the note section. It frustrated him that there weren't any of his crew at the party. Of course, months had passed since *Interceptor* had a crew. The Navy just couldn't sit on 130 crew while they waited for a party. He'd make sure each and every one would get a copy of the speech... at least.

I should have asked how long until they needed me.

Three bells chimed, bringing the gathering to attention. A chief petty officer Jacob didn't recognize walked formally up to the large bay window. He came to attention, *Interceptor* silhouetted behind him. He was about to speak when some admiral began to cough. Only a little at first, but within seconds he was coughing so hard the entire room looked his way.

Jacob turned back to his notes, jotting down a few lines, trying not to focus on what Nadia had done to buy him a few more minutes.

When the admiral had finished, the chief began.

"Attention. All hands, now hear this. The decommissioning of the DD-1071, USS *Interceptor* begins now." He turned, took three measured steps to the bulkhead, and stopped.

Admiral Villanueva walked gracefully up onto the stage, her immaculate uniform a testimony to her career in the Navy. "Twenty-five years ago, I served aboard the heavy cruiser USS *Vulcan*. She was a fine ship. During the last battle of the Great War, she was badly damaged. The captain ordered all hands to abandon ship. As a deck officer, I'd done my best to get my people to safety. However, in doing so my suit took a hit. As I crawled to the lifeboats with my oxygen rapidly depleting, I knew for certain—I was going to die."

She paused for a moment, looking around the room, meeting virtually every eye. Jacob knew there wasn't a spacer in attendance that hadn't gone through that experience or at least had nightmares about suffocating.

"As my atmosphere ran out, a strong hand grabbed my harness and hauled me up. She pushed me down the corridor to the lifeboat and shoved me in. Master Chief Melinda Grimm saved many lives that day. I'm here because she did her duty, no matter the cost. Ultimately, the cost was her own life. However, many years later I was able to return the favor and put an unknown, if slightly tarnished"—light chuckles filled the room, including Jacob's—"young officer in command of an old, battered destroyer stationed in a backwater system no one wanted."

Memories of his time in Zuckabar flashed through his mind, whirling around like a tornado. The deaths, the victories, the defeats, all swirling in one mass.

"Lieutenant Jacob T. Grimm not only did his duty to the letter, but he also exceeded my every expectation. Because of his actions and the tough little ship we honor today, the Alliance stands in the best possible position to put an end to the war that threatens to engulf our galaxy.

"Signing the letter of decommissioning for *Interceptor* was one of the hardest decisions of my life. The best I can do is send her to service at Blackrock, where she will train, inspire, and protect the next generation of spacers."

The audience broke out in spontaneous applause. Jacob joined in for a moment. He hadn't finished with his speech, but he didn't want to disrespect the admiral by ignoring her.

"My fellow officers, it is my privilege to introduce Captain Jacob T. Grimm, the last commander of the *Interceptor*, to give the farewell address for the most decorated destroyer in Alliance history."

Applause echoed through the small room. Jacob nodded and smiled as he made his way up to the pulpit. He placed his NavPad dead center on the podium and rested his hands on either side for a moment. He saw many faces blurring into a mass. Probably a hundred people, half in white uniforms, the other half in civilian clothing. Seconds ticked by as he looked, seconds in which the audience began to shift uncomfortably. He found Nadia in back, smiling, looking on him adoringly. With a deep breath, he rested his hands by his side and began to speak.

"Honored guests, fellow officers, and friends. Today we gather not to bid farewell to an inanimate object of steel and circuitry, but to celebrate a vessel that has been our shield, our sword, and our home. The USS *Interceptor* is more than a ship—she's a testament to the valor and spirit of every man and woman who has ever served aboard her.

"For the past five years, the *Interceptor* has been my command, but she belongs to her crew. She's carried us through battles and through storms, both literal and metaphorical. Her hull has absorbed the blows meant for us, her engines have pushed us beyond what we thought was possible, and her very name has struck fear into the hearts of our adversaries.

"In her corridors, we've shared laughter and tears, victories and losses. Each deck plate bears witness to our stories, to acts of courage that will never make it into the history books but are etched deeply into the legacy of this ship. We honor today those who've given everything. Their sacrifice is the beacon that guides our resolve. We privileged few who've survived will bear these stories to our friends, our family, and our children.

"The *Interceptor* has not just been a part of our military engagements; she has been a sanctuary where bonds were forged in the fires of duty and honor. Here, we learned the true meaning of service—not just to the Navy, but to each other.

"As we decommission the last Hellcat, we do not lay her to rest. Instead, we pass her on to the next generation. At the naval academy on Blackrock, the *Interceptor* will continue her mission. She will teach. She will inspire. Future officers will walk her decks, learn her stories, and, through her, understand the weight of the uniform they aspire to wear.

"Let us remember, the *Interceptor*'s journey doesn't end here. Ships are decommissioned, but their legacy, their spirit, soar on. It exists in the hearts of those who served aboard, in the skills of the cadets she will train, and in the future missions that those officers will command.

"To the USS *Interceptor*, to her crew—past and present—thank you for your unwavering service. Here's to the honor you've upheld, the courage you've shown, and the sacrifices you've made. May these walls continue to echo with the principles of naval tradition. Duty. Honor. Courage.

"May the *Interceptor*'s legacy guide us, as she moves from the frontline of battle to the forefront of education.

"Fair winds and following seas, *Interceptor*. Your watch may end, but your watchword echoes. 'First to Fight.' Here's to the next chapter in your storied life. Thank you."

Dead silence followed his words. His nerves had vanished while he spoke, but when he finished, he briefly wondered if he had said too much.

Nadia's smile lit the room for him, her wet eyes on the brink of tears. At the moment he made eye contact with her, he had no doubt he'd spoken well.

Applause rippled through the hall. Vigorous clapping and shouts of praise.

The chief petty officer behind him yelled, "Three cheers for the *Interceptor*. Hip, hip, hooray!" What followed was a moment Jacob would cherish for the rest of his life. He turned to watch his home, his love, his very redemption, flash her lights one last time before going dark. Her legacy would live on.

CHAPTER SIX

Gunny Jennings hefted her bag up the gangplank to her new home. Try as she might, she couldn't get Marine Corps Manpower and Reserve Affairs to station her with the captain. In her contact's defense, there just wasn't a call for a naval captain on a training assignment to have a gunnery sergeant attached to him.

Mendez probably figured out a way, she thought.

At the entrance to the ship, she held up her NavPad. The Marines on duty gave her Service A uniform a once-over. It wasn't her favorite—she preferred the grey and black combat uniform. Though she had to admit, in the blue dress uniform with all its gold buttons and shiny medals, she cut quite a figure. The marine ogled at the numerous medals for combat displayed on her chest.

"Gunnery Sergeant Allison Jennings reporting for duty."

The two Marines, a pair of PFCs, snapped to attention. "Yes, Gunny," they said in unison. "Lieutenant Poole is in his office on Deck 2, frame 25, port side, Gunny." He scanned her NavPad, ensuring she was in fact Gunnery Sergeant Jennings before allowing her to pass.

She liked that they took their post seriously. Too many Marines, especially PFCs, had a tendency for familiarity that impeded their duty. As if nothing could happen to the ship as long as it was docked, so why bother?

She stopped inside, taking a deep breath. While she'd seen the inside of a battleship before, they were Alliance-built. This currently unnamed monstrosity was built by the Republic. Her lines were... wrong. Off. She decided it wasn't for her. Luckily, assignments didn't usually last that long, and she would be transferred as soon as the captain finished his training assignment and had a real ship again.

The gangplank led to deck three, where Jennings had to stop and get her bearings. The ship was massive, bigger than any she'd served on. Nine decks went from the keel gravcoil to the bridge. Unlike *Interceptor*, the bridge was amidship... not that she expected to go there often. When it was all said and done, there would be twenty or more Marines aboard. She would be one of many. A platoon gunnery sergeant, no more. As much as she had balked at her promotion, she'd grown use to command.

Also unlike *Interceptor*, she was forced to take the lifts. Aboard the smaller ships, the lifts were reserved for wounded or guests. Never for Marines who were able-bodied and could walk or run where they needed to go. She couldn't shake an uncomfortable gnawing in her gut as she rode the lift. It moved swiftly, whizzing her to frame twenty and depositing her on the port side.

The passageway's dull grey bulkheads all blended together. Every frame was stenciled with a number indicating the deck, frame, ship's side, and use. In the case of Lieutenant Poole's office, the designator was 2-25-2-O.

She found it quickly enough, then paused to put her bag down and move to attention before wrapping her bare knuckles on the hatch three times—as hard as her McGregor's World strength would allow.

The hatch slid open, revealing a tight compartment with a desk built into the bulkhead. Lieutenant Poole hunched over his desk, fitting neatly into the small space. She decided he wasn't much taller than her, and that worried her. She marched in, stopping two paces from his chair. Snapping to attention, she brought her hand up in a parade ground salute.

"Gunnery Sergeant Allison Jennings, reporting as ordered, sir."

Poole looked up at her for a moment before giving her a lazy salute. "Stand at ease, Gunnery Sergeant."

She dropped into at ease and waited. Looking back at his own NavPad, he typed a few words. "Gunnery Sergeant, huh? For two years now? That's a little young for the rank, don't you think?"

Jennings wasn't sure if he was asking or telling, so she decided to err on the side of caution and say nothing. He continued to scroll through his NavPad, looking at her jacket. She could tell he saw her awards section when his eyes widened.

He looked up at her uniform, narrowing his vision on the salad displayed across her chest. "I see you've seen some action," Poole said.

"Aye, sir."

"I have yet the privilege of combat, Gunnery Sergeant."

Jennings kept her mouth shut. There wasn't anything to say.

"We have just fourth platoon aboard this ship. B company, 3rd Battalion, 6th Marines. Our primary three platoons came whole cloth from other units, and they will be reporting to their respective ships. Fourth platoon are stragglers. Individuals brought from disparate units. No other sergeants or platoon leader yet. I need them whipped into shape. Understood?"

"Oorah, sir."

Poole frowned at her use of the battle cry. "In my unit, Gunnery Sergeant, you will say 'yes sir' or 'no sir,' and nothing else. We're not some gang of thugs grunting our replies."

Jennings clenched her jaw. She liked to think she knew exactly what the Corps was. "Yes, sir."

He frowned again.

"Yes, sir, what?"

She blinked. Was he serious? "Yes, sir. I will."

His frown lingered, but when she didn't offer anything else he continued. "Good. I'm not going to have a problem with you, Gunny? I know your previous commander's reputation, and I don't want that kind of familiarity in my command."

"No, sir."

He nodded. "Good. Dismissed."

Jennings picked up her bag, came to attention, performed a perfect about-face and marched out of the office. She'd spent too much time in charge of her own unit. Taking orders from officers with no practical experience rubbed her the wrong way.

Halfway down the corridor, a familiar face turned the corner and almost collided with her.

"Ma'am?" Jennings said, shocked.

Commander Kimiko Yuki looked up from her NavPad with a smile on her face.

"Jennings!" Yuki leaned forward and embraced the Marine in a hug before she could object.

"I didn't know you were here, ma'am."

"I didn't either until this morning. I already miss *Apache*, but I can't say no to an XO billet on a *battleship*. Is all of Bravo-Two-Five here?"

Jennings, while happy to see a friendly face, also needed to find her bunk. "No, ma'am. At least, not as far as I know."

Yuki looked like she wanted to say more. "It's good to know you're aboard, Gunny. No one I would rather have at my back."

Jennings cracked a rare grin. "Nice one, ma'am." She slipped past the officer, remembering the incident on the freighter where then-Lieutenant Yuki almost turned into a burnt marshmallow. Jennings refocused on finding her bunk and changing uniforms before she met her Marines.

———

Lieutenant JG Misha Gabriel looked up the gangplank as his mind wrapped around what was happening. Only one tour out of the academy and the Navy had him assigned to the newest battleship. Even if it was as a trial run, they wouldn't hand a ship to a crew they didn't trust. A ship with only a naval construction contract number, not even a real name yet.

"Can we help you, sir?" A Marine PFC said from the top of the gangplank.

"Uh, yes. Sorry." Misha fumbled for his NavPad as he started up the ramp. It was a little steeper than his last command; he didn't know why. Once at the top, he finally managed to pull out his orders.

PFC McClaren took his NavPad and ran his orders. Both Marines snapped to attention at the same time. "Welcome aboard, sir."

"Thank you, uh, private…"

"PFC, sir. That's okay. It's a weird rank." McClaren gave him a sympathetic smile.

Part of Misha hated his rank. Officers were supposed to be imperious, perfect, and indefatigable. He always felt like a kid playing with his parents' stuff. "Can you tell me how to get to the officer's quarters?"

"Certainly, sir." McClaren programmed in the route to his rack. Misha made a mental note to thank the Marine in a more substantial way in the future, and hefted his bag, careful not to crease his dress blue jacket. Once positioned, he entered the ship.

He'd read up on her. It was a weird amalgamation of Republic and Alliance technology. According to the manuals he'd read on the trip from Blackrock, most of the systems had been replaced with Alliance tech. The only thing left that was Republic were the engines—which would have required more than a six-month refit to replace.

He wished they could have kept the Republic weapons technology, but he understood the reasoning. How could anyone ever trust it? All the turrets were replaced, the torpedo launchers, and even the main guns were ripped out in exchange for Alliance coil tech.

The more he thought about it, the more he marveled at how much they achieved in six months. Engineers and yard dogs must have worked overtime to get it done. He took the first lift to deck three, officer quarters, and ran smack into a pack of wrench monkeys with the bulkheads pulled off, elbow deep in the ship's guts.

I guess they're not quite done.

He scooted his way past them, giving a nod to the senior chief, a tall, dark-haired man with a whip thin frame and vaguely red-tinted skin. Etiquette dictated a work party should not stop to acknowledge his presence. Once past them, he found his cabin: two bunks fit against the bulkhead, with a small work area next to them for whoever wasn't on duty to get through paperwork. The head was right next to the door. It wasn't huge, but it was better than the four-man bunk he had on his last deployment.

"Anyone here?" he asked. No answer. *First come, first served.* He tossed his bag onto the top bunk and started unbuttoning his dress uniform, eager to get into a ship uniform. "What if the captain wants his officers in dress whites all the time?" Misha groaned.

"You don't have to worry about that, Lieutenant," a voice said from behind.

Misha turned to see a man of average height, with close cropped blond hair and sharp eyes. His dress whites were immaculate. Lieutenant commander's insignia adorned his uniform, along with a healthy number of ribbons for a man who couldn't be but a few years older than Misha.

Misha shook himself from shock and snapped to attention.

"Officer on deck," he said out of habit.

"As you were," the man said as he held up his own bag. "We're bunk mates." He held out his hand. "Mark West."

"Uh, Misha Gabriel."

They shook, and Misha felt West sizing him up. The senior officer glanced at the bunk. "You were here first, you sure you want the top bunk?"

"Yes, sir, I would appreciate it."

"Listen, Misha, while we're in here and it's just us. Mark is fine. In this sacred chapel we're bunk mates, not senior and junior officers. Okay?"

The young lieutenant cleared his throat before answering. "Yes, sir—Mark. That feels weird."

Mark gave him a genuine smile and a clap on the back. "Get used to it. Now, one more thing. What we say in here, stays in here. I'm the Ops officer, and the last thing I need is to worry about the grapevine. Understood?"

"Yes, of course. And if I sometimes bitch about my fellow crew, I hope you will do the same."

"Oh, hell no. I'll write everything down and run it up the mast."

Misha froze, his heart pounding in his ears.

Mark laughed. "Of course. Privacy goes both ways."

"You had me, Mark."

―――

Lieutenant Boudreaux stood over her boat bay in amazement. Two massive doors curved along opposite sides of the hull. If both were open, a ship could fly straight through the battleship. Four Corsairs were parked alongside six Marine combat-outfitted Mudcats.

She let out a low whistle. Someone at NAVPER loved her. She thought her flying days were over. Here she was, the officer of the deck in charge of the Corsairs and everything that flew or drove aboard her new ship. Its lack of a name bothered her. Just a number, *BB-17*.

Her orders had specified they were crewing her for the ship's trials. Which could take months. They had to test her space worthiness, engines, weapons, damage control... the list went on. She'd done it with Corsairs brand-new out of the box, but never with an entire retrofitted ship from a foreign power.

"She's a big bay, ma'am." A familiar voice said from behind.

Viv turned to see PO Stawarski. Strike that, Chief Petty Officer Stawarski.

"You made chief? Congrats!" she said with genuine enthusiasm.

"Thank you, ma'am. I see you nailed officer school." He gestured to her rank. Most of the officers rolling out of officer school made JG at best. She was senior grade.

"Well, I had a lot of prior service to make up for. This is some boat bay. Have you met the crews?"

"Not yet. There's only about 300 personnel aboard at the moment. They're trickling on as NAVPER gets them here. I've seen a couple of lists and was surprised so many of our shipmates were aboard."

Viv frowned as she realized it was strange to run into someone she knew. The Alliance Navy had hundreds of thousands of spacers in it. What were the odds her boat bay chief would be a spacer she'd served with? "What do you think that means?" she asked.

"I wish I knew, ma'am. We waffle between recognized for our skills and being shunned for our association with... you know."

Viv did indeed know. More than one officer in her six-month course candidate school had muttered about Jacob T. Grimm. Like Chief Redfern, Vivienne Boudreaux was no stranger to back channels. She knew the captain made enemies—more than he realized.

"Regardless, it's good to see you again. Now we've got a job to do. Let's get it done."

"Aye, aye ma'am!"

CHAPTER SEVEN

"Out of the fire and into the frying pan," Jacob muttered.

"Come now, it's not all that bad," Nadia said.

Jacob looked at her like she'd grown a second head. "Let's see. Yesterday we bore witness to my ship, *Interceptor*, losing her commission to go teach some snot-nosed cadets how to fly. On my way to the office, I receive notice of a formal dinner at"—he held up his NavPad as if he needed a reminder, and Nadia broke out into a giggle—"right. The Palisades. You know, where the president lives." He tossed the NavPad on the bed.

"Jacob, hon, I've attended a million of these things. You go in, you nod, you smile, and once you've hit your third drink, it all blurs together."

"Is that why people drink?"

"Oh, right. I forgot." Her smile clearly indicated she hadn't forgotten. "Oops. I guess you'll just have to suffer."

He closed his eyes. "Why did I marry you again?"

"Because I'm the most beautiful woman you've ever seen."

"Can't be that. Has to be your personality."

The pillow hit him square in the head.

An hour later, they walked arm in arm to the security checkpoint leading into the Palisades grand ballroom. An armed Capitol police officer checked their identity before letting them in.

Jacob stopped in awe of the tremendous decorations. The official Army band played stringed music that seeped over the room like a soft blanket. Vaulted skylights showing the constellations of the Alliance gave the effect of a ceiling reaching for the stars. It lit the room in uneven but lovely blue light. Clearly some kind of holographic technology enhanced the shining stars.

"Keep moving, my love," Nadia murmured.

"Right." While he'd attended several official Navy dinners, the grand ballroom was something else. A whole other level of class and sophistication.

Nadia leaned in close to him, filling his nose with her delightful scent and grounding him in the moment. "Do you know anyone here?" she asked.

He surreptitiously looked around the room for familiar faces. There were more people in uniform than not, but he found no one he recognized. Circular tables with blue and gold tablecloths were set up in one corner of the ballroom. The majority of the space was taken up by a dance floor where several couples gently glided through a traditional waltz.

On the far end of the room was the second most popular location: the open bar. Jacob smiled at the gaggle of Marine uniforms around the free drinks. *Of course. They're probably the only ones having fun.* "No. Not that I can see. I'm sure your old boss is here—"

Nadia shuddered when he mentioned Wit.

"Everything okay?" he asked. Nadia didn't give away emotions easy, he knew that.

"I've ignored several messages from him. I don't want to talk to him, not after... not after last time."

Jacob took what she said in stride. He didn't know the details, couldn't know them, but he figured whatever happened had to be traumatic. Even after he returned from Cordoba, she had remained hospitalized for over a week. When he tried to talk to her about it, she shushed him and hugged him tight. He'd never seen her so fragile and needy.

She hadn't left his side since. He'd be lying to himself if he said it didn't trigger his protective instincts.

"I'm going to go find us some drinks." She broke free and glided across the room.

His heart thumped hard as he watched her go.

"That is a look of a man in love," Archer Ban said.

He was delighted to hear his old friend's voice.

"Archer, you son of a gun." Jacob clasped the man's hand and leaned in for hug.

"How are you, *Captain*," Archer said with a nod to the silver rank insignia contrasted on the white epaulets. "I should have known you'd find a way to outrank me."

Jacob's friend cut quite the figure. Archer had the kind of easy good looks the girls in the academy always loved. If his career in the Navy hadn't worked out, he could have been a vid star.

"You're not doing so bad yourself, *Commander*," Jacob said. While his own uniform bore the insignia of Education and Training Command, Archer's had his ship's insignia. "USS *Tsunami*..." He let out a whistle. *Tsunami* was the latest and most powerful heavy cruiser in the navy. "Not bad my friend."

"Some damn fool must have recommended me for the job. I can't imagine who that was."

"Don't look at me. If NAVPER asked, I would have told them to put you on a barge."

Nadia returned, holding two drinks. "Jacob, who's your dashing friend?"

"Nadia, this is my oldest friend, Commander Archer Ban."

Archer took on a formal countenance and bowed. "It's a pleasure to meet you, ma'am. My apologies for not attending your wedding. I did receive the invitation, but I was at the yard, taking command of my new ship. Had I known he was marrying such a stunning woman, I would have absolutely stood up and demanded a chance to woo you away from him."

She gave him a dazzling smile and handed him one of the drinks. "I don't miss 'needs of the service' excuses, that's for sure."

Archer raised an eyebrow. "Jacob didn't tell me you served?" He carefully sipped his drink. Upon tasting the beverage, his face lit up in appreciation.

"Chief Petty Officer (Ret.), Nadia Grimm, Fleet Logistics."

Jacob's heart swelled with pride at hearing her use his name. He pulled her tight, resting his hand on her generous hip.

"What brings you to the party? Other than your goofy-looking face?" Jacob asked.

Archer feigned hurt. "As a matter of fact, *Tsunami* is assigned to a new task force forming here."

Jacob couldn't have been happier for his friend. "Archer, that's fantastic. Being part of *Alexander*'s battle group is prestigious as heck."

Archer looked around the room for a moment. He stepped a little closer to be heard and keep his words from straying too far. "*Alexander* is still in Praetor. My orders didn't specify which battle group we're assigned to. Which leaves me wondering if we have a new flagship taking the position of defender of the capitol."

Scuttlebutt had missed the mark big on the comings and goings in the system. Jacob hadn't heard a whisper of a new battleship. Then again, he was elbow deep in training crews with the giga-pulse systems. Hell. Between the training, wedding, and abbreviated honeymoon, not to mention decommissioning of *Interceptor*, he didn't know if he'd even had time to stay up on rumors.

"That's exciting. I hadn't heard."

Archer cocked an eye at him as if he didn't believe what Jacob said. He clapped his friend on the shoulder and nodded his chin in the direction of the dance floor. A pretty blonde civilian, obviously bored by the conversation around her stood by herself.

"If you'll excuse me, I was never one to let a beautiful woman feel ignored." Archer walked toward his target, every inch the dashing Navy officer.

"He's quite the character," Nadia said.

"Who? Archer? Oh yeah. He's always had buckets of charisma."

She slid her hand into his and squeezed. "Not as much as you."

"Ha. Please. Archer could sell sand on Ohana and turn a profit. I've never met anyone with more natural affinity for making people feel at ease than him."

Archer walked up and spoke to the young woman. After a moment, she took his hand and let him lead her to the dance floor.

"True. But I've never met anyone who can give a room full of strangers goosebumps with a speech about a ship none of them ever served on."

"Touché."

The band stopped playing, causing everyone to turn their attention to the stage. President Axwell ascended the stairs and stood at the microphone.

"Ladies and gentlemen, thank you for coming to our

welcome gala. I could give some big speech, but since I'm not running for reelection, I don't see the point." Light laughter echoed through the crowd. "We're here to welcome Crown Prince Heinrich Faust of the Iron Empire."

Applause broke out, including from Jacob. He was more than happy to have whatever help they could in the war effort. With the Republic seemingly abandoning them, having the IE and their impressive fleet join would be welcome.

After the clapping died down, Axwell continued. "A few years ago, members of our esteemed Navy were able to assist the Iron Empire with a problem. Since that day we've worked to solidify our relationship. Today, I'm proud to announce the Iron Empire will allow an Alliance embassy to open on their home world, and..." He paused for a moment. "...joint naval training with their current ships in our system."

Jacob heard the president, but his mind was far afield. What great service had the Navy helped with? He looked to his chest and the gold cross hanging off the black and gold ribbon: the Badge of Honor of the Bundeswehr.

The raid on Medial? But... what could they have had to do with it?

Nadia gave nothing away as he examined her. She was neither stiff nor too loose. Her face didn't twitch. She simply smiled at the president's words and clapped when required. *She really is an amazing spy. A computer couldn't read that woman.*

"I know your answer is likely going to be something along the lines of 'I have no idea,' but do you know what he's talking about?" Jacob asked.

She looked up at him, a twinkle in her gorgeous brown eyes. "I have no idea," she said. Her eyes, though, flicked to the medal on his chest. "You might ask the prince, though, since he's the reason you're here."

Jacob's attention shifted back to the president as he pointed into the crowd. A light flared to life, softly illuminating Heinrich. He was of average height with the standard black Imperial Navy uniform. Silver buttons gleamed down either side. It all contrasted mightily with the mainly white Alliance uniforms. Half a dozen similarly attired IE spacers were scattered through the crowd.

A tall, lithe blonde woman in a striking red dress broke from the crowd of IE navy, clearly walking his way. He frowned. He'd never seen her before—he was sure he'd remember such a beautiful woman. Her tanned skin contrasted with her almost white, blonde hair.

Nadia suddenly broke away from him. "Elsa," she practically squealed. Managing, somehow, to be both excited and quiet at the same time.

President Axwell resumed speaking, but Jacob couldn't give him the full attention his commander-in-chief deserved. Nadia, holding Elsa's hand, dragged her over. Jacob was almost always taller than everyone around him. He'd only met a handful of men who exceeded his 193 centimeters. In her red high heels, Elsa towered over Nadia and looked him directly in the eyes.

"Nadia! You never told me how handsome your man is."

He wasn't sure if he was supposed to hear that or not but couldn't stop himself from reacting; his heart thumped, and blood rushed to his face. He was never going to grow accustomed to compliments from women.

"As if I would settle for a man who wasn't heroic *and* handsome," Nadia said. "Jacob, this is Princess Elsa Faust."

Elsa held out her hand. Jacob took it, bowed, and lightly brushed his lips across her knuckles. "It is an honor to meet you, Princess Faust."

Nadia giggled with excitement.

"The pleasure is all mine, *Herr Captain*."

Jacob released her hand. "How did you two meet?" he asked nonchalantly.

Without missing a beat, "Dear Nadia allowed me to hitch a ride on her ship after I was accidently dropped off on the wrong planet. We've kept in touch ever since. Though this is my first time to visit her—with the long transit times it can be difficult to get this way."

Jacob's experience told him she wasn't *quite* lying. Obfuscating, yes. Perhaps approaching the truth at an oblique angle. But not outright lying. He didn't miss the mischievous grin the two gave one another when they thought he wasn't looking.

A word from the president caught his attention just in time to see President Axwell gesture to Heinrich. More applause, and Jacob decided it was a good time to focus on the social occasion. After a few minutes, the president finished speaking and the large ballroom doors slid open to reveal the East Lawns veranda that stretched out to the ocean. Lights decorated wooden posts, making them all look like masts from ancient sea faring vessels.

"Let's go enjoy the night air," Nadia said. She took Jacob's hand, and to his surprise, Elsa took the other, and they walked toward the sea.

He leaned down to his wife. "What's gotten into you?"

She gave him a wicked smile. "With any luck—"

"Don't finish that sentence. I'm in uniform."

Outside, Nadia found a table with a gorgeous ocean view. The temperature perfectly enhanced the night—not too hot or cold, with a light breeze bringing the smell of salt off the water.

More and more people arrived; ambassadors, civilian workers, and even celebrities. Jacob spotted an actor he'd seen in a vid the year prior.

"Is that Georgia Saint?" Elsa asked. She indicated a young woman with dark hair and skin that was only a shade lighter.

"I think so," Nadia said. "Let's go introduce ourselves."

"I couldn't," Elsa said.

Nadia had a look Jacob knew well.

"Elsa, you're a frigging princess. What good is that if you can't go say *hi* to a famous singer you admire?"

Convinced, Elsa agreed to chase down the entertainer they both seemed to like. While Jacob considered himself a musician, it was mostly with his guitar and folk songs. He didn't exactly follow popular music.

A strong voice broke him out of his thoughts. "Is this seat taken, *Herr Grimm*?"

Prince Heinrich Faust stood above him, drink in hand.

"Your Highness," Jacob said. He rose and gave the prince a semiformal bow. "Not at all. Take any seat you like."

"Please, Henry will do just fine." Sipping his drink, he watched his sister and said nothing as he sat.

"I was hoping I'd have a moment to speak with you," Jacob said.

"Oh?"

He unclipped the golden star for his uniform and placed it on the table between them. "I received this without any explanation. Just a note that said, 'From a grateful nation.' I had to look it up to know what the star meant."

Henry picked up the golden cross. "Know this, Herr Grimm—"

"Jacob is more than fine."

"Jacob. So you know, I'm not bound by secrecy. You saved my sister's life on Medial. Pirates had taken and sold her to the slavers there. Your actions led to her escape."

Leaning back, Jacob let out a whistle. His mind reeled at the revelation.

"Wow. I had no idea, Henry. We freed a lot of prisoners that day. Though we suffered losses, I know those who didn't make it back were proud of the work we did."

Henry placed the medal carefully on Jacob's chest, next to the many others he wore.

"You're no stranger to combat, Jacob. As anyone can see. You have a noble spirit as well. That is a rare combination."

Whatever Henry meant, Jacob didn't have time to ponder. Motion caught his eye as four men in IE uniforms, arm's length apart, moving through the crowd.

"How many men did you bring to the party tonight?"

Henry frowned at the non sequitur but answered all the same. "Myself, Elsa, and four others; they're over there by your president."

Jacob was up and moving before he even realized what he was doing.

CHAPTER EIGHT

Nadia was incapable of suppressing her awareness of the events around her. She wished she could. Her therapist called it PTSD in the form of hyper-vigilance. Simple tasks for anyone else were complicated for her. Walking into a store, driving her aircar, even cuddling on the couch with Jacob—they all became exercises in anxiety management. Where were the exits? Where was her nearest weapon? Was there cover from the windows or just concealment?

Jacob's sudden movement triggered her awareness, and she turned to see him charge—full on, like a linebacker—across the veranda. Prince Henry followed three steps behind him. Her body kicked in before her brain registered the events, and she discarded her heels and ran just as hard after them.

With Prince Henry right behind him, Jacob plowed through the crowd. Nadia spotted their targets: four men dressed as Imperial Navy, beelining for the president. Jacob pushed a guest aside, and the man yelped, alerting the four assailants.

They turned, pulling their jackets aside and revealing long blades that reflected light like a pond covered in scum.

Poison. They have poisoned blades.

Nadia's mind whirled through a dozen reasons they were using blades. Range weapons would be too difficult to smuggle in. The Palisade's air defense was second to none, and after what the Guild and Caliphate did, multiple light cruisers were in geosynchronous orbit ready to defend against orbital bombardment whenever the president was on planet.

All of this flashed through her mind as it swirled to the only possible explanation: assassins. While Nadia's training in hand-to-hand was world-class, her body's lack of muscle mass related to a comparable sized man put her at a disadvantage. Or it would, if it weren't for her cybernetic arm.

Her petite size allowed her to slip between guests, and she actually reached the men at the same time as Jacob. Leaping in front of him, she held up her cybernetic arm as the assassin struck.

Globs of a green viscous goo splashed against her dress. Jacob's strong hands latched on to her shoulders and heaved her back. With the blade embedded in her arm, the sword jerked out of the assassin's hand as she fell back.

She barely had time to register the stunned look on her assailant's face before Jacob shoulder-checked him into his partner. Nadia caught her fall, careful to keep the imbedded blade away from her flesh. Her vision wobbled. Trying to stand, her legs gave out. A man was there, holding her real arm, attempting to help. The more she tried, though, the more her vision swam, and darkness encroached.

Jacob recovered from the blow, backing up the way Jennings had trained him, keeping his hands up. If Nadia hadn't warned him about the poison, he'd be dead. The man he shoulder-checked wasn't getting back up, but there were still three remaining.

Henry went after one, charging right in. Ducking the swing of the sword, he grabbed the man's wrist and broke it with one smooth motion. To the assassin's credit, he made no sound; he simply dropped the sword and lashed out with his free hand.

One of the remaining men, enough like the others that Jacob doubted he could tell them apart, took off in a dead run for the president.

Alliance Presidential Protection Services already had the president in a huddle, dragging him to the exit. There were too many civilians in the crowd for them to shoot indiscriminately, but Jacob knew they would if the threat became imminent.

Archer Ban stood next to the outdoor bar. "Archer!" Jacob shouted and pointed.

Archer grabbed a bottle of champaign and charged after the man heading for the president, leaving the final assassin for Jacob to handle.

Leading with his blade, the assassin charged. Thankfully, the crowd had dispersed around the brawl, saving any bystanders from exposure to the poison.

Commit to the goal. Jennings words rang in his mind. He didn't need to beat the guy, only hold him up until APPS could shoot him.

Jacob skipped back as the assassin slashed his blade then reversed the swing for another swipe. Backpedaling as fast as he could, Jacob lost his balance. The hard flooring smacked his backside. Taking advantage of his fall, the assassin came at him with an overhand chop.

Jacob's tall frame saved his life. He struck out with his foot, hitting the underside of the man's ribs with the heel of his boot. Strength born from a lifetime of hauling around 108 kilos cracked the man's ribs and sent him flying back, his sword clattering to the ground.

Henry had his opponent in an armlock, swinging him around whenever the assassin attempted to escape.

Jacob rolled to his feet, spinning to keep his opponent in front of him. Fists up, he held them close to his face and charged in the way Jennings taught. The assassin struck with lightning speed, but Jacob had thirty kilos on him—and routinely trained with Gunnery Sergeant Allison Jennings. The man's blow landed, and pain blossomed from Jacob's stomach, but he was close. He jabbed out hard and fast, smashing the man's nose.

"Jacob! Down!" Archer shouted.

Without hesitation, he threw himself to the side, covering his head and hitting the deck.

Coil guns cracked, spitting 10mm death through the air, blasting gory holes in the man's chest. No wearable body armor in existence would stop a coil-accelerated round.

Jacob looked up from the ground; all four assassins were down, likely dead. The guests huddled on the sides of the veranda—all except Nadia. The sword still stuck out of her arm, and a Navy chief knelt next to her. Scrambling on all fours he slid to a stop next to her, grabbing her flesh hand in his.

"Nadia?" He looked at the chief. "What's wrong with her?"

"I don't know. I thought she was poisoned but her arm is cybernetic."

Jacob touched her face. Cold and clammy skin met his grip. He whipped out his NavPad and called emergency services.

Prince Henry, son of the Iron Emperor, fumed over the bodies of the dead men.

"Dieter, where are you?" he shouted in his native language.

His aide-de-camp, disheveled and clearly stressed, appeared at his elbow. "Yes, *Eure Hoheit*."

"Who are these men? I don't recognize any of them."

To be fair, there were only three with intact faces. The one Captain Grimm had fought, had taken several rounds to the head. Not much of his skull remained to identify.

"I don't know, Mein Herr, but we will find out." Dieter knelt, using his handheld to scan their bodies. Several of the Presidential Security detail hovered nearby, not sure what they should do. Henry couldn't help but notice they kept their weapons pointed in his general direction.

If they were in his home, and Alliance assassins attempted to kill his father, he wasn't sure he wouldn't throw every single member of the Alliance in prison first and ask questions later.

Captain Grimm was kneeling next to his wife, holding her hand as the medics worked on her. Blue and red lights flashed as an air ambulance came to a hover fifty meters above. Two security skimmers with manned turrets flanked it.

Two doors slid open on the underside of the ambulance. A gurney lowered with an EMT hooked into it. Henry, wanting to know if the woman would live, left his aide to identify the assassins and went over to Grimm.

"...some kind of neuro toxin." The medic rapid-fired medical jargon that Henry failed to catch.

"Step back, sir," the EMT told Grimm.

"Hang in there, Nadia," Jacob said. His plea fell on deaf ears—she was unconscious.

"Will she make it?" Henry asked.

"Hard to say until we get her to the hospital. Her breathing is shallow, and she's unresponsive. Move back, please," the EMT said.

Preparing her for transport, the two medical professionals

sprayed her down with cleansing nanites designed to remove surface toxins and collect them for analysis. As one, they carefully lifted her into the gurney, hooked it on, and raised her to the ambulance.

Captain Grimm seethed, fists impotently opening and closing.

"I'm very sorry, Herr Grimm."

"Not as sorry as whoever sent them is going to be," Jacob growled.

Henry expected the naval officer to automatically blame him for the assassination attempt and was mildly shocked that he didn't seem to be making that connection.

An armed APPS man approached them. He wasn't nearly as tall as Grimm, but he oozed danger. "Captain Grimm. Prince Henry. The president would like to speak with you."

Jacob did everything he could to shove down the sheer rage boiling in his blood. If he were in command of a ship in that moment, he'd order a bombardment of... something. He followed Prince Henry through the crowd toward the Palisades—likely the most secure building on the planet.

Elsa broke through the crowd and joined her brother, taking his hand and whispering something to him. They were striking, Jacob admitted. Not as tall as himself, but tall and statuesque.

Heading for the hospital, the ambulance disappeared behind a building. *Dammit, I should be with her.* For the first time in his adult life, Jacob felt a conflict building in his heart. Since he joined the academy fresh out of high school, he'd thrown himself into the Navy life. *Duty, honor,* and *courage* were far more than words. They were his creed. Words that were ingrained to his very soul. Words that had led him to face terrible odds and put his crew in danger more than once, all for the pursuit of those glorious words. The ideals he felt he had to live up to because of his mother's legacy.

As the flashing lights of the ambulance faded, Jacob wished to God he had gone with her instead of staying to report or listen to some lecture on the current state of political affairs.

"She's tough. She'll be fine," Archer said from beside him. So lost in his own thought, Jacob hadn't even realized the charismatic officer shadowing him.

"I should be with her," he said.

"Captain Jacob T. Grimm, you wouldn't know what do with yourself if you were with her. Smarten up, Mister. We've got to meet the president."

APPS led them through the exterior door; two civilian-clothed guards with drawn coil pistols watched their approach with suspicious concern. Past them were ten Marines in full combat kit.

"Princess Elsa, you may stay here. These men will make sure you return to the embassy safely," the APPS man said.

Elsa turned to her brother and kissed his cheek in the way some cultures did. They looked at one another for a long moment. She turned to Jacob. "Herr Grimm, I'll go to the hospital and be there for her. It is the least I can do. I owe her everything."

Very glad someone would be there with her, but not trusting his words, he could only nod his thanks.

"Marines, move out," their Gunny hollered. They bracketed the princess, escorting her to the roof where her armored aircar awaited.

More APPS fell in with Jacob, the prince, and Archer, delivering them to the office of the president. When the doors opened, the guards took up a perimeter. The big office was full of men and women. He immediately spotted several uniforms, including one he didn't recognize—a short bulldog of a man in a brown military outfit. SECNAV DeBeck stood near the president, along with Fleet Admiral Villanueva. Among the civilians, he recognized Talmage St. John.

"Sir, I must protest Heinrich Faust's involvement in this meeting," a balding man with a pitted face said.

"Oh please, Charles, do you really think the assassins were sent by the man who fought them off at great risk to his own life?"

Charles, who Jacob realized was Defense Intelligence Director Charles Gradford, shook his head. "It doesn't matter what I *think*, sir. It matters what my investigators can prove."

While no stranger to investigations, Jacob wasn't versed in the rules and regulations of civilian security. However, the man's logic made a certain sense. It could be an elaborate attempt, designed to fail, just to make the prince look good. But... no. Jacob always trusted his instincts on people. He didn't think for a single second that Henry was behind the plot. They'd fought side by side, faced death together. A man could hide a lot of things, but not how he faced death. In that moment, they were either courageous or cowards.

"Your objections are noted and overruled." President Axwell said. "Prince Faust, Captain Grimm, Commander Ban, thank you. If it weren't for your quick action, the assassins could have done much more damage.

"Mr. President," Henry said, "—from the bottom of my heart, I promise you we had nothing to do with this. Right this moment my men are looking into who they were and how they acquired our uniforms and identification."

President Axwell had a fatherly look about him. Jacob had met him once before, when he'd returned from Medial. Axwell had told him then that he was a career politician and would do what was best for his career. After the last few years, Jacob wondered if that was still true.

"Prince Faust—Henry—I know. You provided a comprehensive list of your people on the planet. You were very generous with the information. The preliminary report shows those men's appearances were altered. We'll know more after the forensics is done."

Jacob glanced at DeBeck and Villanueva. Something was off. They were... pensive. In fact, he realized everyone in the room held a kind of tension. Sure, the president had just survived an assassination attempt... but the attempt was only minutes old, yet all these high-level people were in the room. Something else nagged at him.

Fleet Admiral Villanueva wore her mess dress, and DeBeck was in his civilian suit that Jacob had never seen him without. But the rest of the president's cabinet were in regular clothing. They were already there before the attack. What was going on?

"Of course, my people will cooperate in any way you require, Mr. President. My father's honor demands no less."

"With that out of the way... I want to thank the three of you, and Ms. Dagher—"

"Grimm..." Jacob blurted out. "...sir. Mrs. Grimm. We were married recently."

President Axwell's broad smile touched his eyes. "Congratulations, young man. I'm happy for both of you. I'll make sure she has the best doctors."

"Thank you, sir. Without her, we wouldn't have known about the poison blades. I hate to think what would have happened if they managed to cut someone with them... just contact on her skin sent her into shock. If it wasn't for her quick thinking, I'd be dead."

For a long minute, silence hung heavy in the room.

"We're all familiar with Dag—Mrs. Grimm's leap-before-you-look approach," Director Gradford said.

It was only through years of practice, training, and an extreme amount of self-control that Jacob didn't verbally, or physically, lash out at the man. Even with the tumultuous state of his emotions he had enough sense to keep quiet. *If this is what politics is, no thanks.*

"That's enough," DeBeck said. "Nadia *Grimm* has served her nation with distinction. If it weren't for her investigation—"

"Illegal investigation," Gradford interrupted.

"All the same. Without her, we would still be infiltrated by both the Guild and Caliphate intelligence."

Gradford's face grew dark. "You would say that. She is your protégé."

What had Nadia done that upset that man so?

Before DeBeck could retort, Axwell broke in. "Enough. I won't have two of my cabinet trading barbs at a time like this. You two want to go find a closet and settle who has the bigger flex? By all means. But do it on your own time. Understood?"

The sheer amount of command that rolled off President Axwell made Jacob want to snap to attention.

Both men muttered, "Yes, sir," and stopped talking.

"Now, Prince Faust. On behalf of the Alliance, we invite you, your ships, and their crew to continue enjoying our hospitality. You were scheduled to stay for a month, and I see no reason to change that. Do you agree?"

With a severe nod of his head, Henry snapped a formal bow. "Yes, Mr. President. Your understanding in this matter is beyond reasonable. Thank you."

CHAPTER NINE

The news of the assassination attempt spread through the fleet like a wildfire. As usual, scuttlebutt was faster than the media. Every Navy and Marine ship in the system went to Condition Zulu for the next twenty-four hours. Even the Marines on the ex-Republic battleship.

Jennings stalked into 4th platoon's berthing area, flipping on the lights. Sixteen racks for her platoon, one cabin for her two squad leaders to share, her room she shared with a PO from engineering, and the platoon leaders' cabin somewhere in officer country. Thankfully, she shouldn't have to deal with Lieutenant Poole often. From here, she would go forward and wake up the four females in the squad who had their own cabin.

She grabbed the first Marine she came to and slid him bodily out of his bunk. He yelped as he hit the cold deck

"Fall out," she bellowed. "On the bounce, Marines."

One man, a lanky private with scruff on his chin, rubbed his eyes. "It's 0500, Gunny—"

Jennings froze. Her head slowly turned like a weapons

turret until her eyes locked on to the private. "Do you think the enemy gives a damn what time it is?"

He gulped, suddenly aware of the danger he was in. Jennings grabbed his blankets and ripped them off the bed, revealing his shivering boxer short–clad body.

"Gunny!" the private yelled.

"Drop and give me fifty. Sound off."

"Yes, Gunny," he said. Slipping out of bed, the Marine started his pushups. "One."

Jennings turned to the rest of the compartment. "Anyone else?"

Nineteen Marines leaped out of bed, rustling their PT gear out of their lockers before running for the head.

Eventually she would have her squad leaders for the task, but at the moment she only had privates, a handful of PFCs, and two lance corporals. "Fallout in the squad bay in two minutes. PFC Monahan, take charge."

From there, she marched to the lift one frame over and keyed in the location of the women's berth. Five minutes later, after a repeat of the previous wake-up, Gunnery Sergeant Jennings stood in front of her platoon.

She led them in PT for an hour, smoking them with every exercise she knew they hated. If she was going to lead a new platoon, she needed to know their worth. If there were personality conflicts or weak links that needed shoring up... The way to find out was to work them to their absolute limit—then push them harder.

If they broke, they would break on their weak points.

"Gunnery Sergeant Jennings," a familiar voice called out.

Jennings hopped up from forward leaning rest with practiced ease. She turned, a slight smile on her lips. "Sergeant Naki. You're one of my squad leaders?"

Naki, dressed in his blues with enough ribbons to make any

Marine's jaw drop, snapped to attention. "Staff Sergeant Akola Naki, reporting as ordered, Gunny."

It was a Bravo-Two-Five reunion, the only thing missing was...

Before she could finish the thought, Sergeant Owens entered, followed by Corporal June. Both also wore their immaculate dress blues.

Jennings cocked her head to the side, the mirth in her expression gone as quickly as it had appeared. Something, she decided, was fishy.

———

An Alliance Legion-class battleship, like the *Alexander,* had three general galleys for feeding enlisted, one for chiefs and warrants, and two for officers. A smaller galley was reserved for the captain and his guests, or for a solitary dinner if the captain was that type.

PO Josh Mendez didn't know which way his captain might be. The newly minted Commander-class battleship was a Republic of Terra design, completely overhauled from the keel up by Alliance engineers. She was one of a kind. Republic designed with her hull intact, but all the insides ripped out and replaced. According to his briefing, not a shred of Republic of Terra tech remained aboard. That would include the galleys and mess. One of which he would be assigned to. He needed to find his new department head.

Josh checked his NavPad again, making sure he had the name right. Mike Redelfs. No rank. In and of itself, that was weird. He'd never seen a department head without a rank before.

It took him three lifts to get where he thought it was, only to find out he'd mistaken the wardroom for the main galley.

Several junior officers lounged in the smaller mess and gave him the "what are you doing here?" look when he entered.

Backtracking, he found the ladder between decks, then caught another lift down the keel to deck four where the actual main galley was. The galley, as he had to explain to his sister, was the kitchen; the mess was the dining room. She pestered him about why it wasn't called a kitchen. His only explanation: That wasn't what the navy called it.

Josh stood in the hatchway, absolutely in awe of the room. *Interceptor*'s mess might fit half the crew at any given time—the mess in front of him could fit three times the entire crew of his previous ship.

"Out of the way, dipwad." A rough hand pushed him aside. Josh had to grab the bulkhead to keep from falling. Two men, both broad-chested and well-muscled, pushed past him toward the galley line. One of them wore double stripes, and the other three. Certainly no way to treat a PO.

"Spacer," Josh said. He didn't raise his voice, but he spoke with authority. They stopped as one and turned around. To his amazement, they were identical. The only difference he could see was the spacer had a day's worth of scruff on his face.

"What?"

Josh glanced at his name tag. *Fontenot.* "When you speak to a superior, do you not address them by rank?"

Grins split their faces. "I'll let you know when I see a superior."

This is going to be something I have to nip in the bud. They put him in a bind. Until he reported for duty, he wasn't in the official chain of command. For the moment, his options were limited.

"Watch where you're going, Fontenot. Don't let it happen again."

From the expressions on their faces, he doubted he had any

impact on them. They turned and walked to the chow line as if nothing had happened.

Pushing the incident aside, he looked for the entrance to the galley. Sure as shoot, he found it near the bulkhead.

A rack of ovens as long as the galley itself dominated one side. A prep table stretched the length of the galley, ending at the serving window. While crew could order food ahead, everyone ate mostly the same thing with few variations. They couldn't waste food making six different meals for each spacer. They could, however, put in requests for meals. Of course, holidays always had special meals.

To his right was a massive hatch that looked like it belonged on a tank: the walk-in fridge.

"Can I help you, PO?"

An elderly man, and Josh only assumed that because of his white hair and white mustache, wearing a chef's smock over civilian clothes, approached him.

"I hope so, sir." Josh held his hand out to shake and the old man took it. "I'm looking for Chief Redelfs? Only he might not be a chief. The NavPad didn't show me."

The older man gave him a fatherly smile. "I know him, son. He's me. Chief Petty Officer (Ret.), Mike Redelfs. I work for the civilian contractor who installed all of this. I'm in charge of the galley for her trials—after that you'll get a proper officer."

Josh instantly liked the older man—he had the look of a good man about him. In reality, he was probably only sixty or seventy.

"Well, then, I guess I'm one of your assistants."

Mike frowned. "I don't think so... you say your name was Mendez?"

Josh showed him the NavPad in response.

The retired naval chief motioned for him to follow back to his office—a tiny cubby off the side of the kitchen. It didn't even have a hatch, just a privacy curtain to shield a small workstation and office. Josh was amazed at how much sound the curtain muffled once it slid shut.

"Nice, right? Sound-baffling tech. It gets loud out there."

"How many work in the galley?" Josh asked.

"Oh, I'd say twenty to thirty in the galley, another ten in the mess—"

"Wow, that's a lot—"

"Per shift. Four shifts, so almost 200 when it's all said and done."

Josh looked at Redelfs with awe. He handled six at any given time... total. Redelfs had more spacers working in his galley than the *Interceptor* had crew!

"Quite a lot, huh?"

"Yes, sir, it is. Is that normal?"

"For a Legion class there would be even more. Though the new Whirlwind class has a lot more automation in the galley, so they get by with about half as much staff. We're stuck in the middle. Some of the jobs are automated, but some still have to be done by hand. I never understood the civilians' desire to automate everything. Too many things can go wrong on a cruise. Automate too much, and you might not be eating dinner."

Josh thought back to the galley fire aboard *Interceptor* and the loss of a crewmember. He still sent a quarter of his paycheck to Lopez's family. He'd gone to see them, but they were so stricken in their grief, he hadn't stayed long.

"Aye, sir. I agree. Now, about where I'm supposed to be?"

Mike looked at Josh for a moment as if he were lost in his own memory. "Right. Let's see." He tapped the station to life, bringing up the crew files. "I see the problem. You're not reporting directly to me, son—you're in charge of the captain's wardroom. Did you have one of those on your last command?"

"No, sir, we didn't. Not even a wardroom... just one mess for everyone. What's the captain's wardroom do?"

"You're in for a treat," Mike said. "You prepare all the meals for the skipper. If he has guests, you do that too. You should have at least three assistants, but who knows with the ship still awaiting trials. I'm not your supervisor, but if you need anything come to me."

Josh thanked the retired spacer and started to leave when he realized something important. "Mike... who is the captain?"

Redelfs shrugged. "Not assigned yet. Even better for you. Give you time to learn the wardroom galley."

When Kimiko Yuki first received her orders to *BB-17*, for a brief shining instant, she thought she was the CO. Reality struck her, though, before she even opened her orders. Even with her mostly stellar record, there was no way NAVPER would put a commander in the big seat of a battleship. None.

But as executive officer? Yes.

She'd spent the last two years on *Apache* as CO. Destroyer skippers had a level of autonomy only dreamed of by other ships' captains. Sailing into the unknown, often days, or even weeks, without messages from command. Stationed on a BB for her trial runs in the home system was a huge change. It was going to be hard to answer to someone. Anyone.

Thinking of Alexandria made her long for Rōnin, her own home planet. How long had she gone without stepping foot on her native soil? Almost a decade. Stellar mechanics put Rōnin months away; even with the Navy's generous leave packages, it was too far for her to go home. She would need to correct that soon.

The XO's cabin—hers alone—was almost as large as *Inter-*

ceptor's bridge. The amount of space on the ship blew her mind. Her favorite feature, though, was the massive transparency allowing her to see out into space on the starboard-side bulkhead. Stars glimmered like diamonds in the dark. If she moved close enough, the edge of Utopia stuck out below.

"If my dad could see me now," she whispered. Thinking of her parents, she recorded and sent them a quick greeting, letting them know she was well and that she had a new assignment. They would be too embarrassed if she lingered longer than it took to say hi and show them her cabin. Despite not having seen them in ages, Rōnin society wasn't one to spend time on emotional displays.

As she pushed send, her cabin hatch chimed. "Open," she said.

"Lieutenant Commander Mark West and Lieutenant SG Owusu reporting for duty," Mark said from the hatchway.

Kim sprang to her feet, matched the two men's attention, and returned a sharp salute. "At ease and come in!"

They did just that.

"Mark, Owusu, it's so good to see you. It's been, what?" She paused to remember the last time they'd all served together.

"Two years, ma'am," Owusu said in his deep baritone. "I was working as an aid to Admiral Webster when my orders came in this morning."

Mark clapped the black man on the shoulder. "I was weapons officer on board *Typhoon*. She's shipping out tomorrow, and they pulled me off at the last second. When I found out why, I can't say I'm unhappy."

"You two had chow yet? There's plenty of room. You know this ship comes with its own officer's wardroom and a private wardroom for the captain?"

The two men took a seat on her couch, facing the transparency to space. Mark let out a whistle. "Ma'am, I know this is a warship, but I can't help but feel like it's a luxury liner. The Republic sure put in a lot of extra space."

Kim grabbed a couple of sealed drinks from her private fridge and handed them to the boys.

"I ran into Jennings. She's aboard."

Mark raised an eyebrow, looked at Owusu, and back to Kim. "That's... strange. The three of us, and one from Bravo-Two-Five—"

Her hatch chimed again. Kim glanced at Mark and shrugged. "Come in."

The hatch slid aside with a customary hum, revealing Lieutenant SG Vivienne Boudreaux. The former aviator stepped into the hatch and saluted. Hand halfway to her temple, she realized who was in the cabin. Despite her shock, she managed to spit out her official words. "Lieutenant Boudreaux reporting as ordered."

Kim returned the salute for the second time that afternoon. "Stand at ease, Viv. Come on in. We were just reminiscing."

The petite French woman entered. "Mon Dieu. Is the entire crew here?"

"Wait..." Kim said. "You ran into others?"

"Oui, ma'am. PO Stawarski is onboard, and I swear I saw Chief Redfern coming aboard as well."

"Well, well, well. Looks like we might be in for more surprises."

Mark took a long pull of his beverage, a fruity, carbonated concoction popular on Ohana. "How so, ma'am?"

Kim went around her desk and activated her terminal to type in a query. "Almost all of them." She was delighted.

"What is it?" Owusu asked.

"*Interceptor*," she said. "Almost everyone who served aboard her in the last five years... they're here, on this ship."

Mark hurried to her side to see the list. "There's a few missing, but that's probably because they couldn't be brought in-system in time. I know Fawkes has his own DD now."

Boudreaux cleared her throat. "Ma'am, is the captain..."

Kim shook her head. "Until NAVPER assigns someone, I'm the acting captain. However, my official assignment is first officer. Which means we're still waiting on our CO."

The four officers exchanged grins. If there were that many members of the *Interceptor* aboard, with the captain's luck, he would be too.

CHAPTER TEN

Hamza marveled at the technology of the massive *Mecca*-class Dreadnaught, *Al-Baraq*. The first of her kind: 1,300 meters long, a crew of eight hundred souls, and more weapons than he could have imagined even as a child. Eight-terawatt plasma lasers, twenty forward torpedo launchers, and enough turrets to turn a planet to ash. Not to mention the almost four companies of Immortals, each with their own dropships and heavy weapons. No other civilization had reached such greatness.

Al-Baraq was designed to be a self-contained fleet, capable of smashing the enemies' defenses and taking their planets. With his support ships—six heavy cruisers, two troop transports, eight light cruisers, and six destroyers, two of which were the new missile boats—that was exactly what Hamza intended to do.

The U-shaped bridge layout emphasized each crewmember's role to play in the whole. Sitting shoulder to shoulder with nothing between them, there was no hiding laziness. Hamza's chair sat a meter above the deck, allowing him to see every screen and man at their station.

His chair also came with multiple screens he could use to mirror whatever station he chose. At the bottom of the U, elevated to eye level with Hamza, an enormous three-dimensional holo player showed local space around the immense dreadnaught.

Never before in history has a man controlled such destructive power as I wield. The thought sobered him. Pride flared in his chest that his uncle would entrust such a weapon to him.

"Prepare the fleet to depart," he ordered, his voice not quite as authoritative as he wanted.

"Yes, sir."

The bridge turned into a hive of activity as the ships of the fleet were contacted. Courses were plotted, engines activated, and crew buttoned up at their workstations.

Thirty minutes passed; he waited with decreasing patience. *Is this how my uncle feels? Orders were given, yet the men below him simply fail to follow them.*

"What is the delay?" he bellowed when the clock ticked over to the forty minutes.

"My apologies, Admiral. The crews of the ships are new and we're having trouble linking them all up. Only a few more minutes."

"Very well, but no more than ten," Hamza said. He didn't know the man's name, nor did he think he needed to. He was the admiral; they were the subordinates. If he called them by name, they might think they mattered.

Finally, with seconds to spare, maneuvering thrusters fired, and the massive nose of the dreadnaught began to move. Slow at first, but picking up speed.

"She's a pig, Admiral. Moving this thing is like getting my wife to do the dishes," the helmsman said.

Hamza laughed at the joke. "Agreed. Do your best." If the maps he'd consulted earlier were correct, and if he headed directly there with as few stops as possible, he would arrive at his destination in a little over a month—just a few days after his cousin struck Praetor. With Allah at their backs, they would meet soon after.

He could not fail. This was his only chance to prove himself. To show the Caliphate that he was worthy of his family's legacy. Hamza heaved himself up, confident the fleet headed in the right direction.

The holotank displayed their target star system in bright colors and vivid detail. It felt wrong to him as he gazed at it. The Alliance, through random chance, had received not only a planet like Alexandria, with its massive surface area, vast oceans, and mineral rich crust, but also the surrounding moons and planets... and on top of all those blessings, a thick asteroid belt with everything they could ever want to mine.

As a kid, Hamza had wondered if perhaps the first Caliph had somehow angered Allah. He'd since repented for his blasphemy—the Caliphs didn't make mistakes. The hundreds of barely habitable planets the Caliphate controlled were chosen by design. If they had colonized closer to the Alliance or Republic, the wars might have started long before they were ready for them.

CHAPTER ELEVEN

After the meeting and a few questions, Jacob was ushered into the side room. The prince, who Jacob seriously doubted was in on the assassination attempt, had exited a different way.

Waiting outside the presidential office, Jacob fumed. He checked his NavPad for the tenth time, hoping for an update, praying one didn't arrive. If she died saving him... no. Thinking like that would only spiral into madness. Rubbing his face with both hands, he pressed his eyes hard enough to hurt.

Jacob stood, stopped midway, started to sit down again, then changed his mind. He needed to do something. His heart raced as he walked nonstop around the small room.

"Sir, can I get you a coffee, or snack?" an aide asked.

"No—yes. Do you have any Navy-issue orange drink?"

"Let me see what I can do, sir."

Jacob leaned against the window, staring out at the New Anchorage Bay. The city slept, oblivious to the plight of the most important person in the world... himself. His reflection hit him hard. Haggard, with a bruise forming where he must have been clipped. He hadn't even realized it until that moment. A glance told him his dress mess was disheveled, the lapel torn. Some of his medals were missing.

Jacob closed his eyes, turning inward to feel himself. His heart raced and his joints hurt. The pain of multiple blows throbbed through him, grounding him. "Okay," he said aloud. Letting out a long, slow breath, he eased his heart and mind. "She's going to be okay." Saying it made him mean it. Feel it.

"Sir?" The aide returned with a tall glass of Navy-issue orange drink.

"Oh boy. You're a lifesaver."

"My pleasure, sir."

Jacob took a long pull of the drink. The mild stimulant swam through him, pushing the pain and cloudiness of exhaustion away, clearing his head.

Moving slowly to keep it from ripping further, Jacob slid his jacket off his shoulders. He did what he could to clean it and straighten his rank and medals. His right cuff was a total loss. All he could do was tuck it in.

"Captain Grimm?"

Jacob turned to see the backlit form of the president's Chief of Staff Leilani Kahale. Her black dress hung around her in the right places without being overtly sexual. She had the professional look down pat.

"Yes, ma'am." He slipped his jacket back on and fastened the large brass buttons. It wasn't great, but he was at least presentable.

"The president can see you now."

Jacob walked forward, head slightly down, as he prepared to meet his commander in chief for the second time that night. Surprise hit him as he entered the office: Only the president and Admiral Villanueva were present.

Leilani closed the door behind her, leaving only the four of them in the room. Jacob did as countless hours of training told him; he stopped in front of the desk, right over the symbol of the Alliance, spun, and saluted.

"As you were, son. Have a seat," President Axwell said.

Not sure how to proceed, Jacob did as bid and sat on the couch, practically at attention. A part of his mind wondered if this was how Gunny Jennings always felt. Sitting, ramrod straight, ready to spring into action at a moment's notice.

"For pity's sake, son. Relax," Axwell said.

"With all due respect, Mr. President, relaxing isn't something I can do right now... even if I wasn't in this hallowed place."

Axwell walked around to the front of his desk and sat half on it. "I suppose most people feel that way. For me, this is my office. If I were on the command deck of *Interceptor*, or some other ship, I would feel as you do now. Even if my wife wasn't in the hospital. Don't worry, Captain. Our best people are helping her. The very best."

Jacob nodded, which was almost more than he could do. He wanted to be there with her, but instead, he was in a secret meeting.

"Thank you, sir. I appreciate that, as would she, I'm sure. May I ask the purpose of our secret meeting?"

"How do you know it's a secret meeting?" Leilani asked. She moved around the desk to stand opposite Jacob, next to Admiral Villanueva.

"When a mere captain is called into a private meeting with the President of the Systems Alliance, his Chief of Staff, and the Alliance fleet admiral with no one else present? It's secret. That and... I am who I am. This isn't the first time someone has asked me to do something secret... and quasi-illegal."

Villanueva suppressed a grin. Axwell let out a hardy laugh. "Good enough, Leilani?" Axwell asked.

"I don't like that he already knew," she said. Reaching into her pocket, she handed Jacob a card. "Insert that into your NavPad."

He did as she asked, and the ubiquitous device beeped once. A new screen appeared, with his profile displayed followed by a long wall of text. It quick scrolled to the end, asking for his thumbprint.

"Am I supposed to read all this?" Jacob asked.

Leilani shook her head, dangling earrings following her movements like little birds in perfect orbit. "You read it the first time you were granted a secret clearance. This elevates your security to *Top Secret – Yankee Black.*"

Jacob didn't bother to hide his confusion. "Yankee Black? I thought clearance with the President was Yankee White?"

"Once you thumb the acknowledgement, I can tell you the difference," Leilani said.

Jacob placed his thumb dead center. Red light flashed as it read his print and biometric data. Duplicating a person's thumbprint was beyond easy; duplicating their blood type, oxygen content, heart rate, nerve conductivity? Impossible. Or at least far harder than most could do.

"Accepted. Grimm, Jacob T. Captain. Top Secret - Yankee Black," said the feminine voice of his NavPad.

"Jacob," Villanueva spoke for the first time since he entered. "What I'm about to tell you stays in this room and this room only." She looked up at Leilani and nodded.

"Yankee Black is for direct communications with the president and his selected team. Not even the SECNAV has this information," Leilani said.

He sat up straighter, as if he could. "Yes, ma'am. Of course."

The lights dimmed and the admiral's NavPad sprang to life, showing a holographic map of the galaxy. It autorotated and zoomed in until only the Alliance and close surrounding systems were visible. Several stars lit up; Jacob recognized them without having to read their labels: Cordoba, Rōnin, Zuckabar. All spread across the Orion's Spur.

Admiral Villanueva highlighted several stars. Small triangles indicated the Alliance ships. Larger white triangles surrounded by little yellow ones showed the six battle groups of the Alliance. One was in Cordoba, one in Zuckabar, one en route to Seabring, and one on the way to join the two battleships that were already in Medial, bringing the total there to three.

Jacob took in the entire force movement, processing the results almost instantly. "We're taking the fight to the Caliphate?" No wonder they were putting him under such intense scrutiny. Why would they tell a mere captain the current battle plan of the Alliance? No matter what missions he'd carried out in the past.

On the holo, the three battle groups merged into a task force and proceeded into Caliphate space. Behind them, transports appeared, moving the newly enlarged Army of the Alliance to hold taken planets while Marines did the main fighting on the ground. A small clock counted down in the top corner, showing him the actual time frame of the assault. Between each system, the ships barely stopped to land troops before moving on.

"This isn't just an attack. This is an endgame operation," Jacob said.

Villanueva waved away the hologram. The lights rose gradually, like a technological sunrise.

"Yes. And we need every ship that can fight. Every single one. Including the ones defending *this* planet." She let those words hang in the air.

"What?" Jacob said.

"We simply don't have the ships to spare. We need them all in the front, which puts us in a dangerous position," President Axwell said. "We need to send everything, but we must appear to have something at home. If the Caliphate were to learn of this bluff, they could send a fleet directly here and smash us."

Jacob had no idea things were that... advanced. If Admiral Villanueva was willing to risk everything in a desperate bid against the Caliphate, it had to be bad. "How long?" he asked.

"How long until what?" Leilani said.

"Until we lose the war." He'd said it. Put the words out, and they could never come back. Every battle he'd fought, every mission he'd completed? He thought they were winning.

"How can you know that?" Leilani asked.

Admiral Villanueva answered him. "A year, maybe more. We can't outbuild them. They've practically replaced the fleet Admiral Webster destroyed when we took Medial. They have more people, resources, and ships. Our advantages, while many, can't outweigh that. How did you know?"

"This is a move of desperation," Jacob said. He gestured at the faded map. "I take it the Consortium is attacking as well?"

She looked uncomfortable for a moment. "Despite our close relationship with them, ONI feels they can't be trusted. Too many leaks. We've *encouraged* them to pick up the pace of their actions, but... they're concerned about counterattacks over their long border."

We're on our own, Jacob thought. "What do you need of me?"

Villanueva cleared her voice as she re-engaged her NavPad. "This is the battleship you brought back from Cordoba. It's a Republic design. We've spent the time since your return stripping out all the Terran technology and refitting it with our equipment. We've given her the number *BB-17*. By law, she's just the number until she completes her builder and Navy trials."

Jacob didn't need to be led to water; he knew where this was heading. "You want me to run her through the trials?" he asked.

"Yes and no," President Axwell said. "Anyone could do that. We need you to do it while showing the flag. Don't just sit in Utopia's moorings and run simulations. Put her through the paces where everyone in the system can see you doing it."

Admiral Villanueva filled the silence left by the president. "Jacob... *Mon ami*... we need everyone to *believe* there is still a battle group guarding Alexandria. We especially need the spies we know are in system to believe it as well."

He pondered the problem like it was a fleet war game. How to fool everyone into thinking Alexandria had its mobile defenses in place, while not actually having them? As usual, his subconscious was two steps ahead of him; he found himself looking at the door Prince Henry had exited through earlier. "How long, ma'am?"

"A month or two. Long enough for *Alamo* to patrol Seabring and Ohana and return. Then we can get you on a regular command."

Jacob sighed. "And it has to be me, doesn't it?"

"Why do you say that?" Leilani asked. "Maybe you're the only captain available."

Jacob shrugged. "Possibly. But I'm... I am who I am. I'm visible. After tonight, even more so. No matter where I go, someone will be watching. Having a visible captain of a battleship in-system solves many of these problems."

Axwell laughed again. "Grimm, I swear, every time I meet you, I'm more impressed. When you're done in the Navy, I certainly hope you go into politics."

"No offense, Mr. President, but I'd rather die."

"I know you, Jacob," Admiral Villanueva said. "But I need to hear you say it."

Deception, subterfuge, strategy? It all sounded perfect for him. On top of it all, he also would remain in-system. Which meant, at least every once in a while, he could pop down to Alexandria and see Nadia... assuming she lived.

Don't think like that. Of course she's going to make it.

Jacob stood to attention. "I stand ready to serve, as always, ma'am."

Hospitals never bothered Jacob. He'd certainly spent enough time in them over the years. Naval hospitals mirrored civilian centers, with the added difference of military personnel from top to bottom. While there were civilian contractors, most of the medical people were Navy.

He'd spent all night in the briefing with the president, then with Alliance Presidential Protection. They'd finally let him go at 0600. The sun was just cresting the horizon as his aircar circled the tall, gleaming white building with the universal red cross and the name painted on the side: Naval Hospital Anchorage Bay. Flags of every planet from the Alliance hung proudly from the side of the building, with the flag of the Alliance flying tall above them all. To the protest of the driver, Jacob popped the door open a meter above the landing pad, then leapt out and ran for the door.

Archer's last message told him where to go: the eighteenth floor, Toxicology and Poison Center. The lift didn't descend fast enough, and Jacob found himself on the verge of swearing. His heart ached and emotions ran raw through his veins.

He was so anxious, as soon as the door started opening, he slid through sideways. Archer was there to greet him.

"Where?" Jacob said.

"This way," Archer said.

He heard her before he saw her. The laugh, her unmistakable laugh. Her room faced the rising sun; its rays lit her face. She was alive. *Alive.*

Jacob went to her, wordlessly wrapping her in a hug and burying his face in the soft confines of her neck. Nadia froze, as if she didn't know how to respond to his overt affection.

"I'm okay, Jacob," she said. "Just a weaponized palytoxin designed to kill on contact."

He pulled back, looking her in those big brown eyes. "Just?"

She shrugged with one shoulder. Her cybernetic arm was missing, leaving her with no real shoulder to speak of. "Okay, slightly more serious than 'just.' If it weren't for this"—she raised her shoulder—"I'd be dead for real."

"You saved us, Mrs. Grimm," Archer said. "We would have barreled into those men full speed. Forcing them to attack you was pretty clever."

She shook her head. "Thanks, Archer, and it's just Nadia. While I suspected the green goo was a toxin, I thought I could get in there and take out a few. It wasn't until I hit the ground that I realized it was a paralyzing agent as well."

"Do me a favor, Nadia. Next time, just shout a warning. I had to speak to the president afterward, and I think I would have agreed to anything, no matter how crazy, if it got me out of there to come see you."

She glanced at Archer and made a small gesture that meant "excuse us for a minute."

Archer coughed politely. "I'll, uh, be outside if you need me, buddy."

When he was gone, Nadia looked Jacob square in the eyes. "What did you agree to... and was Wit there?"

Jacob couldn't help but smile. "He wasn't. They want me to run the new battleship through her trials. The more public the better... that's all I can really say..." *Here* was the unspoken word at the end of the sentence. Even though they were in a naval base, it didn't automatically make them secure.

"You're staying in system?"

He heard her hopefulness. "Yes. I don't know how often I'll get back to Alexandria, though. I'll make sure I get here every chance I can."

———

After an hour of him doting on her, Nadia forced Jacob to leave. She pretended to be tired and once those magic words came out of her mouth, the nurse did the rest. Her body ached in a way she couldn't describe, like her skin was exhausted.

Someone had tried to assassinate the president at a diplomatic event. It made no sense to kill Axwell now. It was his last year of his last term. Even if he died, Vice President Shuemaker would just take over and that would be that until the elections in the fall. Her mind clawed at the incongruity. Then she reminded herself that she wasn't in the Navy or ONI anymore. It wasn't her problem.

Still... just thinking about it wouldn't hurt. Four men dressed in Imperial Navy uniforms, complete with archaic swords coated in a weaponized toxin that caused paralysis on skin contact—death if it hit the bloodstream.

Nadia reached over with her stump... then remembered and used her actual arm to grab her NavPad. While technically not in the Navy anymore, she still had her pad from when she went on the run. There was no reason to return the state-of-the-art device, especially since no one asked for it. She thumbed it on; the home screen showed a pic of Jacob and her at the lake.

She activated voice mode and started searching. While not a scientist by any stretch of the imagination, she didn't need to be to find where something came from. The search returned an organized list of all the planets the toxin could have originated on... and it was all of them.

"Oh boy," she whispered. "This might take a while."

CHAPTER TWELVE

Presidential candidate and current sitting Senator Talmage St. John found himself in uncharted waters. His candidacy wasn't going well. For the last four months, he'd toured and pontificated about the state of the union. Despite his popularity as a senator, his opponent, Mia Patel, was three to five points ahead of him in almost every poll... except on New Austin, where he hailed from, and a number of smaller worlds. She simply had more money and more support. Not to mention she looked every inch the regal president already, a genetic trait common of Weber's World. They were mostly of Scandinavian descent, and the people the planet produced tended to be tall, thin, and blond. Not to mention rich. As the main shipbuilder for the Alliance, the planet's GDP was greater than two-thirds of the Alliance combined.

"Sir, you need to think about a different strategy," said Liam O'Connor, St. John's chief advisor. Liam came from Glenanne, one of the smaller worlds that were in his corner.

It was a constant theme of his candidacy; the rural planets loved him. Sadly, they didn't have the votes to elect him.

"I know, Liam, and if you have any ideas, I'm all ears."

He should never have accepted Wit's offer to run for president. Not only was it taking away from his work as a senator, but he couldn't even remember the last time he had seen his wife. He had just returned to Alexandria when the news broke about the assassination attempt.

"We could try moving more to the center. Polls show that Seabring doesn't support the continuing war. We could—"

"No," Talmage said more forcefully than he intended. "I won't for an instant appear to be backing off defeating the Caliphate. We're not going to give an inch on this, Liam. Don't even ask."

"Without more support on the big three, you're not going to have enough votes to win, sir."

The big three referred to Alexandria, Seabring, and New Austin. The most heavily populated planets in the Alliance. A candidate could win without them, but only if he pulled in the majority of the rest of the members. Which St. John wasn't. New Austin and her one hundred votes were his, easy. Seabring, though, was polling heavily for Mia. Unless it changed, their one hundred votes were hers. Alexandria was split right down the middle. Without a larger population planet, he would need to win over more remote places like Rōnin and Cordoba—which were too far away for him to visit and campaign in person. The election was only two months away and both those planets were a month just to travel to. More than likely, he would take the majority of both planets, but not all of them.

"What about more appearances with President Axwell? He's popular enough it might swing the vote here on Alexandria," Liam suggested.

Talmage hated to go back to that well. He'd already had more events with the current president than he was comfortable with. There was a fine line between having Axwell show his support and looking as if he couldn't do anything without him. Not to mention, appearing with him right after the foiled assassination would be seen as pandering.

"What about McGregor's World?" he asked

Liam shook his head with a wry smile. "I don't know what possessed you to pick a running mate from that hole, but it worked. They're almost a hundred percent behind you... which is something they've not done for any candidate since they first joined the Alliance."

"They're a small world, and to be honest, their backing is more of a political stunt than a practical one. Let's focus on the planets we have time to visit, and where we might do the best."

Liam pulled up the core worlds of the Alliance on holo. "Seabring should be our—"

"No. We might convince five or ten percent of the population to swing our way, but I won't waste time trying to convince people who will never vote for me. Let's go someplace where we have better odds. I want to send a series of commercials to Rōnin, Cordoba, and Zuckabar. We'll do personal visits on—"

Talmage spent the rest of the night working out his next month's travel plans. There were a handful of planets he could reach and spend a few days on. It was a desperate move, but he was all out of non-desperate ones.

His missing eye itched.

This isn't going well.

―――――

Someone, Nadia had no idea who, leaked footage of the night's events. Looking at the angles and their ability to zoom in, they had been close to the action—but she couldn't for the life of her figure out who. It was all over the news channels, with headlines ranging from "Heroic Navy Captain and Imperial Prince save the Alliance," which was blown slightly out of proportion, to less favorable ones like "Imperial Navy stages assassination against unpopular lame duck president."

Politics wasn't her thing, but she liked Axwell. She had even voted for the guy; most people in the military had. Unfortunately, there were more of the latter headlines than the former. She reviewed the footage once more, wishing that the person who leaked it would have released the entire thing. They started it right after she was thrown back by Jacob—making it look like she was an innocent bystander—and ended it before the APPS shot the final assassin. The angle missed the sword stuck in her arm.

In fact, it was cut in such a way that if a reporter wanted to be negative or positive, they could do so with little effort. She flung her sheets aside. Her doctors wanted to keep her for another day, but she had work to do. Whoever leaked the footage had the whole video. It wasn't APPS... too cinematic for that. And it wasn't from a NavPad. It was someone with a microdrone... which meant they either knew the fight was coming or just happened to have everything they needed to record the assassination of a sitting president.

Nadia Grimm, former ONI agent, spy, tramp freighter captain, and all-around loyal citizen of the Alliance, didn't care that it was someone else's job to investigate these things. All she cared about was someone tried to kill her man.

She reached for her pants, her brain still convinced she had two arms. "Well damn, this is inconvenient." It took her fifteen minutes just to pull on her pants, and by the time she finished, she was out of breath and her heart was pounding.

She looked down at her taut stomach; the button on her slacks was undone. "Sonofa—"

"You need a hand?" Archer Ban said.

Nadia blushed, pulling her shirt down to cover the few centimeters of her stomach.

"Nice. Yes I do, actually. But not from you."

Archer put a hand over his eyes, his fair skin burning bright red. "I... I didn't mean it either of those ways. I'm so sorry. Let me go get a nurse."

She chuckled to herself as he stumbled out of the room. Having only one arm was going to slow down her investigation; if she had to stop just to... *sheesh I can't even load my pistol.* She took her cybernetic arm for granted, assuming it would always be there. While some of it still was, it was just a stump, the anchor that attached to the rest of her body. She'd never had to manage without the arm.

A moment later, a nurse with the silver entered with a disapproving frown on her lips. "And where do you think you're going, Chief Dagher?"

Nadia pushed down her annoyance, channeling her inner Jacob. "I appreciate your concern, but it's Mrs. Grimm, and I'm not in the Navy. I'm leaving."

The nurse, whose nametag read Laskaris**,** took a step forward, as if she planned to stop her. Nadia shot her a baleful glare. "I'm trying to be patient, I really am. I'm tired, my missing arm hurts, and I've got a headache that won't stop. Can you please help me button my slacks, put on my shoes, and let me get out?"

Laskaris' eyes softened a smidge. "I'll help. You really should stay, though."

"Believe me, lounging around in a comfortable bed with nothing to do but read and watch vids sounds heavenly. However, I've got a job to do, and it waits for no one."

Half an hour later, with the help of Lieutenant Laskaris, and leaning on Commander Archer Ban, Nadia limped down the stairs leading from the medical center to the public aircar station.

"Where are you going?" Archer said.

"For now, home. Then I have some... things to look into."

He saw through her deception. "Well, I've got my personal vehicle. How about I give you a ride? That way I can tell *Captain* Grimm I did everything I could to look out for you."

Nadia shook her head. "That's sweet, Archer, but it's a three-hour trip to the farm and—"

He raised his hand. "Lucky for you, then, that I happen to have a very fast aircar and I know the way to Jacob's place. We spent every Christmas there."

Jacob had mentioned his friend before, but no one in the Navy had really gone out of their way to keep in touch with him after the media called him the Butcher of Pascal. For that matter, Jacob hadn't ever talked about his post-Pascal time all that much.

"Okay, Ban, but I'm warning you, keep your hands to yourself." The mischief in her voice robbed the comment of sting.

He raised one hand in a mock salute. "I wouldn't dream of disrespecting the captain's wife."

If he realized he'd referred to Jacob the way the rest of his crew did, Archer showed no sign. Once again, Nadia was amazed at the loyalty her man engendered. She shouldn't have been, though; after all, she'd married him.

CHAPTER THIRTEEN

Jacob strapped into the new Corsair's leather seat. Not even twenty-four hours had passed since his meeting in the White House, and he was exhausted. The ship's full complement prevented him from riding up top, so he settled for the seat furthest to the rear. He had work to do and didn't want to be bothered by anyone sitting next to him and getting chatty.

Jacob went over his instructions one more time. *Take command of BB-17, complete her builder and naval trials, and be seen doing it.*

An alert notified him of two incoming messages. One from Nadia, one with the update of his crew list. Plasma engines roared to life, rumbling through the passenger compartment, lulling him to sleep. Knowing he couldn't keep himself awake much longer, he opted to watch the message from Nadia. Her smiling face appeared, and she was in a private aircar, not the hospital.

"First of all, don't be mad. I'm just heading home. Archer was kind enough to fly me out. There wasn't any reason for me to stay at the hospital another day, other than to satisfy the doctors." She looked out the window and momentarily showed him the view. They were at least 1,500 meters up, flying over the vast plains north of his home. He could just make out the mountains in the distance.

"It's beautiful," she said with a sigh. "I'll be home in a few hours. Don't worry, I'll be fine. I'll stay there for at least a day." Her smile lit up his heart. "The MedTech's say they'll have my arm ready in a few days. You take care. Focus on your job, I know it's important..." She looked like she wanted to say more, and he felt like he needed her to say more. She brought the camera in close and mouthed, "I love you."

Jacob lay his head back and closed his eyes. It was an hour-long trip out to his new command, and he needed the rest.

———

A clunk of metal reverberated through the hull, waking him when the Corsair came to a rest on the deck. Machinery whirred as the automated umbilicals attached, refilling the ship's vital supplies of fuel, water, and air. Three dozen spacers hefted their bags and shuffled toward the side door. They were all so young. *Was I ever that young in the Navy?*

What felt like a million years ago, an eighteen-year-old Jacob showed up at the hallowed gates of Blackrock Naval Academy. He'd had nothing but the clothes on his back, a suitcase full of books, and hope in his heart. Contrasting his first command with his latest, things had certainly taken a turn. When he arrived in Zuck to take command of *Interceptor*, hope was nowhere to be found.

While he lost himself reminiscing, the last of the spacers departed the ship. Jacob grabbed his blue duffel and heaved it over his shoulder. As a captain, he could have had the Bosun take care of it, but he would rather carry his own things.

The moment he stepped foot out of the Corsair, the Bosun's pipes played. Two hundred spacers snapped to attention, their boots slapping the deck with enough force to echo in the cavernous boat bay.

Jacob was unprepared for the reception. The first notes of *Eternal Father* played from the speakers, and the crew started singing. His foot missed the first step from shock. He hadn't expected a full-on ceremony. It was a rare XO who pulled out all the pomp and circumstance for a change of command.

Because *BB-17* wasn't officially in the Navy yet, it had no name and no flag; instead, an Alliance Navy Flag hung on the stern bulkhead. Jacob stepped off the stairs onto the ship's deck, came to attention, and saluted the flag. All the while the crew continued to sing.

Turning, he saw the reason for his warm welcome: one Commander Kimiko Yuki, in full dress uniform, standing at attention in the XO's place. Jacob maintained the serious look of a captain as he marched across the small deck to the yellow-and-black stripe where the ship "officially" began. He came to attention with his toes on the line.

The chorus faded, its mournful tune echoing off the bulkhead for a few more seconds longer.

Jacob snapped a crisp salute. "Permission to come aboard?"

"Permission granted," Yuki replied, her salute just as crisp. "Bosun, dismiss the detail."

"Aye, aye, ma'am. Detail!" Bosun Sandivol bellowed. "Disss-missed!"

Jacob stayed still, waiting for the crew to depart. He recognized more than a few faces. Several murmured "Captain" or "Skipper" as they left.

"Kim," Jacob said, the shock of seeing her clear as day. "When did this happen?"

"Believe me, Skipper, I'm just as surprised. Bosun, follow us," she said.

Senior Chief Juan Sandivol fell in step behind them. Jacob didn't miss the opportunity to shake the man's hand; he had served with him for years. "Juan, it's great to see you."

"You too, Skip. This isn't the *Interceptor*, but she's got heart, I think."

Jacob didn't know about that. No ship could ever replace his shark-nosed love.

"When did you get your orders, sir?" Kim asked.

"About twenty-four hours ago. Ironically, right after the assassination attempt."

Kim let out a chuckle, mirrored by the Bosun.

"The moment the word came down that a naval officer staved off an assassination, we knew it was you," she said.

Jacob's wry grin didn't disagree with them. "Well, it was a military party to honor Crown Prince Henrich Faust. There were lots of naval officers there," he said.

"None damn fool enough to charge a sword," Kim said. "Jennings was fit to be tied when the footage came out."

A Mudcat could drive through the boat bay double hatch, and the corridor outside wasn't much smaller. It ran the length of the ship, with airtight hatches on every frame for security. At the moment, they were all open for the ship to take on supplies.

"Allison is here?" Jacob asked.

"Haven't you received the crew manifest, sir?" Kim pressed the call button on the lift.

Jacob was ashamed to admit he had but hadn't looked at it. His call to Nadia was all he had left before sleep overtook him.

"It arrived just before we were airborne. The last twenty-four hours were a little exhausting. I figured I'd read it once I was up here."

The lift arrived, and the doors opened with a whoosh. "These lifts run the length of the ship," Kim said. "Every one hundred meters, there's an intersection that moves up and down. You can pretty much get close to wherever you need to go on any lift you enter. I'll give you the skinny on the crew."

The lift whirred to life, and Jacob grabbed the handle on the side to keep from losing his balance.

"The vast majority of *Interceptor* is aboard. Some from the last deployment, some from the first. It's crazy. Bosun, the SOs, and I have spent the better part of the last three days trying to figure out why."

"Any luck?" Jacob asked.

"No, sir. Until we got word you were assigned, we figured it was random."

"What does my assignment have to do with it?"

"Sir, please. You know how NAVPER loves to keep you with your crew."

Jacob thought back to a previous discussion with Admiral Villanueva. She'd let him know that if it were up to NAVPER, he'd be commanding a garbage scow at the breakers. *No, if my crew is here, it's because of her. No need to spoil it, though.*

"You're right, of course. Or maybe I'm just that unlucky," he said with an impish smile.

"Begging the captain's pardon," Sandivol said, "I think you've got that backward. We're the unlucky ones."

The two officers burst out in laughter until the lift came to a halt and the door opened. Not ten meters away stood the open nano-reinforced steel hatch of the bridge.

"This is it," Jacob whispered, his voice as serious as ever.

"Aye, aye, sir. You deserve this, Jacob. Make it happen," Kim whispered from beside him.

"We both do," he said out of the side of his mouth.

No Marines stood guard outside the bridge—something Jacob would change. There should always be Marines, and they should be armed. The bridge itself, so large that fifty spacers could stand front to back from hatch to fore, looked far too clean. His time on the *Interceptor* was marked with equipment from three generations of Naval operations; everything on *BB-17*'s vast bridge gleamed with a state-of-the-art shine.

As soon as he crossed the threshold, Kim hollered, "Captain on the bridge."

Twenty-five officers, NCOs, and enlisted clamored to their fee... all except the black-haired NCO tucked away in the Pit. Jacob marched formally to the command seat, a leather wrapped chair in the center-stern of the bridge. Four different monitors sprouted from two arms. It would take some getting used to, he knew.

He thumbed the screen on his NavPad, which connected to the ship's computer and verified his identity and the authenticity of his orders. It beeped once, letting him know it was ready.

Jacob thumbed the "all-hands" button on the arm of his chair.

A sharp whistle played in every section of the ship, from the torpedo rooms to the stern maintenance deck. Every spacer, NCO, and officer stopped what they were doing and looked up to listen to the announcement.

He held the NavPad out to Yuki, who glanced at it before placing her thumb on the reader to verify her receipt of the orders.

Then, he began:

"From the Office of the Chief Naval Officer and the desk of the President of the United Systems Alliance,

All who bear witness, know that, reposing special trust and confi-

dence in the patriotism, valor, fidelity, and abilities of Captain Jacob T. Grimm, I do appoint him as master of the vessel bearing the hull number BB-17. As such, from the day these orders are read, this officer will therefore carefully and diligently discharge the duties of the office to which he is appointed, by doing and performing all manner of things thereunto belonging.

And I do strictly charge and require those officers and other personnel of lesser rank to render such obedience as is due an officer of this grade and position. And this officer is to observe and follow such orders and directives, from time to time, as may be given by me, or the future President of the United Systems Alliance, or other superior officers acting in accordance with the laws of the United Systems Alliance.

This commission is to continue at the pleasure of the President of the United Systems Alliance for the time being, under the provisions of those Public Laws relating to officers of the Armed Forces of the United Systems Alliance and the component thereof in which this appointment is made, that being the United Systems Alliance Navy.

Affirmed on the Capitol of Alexandria, this 23rd day of March in the year of our Lord 2939, with power entrusted by the United Systems Alliance, Friends in Peace, Family in War.

Signed, Fleet Admiral Noele Villanueva and President Johan Sebastian Axwell."

Jacob touched the NavPad to the screen, and a copy of the orders was sent to every crew member's screen. He turned to Commander Yuki and snapped to attention. She followed suit.

"Commander Kimiko Yuki, I take command," he said with a confidence born of years commanding a ship.

"Captain Grimm, you have command, sir."

Chief Echo Redfern scolded the two spacers before him for the *second* time that day.

"Miller and Kolchak, you don't know the crap you two are in. Not only did PO Baptiste specifically tell you to clean the suit lockers, but he even walked you through the procedure to do so. Tell me, please, why then are there eight ELS suits on the deck and not a damn thing has been done?"

Miller, a short fellow with narrow brown eyes glanced at Kolchak who, to Echo, looked like a troublemaker from Zuckabar if he ever saw one.

"Chief, no excuse, Chief," Kolchak said in his Zuckabar accent.

Redfern frowned. If he had to guess, Kolchak had talked Miller into something. Miller looked back straight ahead, a bead of sweat rolling down his face.

Chief Redfern unfolded himself from behind his desk. He was tall, with a lanky frame and a serious set to his brow.

"That no excuses felgercarb might have flown in A-school, but you're not 'prentices anymore, are you?"

Miller gulped loud enough that Echo heard, but Kolchak took it in stride. Neither answered.

Echo couldn't remember the last time he'd let a spacer get under his collar the way these two were. Maybe it was because they were on a battleship, and he expected better of them. Or maybe he just didn't like people from Zuck. Which he knew was stupid. He had plenty of friends from his time there.

That's it, isn't it? You know what kind of people they are, and it has nothing to do with Zuck. "I asked you two worthless sacks of carbon a question. I expect an answer."

"No, Chief," Miller replied, his voice barely above a whisper.

"No, Chief," Kolchak said more casually.

"Why then, did Spacer First Class Merrick find the suits unsecured with you two clowns nowhere to be found?"

Miller glanced at Kolchak again.

Echo understood what was going on. "Miller, dismissed."

Miller instantly spun around and marched out of the office. Echo triggered the hatch closed behind him. It wasn't a big office; even on a battleship, space was at a premium in the engineering section.

"Kolchak, we have a problem." Echo moved to stand directly in front of the spacer. With his flat face, broad shoulders, and big nose, he looked down at the Zuck native.

"How so, Chief?"

He could almost see the spacer's thoughts. Once upon a time, a much younger Echo Redfern had acted exactly the same way. Screwing off at every opportunity, avoiding work whenever possible, and making sure that others took the blame for his bad choices. Lucky for Redfern, he had a chief take an interest in him and beat the bad habits out of him before they got him kicked out of the Navy... or worse, in the brig.

"I said we, but I meant you. You have a problem. What is it?"

"No, Chief. No problem."

"Uh-huh. Did you want to be assigned to another station?" Redfern knew from experience that engineering wasn't for everyone. He considered it the hardest department on the ship.

"No, Chief. I like *engineering*."

"So, is it me you don't like?"

That threw Kolchak for a loop. The hardness in his eyes faltered for a moment. "Uh. No. I like you just fine, Chief."

Redfern eyeballed him for a moment. It wasn't easy, trying to figure out how his past self would have dealt with the situation. If he was too hard on Kolchak, he'd reinforce the man's mentality. Too soft, and nothing would change.

"How long have you been in the Navy, Kolchak?" Redfern asked. He already knew, having read his file.

"Eight months, Chief."

"You like the Navy, you like engineering, you like me... then why are you determined to sabotage your own career?" Redfern held up his hand. "Don't answer that. Other than your official duty, and chow, you're confined to quarters for twenty-four hours. I want you to think about what you want out of your time in the Navy, Kolchak... if you want anything at all. Dismissed."

CHAPTER FOURTEEN

Two days was all Nadia could wait. Theoretically, all they had to do was fix the arm and send it to her. She spent the two days cleaning Ben Grimm's kitchen, practicing her cooking, and drinking copious amounts of coffee. It was all good practice for her remaining arm.

What she couldn't do—wouldn't do—was nothing. In between making meals for Jacob's father, she searched her NavPad for official information about the investigation into the assassination attempt. According to sources inside the Palisades, DNI had its full resources bent on discovering who was actually behind the plot.

On the surface, the announcement by the DNI spokesperson, a statuesque blond with striking eyes who clearly used to be military, sounded completely reasonable to the average Alliance citizen: The powers-that-be were looking into it.

Nadia was anything but an average citizen. On the third night, she cuddled up on the couch with Jacob's blanket that still smelled of him and set to work on her NavPad. To make sure she didn't lose track of anything, she listed her problems in the notes feature:

Foreign agents faked Imperial Navy uniforms to gain entrance to the gala. They had the correct ID and biometric data to enter through any of the dozen checkpoints. They used swords made of undetectable material, coated in a contact toxin guaranteed to kill if it broke the skin. The men were highly skilled and willing to fight to the death.

She thought about the entire situation—everything she remembered and everything she'd read after the fact. Then she added one more thing. They knew exactly where the president would be. Not just at the party, but where he was in the party.

Nadia's next step was to find out what DNI already knew. Which, for her, was far easier than for anyone else. Her NavPad logged into the backdoor of ONI's system and piggy-backed over to DNI. She pulled up the file on the assassination and...

It was empty.

She looked to see who the assigned agent was. Agent Friendly. Either DNI was playing the case extremely close to the vest, or they were keeping their files offline for this exact purpose. They didn't even have pictures of the assailants, their weapons, or their clothing in the file. Nothing.

Sensing something wasn't right, Nadia backed out of the system, making sure her countermeasures were on. She left no trace of her intrusion before shutting her system down completely.

Her next call went to the hospital. The cybernetic arm she needed to function as a complete person was still under testing. Since she'd received the arm from ONI after she lost her flesh-and-blood one in Zuckabar, she'd almost forgotten it was metal. Without it... she felt less than. It was possible the hospital wasn't lying, that the toxin on the blades somehow interfered with the working of the sensitive and complex systems.

Or... it was possible someone was deliberately keeping it from her.

Above the front door, a red light blinked, letting anyone in the room know an aircar was closing with the property. One of the things she very much appreciated about the older Grimm was his healthy sense of mistrust. Nadia grabbed her coil pistol, checked the readout to make sure it was fully charged and loaded.

She heard the whine of the engine before she saw the vehicle. She stood next to the window and used defilade to keep behind cover—only peeking out enough to see what was coming.

It wasn't an Alliance model. The Alliance aircars had a sleek, minimalist look, like someone took a ground car and removed the wheels. Often, their ground vehicles and air models were only distinguished by the name of the vehicle.

Whoever made the shiny black monstrosity currently hovering over the front drive, they weren't from the Alliance. Light glinted off the metal frame as it turned slowly to face the house, and she had her answer; the golden crown and sword logo of the Iron Empire flashed in the sun. The ship settled onto its landing gear in the dirt, then a door appeared and stairs extended down.

Nadia wasn't at all surprised to see the tall, graceful form of Elsa Faust step out. Elsa wrinkled her nose, probably at the smell, and descended. Nadia stifled a laugh. Elsa wore a very stylish hiking outfit, including cargo pants and high-heeled boots. Her outfit looked like she'd stepped out of the adventure vid about the famous archeologist who just happened to find another mind-blowing alien discovery week after week.

The ex-spy stuffed the fifteen-centimeter coil gun in the small of her back, plastered a smile on her face, and went to the door. She opened it just as Elsa lifted her knuckles to knock.

"Nadia," Elsa said. "Imagine my surprise when I went by the hospital, and you weren't there!'

"I bet it was more like, 'I would go to the hospital, but my brother's intelligence service already knows she's at Jacob's ranch.' Or something like that. Close?"

Elsa fidgeted for a moment before her full lips grew into a big smile. "Actually, I never had to ask. He's keeping me updated on you in real time. May I come in?"

Nadia hesitated for a moment. She'd risked her life to save Elsa from Medial. Risked more than her life. And the princess had fought just as hard to escape the planet. That kind of action created something, but at the end of the day, did Nadia really know her? What if Henrich was behind the assassination attempt? What if she were here to kill Nadia and make it look like a suicide?

In that case, she would find out just how good Iron Empire training was. Nadia smiled and let the woman in. As Elsa passed, Nadia hid behind the door, only peeking out enough to make sure no one followed her. When she turned, Elsa was a meter away, looking at her.

"What's going on?" Elsa asked. Something around the girl's eyes had changed. They held a seriousness not there the night of the gala. Nadia recognized it from Medial—when they escaped.

A million and one calculations ran through Nadia's mind. She needed help. She couldn't turn to Wit or anyone in the government. Jacob would be gone for some time. She made a decision.

"I don't think the people who are supposed to be investigating the assassination attempt are."

Elsa turned to see if anyone else was in the room. When she thought it was clear, she sat on the couch, patting the spot next to her. "Walk me through it."

Nadia joined her and began laying out everything she had found or suspected—which she knew wasn't much.

"That's thin, Nadia," Elsa said. "Maybe your..." She waved her hand at the NavPad. "...made a mistake. Or maybe they keep their files elsewhere. If you found they were investigating it, would you continue to look into it, or would you let it go?"

Nadia opened her mouth to respond, then stopped. The answer was simple. She'd look into it no matter what. Not because she thought the people in charge weren't competent, but because no one could do as good a job as herself. Whether they knew it or not. She let out a long sigh. "Yes. I'd investigate no matter what."

"Great!" Elsa said with a little clap of her hands. "Let's get looking. Despite your president's generous offer, my brother has recalled all of our people to do a vigorous head count. He's sure those men weren't ours, but he wants to *know*. When that's done, he plans on returning to the surface to aid the investigation in any way he can." Her eyes twinkled for a moment, and an impish smile appeared on her face. "It would do me no end of good to have solved this before he returns. Where to first?"

Nadia thought about saying no and telling her visitor from another nation she shouldn't get involved, but an idea hit her. "Tell me, Elsa. Do you have diplomatic immunity?"

CHAPTER FIFTEEN

CALIPH LIGHT CRUISER AL-HIKMA

"Unbelievable," Captain Kareem said as he stared at the planet in awe. The gas giant's size surpassed his home world by a thousand times.

"How many moons does this thing have?" XO Al-Zaheem asked.

"Too many," Kareem replied. "But we're only interested in one."

Despite the Alliance's best efforts, which were pitiful, the ISB still had intelligence gathering capability in Alexandria. They had located the only remaining base that could alert the Alliance to the impending attack. *Al-Hikma* had already destroyed or disabled three early warning stations.

The frozen moon was the last one that could alert the Alliance. Once it was taken, not only would they have access to an Alliance communication node, but they would also clear the way for the fleet. The distant gas giant, out of the way and not currently in the path of any starlane, was the perfect spot to rally the coming ships. From there, they could strike out in one massive sweep toward the Alliance Capitol, destroying vital infrastructure along the way. Whatever defenses the Alliance mustered would be useless against the might of their dreadnaught and her accompanying fleet.

"Captain, the gravity fluctuations of the gas giant do pose a danger," Al-Zaheem said.

"Understood. Instruct navigation to keep the appropriate distance. However, under no circumstances can we reveal our presence."

His crew set about to carry out their orders. *Al-Hikma* crawled ahead at a meager ten gravities per second, a slow acceleration aimed at preventing detection of their grav wake. Even a ship only ten thousand klicks away wouldn't pick it up at such low power.

Kareem eyed the display showing their progress around the gas giant, toward the frozen moon that was his destination.

"Sir," Vizer, his weapons officer, said. "I'm picking up a satellite at bearing zero-two-one, mark three-zero-zero, range... one-five-zero thousand kilometers."

Close, Kareem thought. *Too close.*

"Lieutenant Vizer, destroy it before they detect us."

"Yes, sir."

Vizer turned to his panel. Using the sophisticated detection apparatus and his skill with the ship's weapons, he quickly had a targeting solution. "I'm prepared to fire."

"Fire!"

Turret four blasted out an electrostatic laser plasma that spanned the distance in less than a second. Gigawatts of energy dumped into a satellite no bigger than an aircar. The result was instant and fiery.

"Target destroyed," Vizer said.

"Inserting into orbit over the target moon, sir," Al-Zaheem announced.

"Prepare the landing craft. Have the technicians interface with the communications equipment. Once we have access to the network, we'll get some distance and listen in."

CHAPTER SIXTEEN

DAY ONE OF COMMAND

Jacob leaned against the built-in sink while the cold water ran down the drain, swirling away toward the water reclaimer. In all his time in the Navy, commanding a battleship had always been his goal. Always.

The day had come. He was the captain now.

Turning the water off, Jacob leaned against the sink, looking around the head. Including a full sink, walk-in shower, and an automated closet that not only stored his uniforms but laundered and ironed them, it was almost as big as his entire cabin on *Interceptor*.

The main cabin had a desk, with three screens and a couch facing the translucent wall. He could even press a button and have a table rise out of the floor for an in-cabin meal.

Lastly was the bedroom. A queen-sized bed, giant screen, and a secondary head just for a toilet. He felt like it was too luxurious; part of him didn't think he deserved it. Had he done the work? Going from a destroyer to a battleship felt like cheating. After all, there were other captains in the Navy with many years more experience than him.

He pushed the negative thoughts behind him. There would be time for self-recrimination later. Either he did the job, or he resigned and ran back home. Part of him—the traditional man—ached to head to his family home and take care of Nadia. See to her needs. Fetch her slippers. Thinking of her brought a smile to his face.

But as much as he would enjoy taking care of her, he had a job to do.

Jacob pulled on the space-black sweater with GRIMM on the left breast and NAVY on the back. His rank was on his epaulets. Lastly, he affixed the bloodred watch cap to his head, making sure the line ran parallel to the deck.

A buzz from a hatch he thought led to extra storage interrupted him.

"Yes?" he said.

The hatch slid open, and Petty Officer First Class Josh Mendez pushed in a cart. On it was a plate with eggs, bacon, sourdough toast, and a carafe of orange drink. "Good morning, Skipper. Breakfast is served."

Shock at seeing the young man froze him to the deck. His mind finally caught up. Not only was Josh there serving breakfast, he came through a hatch connected to his quarters. "What?" Jacob managed to say.

"Imagine my surprise, sir, when they told me I'd be the captain's cook. Any specific meals you want, alone or with guests, I'm at your disposal. Otherwise, my crew and I make your meals around the clock."

Despite all the chaos of the last few days—the assassination attempt, Nadia's near death, and his sudden assignment—the young cook's appearance created a sea of normality in Jacob's tsunami of a life.

Josh pushed the cart in front of the couch, facing the translucent screen. He took the transparent top off the food, releasing the mouthwatering smell of Jacob's favorite breakfast.

"You know," Jacob said as he skirted the couch to sit down, "when I first met you, I asked Chief Suresh if you were for real or just angling for a promotion."

The young man carefully poured orange drink into the mug labeled *Skipper*. "What did she say, sir?"

"She said you were too earnest for your own good." That wasn't what she actually said, but he liked to think it fit the spirit.

Josh chuckled as he took a step back. "Sounds like the COB. I'm happy to be here, sir. I wouldn't still be in the Navy if not for you."

Jacob's guilt at all the men and women who were no longer with them in no way diminished the pride he felt in PO Josh Mendez and the man's journey since they'd met.

"Captain on the bridge," Lieutenant JG Misha Gabriel said. His voice rose an octave, and he kicked himself for almost shouting the announcement... like a midship on his first cruise.

Captain Grimm swaggered onto the bridge. His black uniform, contrasted by the two blood stripes and red cap, looked as natural on him as spots on a leopard. He stopped and turned Misha's way.

"As you were," he said in a clear voice. "From now on, there's no need for everyone to come to attention—just the duty officer or officer of the watch."

A chorus of "yes, sir" echoed throughout the bridge. Misha mentally kicked himself as his "yes, sir" came a second late, making him stand out.

Captain Grimm took it in stride, giving him a smile before heading over to the captain's chair. Misha hadn't sat in the chair—yet. He looked forward to taking a watch.

The bridge of *BB-17* dwarfed any of the ships Misha had served on in his short career. Though, it didn't feel short. At twenty-seven, he felt like he should be much more of a man, but half the crew on the ship wore blood stripes—not one, but two.

As the ship's weapons officer, Misha was in charge of all the weaponry. All of it.

Three main turrets, each with three gigantic 400mm coil guns: massive ship killers that launched like Long 9s, but from actual turrets.

Twelve single-barreled 120mm turrets, firing the more conventional armor-piercing tungsten penetrators at 20,000 KPS.

Eight 20mm quad turrets that were exclusively for torpedo defense and close in targets. He shook his head trying to wrap his mind around that fact. His last ship, the Light Cruiser *Ursa Lieutenant*, had 20mm quad turrets as their primary armament... and only eight of them.

For torpedoes, she had twenty forward tubes and ten aft, all launching the Alliance new standard torpedo.

The final weapon system was the giga-pulse defense lasers. A system Misha had practiced with only briefly, when Captain Grimm had boarded the *Ursa* for two days to train the weapons crew on them. Three of the GPDLs were mounted on the bow, amidships above the bridge, and on the stern deck next to the towed array system.

BB-17's fire control systems were almost as complex as the weapons themselves. Misha sat in his molded bucket seat, his hands on the console. A wall of screens showed him the inside of every turret and their ammo stores, along with the location of his on-duty personnel.

Like most Alliance computers, there was a mix of touch, holo, manual, and automated controls. He wished the Alliance contractors would just pick one. However, he couldn't fault their logic. Any given system could fail during combat. Redundancy was built into the Navy way of life.

While his fire control radar/lidar showed him a clear picture of everything within a million klicks, he knew the real sensor work happened at astrogation. The chief with the painted face had spent the better part of three days taking his system apart and putting it back together.

Misha wasn't ops. That was Lieutenant Commander West's gig—astrogation answered to him. Weapons were their own department, and Misha had two junior officers, a midship, and the NCOs who ran his turrets. Spacers, while assigned to different posts, all answered to the Ops officer, not the department they were in while performing their duties. There was just too much to do on a ship as large as *BB-17* for him to have all the spacers manning the turrets only answer to him. They had multiple duties and stations depending on the watch.

He pulled up his list of NCOs. They all seemed solid. Three chief petty officers for the big turrets, with the rest commanded by POs. The only other NCO he had was Master Chief Petty Officer Jimenez—"Master Guns" as the crew called him.

Misha wiped his forehead. Just thinking of all the responsibility he had, the sheer number of people he had to manage, made his heart race and his brow sweat.

"Lieutenant Gabriel?"

Misha spun in his chair to come face to neck with the XO, Commander Kimiko Yuki.

Kim walked onto the bridge a few minutes after Jacob. The skipper was busy catching up on the reports and the plan for the day. *BB-17* was still moored against Utopia, and would be for another week while the builder finished her trials. Once the yard dogs cleared her, the crew could start the next phase and take her out for the Acceptance Trials. That involved a steady run of her engines, navigation, sensors and comms for at least a month, pushing the equipment to the absolute limit to see where the weak spots were. After they finished, the real fun began: Space Trials. Live fire exercises, war games, and other real-world tests to see if the weapons could handle everything. The list went on. It was a lot of work to finish in a short amount of time, with a massive crew and an untested ship.

Kim checked her NavPad for the next thing on her list. Since she was in charge of the crew and the day-to-day running of the ship, it was important for her to meet with all the officers and as many of the crew as possible. First on her list was Gabriel, Misha, LT SG. Top marks from his previous commander, top twenty percent of his class. A little shy according to his FITREP. Nothing big, but it could keep him from line command.

It was the same for her years before. Until Kim came to the moment where she had to force herself past her own instincts, she hadn't known if she could do it. Her people were very much a closed society. Don't speak, don't share, don't look people in the eye. It was certainly something she had to overcome in the Navy... and remember to go back to when she was home.

"Lieutenant Gabriel?" she said.

Gabriel spun around in his chair a little too fast, trying to stand before the chair was finished and ended up faceplanting into Kim's neck. She took a step back, more from surprise than outrage. Gabriel had the decency to freeze like a rat caught stealing an egg. His face bloomed bright red, and she was sure the ship's thermal sensors could pick him up a klick out.

"M-m-ma'am," he stuttered. "I'm so sorry."

Kim let the humor of the moment win, not the embarrassment. An amused smile played on her lips. "If we didn't have missteps as junior officers, what would we have? Come with me, Gabriel." She didn't wait to see if he followed—it was part of her assessment. Would he follow? Call for relief?

"Bosun, could you have a relief come up and man weapons, please?" Misha said.

"Aye, Lieutenant. On it."

Kim liked that he said *please* to the Bosun—and liked even more the tone he used to address Chief Sandivol. That spoke volumes for the young man.

Unlike any of the other ships she'd served on, *Seventeen*, as she called it, was huge. No Alliance vessel would ever be built with a bridge as large as this battleship, nor with two conference rooms attached—one for the general crew, and one for the captain and his guests. The ship's superstructure above the bridge was sharply cut, giving the ship a sort of flat-top look, like the barber had shaved the top off. Alliance engineers, not letting any open space go to waste, installed a bevy of antenna, external gravity wave detectors, and a giga-pulse laser system solely for protecting the bridge.

The hatch slid open with an audible hum, revealing the six-meter-long black obsidian conference table with enough seating for twenty people. Just enough to fit all the senior officers and some of the senior enlisted for meetings and gatherings. The table's material was an extravagant luxury for a military ship. Her understanding was the Republic fused the material with the hull, and it would've taken more time and work than it was worth to remove.

"Have a seat." Kim gestured at the closest chair and walked around to the opposite one. She sat and pulled up her NavPad's holo of his file.

Misha sat like he was at attention, further amusing Kim. "Relax, Misha, I won't space you on your first day."

"Aye, ma'am. I—is there a day you would space me?"

Kim chuckled. "Disappoint the captain and you'll want to space yourself, trust me."

She let him chew on that for a few seconds. While the silence grew, she fiddled uselessly with the file, moving notes back and forth, making appropriate noises. Whatever she could do put him on edge. She needed to know how he operated under pressure. It worked. When she thought he was about to pass out, she struck.

"Why did you join the Navy, Misha?"

His eyes went wide. Was he trying to decide which surprised him more, the question or her use of his first name.

"Uh, ma'am?"

"It's a pretty simple question, Misha. I can repeat it if you like…"

"Uh, no, ma'am." He cleared his throat. "It seemed like a good career path."

Kim shut off her NavPad and leaned back. "No one pursues a degree in physics, graduates the top of their class, then immediately joins the Navy—the same day I might add—because 'it seemed like a good career path.'" She watched the cut of his shoulders, waiting for the moment they relaxed. It was important to know where that point was.

"True. I guess not. I don't know a whole lot about the other planets in the Alliance. Um, well, except Zkron, my home, and Alexandria, where I went to school. My family put an emphasis on education. Most good Jewish families do," he said with a sad smile. "My father had wanted to join the Navy. He even dreamed about it as a kid. He was born with Fragile-X syndrome."

Kim interrupted, "I thought they'd cured that?"

"Yes, ma'am, they did. Now it's screened for in the womb, and genetic restructuring can fix it. But that's new, my dad was already forty when the cure came out. He doesn't have it anymore, but he also doesn't want to leave his wife and kids to go galivanting around the galaxy. This is going to sound strange, but that's really why I joined. He couldn't, but I can for him. I write to him every week. Detailed letters and holos of my daily life. What I'm seeing and doing. It's made him happier than I've ever seen him. At the end of the day, I joined to make my father feel better about his life."

Kim had heard a hundred—maybe even a thousand—stories of why people joined. Everything from "I needed a job" to "I wanted to serve my nation." Most people fell somewhere in the middle. Misha Gabriel wasn't on that scale. He joined to make his dad happy. She respected that.

Jacob stood next to his command chair. Had no idea who had sewn the *Interceptor* patch onto the middle of the headrest. He ran his fingers over the image of the shark and the words *First to Fight*. Oh how he missed his little ship. He took a moment to scan the bridge surreptitiously—as well as a two-meter-tall master of the ship could. No one looked back. No one made eye contact. Perhaps it had been placed there by the same person who had disabled the conference room door of his old ship. He'd never know, and he didn't need to. The spirit of his shark-nosed destroyer lived on.

The captain of the *Seventeen* took his seat, getting a feel for the chair and how it moved. The new leather creaked. Like everything else aboard ship, it was straight from the Alliance logistics center. As he gently rocked back and forth, it struck him as odd. *Seventeen* had a new-ship smell, yet he'd faced her in battle. With different armament and a Guild crew... the Alliance engineers had outdone themselves, gutting the ship and rebuilding her in the six months since his return.

"Outstanding," he muttered. "Helm, can you tell me where I can find Chief—" Jacob stopped when he looked into the mirror that showed the person in the Pit. He had been about to ask Chief Suresh where he could find Chief Suresh. The girl in the mirror looked back at him with too-young eyes and a face that belonged on a high school student.

"Which Chief, Skipper?" she asked as if nothing was wrong. Jacob coughed to cover his hesitation and rudeness. If Chief Suresh wanted to look like a kid again, it wasn't his place to say anything. But still... he wanted her to be the COB. It was kind of hard to be the old lady if she looked eighteen.

"Uh, right. Chicf..." Jacob closed his eyes to clear his mind. "...who is your relief?"

"I just got here, Skip. I can call up PO Collins or one of the spacers."

"No, that's fine. You know what, never mind. I'll talk to you about it later." Jacob stood up, spun, and marched straight out of the bridge in a vain attempt to cover his embarrassment. He hadn't handled that well. Devi Suresh was as fine a chief as the Navy had—no one deserved to stay flying longer than her. But... she looked so darn young! He'd make it up to her. Somehow.

In the meantime, he had several orders of business to attend to, the most pressing of which was to meet with his Marine contingent commander.

"I'm sorry, Captain Grimm, I know we said today... but it's just not going to happen," Mr. Connor said over the comms.

Jacob could only nod in agreement. The civilian and military yard dogs had worked their fingers to the bone over the last months just refitting the ship. Asking them to work any harder to kick her out of the yard was unreasonable.

From what Jacob could tell, Greg Connor was a good man doing a hard job. The log showed the engineer only took Sundays off and had inspected every inch of *Seventeen* personally. He couldn't fault the man's honest assessment.

"What can we do to help?" Jacob said. "We're still two-ten shy of a full complement, but I can put my people to work on whatever you need." The conversation was private; Jacob sat on his rack, holding the NavPad up to speak. It was the end of a long day... lost in a slew of many long days. He pulled off one boot and started undoing the other.

"That's very generous of you, sir, but my people have it in hand. We need seventy-two hours with the reactors, and another five days on the armor plating checks. After that, I'm comfortable signing off on you taking her out for a propulsion trial."

Jacob scooted back until he rested against the slightly curved bulkhead. "Are we concerned about the reactor?"

"Your chief engineer hasn't arrived yet, and it's the only major piece of technology we couldn't replace. You have three Terran Republic HIT7 reactors, each with a much higher impulse rate than our own. Matching the flow of fuel through our anvils and the production and storage of energy is a bit of a challenge. We can't just plug in an adapter—"

"Listen, Greg, I get it. You don't have to sell me. Your people do good work and so do you. I know you probably hear this all the time..." Jacob made an exaggerated expression like he was telling an old story. "...but we appreciate you and we're here to help. Whatever you need."

He was pretty sure those particular words had never come

out of a Navy captain's mouth before—at least not when speaking to a civilian contractor.

"I don't know what to say. Uh... thank you. When your chief engineer does report, have him contact me."

"Will do."

Jacob closed the connection and tossed the NavPad on his queen-sized rack. It felt weird, having such a spacious quarter. He almost wanted to give it to Kim and her bunkmate and go find a single room somewhere. Moving from the bridge to the main deck would also take some getting used to. His quarters were on the same deck and right next to, turret #2. The deck vibrated when the turret turned. Lucky for him that was only likely to happen when he was on the bridge and ordering them to fire.

Someone rapped on the hatch.

"Yes?"

"Lieutenant Poole to see you, sir," a familiar-sounding voice said.

Is that... Jennings?

Jacob, excited to see his Gunny again, leapt off the rack and quick-stepped to open the hatch, a stupid smile on his face.

"Gunny!"

She stood with her back to the door in textbook parade rest, dressed in her pressed grey camouflage combat uniform. Wrapped around her waist was the brown leather combat holster and belt the Marines favored with the MP-17s in pistol mode.

Beside her was a frowning lieutenant, also dressed in combat grey. His pressed and crisp uniform cut all the right edges. MARINE and POOLE emblazoned his chest, along with his rank on the collar.

"Lieutenant Poole reporting, Captain," Poole said.

"It's a pleasure to meet you, Lieutenant." Jacob shook the

man's hand and gestured for him to come inside. As he passed, Jacob patted Jennings on her shoulder with his fist. "Good to see you... Gunny."

"Oorah, Skipper," she whispered back.

The hatch slid shut with a whoosh. Jacob went over to the small bar that was his privilege to have and opened a container of orange drink. He hefted the drink box up to offer the Lieutenant.

"No, thank you, sir."

All business, I can respect that.

Once they were seated, Jacob started. "This is an informal meeting, Lieutenant. Do you prefer Malcom?" Jacob asked.

Poole frowned, glancing at Jacob's shoeless feet. He felt a small rush of embarrassment that he quickly squashed. He'd already taken them off before the lieutenant arrived—he wasn't going to double down by rushing to put them back on.

"I prefer 'Lieutenant Poole', sir."

Those words, repeated by different officers throughout his time as a ship's commander, were familiar to him. Jacob gave the young lieutenant a sympathetic smile.

"I appreciate that. I certainly encourage formality in formal situations. Of course, informality can only flow one way. I may call an officer or enlisted by his or her first name, but the reverse, of course, wouldn't be true. Wouldn't you agree?"

Poole managed to keep his spine straight, but his face faltered for a moment.

"I would agree that professionalism is the order of the day," he said.

"Excellent. I encourage that, Malcom. Now, tell me about the Marines aboard *Seventeen*."

Poole opened his mouth to protest but stopped. Instead, he lifted his MarPad—Jacob made a mental note to have Bosun issue him a NavPad—and went over his notes.

"Right now, we have one platoon at full strength. My understanding is a ship this size would normally have a captain or major as the Marine contingent commander and a full company of Marines."

Jacob continued to ask him questions about equipment, readiness, and performance. Poole had an answer for everything, and Jacob quickly decided the man knew the textbook—and the numbers—of his job. As a captain, Jacob appreciated that.

Bells quietly rang over the comms, signaling first dog watch.

"Well done, Malcom. I'm impressed with your organization and level of detail. I look forward to hearing more at the next general officers staff meeting."

Poole cocked his head to the side, a quizzical look on his face. "Sir? Why would I be at a general staff meeting? My Marines aren't part of the ship's crew... not really."

Jacob understood Malcom's concern, but he also needed him to know that as an officer on his ship, he was expected to be involved. Anything could happen, and while the chances he would ever need to know about operations outside of his Marines were low, they were not zero.

"Look, Malcom. We might be here to run the ship's trials, and I don't even know if we'll be the crew once we're done. Until then, though, we're going to do the best job possible, and we're going to do it by the *Book*. Understood?"

Malcom looked uncomfortable at the declaration. "Yes, sir. If you say so."

"Good man. Get the XO a list of anything you need. It looks like we're going to be in the dock for at least another week."

CHAPTER SEVENTEEN

Nadia closed her eyes, breathing in the heavenly aroma of the cappuccino that Elsa sipped from the passenger seat of the aircar.

"Can I get you one?" Elsa asked.

"No. I'm trying to quit."

"Coffee is a universal truth, Nadia. You can't just *not drink it*." Her tone wasn't mocking, but there certainly was amusement in her voice.

Nadia's aircar was parked on the top floor of a parking garage opposite the Palisades. Clear ground for five hundred meters gave them an excellent view of the building. The view of the Palisades at midday was truly epic. Designed in the Georgian style, the long building had symmetrical windows, long walkways, and gently sloped roofs. She knew that hidden behind those artistic choices in brick and concrete were military-grade materials capable of withstanding immense weapons fire—and a small army of men and women who could fight back.

"I get it," Nadia said. "Everyone loves coffee. So do I."

"Then why quit?"

Nadia leaned against the inwardly curved window, gazing out at the side yard where the assassination attempt had taken place. "Because Jacob doesn't drink it, and I don't want to be the person always reminding him that he's different."

"You don't mind if I continue to drink, do you?"

Nadia smiled at her friend. "No. Of course not."

The rectangular property had streets running up and down beside it, but none closer than two hundred meters.

"What else do you give up for your husband?"

Nadia took her eyes off the Palisades for a moment. She squashed an irrational spike of irritation.

"For? Nothing. Jacob and I are the same person. I know it sounds cliché and trite, but we are. Do you know we've never really argued about anything? He's such a north star that I know, in my heart of hearts, if he truly believes in something, then it is more right than anything I could know. Even when he's found out some of the things I've... done, as part of my job, he's never spent one second judging me. He's like a man born two thousand years too late."

Elsa's snort turned into a giggle, which produced a round of laughter both women enjoyed.

"*Mein Gott*, he sounds like my father."

Nadia balked at that. "No, he's—" Then it occurred to her: She didn't actually know anything about the *Iron Emperor* other than his title... and too many rumors to be true.

"You might think my father a cruel, heartless man, and that may be right. His back, though, is as rigid as any *ritter* who ever road a horse," Elsa said.

"I don't know what half that means. Ritter?"

"Knight. Like a... knight?" She mimed riding an animal.

"Uncompromising," Nadia added. "Yes, that's Jacob. He would risk everything he has to save one stranded spacer. He has his code, and damnation be upon those who violate it."

The two women sat in silence, observant eyes staring out the windscreen toward the Palisades.

"I wonder," Elsa said. "Would your Jacob get along with my father? Or would they be enemies?"

Nadia thought of the people Jacob had encountered in his career. Men like Rasheed, who went from enemy to ally over Jacob's unaltering personal code.

"Maybe both," she said.

Nadia wasn't quite sure what brought her to the Palisades. Something nagged her. When Elsa showed up at her home eager to aid her in the investigation, she wasn't sure what to do. It wasn't like she had ONI resources or DNI authority. All she had was her very illegal NavPad, and a desire to find the truth. With Jacob off-planet for the foreseeable future, it felt like digging for answers was the right thing to do. Especially since DNI didn't seem to be investigating the situation.

"Elsa?"

"Hmm?"

"How did you and your brother arrive at the Palisades that night?"

"Kannon's... uh, our version of the Corsairs. We landed at the commercial space port west of the city. Ambassadorial vehicles from our embassy ferried us to the actual party."

"How many Kannons?"

"Only the one. My brother and I, and about a half dozen navy personnel, along with the ambassador and his family."

Nadia wasn't sure where her mind was going, but in her experience, letting her thoughts play out produced the best results. "Your brother already confirmed the four assassins didn't come from your party, yes?"

"Yes. We haven't figured out who they are yet, or where they came from. I mean, technically, they are Imperial Navy. The uniforms aren't fake. But no one on the ships we brought knew who they were or ever recalled serving with them. Why?"

Nadia let all the lines come together. It wasn't a major revelation; perhaps it was something someone at DNI had already pieced together. But still... "How did they get to the party?" she asked.

"What do you mean?"

"If they didn't ride down with you on your Kannon, and they weren't in the vehicle with you... how did they arrive at the gala?"

"Indeed, how?"

Nadia scanned the neighborhood around the Palisades with her NavPad, finding every camera with a view of the presidential residence. Two covered the parking area leading directly into the gate of the gala.

She pulled up their feeds.

"These should have..." Both camera's memories were wiped, only going back to the morning after.

"Nothing strange about that," Elsa whispered.

Nadia felt she was missing several things. Maybe it was time to go back to the very beginning. "Why would the Iron Empire want to assassinate the President of the Alliance?" she asked.

"Nadia, I'm not just the emperor's daughter. I'm heavily involved in our espionage and security programs. I'm telling you, we didn't do this," Elsa said.

Nadia looked at her, really looked at her, past the facade of the innocent girl or party-happy woman. Nadia had seen Elsa in the depths of despair; she liked to think it mattered.

"I know that. But humor me. Why?"

Elsa frowned, not even wanting to think about the ramifications if her people were involved.

"I suppose the obvious reason would be to stop any treaty. If there were separatist forces in the Empire—which there aren't—this would be their way of keeping us apart."

Low-hanging fruit, Nadia thought. The obvious answer. Not necessarily the simplest, but certainly the most obvious.

"It could be ISB, to keep you out of the war. It would be much easier to reach us here than anyone in the Empire. They have gene-editing technology, as we know. They could have edited four assassins to be from the Empire. Used them as disposable tools. Succeed or fail, it would put a wedge between us. Delay or even stop our Alliance."

Elsa frowned at the idea.

"Are you on the edge of victory or defeat?" she asked.

"I don't know. Maybe both. Regardless, the Caliph has the most to gain from keeping us from working together. I can't really see anyone else—outside your separatist theory." Ignoring Elsa's strangled protest, she went on. "Your Navy is formidable, as we all know. The last thing the Caliphate needs is the Iron Navy rolling on our side. Even if you just took a defensive roll, it would free up our ships to be much more aggressive."

"Doesn't the Consortium do that for you already?" Elsa asked.

On her NavPad, Nadia brought up a map of the current fleet distribution. If Elsa wondered how a civilian had access to such things, she made no mention.

"Consortium forces aren't playing aggressively. They're defending their territory—moving all their available ships to the border but not actively fighting."

"But they're your allies... I thought."

"Yes. They're doing everything they're legally obligated to do, just no more. Part of the problem, I suspect, is that our last SECNAV did the same—everything the treaty obligated, but no more. Under that policy, the Consortium lost millions of her people to slavery in the Caliphate. This may be them playing it safe in return."

Elsa was acutely aware of the Caliphates role in human trafficking. They were the number one recipients of all trafficked people in the entire galaxy. "Bastards," she said. Probably unconsciously, she rubbed her throat where the collar was once placed on her.

Nadia had her own demons because of the Caliphate. She knew all too well the human cost involved. And she couldn't blame the Consortium for defensive posturing.

"Let's assume the ISB's involvement, then. Since there are no abandoned aircars or ground vehicles, we can assume someone dropped them off."

"Automated car?" Elsa asked.

"Without footage, it's impossible to tell. I could hack all the rental car companies in Anchorage Bay, but that would take a while. I think, though, they either owned the vehicle or rented it but had their own driver. Which means—"

"There's more of them," Elsa finished.

"That would be my guess. Since they had legit uniforms and papers to get in the gala, I'm going with them having serious inside support. So *how they arrived* is our key to finding them."

Elsa finished the last of her coffee and dropped the cup into the small recycler. "Where do we start?"

"Someone let them in, and that someone will know how they arrived. They had swords laced with toxin. Even if they had all the papers in the world, someone had to look the other way. That's where we start."

"Who handled the door security for the gala?" Elsa asked.

Nadia thought back to the night and remembered uniformed police officers working the entrance.

Going back to work was a risk Ahmed was willing to take. The assurance that his cover wasn't broken meant nothing if he suddenly quit his job with Anchorage Bay Police Department. He'd spent years toiling for law enforcement, his spotless record allowing him a choice of assignments. Whenever anything came up that offered extra money, Officer Ahmed Al-Qahtani had dibs.

He couldn't quit now. Couldn't risk the cover he'd spent years building. The Caliph might need him again. The last time the Alliance dogs started rounding up everyone with a Caliph name, he'd worried his deep cover was blown, but his skills, and the fact that he'd done nothing wrong and had a stellar reputation, freed him from scrutiny.

If only they knew. No true son or daughter of Allah would ever bow to the infidels of the Alliance. He scoffed at those he passed in the morning. The Mosque was full of cowards and liars, women whores and men who allowed them to fornicate.

Ahmed shook his head. He needed to keep his mind focused. Allah forgave him for his transgressions while under muruna. After all, if all one had to do to find a spy was make them eat pork, it would be easy to find all of them. However, the infidels were easily fooled by Ahmed drinking a beer with them after a long day's work or hitting the clubs and picking up loose women. Even his partner didn't suspect anything. More precisely, Ahmed thought, *they didn't want to suspect.* It was a kind of willful ignorance. Everyone in his department was willing to believe he was one of the "good ones." They didn't realize how racist they were.

Ahmed closed the door to his patrol aircar; recognizing him, the computer instantly lit up.

"Good morning, Officer Al-Qahtani, your patrol starts in five minutes. Would you like to prepare your shop?" the onboard computer informed him. Shop was police slang for the aircar.

Ahmed keyed in his override, turning the AI off and allowing him to control his shop manually.

"Dispatch, twenty-four is ten-eight."

"Roger, twenty-four available."

He eased the aircar out of the garage and into the sky. Nothing quite beat the feeling of—

At three hundred meters, an altitude sensitive trigger ignited, activating a pen-sized laser. For a split second, plasma as hot as the sun burned on the surface of the four kilograms of explosives under Ahmed's seat. Twenty-five thousand kilojoules of energy detonated at ninety-four thousand meters per second. Ahmed didn't even hear the explosion as he and his aircar turned into a cloud of debris spread out over a kilometer of downtown Anchorage Bay.

CHAPTER EIGHTEEN

"Finally," Jacob whispered to himself. With the yard's clearance, *Seventeen* was free and clear to depart her moorings.

For the final week, his crew had struggled alongside the yard, working around the clock, through all bells, to make the seized battleship space worthy.

From problems with the hatches to the gravcoil housing, it hadn't seemed like it would ever end. But here they were, ready to strike out on their own and prove that their hard work and lost sleep resulted in something spectacular. The renovation of a battleship built by the Terran Republic was a feat of the ages. In the founding days of the Alliance, retrofitting enemy ships was common; the resources required to build a hull from scratch were far greater than filling out the interior of an already built ship that had belonged to the enemy.

He smiled at the hum of the gravcoil coming online. Tapping his fingers gently on his armrest, Jacob prepared himself for departure. Utopia shipyard was alive with activity. Hundreds of ships—military and civilian—were in various stages of construction and repair, either moored upon the surface of the moon or in one of the many grid-like hangers orbiting above the surface.

"All moorings are cleared," Chief Suresh notified him.

He was still getting used to her very youthful face in the mirror they shared, but he liked to think he'd done a good job of not showing his shock at her appearance. "Thank you, Coxswain. Ops, set condition Yankee, underway."

Alarms blared throughout the ship.

"All hands, set Condition Yankee. Prepare for underway," Mark West said in the calming clear voice all officers trained for.

"Helmets, Skipper?" Yuki asked from her chair to his right.

"No. Keep them handy, but the suits should be enough." With the war raging on, several changes had swept through the Navy. One in particular Jacob was glad for. With crew spending more time in their ELS suits than before, the Navy had rushed a new version to the field. Thinner, more comfortable, and, more importantly, the plumbing connections were automatic and barely felt. There was also an option to not connect the plumbing, allowing the new ELS suits to be worn under standard uniforms for extended periods of time.

The helmets were still the same, though. There wasn't a lot to improve on a nano-reinforced steel box designed to protect one's head from violent impacts.

Jacob eyed the timer on his primary MFD. The moment the announcement to set condition Yankee blasted over the ship's speakers, a timer started. Back on *Interceptor*, the ship's readiness goal was two minutes. That was with a hundred odd crew and a ship that was only a hundred meters long. *Seventeen* was literally ten times as big, with ten times as many crew.

He would give them three minutes.

As the timer approached the mark, Jacob swiveled his chair to face Ops. The screen beyond Mark West's chair, flashed half green and yellow. They weren't going to make the time.

Knowing that, he turned back to Kim. "Set up regular drills, all watches. No one knows when but me."

"Aye, sir," she said. "I've already got a schedule setup."

Jacob smiled at his diminutive XO. "I'm tempted to add something just so I don't seem predictable."

She let out a stifled laugh.

"Predictable is good when it comes to leadership, Skipper. I've gone through the files on all our crew—we've got people from a dozen ships and multiple naval stations. Hell, sir, we even have some civilians. It's going to take time to make them all into gel. You and I both know, though, you're the man for the job. If I can make things go a little quicker by anticipating your commands, then we can make this happen faster."

Commander Yuki never ceased to amaze Jacob. From the moment he'd met her back on *Interceptor* all those years ago, he'd felt she was an outstanding officer. It was nice to know he was right. "Okay, Kim. You've got me. Set up the training schedule along with the alerts and have it on my desk by 1900."

She tapped a key on her NavPad. "It's on your desk now, Skipper."

Red letters turned green on his MFD as Mark West announced crew readiness. "All stations reporting ready, sir."

"Forward view," Jacob ordered.

The massive, curved screen dominating the front of the bridge sprang to life with a view immediately outside. From below, the long nose of *Seventeen* stretched out encased in the scaffolding of the yard.

"Helm, five g's on the gravcoil."

Misha Gabriel turned to face him. "Sir, we're only supposed to use maneuvering thrusters in dock—" He stopped abruptly when half the bridge looked his way with various shades of grins.

"I understand, Mr. Gabriel," Jacob said. "It's an old tradition. Take us out, COB."

"Aye, aye, Skipper," Devi replied. "Zero-five gravities on the gravcoil in three—" At one, she eased the throttle forward to the first hash. Power thrummed to life, and the ship trudged forward at fifty meters per second per second and shooting out of the dock.

"Set course for Pandora Station," Jacob ordered. Pandora orbited the closest asteroid belt to Alexandria and was the Navy's official range used for target practice.

"Aye, sir, course calculated and sent to helm," Lieutenant Brennan said.

Jacob made a mental note to praise Fionna at his first chance. She must have calculated every possible course to have it ready as quick as she did. "Course change. Come to two-seven-five at two-five g's for one-one-five minutes," Brennan said.

Devi repeated back the course. "Ready when you are, Skipper."

"Execute," Jacob ordered.

The nose of *Seventeen* swung around, on course for the distant logistics station in the asteroid belt of Alexandria. In the vicinity of the planet, the moon, and the shipping lanes, they were restricted to no more than two-five gravities until they were outside the shipping lanes and the gravwake wouldn't disrupt other vessels.

Once they confirmed their course was clear with space traffic control, they could increase their maximum velocity to one thousand KPS. After another hour of travel, they could bump it up to one-zero-zero g's and increase their max velocity to something that would get them around the system before they died of old age.

Jacob leaned over to Kim, pitching his voice just for her.

"Have a word with Misha, not for speaking up, but for speaking up publicly. I'd rather have a private note than an officer who questioned my orders in the open."

Kim gave him a curt nod. "Aye, sir. Though I doubt I'll have to say much." She nodded toward the weapons officer. He had buried his face in his console, not making eye contact with anyone, and was so bright red his neck looked like a cherry.

"Poor kid," Jacob said.

"I'm sure the experience will be good for him, sir."

Jacob hit the ship-wide comms. "All hands, this is the captain speaking. We are the first crew of *Seventeen*. Over the next month, we will put the Navy's newest ship through her paces. I expect nothing less than maximum effort from everyone aboard. Most of all, from myself and the officers.

"A ship is nothing without her crew. From the newest spacer's apprentice to her captain, we all have a vital role to play. I want each and every one of you to feel heard. If you have a problem, we have a problem. Use the appropriate chain of command, but I want you all to know, my door is always open. You give me one hundred and ten percent, and I will do everything in my power to give it right back."

He looked around the bridge, suddenly realizing that every officer, NCO, and enlisted was watching him with rapt attention.

"Some of you have served with me before and know this to be true. I look forward to proving it to the rest of you. Good luck. Captain out."

Life returned to the bridge after he finished... almost as if the crew held their breath while he spoke.

"How do you do that?" Kim asked.

"Do what?"

She twirled her fingers in the air. "The speech. Do you have a book or something?"

"Just one? No. Hundreds. I like reading."

"So you come up with them off the top of your head?"

"Usually."

What he wouldn't tell her was that he had spent hundreds of hours reading about the great leaders of history. He did, in fact, make notes and jot down ideas for speeches. However, it was better if everyone thought he just came up with them off the top of his head.

Seventeen cruised through space, her grav wake spreading out behind her. They weren't going fast enough to see the planet visibly shrink, but if he looked away for a moment, it would. Jacob leaned back, squeezing the handrests. This was where he belonged. "Kim, I'd like a general officer briefing at 1900 hours in the conference room."

"Aye, sir. General officers briefing. May I suggest the wardroom, Skipper? Now that we have one."

Jacob liked the idea and agreed. "Make sure Josh prepares the dinner."

"Mendez?" Kim perked up. "He's here?"

"I'm afraid I have him all to myself. He's the captain's cook. I didn't even know they assigned cooks to captains."

Kim stood up, making sure her uniform was straight. "You're a BB skipper now. There are a thousand spacers aboard, and they were all just told you have an open door. You're not going to have the time to dress, let alone walk to the mess."

As she walked toward the bridge hatch, Jacob realized what she meant. He was *the old man.* He'd have to get used to having assistants take care of his chores the same way he had to learn to shuffle paperwork off on his subordinates.

He left the bridge in West's capable hands. With the ship on course and many hours to go before they were able to accelerate, he decided it was the perfect time to walk the ship. After all, he couldn't break his tradition just because the ship was a klick long.

Two armed Marines guarded the bridge, their gunmetal grey fatigues pressed and creased. At their hips they had the standard brown leather holster with the MP-17 and accessories. He stopped to admire them for a moment.

"John and Derrik, right?" Jacob said.

The two Marines snapped to attention. While their heads didn't move, their eyes darted to the side.

"Yes sir, that's right," the taller of the two said. "I'm Private John Washington." Washington's broad shoulders made Jacob think he'd played football or something like it. Shorter than Jacob, but certainly more muscular.

"I'm Derrik Samuels, sir." Derrik had a lithe figure of a man who ran... a lot.

"As you were, Privates. Have you met the Gunny yet?"

A sour expression flashed over their faces. With all his might, Jacob resisted smiling.

"Yes, sir." They said in unison.

"Give her time, men. I promise you there is no finer Marine."

"Semper Fi, sir."

Jacob took the ladder down to the main deck. Alliance ships had their bridge in the stern; it took Jacob some getting used to having the superstructure in the midship. While he could traverse the ship using ladders and passageways, it would take hours. No single passageway ran the length of the ship. Unlike *Interceptor,* he would have to switch back and forth, up and down, to physically walk to the boat bay. However, he could hit the highlights—like the massive turrets on the main deck and the main gun. From there he could take a lift to the stern and see the boat bay and its crew.

Jacob disliked formal dinners, but no officer escaped their grasp—especially his first meal with the officers who ran his ship. It was important for *esprit de corps* and for his own personal knowledge.

Thankfully *Seventeen* was his ship, and he could modify the rules slightly. They were less than eight hours from Alexandria; every single crew member had been working their fingers to the bone. He wasn't going to make them change into a dress uniform.

It wasn't entirely unselfish. He hated showing off the medals on his dress uniform. Some officers were insecure about their own lack of combat experience, and he hoped to head off any issues with that.

Seventeen's wardroom spanned more space than the entire mess on Interceptor. Someone had taken the tables and made one long line, just like the CO of Naval Station Bethesda had done. The most junior officer sat on Jacob's right, then counter-clockwise in ascending order to Kim, who sat on his left.

The only interruption to this officers-only meeting was the sole civilian aboard, who ran the galley. Jacob had been surprised when he learned about him. A retired chief petty officer, no less. Since he wasn't technically an officer, Jacob put him at the opposite end of the table, dead in the middle.

Gunny Jennings manned the hatch from the inside. Jacob hadn't requested a Marine guard; Gunny decided on her own. After all they'd gone through together, he certainly couldn't blame her.

Josh rolled in from the small galley, Spacers Zach and Perch behind him like little ducklings. However Josh Mendez had managed to stay with him, his staff did the same for Josh. They stopped with the carts parallel to the table, waiting for the XO to perform her duty. Normally, a ship of *Seventeen*'s size would have several midships, but none were assigned.

Kim nodded to Lieutenant Misha Gabriel who sat on Jacob's immediate right. Gabriel stood and picked up his glass of pseudo-wine. "Ladies and Gentlemen, the President." He held the glass up high for a moment. All present lifted their glasses and uttered the same line in unison and took a sip. Once done, Misha sat down.

Next, Lieutenant Brennan stood. "Ladies and Gentlemen, the Navy." The same procedure followed.

Jacob could choose to let the meal begin, but he felt in his heart one more toast must be said.

He stood, instantly bringing the entire room to their feet. Jacob raised his glass of orange drink. "Not only are our fallen comrades commemorated by columns and inscriptions, but there dwells also an unwritten memorial to them, graven not on stone but in the hearts of men." He let the silence linger for a moment. "To absent friends."

Once they were seated again, Kim nodded for Josh to serve the first course. The young chef had knocked the appetizer out of the park; delicious crab cakes, along with a small serving of remoulade sauce.

The meal only improved from there. A succulent beef wellington, served with garlic mashed potatoes, carrots Vichy, and fresh bread that Jacob didn't know was possible aboard ship. Taking a cue from his old station CO, he remained quiet, letting the officers chat amongst themselves. He was more than happy to respond to any questions, but he knew that if he started talking, his position would put an end to all other conversation.

As good as the food was, and it was mouthwatering, he restricted himself to a few bites. His uniforms were already tight around the middle. Since he was back aboard ship with Jennings, he expected her to schedule daily beatdowns again. He couldn't afford the extra weight.

As the captain's cooking crew cleared the main dish, Jacob touched Josh's elbow.

"Outstanding, young man," he said.

PO Mendez beamed with pride. "Thank you, sir. I'm not done yet."

The coup de grace was a single serving of key lime pie. There was no way he could have known how many exactly would have dined that night. *Did he bake enough pies to cover everyone?*

One bite, and Jacob wanted to die. Tangy and sweet, with a flaky crust and whipped cream so soft it dissolved on his tongue.

A twinge of guilt hit him mid-bite. Nadia was in his home, recovering from almost dying. Assassins had tried to kill his president. And there he was, enjoying a gourmet meal aboard ship.

Jacob chided himself for his reaction. The traditions of the Navy were what kept it going in hard times. He needed his crew to come together, and that happened from the top down, not the bottom up.

Coffee came next, and it was time to get down to business.

"Thank you, PO Mendez. Well done." Jacob lifted his glass of orange drink to the retreating petty officer. "Now that we've eaten entirely too much"—light chuckles broke out—"let's talk business. We're still shy crew, and I don't see that changing any time soon. We've all served aboard ships that weren't staffed to the right numbers. Assume for now that won't change. Mark, your department is the largest; let's start with your report."

"I've had PO Tefiti and Oliv go over every square inch of our EW capability—we're good to go, sir. All systems are squared away. I was surprised myself, but we've thoroughly tested everything from the laser comms to the towed array. I'm pleased to say we are ready for trials."

Jacob was glad to hear it. He doubted every department would be as ready as Mark's, but he could hope.

Kim singled out Marino, the diminutive Hispanic woman who Jacob knew well. "Lieutenant Marino?" Kim said. "How's the medical staff?"

"Ma'am, I've got good people down there, just not enough of them." She raised her hand to forestall objections. "I know... I'm not complaining. But staff really is the only thing we need. I'm the only doctor. I've got four PAs, but none of them are surgeons. Equipment-wise, we have everything we need. However, engineering is having trouble keeping power to the recovery wing."

"That seems important. Beech?" Kim asked.

"Ma'am, I've got Chief Redfern on it. If anyone can figure it out, it's him."

"Good to hear. I imagine your report is going to be the longest, Beech. Let's save you for last. Brennan, how's our navigation equipment?"

Fionna flushed slightly. "We've got state-of-the-art equipment, ma'am." Her Irish lilt was pronounced. "The COB says the throttle doesn't *feel* right." She smiled. "Her words, ma'am. I've got PO Collins looking into it."

The rest of the meeting went as Jacob expected, with each department either having equipment troubles or staffing troubles. Every spacer could cover any job... except medical. He reminded himself, though, that they were just out to show the flag. Nothing more. Not a single shred of intelligence suspected an attack on Alexandria.

Of course, they thought that before the Caliphate nuked Anchorage Bay.

That wouldn't ever happen again. Ever.

After Beech finished his rather lengthy and exhaustive report, Jacob stood. "A training schedule is on each of your devices. Please review it and get back to the XO if you have any questions or need changes."

"Sir, may I ask a question?" Lieutenant Poole raised his hand.

"Go ahead."

"Why are there hours labeled *repel boarders* blocked out for my Marines? Surely that's some kind of mistake? No one has boarded an Alliance vessel as a hostile in over a decade."

While Poole's statement wasn't technically true, Jacob gathered the Marine's meaning.

"A few years ago, *Interceptor* was badly damaged in a nonaligned system with no hope of help arriving. The only thing we could do was send a few brave Marines to an enemy ship to steal their diamond anvil to replace our broken one. Four Marines and one engineer went aboard and got the job done. In hindsight, I should have sent half the crew—but on a tin can, there just isn't much crew to spare."

"Begging the captain's pardon, but what does that have to do with us? No one boards a battleship."

Jacob gave Poole a fatherly smile.

"You're probably right, but the report I read showed the Caliphate had no idea how to repel boarders. I'd be a fool of a skipper if I didn't learn from my enemies' mistakes. I'll have Bosun rotate crew to act as both OPFOR and defense. I'm sure Gunny Jennings can arrange a good time for all."

Poole twisted in his chair, looking back at Jennings as if he'd forgotten she was there.

"Right. Yes, sir. Though I still think the Marines would be better off doing their own training."

Irked, Jacob thought he did an admirable job of keeping it out of his voice.

"Well, Lieutenant, when you're the captain, you can do as you please."

The slight upturn of Kim's lips told Jacob he hadn't quite succeeded.

"I'm doing well. Stop worrying. Your friend brought me home, and your dad is quite capable of looking after me," Nadia said from the screen.

Jacob wished fervently the recorded message was real-time.

Nadia sat cross-legged in his bed, a tank top on and a thick down comforter pulled up to her chest. She was still missing her cybernetic arm, which was hard for him to look at. He loved her dearly, and seeing her in pain bothered him to his soul. However, he'd married a capable woman. Someone who could take care of herself and knew how to be alone. What other way could there be? He wouldn't be taking a station or ground assignment by choice. She was going to have to live with him being gone for months, sometimes years, at a time.

Still, he wished he could have both. His ship and his woman.

"I know you think I should stay in bed and all, but I just can't. Elsa is going to come over today, and we're just going to look at what happened. Nothing dangerous, promise." Nadia paused for a moment, looking into the camera. "I miss you, Jacob, but I won't message you again. I want you focused on your job, not worrying about me. You do your job, and you come home. I promise I will make your safe return worth the effort." The smile on her lips relayed exactly what she meant. Without another word, Nadia killed the recording.

Jacob sighed. She was right. He couldn't do his job effectively if part of his brain, a large part, was thinking about her and what she was going through. He had to put it in a box and move on. When he got home, though. Boy, was he going to make good on her promise.

CHAPTER NINETEEN

Asteroid belts fascinated Jacob. They varied from thick clusters of fine particulates to widely dispersed larger rocks the size of moons. Pandora station, located in the middle of Alexandria's first asteroid belt, was a hollowed-out asteroid a hundred kilometers in diameter, reinforced with nano-steel to keep it from collapsing from the loss of mass. The station held enough ordnance to refill *Seventeen* three times over—all for target practice on the belt's many, many kilometer-wide asteroids.

"Pandora Station, this is Captain Jacob T. Grimm, *BB Seventeen*. Requesting permission to use any available range," Jacob said over the radio. He could have had Mac make the call, but he preferred to do it himself. He didn't want the range officer to feel ignored.

"*Seventeen*, this is Lieutenant Witwicki, RO for Bravo-Six-Six. I'm sending over the coordinates now. She's all yours for as long as you want her."

"Thank you. Can I talk you into coming along, Lieutenant? It promises to be quite the show."

There was a long pause before the RO answered. "That's the

best offer I've had all week, Captain. However, duty calls. Send me a recording and I'll buy you a coffee next time you're here."

"Will do." Jacob killed the line.

A moment later, Owusu acknowledged a call on his station. "I have the coordinates, Skipper."

"Plot the course, send it to the Pit, and let's go. I want to blow something up."

"Yes, sir," Owusu said with a big grin.

Seventeen, as big and sluggish as she was, accelerated away from Pandora toward her first waypoint.

"Ops, bring us to Condition Zulu, training exercise."

"Aye, aye, Skipper," West replied. "Condition Zulu, training exercise."

Klaxons blared throughout the ship a moment later, Collins' voice echoing behind them.

"Eta to range, COB?"

"Two-five minutes at current velocity, Skip," Devi replied.

There was a lot coming together for the test. The crew needed familiarity with the weapons, as did the ship's captain. He was also eager to try out the new ELS suits. The slim, lightweight garments designed to be worn under the uniform had so far, performed admirably. Each of the crew's stations on the bridge came with a storage compartment for a helmet. Part of reporting for station was bringing your helmet along. It was an extra burden for duty, but not nearly as much as having to leave your station, go to your cabin, and get your ELS suit.

"Gabriel, I would like to run a two-part test. First, fire every weapon one-by-one."

"Aye, sir. Standard readiness test."

"Secondly, I want to fire every turret at once, at the same target."

"Sir, regulations state that while at a range—"

Jacob did everything he could not to discourage the young

man. Instead, he stood and moved over to the station, leaning down to whisper.

"Except for trial runs," he said.

"Sir?" Misha looked shocked that his captain was suddenly standing over him.

"The rule: Three-Seven-Alpha of the training of ship's crews and ordinance. Except at designated weapons ranges for trial runs."

Gabriel audibly gulped as he realized he was mistaken. "Yes, sir. Sorry, sir."

"Lieutenant Misha, I fully encourage my officers to have their own opinions. I certainly want them to speak up if they have a good idea. What I don't want, or need, is a rules lawyer. Understood?"

"Understood, sir," Lieutenant Misha said.

Jacob patted him on the shoulder. "Live and learn, Gabriel. Live and learn. Let me know when you have both firing solutions ready."

Gabriel could die. Not only had he corrected his captain—twice—he'd been wrong this time. Even if he'd been technically right, was it worth it to correct his captain? Like him or not, if he gave him a bad FITREP, his career would be all but over. He shook his head. He was looking at this posting all wrong. This was no punishment. As a mere lieutenant, he was the chief weapons officer of a battleship. What had he been thinking?

Gabriel took a deep breath, giving himself a moment to clear his head before continuing. The last thing he wanted to do was follow up an intentional error with an unintentional one. He needed to get his head in the game.

"Gun crews signal ready on all turrets," he ordered over the gun comms.

As the petty officers replied, he marked each turret as ready. "Weapons, Turret Three-Alpha, PO Ignatius. Sir, I'm getting a red light on main bus five-seven for the turret." Turrets 1- through 3-Alpha were the ship's big guns—400mm coil cannons firing rounds at 30,000 KPS. With three guns per turret, *Seventeen* had nine of these barrels. Losing one turret cut their firepower by a third.

Dammit.

"Roger, PO. Stand down for the moment. I'll signal engineering to take a look at it."

If the main bus was down, the turret couldn't charge the supercapacitor to fire. A power imbalance like that could destabilize the entire grid as the ship's three reactors attempted to compensate. A cascade failure could take out the entire weapons systems. Not something a young lieutenant who was already on the outs with his captain needed.

Gabriel switched his channel to the engineering ready line. "Engineering, Lieutenant Misha."

"Engineering, Chief Redfern. How can I help you, sir?"

"Chief, PO Ignatius is showing a red light on turret three's main bus. How quick can you get down there?"

Redfern didn't miss a beat. "I'll have it cleared by the time we're on station, sir."

Thank you, thank you, thank you. Gabriel silently prayed for the chief's good fortune.

"Roger, Chief. Keep me in the loop."

"Aye, aye, sir. Engineering out."

———

Echo grabbed his toolkit. It consisted of everything he'd need to diagnose a problem and make temporary repairs.

"Kolchak, grab your kit and follow me." Echo scrambled down the stairs from his office, helmet in one hand, toolkit on his back.

The young spacer stuck his head out from underneath a panel they were dismantling. "Chief?"

"Get your kit and follow me."

Echo didn't wait for him—he was out the hatch, pulling his helmet on.

Main engineering sat forward of amidships, between reactor room one and two, giving the engineering and damage control crews easy access to the majority of their area of operations. Turret 3-Alpha was far to the stern.

Echo clicked his NavPad into his suit and triggered the map to overlay the best route. There was a lift he could take all the way down to frame six hundred; that would only leave a handful of ladders to traverse by hand.

"On your six, Chief," Kolchak said. Since their conversation, the young spacer had decided to double down and work harder.

If it weren't for the skipper, Echo decided, he wouldn't want to be on a battleship. He vastly preferred the smaller, more intimate setting of a destroyer. Maybe a light cruiser. If the skip decided to stay with battleships, he'd have to come to terms with letting that part of his life go. Before he knew it, they were climbing the ladder into the bottom of the turret.

Each turret was like a six-story building. From the bottom, the ammo fed to the top, with buffer storage around the base. The first three levels were the superconductor rings, interlaced with the ammo feed. Levels four and five were the gun crews, and six was fully automated, with the ammo feed mechanism loading the insanely heavy projectiles into the 400mm coil launchers. The projectiles were an order of magnitude larger than a destroyer could mount. They were intended for engagement with other capital ships, not light elements.

"What did you do to my guns, PO?" Redfern asked over the turret comms as he pulled his lanky form through the hatch. Level four had nine crewmembers to transfer the rounds from storage to the main loader. Level five, which was really a gunner's chair, was in the back, with ladder access where the gun crew leader could aim and fire the turret manually as needed.

PO Ignatius looked up from his control panel. "Chief, you got here quick. I followed the manual to clear the main bus fault, and it reset after five seconds."

Echo finished pulling himself up into the turret, then turned and helped Kolchak.

"Understood, PO. Kolchak... check panel three-seven. Run your circuit tester down each of the odd number circuits. Copy?"

"Copy, Chief."

Echo pulled off his backpack and headed for the main control panel underneath Ignatius' station. The PO was right—all the lights were green except the main bus circuit for the supercapacitor.

"What have you got, Chief?" Ignatius asked.

"I'm thinking the light is the fault, but we'll see."

"Skipper, Six-Six is approaching," Owusu announced.

Jacob glanced up at the main viewer. With a maximum reliable detection of a million klicks with radar/lidar, the distances involved in ship-to-ship engagement were mind-boggling. Not only was it unreliable to detect a target farther away, but the distances meant the shots would take far too long to arrive. The goal of any engagement was to close with the enemy, trap them into a pattern of movement, and destroy them. Of course, that also meant not being destroyed.

With a battleship, the rules changed slightly. Normally, BBs didn't operate on their own—they were escorted by an entire fleet of heavy cruisers, light cruisers, destroyers, and possibly even frigates with them. Trials were the obvious exception.

"Bring up the scope, Owusu. Put it on the main viewer."

"Aye, aye, Skipper. Telescope locking on and showing on main viewer."

"Helm, cut the gravcoil and coast."

"Aye, Skipper, cutting gravcoil," Chief Suresh replied.

For a moment, gravity distorted the image, and a wash of static passed over the screen. Then there she was. Range Six-Six.

"Take a good look at her people. When we're done, she's toast."

Palpable excitement rippled through the bridge. Live fire exercises weren't normally something to get worked up about, but *Seventeen* had a lot of guns. Blowing stuff up was an age-old entertainment for every spacer. Nothing packed as big a punch as a battleship.

"Helm, thrusters. Bring us about to zero-nine-zero starboard," Jacob could just tell Devi to line the port side up for a broadside, but ship handling was his first true love.

"Aye, aye, sir, come starboard one-nine-zero, maneuvering thrusters only."

"Ops, drop the towed array. If I recall, we need full fidelity recordings for our builder friends."

West acknowledged the order. A moment later, the towed array shot out of the stern like a fly-fishing line, powered by thrusters to keep it taut. Jacob's secondary screen lit up, showing the increase in passive data.

"Weps, throw up a tactical overlay, will you?" Jacob asked. He was really getting into the idea of blowing stuff up, and his excitement translated into his casual tone and demeanor.

"Aye, aye, sir. Tactical overlay."

Distance, location, and time in space weren't as straightforward as calculating on a planet. The location of a ship was a matter of perspective. *Seventeen*'s distance to the rock, her previous course, and the estimated distance to Pandora Station appeared on the screen, along with calculated trajectories for her main turrets, as well as possible torpedo solutions. *Seventeen* came to rest 100,000 klicks from the range—far enough to allow for a test of the weapons without undue risk to the ship.

Jacob couldn't help but smile. The whole thing made him giddy as a kid.

"Ops... drain the can."

"Aye, aye, sir. Draining the can." West's fingers danced across his controls. "All hands, helmets on. Helmets on. Helmets on." His voice rang out in every compartment, every hatch, every radio. While they weren't in an emergency situation, they treated the situation as if they were. Death was part of a spacers trade, but Jacob would be damned if he let a spacer die outside of combat if he could help it.

He placed his own helmet on; the seal activated with a reassuring whoosh of canned air.

"Status?" Jacob asked.

"All lights are green, Skipper. All departments report ready."

"Drain it."

Amber lights flashed overhead, alerting any crew who perchance didn't hear the warning a final chance to see it. After thirty seconds of flashing lights, air whooshed out of the ship. Pressure was reduced to near-zero to prevent any explosive decompression.

"Weps, let's start with the twenties. One by one, then a full sustained barrage for one minute." Jacob leaned forward, focusing hard on the range labeled Six-Six.

"Aye, aye, sir. On cycle, twenty-mike-mike followed by sustained barrage." Gabriel turned to his panel and issued the orders. "Turrets sixteen through twenty-four ready to fire, sir."

Jacob savored the moment. The feel of his new command, the way the air seemed to hold still, the quiet in his helmet, the beat of his heart. "Fire."

One by one, the quad-barreled 20mm turrets fired. In order to reduce the heat load, each barrel fired at a slight delay, taking a whole second to fire four rounds. Eight turrets shot thirty-two rounds of nano-steel wrapped tungsten down their coils at 20,000 KPS. Each round crossed the distance to Range Six-Six in five seconds.

On the main viewer, the impacts rippled along the asteroid like popcorn exploding in a pan.

"Status?" Jacob asked.

"All turrets on target, sir," Gabriel replied.

"Good man. Ops?" Jacob turned his chair to look at Lieutenant Commander West.

"Skipper?"

"Make sure you put this on the big screen on all the galleys for the next couple of meals. Quality entertainment is important," Jacob said with a half smile.

"Aye, aye, Skip. On the big screen for meals."

As a spacer himself, Jacob knew the crew would love it. "Mr. Gabriel, one-minute continuous barrage, turrets sixteen through twenty-four. Fire at will."

Not ten seconds later, all eight twenty-millimeter turrets opened fire with all the ferocity modern technology could conjure. Round after round smashed into the nickel-iron asteroid. Dozens of new craters appeared on the well-worn rock.

Seventeen wasn't the first ship to fire on her, and she wouldn't be the last, but Jacob intended to leave his mark.

"Time," Kim said over the shared command channel. "Cease fire."

"Aye. Ceasing fire," Misha replied.

Jacob checked his own board for turret status. If there were any problems with the firing mechanisms or the spacers manning the turrets, a minute of sustained fire was enough to root out any hints.

All the ready lights for the 20s showed bright green.

"Weps, well done. Now let's get serious. Bring up the one-twenties. "

They repeated the test for the larger, slower turrets. Unlike the nimble 20mm rounds, the 120mms were massive. Far more effective for area denial and close in combat, and capable of damaging the thicker armor on a heavy cruiser and battleship. Impacting with anything less than a HC would result in, at very least, a disabled ship.

His brief combat actions with larger ships when he was the captain of the *Interceptor* burned in his memory. Often times, the only weapon they could bring to bear against a heavier foe was the Long 9.

Seventeen didn't have Long 9s. Instead, she had three massive turrets capable of firing far heavier rounds, any one of which would obliterate a destroyer. She was truly designed as a boxer; close with the enemy and pound the crap out of them.

The 120s had a slower firing rate, mostly due to the tremendous amount of heat each one generated when firing. Single-barreled turrets, they could only manage a ROF of one round every twenty seconds.

Like the 400s, the 120s had a dedicated reactor pathway that made sure the power to the weapons was available as needed.

Six-Six turned into a hellscape as twelve rounds hit one after another. The destructive force rivaled anything Jacob had seen... and he'd seen a lot.

"Holy hell." The voice came over the bridge wide. Jacob didn't admonish them—he was thinking the same thing. He'd fired a Long 9 at a planet more than once. Each time, the resulting crater had impressed him. The 120s made the Long 9 look like pop-guns.

"Cease fire, all turrets. Skipper, we have a fault in power relay junction 5-70-1," Kim said. Always the professional, she could have ordered a meal with the same tone.

"All hands, cease fire," Jacob ordered.

"All turrets, cease fire. Cease fire. Cease fire," Lieutenant Misha repeated. The flustered weapons officer turned to his captain. "Sorry, sir, I'll have engineering check it out and—"

Jacob waved off his apology. "Gabriel, this is why we're out here. Take a breath. Pass the fault onto Lieutenant Beech and tell the gun crews to stand down." Jacob spun his chair around to face Ops. "Mark, fill the can and stand us down from Zulu. I think our success deserves a break and a hot meal."

As Mark gave the order and air hissed back into the ship, Jacob clicked over to the private channel he shared with Kim.

"XO, dinner tonight. I want to go over the performance of the crew. I'm sure Josh can make whatever you want, so let him know."

"Aye, aye, sir. I'll put the PO to the test."

Gabriel removed his helmet, taking a second to make sure it shut down properly before stowing it under his chair. Captain Grimm confused the hell out of him. The ship malfunctioned, yet he called that a success. Any other captain would be furious, as if the universe conspired against them to deprive them of their ship.

"Sir," Bosun Sandivol appeared at the young man's side, holding a NavPad out for his approval.

It was the crew roster for the gun turrets organized by watch. "Looks good, Bosun."

"Thank you, sir."

"Bosun?" Gabriel caught the older man's attention as he turned away. Gabriel hesitated. He wanted to ask the fatherly man for some advice, but Gabriel was an officer... wasn't he supposed to know everything already?

The Bosun, with his thin mustache and greying temples, didn't miss a beat. He gestured to the second chair next to Gabriel, who nodded.

"Does the lieutenant have a question about the command style of his current skipper?" Sandivol said, keeping his voice pitched low as he leaned in.

How did he know? "Hypothetically, Bosun, let's say I did. What would you suggest."

Sandivol's New Austin heritage was obvious in his dark hair and light brown skin. When he smiled, crow's-feet lined his eyes. "I've been with the captain for a while, sir. He certainly takes some adjusting. I would suggest the lieutenant continues to be the outstanding officer he is, and trust that whatever the captain asks him to do, is best for the young lieutenant."

CHAPTER TWENTY

PALISADES

Wit stared out his office window. The twinge in his stomach had persisted since he first learned of the Republic coup. Something was very wrong. He just couldn't put a finger on it. The office of the SECNAV was prestigious and powerful, but it wasn't ONI; he had no clearance for intelligence data outside his purview. But a coup? That should have rung the bell of every news organization in the galaxy. Terra wasn't just the largest galactic power; it was the oldest and the home of humanity. To have a coup on a government that was almost a thousand years old... shook Wit more than he'd thought possible.

His hand hovered over his NavPad. He wanted—he needed—information. Was he the only one out of the loop? Did the Director of National Intelligence know? Did his replacement at ONI know?

Wit forced himself to take a deep breath and let it out slowly, steadying his nerves. There were three questions to ask.

Who perpetrated the assassination attempt? Was it related to the coup? Did his own government know and just not tell him?

Once, two decades before, Wit felt the way he did in the moment: trapped. Like a ratbird on a sinking ship. He and Axwell were out at the end of the year. Were there forces behind the scenes conspiring against the Alliance?

There was too much going on for him to track. At least the Navy was squared away. Foolish as Noele's plan seemed, he thought it could work. With the vast majority of their fleet posed to strike into the heart of the Caliph, he could focus on matters at home.

"Mr. DeBeck?" His assistant's voice interrupted his musing.

"Go ahead."

"Sir, the DNI is on his way. A friend of mine in transpo gave me the heads-up."

"Thank you, Richard. Well done." The kid was fantastic at his job. Wit would be sad to lose him when he eventually rotated out.

What did Gradford want with him? Wit sat, opening his NavPad to show Zuckabar in a transparent holo above his desk. He loosened his tie and unbuttoned his top button. His coffee cup was empty; he half filled it with cold water and poured the remnants of the coffee dispenser into it. Steam wafted off the cup for a moment until the cold water won. Scene set, he took his place behind his desk and waited.

Two minutes later, the Director of National Intelligence entered his office. Gradford was good—not as good as Wit, but still good. He was no lawyer or politician. The man had cut his teeth in the trenches of the Great War, risking his life to spy on enemy planets with little or no friendly infrastructure.

While his body had gone soft with age, Gradford was no fool; thinking him one would be a mistake.

The man frowned the second he walked in. "DeBeck,

working late?" Gradford asked as he stopped in front of the desk.

"Worrying over the operation in Zuckabar and Praetor is all. I'm trying to see if there are any angles I've missed." Wit gestured toward his uncomfortable guest chairs. "To what do I owe the honor?"

Gradford seated himself on the edge of the chair, not leaning back—he was emotionally engaged in whatever he was about to say.

"You and I go back a way, Wit. I don't think we ever treaded the same ground, but we did the same job."

Wit nodded along, mildly surprised at the turn of the conversation. "I seem to recall you were a spotter for that thing in '08," Wit said.

A flash of amusement crossed Gradford's face. "I guess not all of it was bad. We sure riled up that outpost." He paused for a moment. "I respect you, Wit. I can't say that about many people in this town. Out of respect, I need you to call your agent off. Don't try to deny it. Everyone knows Dagher still works for you. She's sticking her nose where it doesn't belong."

Outside a brief hello at the gala, Wit hadn't spoken with Nadia in a month. She'd made it very clear that she was out. "You'll have to be more specific, Chuck. What exactly is she sticking her nose into that you don't like?"

Gradford stood abruptly. "Don't play your games with me, Wit. Any and all investigations into the attack at the gala go through me. Not you. Stick to your bailiwick and keep your pet dog out of my affairs."

"Chuck, I really don't know what you're talking about..." He could guess, of course, but he didn't know.

"Then you won't mind when she's arrested."

Wit would mind, but if Nadia was involved, he seriously

doubted she'd allow herself to be arrested. Unless it was what she wanted.

"Do what you have to, but bear in mind, her husband is a national treasure. Think about that before you act."

Every major news channel covered the aircar accident. For Nadia, it stood out like a supernova on a dark night. Alexandria had few aircar accidents to begin with, let alone a police cruiser exploding over the city. Alexandria wasn't a backwater planet. Within the city of Anchorage Bay, a central computer controlled ninety percent of the flying traffic. The police had their own version of it.

Nadia partially hid behind a ground van parked on the side of the road. Projected yellow markers fended off civilians from the burned remains of the police cruiser. A dozen uniformed officers, and half as many forensics wearing their version of ELS, scoured the scene, looking for evidence. They marked every fragment of the car with an RFID tag showing its exact location.

"You don't think this was an accident?" Elsa asked.

"No. What do you see?" She felt Elsa peer hard at the scene, taking a moment to really look before answering.

"The remains of an exploded vehicle..."

"Yes. Now tell me one thing you don't see, and one thing you smell?"

The younger woman breathed in deep and almost immediately coughed. She buried her face in elbow, hacking for a solid minute. "What is that?"

"Nitrogen. Far too much in the air. Probably trace amounts of other chemicals as well. Now, what do you *not* see."

"I don't get it, Nadia. There isn't much to see at all."

Nadia moved around the vehicle; hands shoved deep into the pockets of her long coat. As she walked, she glanced at the accident. Her casual manner and nonthreatening demeanor made the police on the scene all but ignore her.

"Two things this scene tells us," Nadia said over her shoulder. "The car had enough explosives on it to vaporize the frame... and any body. No body, no trail for us to follow. I can't question a dead man."

Elsa followed along behind her. "If they used that much, won't it show up on their search?"

It could, but Nadia doubted the investigation would go anywhere. "In a day, if I had to guess, forensics will find it was a faulty fuel cell or something else benign, and the case will be closed. This is the kind of thing where the people involved have pull. Lots of it."

Which meant Nadia needed to visit her stash and arm them up. After everything she'd survived, it would be the height of irony for her to die on Alexandria looking into a crime. She needed to be extra careful.

The two women continued down the sidewalk, pretending to be civilians who weren't interested in the police investigation.

"Why?" Elsa asked.

Nadia led them back to her aircar but did not start it. Instead, she sat for a moment, thinking through all the possibilities. Seeing things from an angle most people didn't was what made her a good spy. "Killing your weak link is spy craft 101." She tapped the controls, something on the edge of her mind nagged at her. She could see the explosion, the way the police car exploded over the city. High enough the debris rained down for blocks... and... "Why take the chance to kill him with an explosion? Why not just shoot him?" Nadia asked.

"In my experience, criminals blow things up when they

want to send a message to other criminals. Be quiet or this will happen to you," Elsa said.

Nadia agreed. "Who are they sending the message to, though? The other gate guards? Why blow him up?" It bothered her. Something about it didn't make sense. If they wanted to silence their contact, there were a dozen different ways to do it without drawing attention.

She keyed her NavPad to show the dead officer's information again. Ahmed Al-Qahtani. Five-year veteran of Anchorage Bay PD. Second-generation Alliance citizen. Grandparents immigrated from the Caliphate after the Great War. Other than his heritage, nothing about him stood out.

"I don't know, Nadia. You can't start blaming people just because they came from the Caliph," Elsa said, following Nadia's line of thinking. "Maybe he was working with some deep-cover assets, but maybe he was just in the wrong place at the wrong time."

"There's no such thing as a coincidence when it comes to espionage. Only threads we can't connect. Have you heard from your brother?"

The sudden non sequitur caught Elsa by surprise. She took a moment to answer. "No. Which in itself is strange. The last I heard, he had the squadron on lockdown while they investigated the crews."

"How many ships?"

"Six. His heavy cruiser, three light cruisers, and two destroyers. About 1,800 crew in all. It will take a while to check on all of them."

Nadia realized what was bothering her. Having the assassins altered to look like Imperial Navy would slow down the investigation but hardly stop it. Only a fool would fall for it, especially after discovering the CPD officer who let them in the gala. Yes, the Caliphate and Iron Empire were once allies, but they were allies of convenience, not of commonality. When the Caliph-backed pirates took Elsa, they torched any chance of a future alliance.

"There's a third party," Nadia said. "Ahmed may have worked for the ISB or some other Caliph security force, but they weren't responsible. Whoever is pulling the strings just wants us to think they are."

"Unglaublich," Else blurted. "Nadia, you can't be serious?"

Nadia stretched her knowledge of the Imperial language. *Did she mean unbelievable?* "I've got no proof, Elsa. But if we run down this thread with the cop, I'm sure we'll find all kinds of evidence pointing at the ISB. I'll let the DNI do that. They're good at wasting time. That leaves me free to check places they won't think to look."

"Like where?" Elsa asked.

"That's the million-solar-dollar question. Got any ideas?"

CHAPTER TWENTY-ONE

Chief of Engineering Lieutenant Beech and his second, Chief Petty Officer Redfern, crawled through the maintenance access on deck five, heading for frame seventy.

"You sure this is the quickest way?" Chief Redfern asked.

"You know, Chief, you should trust your lieutenant," Beech replied.

Echo Redfern chuckled at that. He'd known Beech since he was a snot-nosed spacer and couldn't be prouder of the young man. Watching him grow from a quiet, reserved spacer into an exemplary officer was one of his great successes as a chief. "I would, sir, but generations of your fellow lieutenants have proven that to be a mistake."

"Very funny, Chief. This way."

Sure enough, Beech led them right to the faulty junction box. They smelled it before they saw it. Burned relays and melted polymers wafted down the maintenance tunnel.

"Something blew a fuse," Redfern said.

Beech propped himself up against the bulkhead. Redfern

rolled on his side; he was simply too tall to comfortably sit up in the one-meter-tall passageway.

The access hatch hung on melted joints; the metal on them had run down the side like water.

"How did a power junction run this hot and not set off the alarms?" Beech asked.

The kid had a point. Redfern set his NavPad to scan and ran it over the panel. Residual heat lingered in the joints and along the access point... but not on the panel itself. "Weird," he muttered.

Putting on gloves to protect themselves from a live circuit, or a hotspot, the two engineers pulled the access panel open with a wail of bent metal.

Inside, the reinforced nano-steel panel was a burned-out mess.

"What the hell?" Beech asked.

Redfern whistled at the destruction. To him, it looked like a grenade had gone off in the panel. Melted cables, fried leads... even the run where the power cables connected to the nearest supercapacitor were fried. "I've seen worse, but not outside of battle damage," Redfern said.

Repairing the panel was going to take hours.

"I don't think—" Beech looked at it for a moment. "Screw it. We're not repairing this. We'll do a computer bypass and pull the whole unit. Fabrications can make us a new one and we'll just slot it in."

Redfern beamed. It was the right call. Other officers might have wanted to show their skill and commitment, spending hours repairing it. Or worse, ordering their subordinates to do it. Skipping to the correct decision was what made Beech a superior officer in Redfern's mind.

"Aye, sir. You get the bypass going, and I'll cut it free."

Beech held up his NavPad to the panel to access the power flow regulators. The Pad gave him an angry buzz. Redfern pulled out his plasma torch, found the junction where the box connected to the bulkhead, and started cutting. The angry buzz sounded again.

"XO, Lieutenant Beech. Are you near a console?" he said over comms.

"XO, here. I can be. Everything okay?"

"I'm not sure, ma'am. Chief Redfern and I are down in maintenance passageway five-seventy, and we've got a burned-out power relay. I'm trying to tell the computer to reroute, but it won't allow me access."

Redfern missed the beginning of her reply as the box broke free.

"...the access point," Yuki said.

"Aye, ma'am, one second." Beech shook his head. "No joy."

"Can you reroute it manually?" Yuki asked.

Bracing himself, Redfern pulled the panel off the bulkhead and pushed it toward his feet. The maze of connections and wires coming out of the reinforced bulkhead were a kaleidoscope of color codes.

"I'm going to get this down to fabrication, sir," Redfern said.

"Get to it, Chief. As soon as I have this figured out, I'll meet you in engineering."

Jacob bounced on his feet, eager to spar with Jennings. He'd needed more training in hand-to-hand; the last six months of desk duty had left him a little overweight and a lot undertrained. *Seventeen* had a gym large enough to park a Corsair and a couple of Mudcats in it. At any given time, a hundred crew used the free weights, machines, swimming pool, and treadmills. In the center of it all was the regulation-sized boxing ring.

Jacob had his protective gear and his gloves. Gunny Jennings wore gloves but nothing else. He thought about ordering her to wear headgear, but he seriously doubted he'd land a punch anyways.

"Ready, Skipper?" Jennings said.

"As I'll ever be." *Remember Jacob, commit to the fight.*

Jennings came in hard and fast. Jacob instantly curled up, covering his face. She lashed out, hitting his shoulder with a blow that would level a porcuswine on his dad's ranch. He grunted, letting his breath out while he swung at her with his opposite hand. He caught her in the arm; it was like hitting bricks. She gave him a rare smile—as her other hand buried itself in his gut.

Jacob exhaled hard as his air forced from his lungs by her blow. He stumbled to his right and immediately shuffled back as another blow followed it up.

"Very good, Skipper. You anticipated that."

He didn't take the bait again. She swung, but he managed to step back as she came in. Her blow missed him by a millimeter. He lashed out with all his strength, right at her face—

Jacob hit the mat flat on his back. Jennings was on his chest, kneeling, with his head trapped by her thighs. She let out a couple of sharp breaths as she pantomimed punching him in the face.

"What was that, sir?" Rolling off him, she held out her hand.

"I thought I could land a blow..."

She heaved him up to his feet. Jacob stretched and massaged his aching back. He knew it was going to hurt for a few days. Several crew had gathered to watch—ones he didn't recognize. A few were doing their best not to laugh.

Well, you had that coming.

"You're blocking is improving, as is your situational awareness. You actually caught me a little by surprise, which was why I flipped you so hard."

She couldn't have said anything that would make Jacob happier. Caught her by surprise? That just didn't happen.

"Hey, Gunny. Are you sparring with anyone, or just officers?"

Jacob followed Jennings' gaze to a square-shouldered spacer. He was wide, but ten centimeters shorter than Jacob, which still made him above average in height. His arms, though, were like slabs of meat.

"Skipper?" she asked.

Jacob didn't mind the chance to catch his breath. He retired to his corner and waved her on.

"What's your name?" Jennings asked.

"Spacer First Class Fontenot." His eyes were angry, and there was a leer in his face Jacob didn't care for. Jennings wore her typical unitard that covered her from neck to feet. It didn't hide her outrageous level of fitness. Still, Fontenot had to outmass her by fifty kilos.

Jennings watched Fontenot stretch and warm up. "Ohana Jujitsu?" she asked.

Fontenot froze. "You read my file?" he asked.

"Nope. I fight for a living, SFC."

Signaling her readiness, she waited. When Fontenot was ready, he did something Jacob didn't understand, he sat down.

"What are you doing?" Jennings asked.

"Attack me," Fontenot replied.

A knife Jacob had no idea she possessed appeared in her hand, and she threw it with all the force of a lethal strike. The blade whistled through the air. Fontenot screamed. The whole gym held their breath for a heartbeat. Between his legs, mere centimeters from his privates, the blade vibrated from the impact.

"Are you out of your damn mind?" Fontenot yelled once he collected himself.

"SFC, we do not fight in tournaments on this ship. If you step into a ring, it is to kill or be killed. No quarter asked or given. Do you know why?" Jennings didn't quite raise her voice, but she had her full drill instructor effect going. She marched over and retrieved her knife.

Bewildered, Fontenot just watched. "We were just sparring," he said.

"Just sparring..." Jennings repeated with disgust. "Skipper, the last time you fought for your life, did you pull your punches?"

Surprised at being brought into it, Jacob almost stammered his answer. "No, Gunny."

"Fontenot, we train like we fight, so that we can fight like we train. Don't get into this ring with me, or anyone else, unless you intend to fight like your life depended on it."

Jacob was busy listening to her speech and missed where she put the knife. Sure enough, though, it was gone.

She walked over and held out her hand to the SFC, who took it but didn't look happy about it. As he regained his feet, Fontenot grabbed Jennings' collar and started to throw her. Jennings let him, but she controlled how she went over his shoulder and hip, grabbing his legs as she went and landing on her feet, only to rabbit punch him in the stomach three times.

Fontenot went down again.

"That's more like it," Jennings said. Fontenot leapt to his feet, an angry scowl on his face. Jacob knew that look. Fontenot was pissed. When you can't win calm, you certainly can't win angry.

Fontenot charged Jennings with a growl.

Gunny let him, falling back as he swung at her. She kicked out, connecting with his stomach and throwing him upside down with a thud. She was on her feet in one fluid motion. A second later, her knee was on his throat.

"You done?" she asked.

He grunted in reply.

Jacob made a mental note to look up Fontenot. He certainly wouldn't punish the kid, but maybe the right word to his PO could put him on a better track.

"Skipper, I've got to get ready for duty," Jennings said.

"Get to it, Gunny."

Jacob grabbed his towel, using it as an excuse to watch the crew as they worked out. With the show over, they dispersed. Fontenot went to a crowd of spacers that jeered him for failing to bring the Gunny down. Something about them...

"Captain Grimm, bridge," Kim's voice sounded. He picked up his NavPad. "Go for Grimm."

"Sir, we've received a message from the INS Undine. Your eyes only."

Jacob took a moment to recall the name: it was a flagship, the one Henry was on. Did he have news about the assassination attempt?

"I'll take it in my quarters. Captain out." Jacob gathered up his things and headed for his quarters.

Fifteen minutes later he switched on his bulkhead panel and played the message.

Message from INS UNDINE in the open, no encryption.

Jacob keyed the message to play. Henry Faust appeared in his black-and-gold uniform. Where he was, bridge or quarters, wasn't clear from the black background.

"Captain Grimm, I hope this message finds you well. I wish to discuss our joint efforts a while back. However, I haven't had a decent meal since we embarked on this journey. As you know, it's many months from New Berlin to here. Could I trespass on your hospitality and join you for dinner? How do you say... a little bird told me you have quite the chef? I look forward to hearing from you."

The message ended. Jacob wondered what he wanted to discuss? Did he have more information about who attacked the president?

Jacob slapped the comms button. "Bridge, Captain."

"Bridge, sir. PO McCall."

"Mac, can you find out where the *Undine* is in the system, and then have Nav plot a course to meet her. I want to see our distance."

"Aye, I'm on it. It might take a bit to check with central space control, but we'll find her."

"Good man. Captain out."

That settled, Jacob stood to change. When he lifted his arms over his head, he realized he needed a shower. Nothing said *competent captain* like a man who stank of the gym.

By the time he was out of the shower, Mac had sent him the requested information. They could leave Range Six-Six and meet up with the imperial vessel within eight hours, give or take a few minutes.

Jacob typed up a text response to Prince Henry, letting him know when they would be available. He needed to finish testing the ship's weapons before he could leave.

He stopped mid-sentence, realizing he hadn't had an update from engineering about when they would be able to continue testing. That seemed odd to him. Beech was a proficient and detail-minded man.

"Engineering, Captain," Jacob said over comms.

"Engineering, Spacer First Class Valter, sir."

"Valter, is Lieutenant Beech or Chief Redfern around?"

"One moment, sir, I'll find them."

Jacob took the opportunity to finish dressing in his day uniform, making sure that every single bit was oriented correctly.

"Skipper, Chief Redfern. What can I do for you, sir?"

"Echo, what's the ETA on the 120s being back online?"

There was a long pause. "Sir? Didn't Mr. Beech inform you?"

"Inform me of what?"

"One moment, sir."

Another long pause. Jacob had a strange feeling in his gut. Things on a ship worked a certain way. There was order to the chaos of shipboard life. When things went out of order, it was never good.

"Sir," Chief Redfern said. "Lieutenant Beech was finishing the replacement of a blown relay... he should have finished by now and reported back."

"Hang tight, Chief."

Jacob paused the call and switched to another channel. "Bridge, Captain. Can you locate Lieutenant Beech for me?"

"Aye, sir. One moment," Mac said.

The feeling in his gut intensified. He hurriedly finished dressing and was on his way to the hatch when Mac resumed. "Sir, he's not answering his comms."

"Man overboard, Mac."

CHAPTER TWENTY-TWO

Alarms wailed over the entire ship.
"Man overboard, this is not a drill. All crewmembers report to your immediate department head. This is not a drill."

Of course, no one was actually overboard, but the alarm covered a vast number of problems, from missing crew to an actual overboard. With the ship holding station off Six-Six, it made the situation less complicated.

Jacob stormed onto the bridge; Kim was there waiting for him. "We checked all the logs. No external hatches have opened in the last twenty-four hours. That's the good news," she said.

"Captain has the bridge." He took his seat. "What's the bad news?"

"His NavPad isn't responding to pings."

That wasn't good at all. The NavPads were rugged little devices that officers carried with them everywhere. They acted as communicator, assistant, and a million other things. "Redfern said his last known position was on deck 5, frame 70. Anyone gone there yet?"

"PO Cartwright is on his way there right now."

Cartwright frowned at the sealed hatch. According to his NavPad, all the hatches in the maintenance accessway should be open.

"Engineering, PO Cartwright. Can you override the hatch on 5-65-2-M?"

"Roger, PO. I'm on it. One sec..."

The hatch hummed as the electric motor engaged, but it didn't open.

"That's weird," Spacer Sebaz said from behind Cartwright.

Another round of humming came from the hatch, but it still didn't open.

"Engineering, it isn't opening."

"According to my panel, it's jammed. You're going to have to burn through it."

"Great. Sebaz, go back and get a torch."

"Aye, aye, PO."

Cartwright activated the scanner function on his NavPad and ran it around the sealed hatch. Nothing showed up on the screen.

"Sickbay, Cartwright on 5-65. I think we're going to need medical assistance."

"Roger, PO. A team is on the way."

The medics arrived the same time Sebaz returned with the torch. It took Cartwright ten minutes of painstaking cutting to burn through the lock.

The hatch hummed and opened, revealing a still Lieutenant Beech, face down on the deck.

In Jacob's private office off the bridge, Lieutenant Marino and Chief Pierre filled him in.

"There's no question, Skipper," Pierre said. "It wasn't an accident."

"Show me," Jacob ordered.

Marino put her NavPad on the desk in front of him and triggered the holo function. A 3D of Beech's head appeared. It showed, in vivid detail, the massive contusion on the back.

"Beech got lucky, sir," she said. "According to PO Cartwright, the ventilation system to the specific passageway wasn't working. With the hatches on either side sealed, he would have suffocated in another hour. However, when he was hit over the head, it put him in a very deep state of unconsciousness. He was barely breathing, meaning he didn't use nearly as much oxygen as he would have otherwise."

An animation played, showing Beech in the cramped passageway. He fell face-first onto the deck. His heart rate slowed, as did his breathing. Had Cartwright not acted as decisively as he had, the young man would be dead. Jacob made a mental note to award Cartwright for his quick action.

"To be clear, you have no doubt he was assaulted?"

"None, Skipper," Marino and Pierre replied at the same time.

"Here's what I need you to do then. File a full report showing his accident. List it as an accident. At chow tonight, tell whoever you're having dinner with it was an accident."

"Sir?" Marino asked, a confused look on her face.

Pierre caught on quicker. "We have a saboteur aboard, ma'am. They'll be a lot easier to catch if they think they've gotten away with it," Chief Pierre explained.

"But why a saboteur?" Marino asked.

Jacob glanced at her NavPad and raised an eyebrow.

"His NavPad is missing. Whoever did this took it and

destroyed it, then hid the evidence. If someone were simply out to hurt Beech, they would have just killed him. This was planned to look like an accident, but also set up so we couldn't rescue him easily."

"But who, Skipper?" Marino asked.

"It's a big ship, Mariposa. We pulled crew from everywhere in-system to get her up to speed at the last minute. It's possible one of the people we pulled is a spy—or worse. Until we get this figured out, though, remember—it was an accident."

After the two medical personnel departed, Jacob had a decision to make. Obviously, he could trust people he'd worked with before. There was no chance that any of his crew from *Interceptor* were spies. Unfortunately, that left 800 plus crew he *hadn't* served with before. Too many files to go through looking for red flags.

If they wanted to catch the person, they were going to have to flush them out. A good old-fashioned mole hunt. The only problem was, he had no idea how to perform such a hunt.

"The 120s are back online sir, and ready to fire," Lieutenant Misha announced.

"Very good, Weps. Unleash the beast. Fire everything."

Misha cleared his throat. "Aye, aye, sir. Five seconds." He'd already double-checked the power relays to make sure they were green. "All batteries... fire."

Seventeen shuddered as the entirety of the 120s fired. Seconds later, light blossomed on the asteroid range.

"Rapid fire," Captain Grimm ordered.

Misha shouldn't be sweating in his temperature-controlled ELS suit, but he was all the same. If the weapons failed this time, it would be on his head. He just knew it. "All batteries, commence rapid fire."

The ship vibrated from the volume of fire. No sound transmitted through the drained ship, but everyone aboard could feel it.

"Add in the 20s," Captain Grimm ordered.

"Aye, aye, sir. Turrets sixteen through twenty-four, commence rapid fire."

For a solid minute, the bridge crew watched as an almost unimaginable amount of fusion-generated energy converted to kinetic force slammed against a massive rock in space.

Heat warnings spiked on Misha's screens, but they weren't his responsibility. The turrets could actually fire much faster than they did, but the heat build-up would overcome their ability to dump it, making the fire rate pointless. Rapid fire was designed to fire at a rate they could sustain for long enough to make a difference. Too long, though, and a heatsink would have to be ejected. On *Seventeen*, there was one every hundred meters: a total of ten that could be ejected individually or all at once.

"Cease fire," Captain Grimm ordered.

"All turrets, cease fire. Cease fire. Cease fire."

One last barrage went out, then the ship was still. The last wave of explosions rippled along Six-Six in a final wave of fiery death.

"Wow," Lieutenant Brennan said over the bridge comms.

"Indeed," Captain Grimm replied. "Well done, Misha. Damn fine shooting."

It took him a second to realize the captain had referred to him by his first name. Not only that, his praise went over the entire bridge wide.

"Th—thank you, sir," he managed to spit out.

As Misha monitored the weapons systems, super coolant

whisked heat away from the areas that generated it and down to the heatsinks to store and eventually disperse. Radiators around the outside of the hull vented as much as they could, but it was only a backup to the heatsinks.

"Alright, Weps, playtime is over. Cycle up the four hundreds."

Misha gulped. This was where it went wrong last time. "Aye, aye, sir." He flipped the comms over to communicate with turrets one through three. "Turret officers, verify readiness."

All three junior officers responded immediately in the affirmative.

Misha double-checked the targeting computer, making sure each turret was locked onto *Six-Six*. "Sir, the 400s are locked and loaded."

Captain Grimm focused on the main viewer. It was an important moment, Misha understood that. Not only for the ship, but for him as well; the battleship's big guns were what she was for.

"Fire," Captain Grimm ordered.

Misha relayed it.

A second later, the ship shuddered like nothing before. One by one, each turret fired its 400mm nano-steel-wrapped tungsten penetrator. Heat spiked to the top of the screen as each one fired. Before he had time to register the results, the asteroid's surface exploded like God had kicked it. By the time the last turret finished, Six-Six had lost more than ten percent of her mass.

Heat levels dropped and all batteries reported green.

"Test passed," Lieutenant Commander West said over the bridge wide.

"I'll say," Captain Grimm replied. His next words were transmitted to the entire ship.

"Crew of *Seventeen*, this is the captain speaking. We've officially passed the builder and yard trials for the weapons systems. Well done, everyone. I've arranged for a special meal tonight. We will have double the time for evening mess. Congratulations. Captain out."

Misha put all the turrets back on safe, making sure each turret crew checked in and verified they were unloaded.

"Ops, fill the can," Jacob said. "Nav, send our pre-arranged course to the Pit."

A chorus of aye, ayes filled the bridge. A moment later, air hissed back into the compartment. Once atmosphere was confirmed, Misha removed his helmet. Wiping his forehead, he breathed a sigh of relief. He half expected all the systems to crash as one.

"Course received," Chief Suresh said. "Ready to engage."

Captain Grimm stood, stretching as he did so. "Chief, Execute."

CHAPTER TWENTY-THREE

Nadia had her NavPad out, the holographic display showing the four men who attacked the president. The file contained everything she knew about the assassination attempt—which wasn't much.

"What are you thinking?" Elsa asked.

"That I can't hold the DNI to a higher standard than myself. The toxin is so common, anyone could make it. The police who manned the gate the assassins entered through are dead, and they only point to a possible ISB presence—something DNI says isn't likely. Finally, why? Why assassinate an outgoing president? You'd almost guarantee to push his political agenda through."

The two women sat, curled up with cocoa and coffee in leather chairs in Jacob's living room. Grimm Sr., kind as he was, didn't like people all that much, and made himself scarce as soon as she showed up with the statuesque blonde.

Besides, something Nadia realized when she stayed on the ranch, there was always something needing doing.

"If my father were killed, I certainly wouldn't suddenly repeal all his political positions. If anything, we would double down. My brother even more so. He's far more militant than I. He fancies himself an expert in all things espionage and warfare."

Nadia resisted the urge to giggle. It wasn't appropriate, and she hated how it made her sound like a little girl. "How old are you, Elsa?" she asked out of the blue.

Elsa smiled at her friend's non sequitur. "Why would you want to know?"

"Curiosity. You're resourceful, skilled, and composed. However, you're also very beautiful, with little to no signs of aging—" Nadia pointed to her own eyes where slight crow's feet could be made out—"and you have a youthful vigor."

Elsa smiled mischievously. "I might just have an excellent skincare routine..."

Nadia giggled despite her best efforts not to. "You better share if you do."

The mirth fled from Elsa. "Nadia, there's something you have to understand about the children of the Iron Emperor... We're raised to lead. Don't get me wrong, I love my father..."

Nadia sensed a rather large "however" approaching. "If you tell me you're sixteen, I'm going to lose my mind," she said, trying to defuse the tension.

"No, not that young. I just mean, I never was under the impression I would lead a normal life. My earliest memories are combat training, public speaking, history lessons, etcetera. My whole life has been dedicated to service. I've had exactly two vacations. The first was when I was fourteen and I went on a state-sponsored review of our planets. The second is right now. Not that touring our empire was a vacation, but it was a break from my daily duties as an imperial princess. My family is about service and duty. I've literally dedicated my life to the goal."

Nadia was impressed. The kind of dedication Elsa spoke of wasn't often found in young people. How did her father instill such loyalty in his children? Elsa's family seemed dedicated to the well being of their nation.

"You didn't answer my question?"

"Twenty-four," Elsa said.

"Wow, color me impressed. When I was twenty-four, I'd just hit petty officer and was heading to military intelligence school. I was thinking about what I wanted from my career for the first time."

They sat in silence for a moment. Nadia sipped from her steaming mug of cocoa. *Why kill him?*

"This just doesn't make sense. We're missing something. The four men come to the gala to kill the president, yet they don't bring anything other than poisoned swords. An excellent weapon, for sure, but did they really expect to get close enough to the president for a sword? Whoever organized this knew the ISB had an agent on Alexandria. Knew how to contact him and use him. But they weren't in the ISB." Pieces clicked together for her, like the puzzles she played with as a child.

"What?" Elsa asked.

"We're going about this all wrong. We keep asking who tried to kill the president, when we should have asked who had the most to gain?"

"I thought that was the same question?"

"Not quite. If the Caliphate assassinated Axwell, any resistance to total war would be out the window. My people would want blood, and we would get it. Right now, we're playing by civilized rules. No orbital bombardments, no nukes, treating our prisoners fairly, etc." She held up her hand to forestall the obvious question. "Yes, warfare isn't civilized, but you know what I mean. We *could* beat the hell out of them if we wanted."

"How would provoking the Alliance to do orbital bombardments help the Caliphate?"

"It wouldn't—it would hurt them. Bad. For now, we're

fighting in their territories, on their planets, in their space. If the fighting came to the Alliance, they would nuke the hell out of our planets without batting an eye. We're following the conventions and not bombing from orbit." Nadia considered a different angle for a moment. "You know what else it would do, though?"

"What?"

"Put all of our resources on the single goal of destroying the Caliphate. It would galvanize our people. Even when they nuked the capital there was so much confusion about who did it, we couldn't really focus. If they murdered the president, every ship we could build, every Marine, all but the barest of units would be sent to fight the Caliph."

"But that seems extreme," Elsa said, "to leave your planets undefended."

"I'm not saying we would entirely, but I think the navy would certainly take more risks to end the war while public sentiment was on their side."

"Which begs the question, who would benefit?'" Elsa asked.

Nadia flipped through her NavPad until she found the counterintelligence file and activated the privacy screen. The pad went full power, blocking every known kind of listening device. She placed it back on the coffee table.

"You didn't hear this from me, understood?"

Elsa nodded solemnly, if a bit enthusiastically. Who didn't want to be let in on secrets? "Understood."

"Last year, we destroyed the Guild."

Elsa gasped. "How?"

"They had an unfortunate accident with their Dyson's Swarm collector array. What's germane here, is that while that was happening, the Guild and the Republic of Terra attempted to take Cordoba—a planet situated between Alliance and Terran space."

Elsa searched her memory. "I think I saw an intelligence report about that. Terra sold a pair of battleships and some light units to the Guild... I take it they didn't actually sell them?"

"Oh, they sold them. Jacob blew up one and captured the other. However, the ground forces on the planet were pure Terran. It turned out—" Nadia stopped. She risked much sharing this information with Elsa. However, she trusted the young woman, and seriously doubted the Iron Empire would make a move on the planet, even though Cordoba was, without a doubt, worth going to war over. "Cordoba has massive, easily minable Osmium deposits close to the surface. Pure enough to make gravcoils for *any* size ship."

"Osmium? On a planet? I'm surprised Terra didn't invade with force!"

Nadia agreed. Osmium was rare, and it was the key component in gravcoils. Entire asteroid belts were mined for the rare element. To mine it, without destroying Cordoba's ecosystem, would take a decade or more, but eventually, the planet's GDP would equal the rest of the Alliance combined. "It was pretty rough, but you're right. They allied with the Guild and tried to be sneaky—something the Guild was good at. They just couldn't follow through with any kind of battle force. What if Terra blamed the Alliance for the failure and still wanted the planet? If the assassination worked and we went to total war with the Caliphate, they could easily move in and take Cordoba. If it failed, we would still blame the Caliphate and move more of our forces to engage them leaving Cordoba with inadequate defenses."

The evidence connected the dots in a way that made logical sense. For once.

"They hate us, no doubt," Elsa said. "The Great War ended for you, but our border is hot to this day. Skirmishes between our navies happen weekly in the DMZ. The only reason their spies aren't more successful is their inability to clean up their..." Elsa's eyes went wide.

"What?" Nadia asked.

"I know how to prove they were Republic spies—or at least operatives," Elsa said, a wicked smile gracing her near perfect features.

"How?"

"I need to examine the bodies. Do you know where they are?"

"No. But I can find out. You need to be sure you can tell—absolutely certain—because I'm going to have to give up something to do this."

"If the operatives are Terran, I'll be able to tell. I'm certain."

THE PALISADES. 1730 HOURS.

Wit DeBeck went through his schedule, angry over DNI's lack of progress investigating the assassins. Or at least, a lack of sharing that information with him. Charles was good at his job... so why was he dragging his feet? Did he think the assassination attempt wasn't important? It was literally his entire job.

Don't be so hard on him, Wit told himself. Alliance Presidential Protection Services was responsible for the president's safety, not DNI. However, finding out who was behind the assassins should be their top priority.

Wit opened his NavPad and searched through the latest reports. It would still be weeks before the first news of the assault on the Caliphate would make its way back to Alexandria. As the SECNAV, he'd hear first; still, it would be a while.

A message from Captain Grimm appeared in his inbox. He opened it.

Mission report: *Seventeen* has passed her engineering, propulsion, weapons, and crew trials successfully. We've fulfilled both the builder and navy trials for the ship. Proceeding to rendezvous with INS *Undine* for JTE. Only one crew casualty to report: Lieutenant Beech hit his head and was accidentally sealed into a passageway. Lieutenant Mariposa Marino ruled the injury an *accident*. Captain Grimm, *Seventeen*, out.

Wit reread the report, then went over it again in his mind. He shouldn't have received it. This was for the CNO, not the SECNAV unless—he checked the routing. Sure enough, it had gone to the CNO, but hidden away in the list of CCs was his official address.

Why would Grimm send it to him? Especially something as mundane as a report on their readiness. It was important, no doubt. But why?

"Mr. DeBeck, you have visitors," Richard said over the comms.

Wit checked his calendar: There wasn't anything scheduled. His curiosity piqued, he replied. "Send them in."

A one-armed Nadia Grimm entered, followed almost in lockstep by Princess Faust. Wit jerked to his feet, both the gentleman and statecraft in him demanding he greet the princess formally.

Stepping around his desk, he stopped a respectful distance from her and bowed.

"Welcome to the office of the SECNAV, Princess."

"Thank you, Mr. DeBeck. It is my pleasure," she replied in her clipped accent.

"Nadia, it's always a pleasure to see you," he said, extending his hand. She took it and smiled, but it wasn't a smile that reached her eyes.

"They haven't given me my arm back yet," Nadia said matter-of-factly.

"I'm sorry about that. They're still running tests on it. I'm afraid it could be some time." *Or never, if DNI gets wind of her presence in the Palisades.* "To what do I owe the honor of this visit?" He returned to his seat and gestured for his guests to sit as well. The women took the two closest seats, sitting almost in unison. From the way Elsa glanced at Nadia, he decided this wasn't a matter of state business for the Empire.

"Purely, hypothetically," Nadia began, "if we wanted to examine the bodies of the men who attacked the gala, where would we find them?"

Wit clenched his jaw, more to keep himself from responding right away than anything else. "Your timing is impeccable, Nadia," he said.

She raised an eyebrow at him. "How so?"

Wit turned his screen to face her, showing the message from Jacob. Her cheeks brightened just seeing his name. The look in her eyes, one she couldn't hide from Wit, said volumes about how much she loved the man.

"Why did he send this to you?" she asked.

"That's the question, isn't it? A crew injury report about one man? They have a crew of a thousand. I'm sure a dozen are in sickbay at any given time. Falls, sprains, illnesses, and other accidents. Why tell me about—"

Nadia's visage snapped shut like an iron trap. Her face changed so rapidly, Wit had to blink to make sure he'd seen it. "What?" he said.

Nadia glanced at Elsa, then back to Wit. "Nothing."

"Nadia, you're here for information. The least you can do is humor an old man and reciprocate."

Betraying nothing, a slow smile crept across her face.

"Despite what you think, Wit, Jacob and I don't have some telepathic connection. No secret codes."

Wit harrumphed at her disclaimer. "I never thought it was telepathic, but you know him better than anyone. Help me out. What does it mean?"

Nadia read the message one more time.

"Beech—a nice young man. I've met him—was injured and it was ruled an accident..." She looked hard at the message. "I can't be certain, but my take is that Beech was targeted in an assault... and Jacob knows it."

Wit looked from the message to Nadia and back. "That can't be. Are you saying—"

"There is a saboteur or spy aboard my husband's ship."

CHAPTER TWENTY-FOUR

Seventeen floated seventy million kilometers from Alexandria, sitting in a Lagrange point between the home world and the fourth planet. Meeting ships in space was always a difficult prospect. Using the gravity manifolds to find the Lagrange points allowed ships to meet without having to use a planet as a reference.

From his cabin, Jacob watched the Imperial Fleet come to a stop. Their black ships were sleek, almond-shaped. Unlike Alliance ships with their turrets and bridges, the Iron Navy went for internal gun ports and command centers, keeping everything in the central hull. It made for sleek ships, with hulls only interrupted by weapon's hatches along the broadsides and the top of the hull.

A rap on his door caught his attention. "Come in," he said.

Gunnery Sergeant Jennings entered. Her grey and white camouflaged uniform's creases were immaculate in the ship's afternoon light.

"Gunnery Sergeant Jennings reporting as ordered, sir." Jennings snapped to attention and saluted.

Jacob couldn't help but smile. Despite their years'-long

service together, Jennings was never an ounce less than professional. He stood, even though he didn't technically need to, and returned her salute. "As you were, Allison."

She snapped to parade rest, then to at ease.

Jacob returned to his seat and pointed at the Imperial ships displayed on his bulkhead screen. "Quite the sight, huh?"

"Yes, sir."

"I never thought we would be this close to really look at them." A wistful expression played across his face as he thought about what the moment represented. His mother had died facing such ships. She had spent her last moments rescuing her crewmates, throwing them in to escape pods until her own ship finally succumbed to damage. *Funny*, he thought, *I never really blamed the Empire. Just the unnecessary war.* Jacob was a spacer, and would be until he retired—or suffered the same fate as his mother. If his president told him to fight a war, he would do so with everything he had. That didn't mean he thought every war was justified, just that he knew his duty.

Jennings didn't reply. Her stoic nature never ceased to amuse Jacob.

"Allison, what I'm about to tell you, only four other people —myself included—know. You're not to tell anyone this. I have a job to do, and I think you, Naki, Owens, and June are the only ones I can trust to help me. Understood?"

Her bright blue eyes practically gleamed. "Not even Lieutenant Poole, Skipper?"

"There are things happening that require a level of trust I can't give him, as much as I would like to."

She gave him a sharp nod.

"The problems we've had with the turrets weren't random. We're being delayed. There's a saboteur aboard."

Jennings' jaw tightened with the news, but she said nothing.

"They did a good job making it look like an accident. Beech was attacked, has no recollection of the incident, and his NavPad was crushed by a malfunctioning maintenance hatch."

"Then how, sir?"

"Cartwright's a seasoned law enforcement officer. He surmised the scene of the accident was staged. Too many things went the way they needed to, from the damaged relay to the maintenance hatches malfunctioning just when Beech was alone. A few things can line up, but according to him, people are sometimes too clever for their own good. Whoever did this wanted to make sure it looked so much like an accident, that it ended up looking too much like one."

"Any suspects?" she asked.

"That's where you come in. We don't have any. What we need to do is set up a situation where the saboteur will have to act. A big fat juicy target, too good to pass up."

A vicious, thin-lipped smile spread across her face. "A mole hunt."

"A mole hunt."

"What does the skipper have in mind?"

"That's why we're here," Jacob said. He waved at the ships in the distance. "I'm going to have Prince Henry come aboard for dinner. If I'm right, they'll try something with him aboard. With all our attention on the guest, they'll think we're not paying attention and go for something vital."

Jacob wished he knew the motivation behind the sabotage —it would make predicting the actions of the person that much easier. So far, they've disabled systems crucial to firing the weapons and attempted to kill the chief engineer. If their goal was to slow the readiness of the ship, then those were good targets. There was only one system, though, that could utterly disable the ship and also be relatively easy to make it look like a malfunction.

"What's your plan, sir?"

"Every ship's system has built-in redundancy. There isn't a single point of failure that can stop us. If we were in combat, we could have rerouted those relays and fired anyway. It would have increased the chance of failure and damage, but we could have done it. The person responsible for the damage has shown a unique knowledge of the ships power subsystems. If the power to the boat bay's Richman field were to drop while we were greeting Prince Henry, then not only would he perish but a large portion of the crew as well."

Allison reacted for the first time, a sharp whistle. "That's quite the gamble, sir."

"Not really. I trust my people. Chief Redfern is already at work. He's going to override the field and use local power to maintain it. The trick, he says, is to fool the ship into thinking local power is already on, then, when the relay goes down, the field would just"—Jacob snapped his fingers—"snap off. We think that's what he'll try."

"The chief is isolating the battery backup and running them while also pumping power through the relay. When the saboteur goes for the relay, I want Bravo-Two-Five there to meet him."

"Aye, aye, sir. We will be ready."

Chief Redfern closed and sealed the panel. "Engineering, Redfern. Relay 3-527-1 is good to go. Tell Lieutenant Beech that's the last check."

"Aye, Chief, will do."

Redfern heaved his kit over his back and headed for the lift. He was glad this particular relay was located only a few frames to the fore of the boat bay in a regular passageway. Crawling hunched over in the maintenance tubes was for monkeys, not him.

Redfern had already set up the maintenance in the log, alerting Lieutenant Beech that the three redundant relays for the Richman field were offline. Normally, only having two points of failure would no-go the use of the fields, and they would open and close the hatches manually. However, the skipper had purposely requested the use of the fields on all four boat bay doors to impress their royal guest.

Using his old set of skills, Redfern had gone into the boat bay's computer log and made a note that the battery backups were temporarily offline and that the boat bay PO had failed to notify engineering.

If I'm right about our saboteur, they know the ship's systems backward and forward.

Echo was... eighty percent sure he was right. Odds like those would have him bet on a hand back in his gambling days. If the saboteur wasn't as knowledgeable as he thought, then they lost nothing. It was a solid chance to catch them.

For the third time in a month, Jacob found himself in mess dress, all his medals on full display. Behind him, Kim and his command crew were also wearing the hated mess. The only person who never seemed to mind was Chief Suresh—whose mess dress came with a sword she'd earned in her youth. Jacob was no aficionado of blades, but he loved history, and he'd read all about the battle that had earned her the ceremonial Katana she wore on her modified belt. He sighed, glancing at it from the side. It looked, for lack of a better word, awesome. With a black handle and red scabbard, it matched her perfectly.

As the COB, Chief Suresh stood at attention in front of the

enlisted and NCOs of Ops, the largest single group of spacers on the ship. Not all of them were there; only a hundred spacers standing at ease in a perfect square. In front of Suresh were his department heads. He and Kim stood before them, only a meter from the yellow-and-black stripe that matched the official embarkation of the ship.

"Now hear this, Imperial Navy Dropship approaching," PO Stawarski said over the bay speaker.

The Iron Navy's dropship looked like a tiny duplicate of their larger ships, but with a few additions. Physics being physics, they had to have wings for dropping into atmosphere, and air-breathing engines along with thrusters. The wings and engines, were folded along the top of the ship, giving it a triangular appearance.

Jacob glanced at Kim. "Here we go. Bring them to attention."

"Chief," Kim said.

"*Seventeen*, atten-SHUN!"

Jacob stifled a laugh. Her voice, like her body, was that of an eighteen-year-old; it didn't have the same impact as someone who had served almost thirty years in the Navy. Her volume did the job, though.

One hundred crew snapped to attention.

The official anthem of the Empire played over the speakers. Jacob thought it would be respectful to welcome the heir of the Empire aboard his ship with the man's own anthem.

Blue light flickered from the Richman field that prevented atmosphere from leaking out of the ship. Static played against the hull of the drop ship as it pierced the field. Landing skids lowered from the belly of the ship. It hovered for a moment before sitting down gently on the deck.

"All hands, stand clear," Stawarski said. It was all procedure

—no one would run out to the dropship before landing had finished.

A panel on the ship's side pushed out and slid up, then stairs gently lowered. Prince Henry Faust, heir of the Iron Throne, stepped out of the ship. His version of the mess dress was every bit as impressive as Jacobs, with a small addition Jacob wished he had: Henry and his party of twelve officers wore black-and-yellow cloaks that extended down to their knees. The black fabric was imprinted with the logo of the Empire, a crown and sword.

"Damn, that's hot," Kim muttered from behind him.

In all the time they'd served together, he couldn't ever recall her commenting on someone's appearance. "XO?"

"Sorry, sir. But damn!"

Henry marched over to the line on the deck, stopped, and snapped to attention.

"Prince Henry Faust, son of the Iron Emperor, and heir to the Iron Throne, requesting permission to come aboard."

Spacer First Class Fontenot walked carefully through the passageway parallel to the boat bay. He was supposed to be there, but with over a hundred crew assembled, no one would miss him. He'd taken some crappy assignments before, but nothing like posing as a navy spacer. He certainly wouldn't do it again.

Fontenot stopped and checked his bearings. He'd spent enormous prep time learning how to get around the stupid ship, let alone how its power systems worked. If it wasn't for the chip in his head showing him which systems he could damage without notice, he never would've figured it out. There was only so much memory he could store on the implanted device without detection. He hadn't expected the Navy to care so much about heat aboard ship that they could detect extra heat coming from the crew.

A line appeared in his vision, showing him the correct path.

"Got it," he muttered.

Between the self-righteous crew, the idiot captain, and the stupid marines, he couldn't wait for them to dock somewhere, anywhere, and let him slip off the ship. His contact had assured him they wouldn't spend more than three weeks in space; that was three weeks too much. He needed off immediately.

If half the crew dies, along with a royal guest, I'm pretty sure we'll return to port, he thought with a sadistic smile playing across his lips.

It wasn't his fault the boat bay PO hadn't requested the battery backups on the Richman field be fixed, nor was it his fault engineering was behind on maintaining three of the four power relays that fed the fields, leaving one carrying the load.

Fontenot took a quick peek around the bulkhead to where the access hatch lay. No one was there. Hurrying to get the job done, he knelt in front of the panel and pulled out his off-brand NavPad. His people at NAVPER had tried to get him a higher rank than spacer first class, to justify having a NavPad, but the risk was too high. Easier just to hide the slim device when he wasn't using it.

He was no computer guy. The thing bypassed local security and allowed him access to hatches he otherwise couldn't. The hatch beeped and slid up, revealing an empty passageway. Just as it was supposed to be.

On his hands and knees, Fontenot crawled into the passageway. Strip lighting embedded in the corners illumined the passageway; he moved slowly until he found the relay he was looking for.

Sure enough, the panel came off as easily as the rest of

them. Inside, to the untrained eye, was a jumble of power cables, optical relays, and molycircs.

Fontenot puzzled over the relays. It would be investigated; there was no way around that with the number of deaths he was about to cause. He needed to break it in such a way that it would look like it failed on its own.

The easiest method would be to make the power relay overload. Fontenot reached in and pulled three of the power relay control nodes. Next, he pulled the molycirc chip controlling heat dissipation partway out, but not quite all the way. If he was right, when power pushed through the relay to the Richman field, the panel would overheat and the field would drop, sending Captain Dipwad and his crew into space.

He closed and sealed the panel, using his micro welder to mimic melted metal.

"Perfect," he muttered.

Fontenot crawled out backward more quickly than he'd come in. Any second, the panel would explode; he didn't want them knowing he was anywhere near the malfunction.

As his head cleared the hatch into the main passageway, a hand grabbed his uniform collar and flung him against the bulkhead. He hit with a groan, sliding down to the deck.

"What the f—" A blow, harder than anything he'd ever felt in his life, slammed into his solar plexus. Air whooshed out of him, collapsing his lungs and sending him to the deck in a fit of sputtering coughs.

Fontenot's eyes watered, and his body tried to recover. He saw the boots: black, polished leather, Alliance Marine issue.

"Spacer, consider yourself under arrest," Jennings said. The MP-17 pointing at his face made her point indisputable.

CHAPTER TWENTY-FIVE

Jacob breathed in the delicious smell of fried bratwurst, scalloped potatoes, and fresh bread. PO Mendez didn't make an appearance in the wardroom, but his assistants did, bringing the food out to the decorated table. The tablecloth was the Alliance flag; the napkins were the flag of the Empire.

As the captain of the ship, Jacob sat on one end. Henry Faust sat opposite him. Between them were the five members of Faust's party and Jacob's top two officers, Kim and Mark. He had also invited Chief Suresh and Lieutenants Marino and Misha. Jacob always liked to include the younger officers in these kinds of functions. It built their confidence and gave them examples of what to expect.

"My compliments to your chef," Henry said in his clipped accent. "This smells amazing."

Jacob subtly motioned for Spacer First Class Zach who immediately came to his side. "Make sure Josh comes out before the night is over," Jacob whispered.

"Aye, aye, Skipper."

Aaliyah Davis, now a full-fledged Spacer, appeared at his

side. She wore the service dress whites with matching white gloves. The sharp looking uniforms were difficult to keep clean, but were impressive to behold. Davis carried a carafe of Navy orange drink just for Jacob. While she carefully filled his glass, Spacer Perch circled the table with the decanter of specially authorized alcoholic drink. In reality, Jacob had asked the crew if anyone had anything from the Empire. To his great relief, a bottle of Kirschwasser Schnapps was aboard and volunteered for the dinner.

Henry held his glass out with a broad smile and Perch filled it.

"My thanks," the prince said, raising the glass in an informal toast. After he downed the alcohol in a quick gulp, he let out a long sigh. He noticed Jacob drinking the orange juice. "I assure you, Jacob, the schnapps you provided is quite good. Much better than the juice you're drinking."

The chuckle started with Devi and ended with a full laugh from Kim. Poor Marino and Misha sat at attention, almost afraid to move.

"I've said something amusing?" Henry asked.

"Yes and no," Jacob replied. "I appreciate my crew finding a bottle of something you would like, Henry. Alliance Navy ships don't generally stock alcohol aboard. While my crew are more than welcome to participate..." Before the word even finished forming, Devi held her glass up for Perch to fill. "...I don't drink."

"My apologies," Henry said. "Of course, you're on duty. I should have known."

Another series of chuckles. Kim and Mark gestured for Perch to fill theirs.

"No need for apology. What I mean is that I don't drink at all. Ever. On or off duty."

Confusion washed over Henry's face. He glanced from his people to Jacob's, then spoke something in his native language.

The five men with him chuckled, as did Devi, which caught them by surprise. They looked at her.

"You pick up a few things here and there," Devi said before knocking back her drink.

Henry nodded to the Chief of the Boat. "I'm afraid my men and I have made fun at your expense Jacob. You see, in my country, drinking alcohol starts when you can reach the stein."

Jacob sipped his favored orange drink, which he genuinely enjoyed. "Again, no need to apologize, Henry. Even here at home I get a lot of strange looks. To each his own. My choice to abstain is not a judgement on anyone who chooses to partake."

"That's very Alliance of you, Captain," the man to Henry's right said.

"Our two nations are more similar, I think, than different, Lieutenant Dieter," Jacob said.

Dieter, a narrow-chested man with a sharp jawline, narrowed his eyes. "With all due respect, Captain Grimm, what do you know about the Empire?"

Jacob, keeping his face neutral looked directly at the man. "Your Iron Emperor produced an honorable son who would risk his own life for the head of state of another nation. What more do I need to know?"

Dieter's face burned crimson, but he said nothing else.

"I would like to think you would do the same," Henry said.

"Without hesitation. It isn't in me to stand by and do nothing. If I see a situation sailing into disaster, I act."

"Brave words from a man who hasn't had to prove them," Dieter said. He had shed his embarrassment and rejoined the conversation.

Jacob gave him a tight smile. If the man only knew the number of times he'd done just that, and the number of spacers who had sailed with him and never returned. He glanced at

Henry out of the corner of his eye. Henry gave him a slight shrug as if he understood.

"Tell me, Lieutenant Dieter, are you in the infantry?"

"Fallschirmjäger, Captain. Drop troopers. An elite branch of the Bundeswehr. We make drops from orbit or low atmosphere on to planets." His smug expression told Jacob the man was quite proud of his status. Who was Jacob to disabuse him of such notions?

"That's very impressive, Lieutenant. I must introduce you to Gunny Jennings. I'm sure she would be fascinated to learn more. I myself am a Navy man. While there are times I've had to go to the ground, it's always surrounded by my Marines. I'm afraid I'm not very good with a weapon, or in hand-to-hand combat. Naval combat is my domain. Attempting to split skills in such disparate areas would be folly, don't you think?"

Henry let out a bark of laughter. "Your blitzkrieg has failed, Dieter. Retreat with honor."

"Herr Captain, you make an excellent point," Dieter said. Jacob appreciated a man who could admit when he was wrong. Either way, the discussion was over, and Jacob was glad for it. Trading verbal barbs with an ally's subordinate didn't make for an enjoyable dinner.

They ate their meal, making small talk along the way. Josh's menu was spot on. After the first course was finished, even Marino and Misha began to ease up.

"Prince Faust, I've heard the medical technology in the Empire far exceeds our own. As a doctor, I'd be fascinated to learn more," Marino said.

"Ahh, Fräulein, if I were only the man to explain it to you. I'm afraid I didn't bring my ship's doctor with me. I believe, though, while our technology branched in a different direction, it is not materially more effective than your little spiders."

Henry held up his hand, forefinger and thumb a centimeter apart.

Lieutenant Marino giggled, a delightful sound that did much to lighten the mood. "Nanobots, Prince Faust."

"Please," he said, gazing at her big brown eyes, "Henry is fine."

She seemed mesmerized by him, and Jacob couldn't help but chuckle. "See, Lieutenant? More the same than different."

"So it would seem, Herr Captain." Dieter acquiesced.

Zach entered, pushing a tray.

"Prince Henry, Skipper. PO Mendez would like you to have a special dessert with his compliments. Cherry Cake," Zach said.

"Excellent!" Henry practically shouted. "Your chef is most skilled, Jacob."

Jacob had always liked Josh, ever since the first time he'd met him all those years ago. How skilled he was, though, he was only beginning to understand.

"Zach, would you fetch PO Mendez for me," Jacob asked.

"Aye, aye sir."

A moment later Josh came out, his face filled with concern.

"Everything okay, Skipper?" Josh asked.

Jacob smiled in delight.

"Our guests wanted to compliment you on your fine meal, is all."

Josh's face turned beet red.

"Your meals spoke to my ancestors, Herr Petty Officer," Henry said. "If you ever find yourself in need of employment, please come see me."

"Sir, that's high praise indeed, thank you."

All the men echoed their sentiments before Josh left to return to the galley with a broad smile.

The hatch to the passageway whooshed open, and Gunny Jennings marched in. The imperial men stirred at Jennings' sudden arrival. She either didn't notice or didn't care. She walked up to Jacob and snapped to attention.

Jacob resisted the urge to sigh. "As you were, Gunny. Report."

Jennings stayed at attention. "Begging the skipper's pardon, but you need to hear this for yourself."

"Prince Henry, would you be willing to join me for a walk?"

Henry eyed the forkful of moist cake mere centimeters from his mouth. With a sigh, he took a bite, swallowed quickly, and stood. "My friends, please stay and finish your dinner."

"My Prince—" Dieter said.

"I'll be fine. I trust Captain Grimm with my life—at least *twice* now."

Jacob quirked an eyebrow at that. Henry had told him that he wasn't bound by security clearances, but perhaps that was just to Jacob, not his own people. It would make sense the Iron Emperor wouldn't want it known his daughter had been kidnapped.

Jacob stood, tossing his napkin onto his plate. "Zach, Perch, Davis, well done tonight. Please see to our guests and their needs."

"Aye, aye, sir," all three rang out in unison.

"Lead the way, Gunny."

―――――

Brigs in the Navy varied from cleaned-out storage compartments with the locking mechanism removed to full prison facilities, complete with interrogation station and one-way glass. *Seventeen* had something in between the two.

Jennings stopped in front of the hatch where an armed spacer stood guard.

"Gunnery Sergeant," Spacer Kazlauskas greeted her, then opened the hatch.

Jacob and Henry followed Jennings in. The brig was one central compartment with three individual cells locked behind reinforced hatches. Each hatch had a large flatscreen imbedded in it that showed the entire cell. In the middle, PO Cartwright sat at a desk with access to more security screens.

Spacer Fontenot occupied the middle cell. He was wearing a standard Navy jumpsuit with no rank. On his chest, instead of Navy, it said PRISONER and FONTENOT.

"He say anything?" Jennings asked.

Cartwright shook his head. "He's on his rack. Hasn't moved since you brought him in. I ran his bios and sent a message to NAVPER to find out who he really is. Even if they respond immediately, it will be eight hours before we hear back from them."

Seeing Captain Grimm and Prince Faust, Cartwright stood.

"As you were, Ethan," Jacob said. "What do you mean, 'who he really is'? He's a spacer..."

PO Cartwright eyed Prince Faust before raising an eyebrow at Captain Grimm.

Jacob smiled inwardly, not letting PO Cartwright see his reaction. "It's fine, PO. Go ahead."

"Yes, sir. He's not Navy, Skipper. I don't think he's military. After his arrest, PO Mendez brought in a meal and mentioned he'd run into Fontenot and thought he acted strange. I did a little test to see what he knew. When I mentioned we would use him for 3M, he asked me what that meant... Pretty obvious he's not an Alliance spacer."

Jacob chuckled at PO Cartwright's clever use of Navy jargon to catch the spy.

"I'm sorry, Jacob. 3M?" the prince said.

Cartwright nodded at Henry. He was another obvious example.

"Maintenance and Material Management," Jacob replied. "It's how we make sure everything on the ship, from foot lockers to the weapons, works when we need it. Spacers love it about as much as cleaning the head."

"We have something similar," Henry said. "That was clever of you, PO Cartwright."

"Uh, thank you, my prince."

Henry chuckled, shaking his head and waving his hand. "You may call me Prince Faust."

Jacob moved to the hatch where Fontenot was kept. He pressed the screen, activating the speaker.

"Fontenot, this is Captain Grimm. I don't suppose you want to tell me who you're working for?"

Fontenot looked up to the overhead where the sound came from. After a moment, he laid his head back without saying a word.

"Is this the extent of your interrogation, Jacob?" Henry asked.

"I'm afraid our options are limited. We'll keep him in the brig until we return to a proper Navy station and can offload him to NCIS. We have his crime well documented; he's not going anywhere."

"Why not have someone question him more...vigorously."

Jennings made no move. Cartwright took that moment to look anywhere else.

"We don't do that without extreme cause," Jacob said. "He sabotaged our ship, but he's caught. Even if he told me who he worked for, there wouldn't be anything I could do about it. I'm not the head of state, just a ship's captain."

"You're too modest, Mein Freund."

CHAPTER TWENTY-SIX

The Alliance communications network proved far more complex to tap into than Captain Kareem had originally envisioned. From the surface of the frozen planet, his team called to report their failure.

"I'm sorry, sir. They're using a key encoded encryption. We could bring the entire Ministry of Science here to work on it, but without the key, we will never get in."

Kareem frowned at the screen. His briefing indicated the Alliance used basic encryption, and that the Caliphate's superior computer technology would allow them to hack in. According to his technician, though, it wasn't even a matter of technology.

"It's not your fault, Fazik. Return to the ship, we'll figure it out from there."

Kareem contemplated what they needed to do. His orders were to gather ship locations and system communications. Something he could do if he took Al-Hikma in closer. Of course, moving the ship in closer came with risks.

He pulled up the ship's loadout. Space aboard ship determined what they could carry. Even with the nano-powered fabrication technology, the raw materials available for the fabricator were still limited. He needed to keep it for ammo and repairs.

"Bridge, Captain. Can you have engineer Jaziri come to my quarters?"

"Yes, sir."

A few minutes later, Jaziri, still in his work uniform, entered with Kareem's permission. Jaziri's head was polished bald, but he had a thick beard.

"I want to turn several of our torpedoes into receiving stations capable of tracking ship movements and sending back the data in burst communications. When the rest of the fleet arrives, I want to be able to give our future Caliph something better than guesses. Can we do that?"

Jaziri stood still, thinking for a moment. "We can pull the warheads, detonators, and even the seeker aids. That should leave more than enough room to put in comms gear—" Jaziri paused.

"What?"

"With your permission, sir, I could alter the torpedoes further and build a gravity wave detection apparatus into them. It wouldn't be able to track in real time, but it could give us general directions and distance."

Kareem sat up sharply. "Jaziri, that's brilliant. You can do this? How long?"

"Perhaps five hours per torpedo? If we distribute them in a wide enough cross section along the ecliptic, it would be very effective."

Five hours. Kareem checked his schedule. If the Caliphate still had FTLC, it would make the operation much more efficient. That was in the past, though. If they altered ten torpedoes, that would leave them with a few days to gather information.

"Do what you have to. Use any people you need. Convert ten torpedoes and we'll start placing them as soon as you're done with the first one."

"Yes, sir!" Jaziri turned but hesitated for a heartbeat.

"What is it?" Kareem asked.

"We'll have to place them closer to the system than we would normally go, sir. Even running silent, we risk detection."

Kareem nodded his understanding. He was both aware of the issue, and also aware of the risk Jaziri took in appearing to question his captain's orders.

"Understood, Jaziri. We'll take all precautions. I'm sure our excellent crew and technology will protect us."

After Jaziri departed, Kareem noted in his log that they weren't able to crack the code but would risk moving closer in system to record findings manually. Under no circumstances would he mention Jaziri's inspired solution. The engineer had taken a huge chance even mentioning it to him. Kareem would make sure all traces of the alteration were destroyed before the fleet arrived.

The last thing either he or Jaziri needed was the Caliph thinking they could spy on their own ships with torpedoes. They would be lined up and shot before they returned home—no matter the success of the mission. Smart officers made sure never to appear to pose a threat to their commanding officers or the Caliph.

CHAPTER TWENTY-SEVEN

Like most of Anchorage Bay, the main hospital was new construction. Nadia grappled with the startling reality of how fast the city was rebuilt after the bombing. Millions had died at the hands of the Caliphate, and yet, somehow, the politicians had managed to keep an all-out war from starting. Maybe, she decided, it was the focus on rebuilding.

Anchorage Bay General Hospital gleamed in the afternoon sun. White paint gave it an immaculately clean look. Red crosses at the top of the building showed where the hover pads jutted out for air ambulances to land. From studying the blueprints, she knew the building could receive as many as twenty air ambulances at once, not to mention the entrances for ground vehicles.

"According to your download, the morgue is in the sub-basement," Elsa said.

Nadia parked the aircar on the roof of the public parking garage. Automated arms grabbed the aircar and pulled it down into the building for storage. Once they'd stopped moving, they were given the green light to exit the vehicle. Nadia didn't. She gripped the yoke with her one hand for a moment.

"What's wrong?" Elsa asked.

How did she tell the princess the last time she got involved in political intrigue she ended up one of the most wanted people in the Alliance? That her once sworn enemy, turned amazing friend, had sacrificed herself to stop the Caliphate. All of it ran through Nadia's mind. A million more reasons why she should go in alone and leave Elsa in the car. If something happened to the princess... "I don't suppose you would stay in the car if I asked you to?" she asked.

Elsa laughed her delightfully musical laugh. "You're serious? All the more reason to go in with you."

Nadia nodded, more to herself than Elsa. She'd expected the answer. Unbuckling, she reached over to the glove box and typed in a code, followed by her thumbprint. The box opened, and the butt of two pistols, along with four spare mags for each, appeared.

"I'm assuming you know how to shoot?"

Elsa barked out a laugh. "I'm an expert marksman with the Navy's standard-issue P3—" She pulled out Nadia's preferred slug thrower and looked at the former spy in disbelief. "Did you raid a museum?"

Nadia took her own pistol, using her only hand to press check it before stuffing it between her legs and loading a magazine.

"Those are bullets," Elsa said. "Why not use a coil pistol or directed energy weapon?"

Once the mag was loaded, Nadia pushed the slide against her chest to chamber a round. "First of all, those are all good choices. I used to fly into a lot of backwater places with just my ship and crew. Access to modern repair facilities was always limited. These"—she hefted her pistol—"are easy to fabricate and repair. Even easier to make the ammo for. Speaking of which, this is a Partlow Arms P2910. It fires self-contained armor piercing ammo, is silenced, and has a twenty-round magazine. No safety, no electronics. It can't be disabled by an EMP. The trigger is soft—you breathe on it and you're shooting."

Elsa eyed the anachronistic pistol like it was a snake coiled in the glove box and ready to bite her. She picked it up, feeling the weight for a moment, then mimicked Nadia's movements: checking the chamber, slamming the mag in, and racking the slide.

"Just like a normal pistol, but without special ammo, without safety features to prevent you from blowing your head off, and without anything to help you hit your target."

Nadia grinned. "This is my safety," she said. The ex-spy held up her remaining hand, wiggling her trigger finger. "I don't think anything is going to go wrong in there, but if we're right, and they aren't actually Caliph agents, or heaven forbid, actual Iron Navy, then whoever sent them might come looking for the bodies—or for anyone who shows too much interest in them."

Elsa opened her door. The lightweight material moved with ease, lifting up and out of the way. "What makes you think they haven't already disposed of the bodies?"

Nadia opened her door with a little more trouble. Once they were both out, the garage arms closed their doors for them and lifted the car up and out of the way into storage. Nadia slid the pistol into the small of her back, having worn a waistband tight enough to hold the gun in place. The spare mags were in her leather jacket. "Have you ever tried to dispose of a body? Let alone steal one?"

"Not really a problem in my line of work. Do you need bodies often?"

"Stealing a body from a hospital comes with its own unique challenges. Add hiding it and disposing of it, and it would be more economical to wait and see if you even need to. Besides, if the bodies went missing, it would raise more questions. They'll be here."

"Then why the *protection?*" Elsa asked.

"If I were running the op, I'd have an insider reporting on the comings and goings of the morgue. If anyone showed up asking questions, I would want to know who they were. Far easier to dispose of them than the bodies. After all, aircar accidents happen. Even in our city, crime is still a thing."

They rode the lift down to the subbasement labeled Pathology Suite. Magnetic guides hummed with power, sending them down a hundred meters in a few seconds. Double doors opened to a grey-painted hallway. A large white sign gave directions to the different rooms on the floor—in three languages.

Nadia knew where to go. Turning right, she headed for cold storage. With the amount of time that had passed since the attack, there was no chance an autopsy hadn't happened.

A small office behind a transparency stood between them and the room they needed. A civilian nurse sat behind a desk. She wore a white smock and a white knit hat to keep her ears warm. If Nadia had to guess, she suspected it was fifteen degrees in the room. Far too cold for comfort.

"May I help you?"

Nadia read her nametag. "Nurse Hensley? I'm Nadia Grimm. I made an appointment. My brother—" she stopped, holding one hand up to her face for a second. She worried Elsa would blow her cover, but the nurse focused on her alone. "My stepbrother, he was a Capitol police officer killed in an explosion the other day... I'm here to see the remains."

Hensley showed genuine sorrow for Nadia. "I'm so sorry for your loss, miss, but... I'm sorry to tell you, there wasn't much in the way of remains left. Are you sure you want to see it? They don't need family for identification."

Nadia choked back a sob, turning to Elsa and pressing her head into the taller woman's shoulder. "Yes," she said between sobs. "I need to say goodbye."

Hensley didn't hesitate. She pressed a hidden button, opening the door. "Through there," she said. "Cabinet C-16B. If you need help I can—"

Nadia waved her away, not trusting her voice.

"I'm sure we'll manage," Elsa said.

The door closed behind them, and Nadia instantly returned to normal.

"Was zum Teufel?" Elsa muttered.

"Sorry, I don't speak Imperial standard," Nadia replied. She walked to the correct cabinet and pulled it out. A stasis field held the particulates in place. There really wasn't much left of the body. Nadia let out a wail like her soul had collapsed, and she sank to her knees beside a stunned Elsa.

Nurse Hensley poked her head in, then retreated at a sharp headshake from Elsa.

"Is she gone?" Nadia whispered.

"Yes."

Nadia stood, whipping out her NavPad, and scanned the lockers until she found the assassins. "These," she said, pointing at four of them.

"Why not just look at the autopsy files?" Elsa asked. The princess grunted with effort as she opened each of the freezers.

"One, I doubt they'll have what you need. Two, again, hacking an encrypted computer is much more difficult than examining the bodies... as you can plainly see."

The four bodies were in stasis, just like the remains of the police officer. Each one looked empty, like a blacked-out light. Intellectually, Nadia knew they'd once lived and breathed, but... they were shells.

"What do you need?"

"Your NavPad set to scan for DNA," Elsa said.

Nadia fiddled with the device for a moment and handed it over.

"Just hold them in the targeting window and scan."

Nadia turned away, unable to look anymore. While her eyes saw the dead men, her mind only showed her the crew who had died serving aboard *Dagger*... even the asshat Pete. She shook her head. Would she ever forgive herself? The events that happened after the capture rarely bothered her anymore. Years of therapy, mostly in the form of a loving relationship with Jacob and sticking it to the Caliphate at every opportunity, had cured her of those.

Her friends were still dead, though, and it was her fault.

"Jawol!" Elsa shouted. "All four of them. Your medical people wouldn't have thought about looking at their DNA. I doubt the agents who hired the assassins thought of it either, but look. Look!"

Nadia turned to see what Elsa was looking at. As she did, the door to the cold storage opened. Three brown-skinned men of clearly Asian descent entered eyes directly on her. Nadia barely had time to swear as she grabbed Elsa with her one hand and yanked her behind the slabs with the bodies on them.

Electromagnetic discharge filled the air as projectiles rained down on their position. In the distant part of Nadia's mind, she wondered what they fired. Coil guns had their own distinctive sound; whatever they used wasn't something she recognized. Nadia shut off the part of her mind that wondered about such things and focused on her more immediate future. Or lack thereof.

"Three tangos, by the door." She knife-handed the positions she last saw them at. "Fire over the top, and I'll peek out when they return fire."

Gun in hand, Elsa nodded.

"Now!"

Elsa raised her pistol over the slab and rapid-fired in the direction of the door.

Nadia leaned out on her side, pistol locked in front of her. She didn't need the sights to aim. The three men stood in the open, compact, rapid-fire pistols out and shooting where Elsa had fired from.

Nadia squeezed the trigger three times, hitting the first one in the chest. Blood and bone blasted out the back of the man, and he stumbled back, a dazed expression on his face as he slid down the wall. Clenching her stomach muscles, she returned to cover. More rounds rained down on them.

"They'll circle us in a second," Nadia said.

Elsa fired a burst to keep them cautious.

Nadia leaped up and ran two steps, then dove behind the next slab. The wall in front of her looked like it had taken a hit from a rapid-fire shotgun. Another shot hit the concrete, spraying her with stinging particles. One hit her in the face, making her wince. A warm trickle of blood seeped down her cheek.

"Keep firing," she yelled. Elsa did as she was told. Nadia took a deep breath, then leaped out the side of her cover to slide across the tile floor. She was right. One man stood by the door, using its partially open state as cover. The other had moved past his fallen comrade and headed for the far side of the room where a mobile toolbox the size of a fridge could conceal him.

Nadia fired until her slide locked back. The one running across the room took six hits, his steps faltering, blood spattering the wall around him. When the final round hit him, he slumped to the ground.

The last man, hiding behind the door, turned his gun on Nadia. He took a moment to get a bead on her. His head snapped back, and his body fell to the ground.

"How did you know I would do that?" Elsa asked, her breath coming in ragged gulps.

Nadia triggered the mag release, the metal box clattered to the tile floor. She pinned the pistol between her legs, swiped up the empty mag, and swapped it for the full one in her pocket. A moment later, she was reloaded and climbing to her feet.

"Let's go before the police or their backup arrive," she said.

"Nadia. How did you know?"

"I didn't. I hoped. Grab the NavPad and—" Nadia froze. Her trusted device, the object by which she had toppled senators, lay in a thousand pieces on the floor.

"I'm sorry," Elsa said. "When they started firing, I dropped it."

"Did you see what you needed to?" Nadia slid the pistol back into her pants as she ran out. She purposely didn't look at the nurses' station—she knew what she would see, and the last thing she needed was another face added to her nightmares.

"Yes. Mein gott," Elsa said as she exited into the hallway.

A few minutes later, they were in Nadia's aircar, preparing for liftoff.

"Aren't you worried about the cameras?" Elsa asked.

"They weren't—which means they had them off."

She lifted off, the turbo fans whining as she pulled hard up into the sky. "Program course for Horseback Mountain location," she said.

"Course programmed," the car's computer replied. "Initiate?"

"Yes. ETA?"

"Three hours, ten minutes, fourteen seconds."

Nadia leaned her head back, a wave of post adrenaline exhaustion hitting her. "Tell me what you found?"

"With the NavPad destroyed, we won't be able to prove it,"

Elsa said. "Despite what you said, now that they know we know, they're probably moving the bodies already."

Nadia knew what Elsa was saying was true. Knowing and proving were two different things. "I'm not law enforcement, Elsa. I don't need to prove anything. What did you see?"

Elsa looked out the window at the fading city. Within minutes, the car was high in the clouds, flying at over three hundred klicks an hour.

"I don't want to start another war, Nadia. You have to understand that. My people don't want war. Not when they don't have to have it."

Nadia did her best to suppress the irritation in her voice. "You told me yourself that the last war never really ended. What makes this different?"

Elsa took longer to answer than Nadia would have preferred, but she did her best to let the woman think it over before speaking.

"If they'd impersonated anyone else, it wouldn't have mattered, but when my father learns of this..."

"Else, who?"

"RISS. Republic Internal—"

"Security Services. I've dealt with them. How do you know, though?"

"Earth is heavily polluted. The Terran Republic only trusts its security agents to Terran-born agents. Stupid, I know, but they're ideologically flawed as far as I'm concerned. All they care about is the party. Those men, they looked like my people, but they had traces of heavy metals in their system consistent with Terran agents. It's why they've never successfully infiltrated my government."

Nadia let out a whistle. Wit was going to be pissed that DNI hadn't discovered this.

DNI was going to be more pissed that she *had*.

"I'm taking us to a safe house. I need to get a message to Jacob, and then we're lying low for... a while. When is your brother coming back to get you?"

Elsa looked up into the sky. "A week, maybe two. You have a safe house?"

"It's more like a cabin up in the mountains."

CHAPTER TWENTY-EIGHT

"I have to say, Jacob. Both your ship and your crew are impressive. Thank you for having me aboard."

Jacob and Henry stood in *Seventeen*'s cavernous boat bay, with Henry's dropship behind him.

"If I'm able, I will always welcome you on any ship where I serve or command."

The two men of action shook hands. For Jacob, it was more than merely a polite gesture. It was a measure of the man, of both of them. Jacob knew, in his soul, that Henry Foust was a man he could trust.

"Before you go, I would like to run something by you," Jacob said.

"By all means."

"Let's do a joint training exercise. We can load up the simulators, make a few runs at each other. Give our crews something to do. Training on the computer only goes so far. They need to feel the hum of the gravcoil beneath them."

Henry pondered the idea for a moment. His men waited impatiently by the dropship. "I think that's an excellent idea."

Unlike when they arrived, there wasn't any fanfare for their departure. Henry bowed once more and was soon on his dropship, heading back for his ships.

"Captain, Gravity. PO Tefiti."

Jacob headed for the nearest comm panel. He slammed it down with his fist. "Captain here. Go ahead."

"Skipper, I'm picking up some odd reading coming from an odd place. I'd love to be more specific, sir; however, I have to show you."

It wasn't like Tefiti to be vague. If the man thought something was odd, it was odd. "What do you need from me?"

"Permission to alter course and deploy the towed array, sir."

Jacob did some mental math. They were well in system from the range. Towed arrays were fine for sparse locations, but Alexandria's inner system was busy enough that it required permission.

"At your discretion, PO. I'll be on the bridge in thirty. Be ready to show me odd."

"Aye, aye, Skipper. Tefiti out."

Eager to change from his mess dress to his day uniform, Jacob walked briskly to the nearest lift. It amazed him how easily using the lifts came. On *Interceptor,* the lifts were for casualties and guests, never the crew. On *Seventeen*, though, he was 800 meters from his quarters and five decks down.

While he rode the lift, his NavPad rang eight bells. He was shocked to see it was 2330 hours. Between the dinner with the prince and the debacle with the saboteur he didn't have—

His NavPad alerted him to an incoming priority message. An image of Nadia_ appeared, tired, smiling, and in strange surroundings. One thing he wouldn't ever complain about: being in the home system and getting messages from her the same day she sent them.

The lift deposited him only a few frames from his quarters. Wanting to both change *and* listen to the message, he hurried to his quarters. The passageways were empty as a ghost town. Alliance ships maintained a day and night system for psychological sanity.

Once inside, he stripped off his mess jacket, tossed it on the chair, then pulled up the message from Nadia and put it on the big screen.

"Jacob, I can only imagine how good you look in your uniform."

He blushed, even though she couldn't see him. He peered at the image. *Is that a painting of a dog playing poker behind her?*

"I know I said I wouldn't send you any more messages so you could focus on your mission, but I can't help how much I miss you." Elsa Faust passed by in the background, pausing only to hand Nadia a beer. It surprised him she was there. They'd left Alexandria weeks ago. Jacob kicked himself for not asking after her to Henry, who surely would have appreciated the gesture.

"We've had a busy few weeks here. Still no arm," she said with a frown, "but they assure me it will be returned at some point. I decided to ask Wit about it—" Jacob hopped on one foot as he tried to pull his boots off while standing and had to lean against the wall to keep from falling over.

She visited Wit?

While she hadn't told him the specifics of her mission while he was in Cordoba, whatever it was had hurt her. Deeply.

"He showed me your message, which was nice of him. I told him where we're planning on going for our honeymoon—if we ever get the time off." Her lips played into a smile, like she was telling a joke only he should get. "I've always wanted to see Terra. We would have so much fun touring the old worlds."

How in God's green universe does that woman know the man locked in my brig is a Terran agent?

"He said something about a coup, but I assured him the

Terran Republic has extremely good security services. We would be as safe there as here. According to Elsa, the only place safer would be the Iron Empire."

They must have identified the assassins as Terran Security Services... which means the Terran Republic wants revenge for Cordoba. Not just on the Alliance, but on me?

"Be careful out there, hon. You never know how many dangers await you in the black. I love you. Message me back soon. Elsa and I are taking a little vay-cay off the reservation. I'll be in touch... Oh, before I forget... I let your dad know about the hole in the south fence. He assured me that he's ready if any of the porcuswine try to get through."

God, thank you for that woman in my life.

Jacob finished dressing, thinking about the volume of information Nadia had given him. The Terran Republic was behind the assassination attempt. They were also most likely behind the saboteur aboard his ship. There could be others. The Iron Empire had nothing to do with it and could be trusted.

How she was able to communicate so much information covertly was beyond him. He would have just blurted it out. Of course, she was a spy and he was a naval officer. However, he reminded himself, he'd sent a cleverly worded message to her before. Maybe there was hope for him yet.

The thought that there could be more infiltrators on his ship frustrated and angered him. It was his ship. Barring combat, his crew should be safe on her.

Once changed, and with all the latest information warring around inside his head, Jacob headed for the bridge to see Tefiti. As he stepped out of the cabin, the hum of the gravcoil vibrated through the ship. He felt himself falling backward and grabbed an overhead bar for a second as acceleration took hold. Of course, it was a trick of his inner ear, but he held on regardless.

A minute later, Jacob walked by PFC Pascal and Private

Washington and onto the bridge. Both snapped to attention, and Pascal bellowed, "Captain on the bridge."

"As you were," Jacob said in response. Pascal wore a large smile. Marines loved yelling at Navy.

Jacob crossed the bridge to Tefiti's station. As he did, he realized how much he missed the smaller bridge of Interceptor. *Seventeen* was a fantastic ship and her crew amazing, but because of her size, she felt distant, subdued. He didn't know her the way he could a smaller vessel. Even if it wasn't the shark, Jacob doubted he would want a battleship assignment again.

"Lay it on me, Tefiti," Jacob said as he leaned over the console.

Tefiti pointed at the center screen. "Watch here, sir. This is us"—he highlighted a yellow icon *BB-17*—" when we arrived at the LaGrange point."

Tefiti let the computer play. Ripples passed from one side of the screen to the other. Each ripple came with a tag identifying the ship type, estimate of distance, and probable speed.

"I wouldn't have even noticed if we weren't sitting on the LaGrange point..."

"Why does that matter?" Jacob asked.

"Traffic around the LaGrange point is limited. Especially this one, since it's so far out from Alexandria. We're already out of the way. These gravity readings are all heavy M-class freighters going to and from the outer system gas giants and the asteroid belts. As you know, the mining in the far parts of the system produce a tremendous amount of traffic—though its nothing near what comes through the starlanes from trade."

Tefiti's fingers danced across the controls, reprogramming the screen. One by one, gravity waves vanished from the display until only a few remained.

"What are these?" Jacob asked.

"These two are coming from closer to the start. It's this one"—he highlighted one coming from farther away—"that's the odd one."

Either there was a civilian ship way out in orbit, or the enemy had infiltrated Alexandria. Jacob prayed to God it was the former. He took a moment to examine the wave. He didn't want to seem like an idiot. Finding out what Tefiti was trying to tell him before he said it would be a coup. One day, that would happen. "Okay, I give. Why is it odd?"

"Every ship's gravity wave is a direct result of her gravcoil. Based on that data, we can identify, to a pretty good degree, the kind of ship that produced the wake. These over here are M-class freighters. When our Imperial friends fire up their ships, we'll know what they are..."

Realization dawned on Jacob like a bell. "Are you saying the computer doesn't know what it is?"

"Not just the computer, Skipper. The harmonic frequency generated by the gravity wave isn't something I've ever heard before either."

"That is odd."

"Exactly."

Jacob clapped Tefiti on the back. "Well done, PO." He walked back to his chair. He had a decision to make.

Battleships weren't small. One-kilometer-long titans of destruction with a thousand crew. Every component on the ship generated heat and electronic noise. She was no destroyer, and Jacob knew it. Sneaking up on the enemy wasn't a possibility unless circumstances were unusual. *If there even is an enemy.*

It could all be a coincidence. The Republic saboteur aboard his ship, the not–Iron Navy assassination attempt on the president. The timing. More than anything else, the timing had him worried.

Maybe assassins and saboteurs could be coincidental... but all while the majority of the Alliance Navy was currently massing to start the largest invasion the Alliance had ever attempted? While the battleships that would normally protect Alexandria were busy showing the flag at systems farther away from the front.

No. Not a coincidence. Which meant... *Yankee Black. I can't tell them anything.* There had to be something he could do to help prepare his crew. He couldn't tell them about the invasion, but he could give them a fighting chance if this were the Caliphate.

"Mark?" Jacob said. He turned his chair to face ops. The four-crew station was currently fully manned: Mark West, PO Collins, and two spacers Jacob didn't recognize. Yet another thing about battleship command he didn't care for.

"Skipper?" West replied.

"Have the XO meet me in the briefing room. You have the con."

"Aye, aye, sir. XO to the bridge briefing room. I have the con."

Jacob departed the bridge, tagging Private Washington as he walked by. "Come with me, Private."

Washington didn't hesitate. "Aye, sir."

He positioned Washington outside the briefing room, with strict orders that only the XO was allowed in. Despite battle stations, they weren't wearing their helmets. With no immediate threat, forcing everyone to breathe canned air was pointless.

Kim hustled in a minute later, coffee in one hand and her NavPad in the other. "You rang, Skipper?"

Jacob gestured for her to sit close. He activated the privacy screen on his NavPad that offered some security against eavesdropping. Kim raised an eyebrow at him. The feature was generally reserved for public locations—not in the captain's briefing room.

He pitched his voice low, despite their privacy. "What I'm about to tell you, I can't tell you. Understood?"

Kim glanced at the hatch, his NavPad, then finally him. "You know I'm with you, Skip. What's going on?"

"I know you are, and I appreciate that. I'm sworn to secrecy on a few things that I can't share with you."

Kim nodded her understanding. Jacob knew he was laying some heavy things at her feet.

"As you already know, our mission here it to show the flag while we run the trials. Part of that was going out to the range and blowing the hell out of some rocks. Part of it was zipping around the system. Having Prince Faust over was completely a coincidence—as was capturing the saboteur."

The next part, Jacob had to be careful with. He couldn't tell her, but he also didn't have to tell her she was wrong when she drew her own conclusions.

"Why, XO, do you think it's important we show the flag?"

His sudden question caught her by surprise, her mug halfway to her mouth stopped midair. "Sir?"

"You heard the question."

"I suppose to keep the morale of the Capitol up. If the Alliance's latest battleship is in system with arguably the most famous naval captain serving, it's good for the people. Especially with the war and all."

Kim was as sharp as they came. "What other reason could there be?"

"Well, since we found a saboteur aboard, I'd say to make sure any spies watching the system... saw... a... battleship here," she finished in a whisper. "Skipper, are we the only ship in the system?"

Jacob made a finger gun motion but said nothing—

confirming her suspicion. "I believe there are a couple of ships in various states of repair at Utopia, so no," he said, deliberately countering his hand movement.

"And the signal Tefiti is tracking... holy crap, Skip. Are the Cali in-system? Here?"

To her credit, she was more stunned at the revelation than panicked. Kim wasn't from Alexandria, and he supposed he should be a little panicked at the thought of them bombing his home... again. That wasn't going to happen, though. He would die and take every Caliphate ship with him before he let them near his home planet.

"I think so. The timing is... unfortunate, but there's nothing to be done about it. If the Caliphate Navy is here, then we have to find and destroy them before they can proceed with whatever mission they're on. No matter what, we can't let them hit us again."

"Skip, this won't be like last time. If they sent any ships, they would have sent a lot of them. Like... a fleet."

Jacob kept his emotions off his face. She was going through exactly what he had the moment Tefiti had shown him the signals.

"I know. *Seventeen* is armed to the teeth. At best they could send a small battle group through one of the less-traveled lanes. If they're here, we hurt them and buy time for Alexandria to prepare. They won't have a stealth ship to make a sneak attack. If they want to get to the home world, they're going to get chewed to pieces. Understood?"

"Aye, aye, sir. What should we tell the crew?"

"For now, nothing. It might *be* nothing. The moment we know, however, the crew knows. Until then, we treat this as training. No one outside this compartment."

Kim stood, gathering her things. "Yes, sir. I've got some prep to do, then."

"Dismissed."

After Kim departed, Jacob stared at the display screen. The blackness of space surrounded the ship. Was he doing the right thing? If the Caliphate was in Alexandria, wouldn't it make sense to retreat to the planet and defend it with them? Except he knew the Caliphate. They weren't just here to attack—they were here to obliterate his home. Given a chance, they would lob asteroids at Alexandria. No amount of point defense would stop them. He needed to take them out, at least cripple them, before they had the chance.

As a backup, Jacob put everything he knew up to the moment, from the saboteur to the possible Caliphate invasion, in an encrypted packet. In the worst case, he could send it to Alexandria with more than enough time for them to react. Stopping the Caliphate was his job. It was why Villanueva put him in charge of the ship.

Jacob let out a yawn that surprised him. He glanced at his NavPad and sighed. His alarm would wake him in four hours. He needed to get some rack time.

CHAPTER TWENTY-NINE

0430 SHIP TIME

Jennings stopped in front of the brig with a sealed mug of coffee for PO Cartwright. She frowned at the lack of Marines on the outside. She'd stationed one after the captain left, replacing the spacer serving the master-at-arms. She'd felt a Marine would do a better job than an under-trained spacer.

Jenings moved to punch in her security code when the hatch whooshed open.

Fontenot and a woman she didn't recognize practically slammed into her.

Slow to respond, Jennings wasn't. She smashed the sealed cup of coffee in the woman's face. The second the seal broke, piping hot coffee splashed across her skin. The woman shrieked, hands going to her face as she stumbled backward.

Fontenot jammed his hand into her sternum, knocking her back a step. He followed up with a right cross, which she blocked. She then stepped inside his reach and brought her knee up with as much force as she could muster. Fontenot danced to the side, taking the hit on his thigh with a grunt.

He swung with his elbow, smacking her in the forehead and sending her reeling.

"That's for the gym," he muttered.

Jennings raised her hands in defense and marched right in. He punched her twice, both blows landing on her forearms, but the mass of the hits rocked her. Fontenot wasn't a large man like the captain, but he was still a man. The third blow he launched, she sidestepped, grabbed his wrist, twisted her body, and yanked with all her might.

Fontenot flew over her like he'd shot from a cannon. His ninety kilos hit the bulkhead with a crack of broken bones. Jennings spun, running for the woman, who had regained her footing. Bright red skin shone where the coffee scalded her. One eye was swollen shut.

Jennings drew her MP-17, firing at point-blank range. Ten millimeters of hardened steel smashed into the woman's gut, doubling her over in a pile of sobs and vomit. Fast as a whip, she fired two shots at Fontenot as he climbed to his feet. The first one took him in the arm, the second in his already broken ribs. He screeched in agony and collapsed to the deck.

"Sickbay, Brig. Medical emergency." Without waiting for a response, she stepped over the choking, sputtering woman and checked on Cartright. Someone, the woman probably, had beaten him over the head with a metal baton. It looked like multiple times. His pulse was faint but steady.

Jennings eyed the two downed saboteurs and briefly contemplated killing them. After all, there could be a third. Instead, she grabbed the woman by her collar and dragged her across the room, tossing her bodily in and sealing the cell.

She turned to Fontenot, who blubbered on the deck, cradling his chest.

"You and I are going to have a talk."

She knelt down next to him. He opened his mouth to swear at her. Before the words formed on his lips, she jammed the MP-17 barrel in his mouth.

"I'm not interested. I only need one of you. She doesn't look like she'll talk, but maybe if I splatter your brains all over the bulkhead and make her clean it up, she'll be more cordial."

His eyes went wide, and he shook his head.

"No, she won't talk?"

He shook his head again.

"You're not being helpful."

He sputtered and coughed.

Jennings looked down at the pistol in his mouth like she'd forgotten it was there. "You want me to take this out?"

He nodded as best he could with the metal jammed into his teeth.

The hatch to the lift opened and Pierre rushed out, followed by Whips. Pierre glanced at her—nodded—and directed Whips to Cartright. "Gurney, now."

She removed the pistol. "Talk."

"I know my rights, I ain't got to say a thing."

Jennings flipped her pistol around and smashed the butt into his face. Fontenot hollered, clutching the side of his face as blood seeped between his fingers. He glanced at the medic who simply shrugged.

"Until I put you back in your cell, you're an enemy combatant. Pierre and I go way back. He won't say a thing. Got it?"

When he didn't speak, she raised the pistol again. He held his hand up and started talking.

"I was hired by an RSS agent. He didn't know I knew, but I did. I'd worked with him before—"

0730

Jacob sat next to Lieutenant Poole in the main briefing room, a cup of his orange drink in hand to shed his brain's exhaustion. Poole had coffee. Jennings, ever in parade rest, reported everything Fontenot had disclosed.

"What? He just decided to start talking? Why the sudden change of heart?" Poole asked.

Jacob reminded himself that Poole was in charge of the Marines and could ask questions however he liked.

"You'd have to ask him, sir."

Jacob cleared his throat. "Gunny, you understand the rules of conduct when it comes to prisoners, correct?"

"I do, Skipper."

Poole guffawed. "Right. Gunnery Sergeant Jennings, did you torture a prisoner for information?"

"No, sir."

"Good enough for me," Jacob said.

"What?" Poole asked. "What do you mean, good enough? The man was beaten to a pulp, Jennings. You jammed the barrel of your pistol in his mouth so hard it broke his teeth. Why were you even carrying a loaded weapon aboard ship?"

"Lieutenant Poole, you may not be aware, but my standing orders are for all Marine's on duty to wear a weapon," Jacob said.

"Are you serious, sir? That's an accident waiting to happen."

Jacob burst out laughing. He couldn't help himself. It wasn't that he thought Poole was being funny, but the irony of Poole's comment was too much for his tired brain.

"Lieutenant Poole, Gunnery Sergeant Jennings is more than qualified to carry a weapon safely, as are the rest of the NCOs. As for why? I think this morning is a prime example of why. I won't entrust the security of my ship to Marines and not give them the tools to do the job."

"But sir! She tortured him."

"Begging the lieutenant's pardon, sir, but he was an enemy combatant during his confession. By the regs, he's not a prisoner until he surrenders or is in cuffs. Or in a cell."

Poole fumed. "That's an egregious reading of the regs, Gunny. I for one will not tolerate torture. I will—"

"That's enough. Gunny, dismissed."

Jennings snapped to attention, spun, and marched out.

"Captain, I protest. You must allow me to discipline my Marines as I see fit."

Jacob held his tongue, going over exactly what he wanted to say before committing to the words. What he said next would determine his relationship with Poole going forward and probably how Poole would treat his Marines.

"Malcom, your command style is yours to decide. However, I'm the captain. The buck stops here." Jacob pointed at his chest. "I won't have you punishing Jennings because of your ego. You've got to let that go. There's no place in leadership for officers who punish their NCOs for taking initiative."

Poole's face turned a shade of red similar to Jacob's blood stripe.

"Sir. She tortured that man."

"She aggressively questioned a foreign spy while stopping him, and his accomplice—who just beat one of my men almost to death—from escaping. Let's not miss the forest for the trees here. I'm having a hard time understanding your logic. Two criminals aboard my ship—one guilty of attempted mass murder, the other guilty of assault at the minimum—were captured by Gunny's quick thinking. And you somehow put all that aside to focus on her breaking regs while doing her duty."

Poole glanced at the hatch, then back to Jacob. "Sir. Torture is strictly forbidden. If I don't punish her, what message am I sending to my Marines?"

Jacob, ever capable of a reasoned approach to leadership and other officers' opinions, leaned back in his chair. At least they were getting somewhere. Poole had given him a rational answer instead of an ego driven one.

"That you value courage. That improvising, overcoming, and adapting will be rewarded, or at the very least, not punished. Do you really want Marines who will fall back instead of attack? Marines that will retreat instead of advance? If they're concerned about a captain's mast or courts-martial, that's what you'll get. If you have a problem with the way Gunny handled the situation, tell her in private. Never go after an NCO in public. It undermines their authority and makes the enlisted distrust their officers."

"How so? That's not what they teach at the academy."

"They do, actually. Just not with that example. Let's say—hypothetically—I were to dress you down in front of your Marines. Deserved or not. What impact would that have?"

"They did teach that, sir. You're never supposed to publicly berate a junior officer in public if at all possible, unless doing so will teach a significant lesson."

Jacob resisted the urge to smile like a predator at the Marine.

"Yes, Malcom. And what does NCO stand for?"

"Sir?"

"The acronym. It's older than the Alliance, by at least a thousand years. You should know this."

Poole fidgeted like a student called out for being late to class. "Uh, you mean noncommissioned officer—oh."

"*Oh* indeed. I will tell you what my Ethics and Professionalism instructor told me. Praise in public, reprimand in private.

If you still feel the need to reprimand Jennings, I won't stop you. But for pity's sake, man, do it in private. Understood?"

"Aye, sir. I think I do."

"Dismissed."

Jacob hoped Poole did indeed get it. He seemed like a bright young man. He might have a career in the Marines. Not, though, if he made it a habit of coming down on his NCOs for doing the right thing... even if it was a little outside the regs.

Alone, Jacob pulled up the information they now had. Fontenot and his accomplice, Nasset, had no knowledge of other spies or saboteurs on his ship or throughout the home system. They knew nothing about a possible Caliph attack, or why they were even hired. Maybe it was the Terran Republic. Or it could just have easily been someone Jacob personally pissed off.

Jacob's eyelids hurt like someone had snuck sandpaper into them. He leaned his head back and, before he realized it, fell asleep.

Kim absent-mindedly rocked the captain's chair gently back and forth. Serving as an XO on a larger ship after commanding her own was perfectly normal. Still, she missed *Apache* the way she imagined Jacob missed *Interceptor*. The destroyers were special. Knowing every meter of one's ship just wasn't possible on a battleship.

She checked their position: humming along at 300 gravities and approaching turnover. "Tefiti, contacts of interest?"

"No, ma'am. Just the usual merchant and civilian traffic. Whatever was causing the gravity wake I picked up earlier is gone. Either not accelerating, or it wasn't ever there to begin with."

Kim guffawed at that. "Right, Tefiti. And if my mother had a rocket pack, she'd be an astronaut. I think you underestimate our faith in your ears."

Through his tattooed face, she couldn't quite tell if he was blushing or not.

"Thank you, ma'am."

It was comforting to be surrounded by so many she'd served with in the past—along with a crop of excellent crew she'd never met before. Jacob had to know it was coming to an end. Most of his senior enlisted were up for promotion. If NAVPER didn't have Chief Suresh promoted to senior chief and teaching at the academy in a few years, she'd be shocked. Same thing with Tefiti, Redfern, Pierre... Hell, Gunny should be on Blackrock running the Raptor school. Yet, somehow, they all managed to find a way to stick with the captain.

Herself included. NAVPER could have picked any of a dozen officers to be his XO. They chose her. Not that she would complain. Serving with Jacob made her a better officer.

"Ma'am, speak of the devil," Tefiti said. "Contact. Zero-two-three mark three-five-zero. Range, six million klicks. Just the faintest of a sound..." Tefiti held the one hand to his ear. "No. It's gone, ma'am. Either they saw us and shut the engine down, or it was an accidental emission. I only had them for a second, but the Cali ship is out there."

Kim checked the ship's clock: 0930. The watch had already changed, but Tefiti hadn't changed with it.

"PO Tefiti, call your relief, mark the log, and get some rack. I want you one hundred percent when we need you."

"Aye, ma'am. Relief and rack."

A few minutes later, when Spacer Hillock arrived to replace him, Tefiti spent far too long filling the spacer in on his job and what to listen for. Kim was just about to send Tefiti away when the PO realized what he was doing, clapped the man on the back, and headed for his quarters.

"PO Roberts, can you come starboard one-zero degrees and down bubble five degrees." If their turn was subtle enough, nothing big, maybe they could lull whatever was out there into a false sense of security.

CHAPTER THIRTY

CALIPH LIGHT CRUISER AL-HIKMA

Kareem sweated inside his uniform. The whole bridge smelled of sweat and stress.

"But it's a battleship, sir," Al-Zaheem said for the fifth time.

Kareem would forgive him because he, too, felt the stress of the moment. He was the captain, though, and the captain couldn't allow himself the luxury of fear. Not even for a moment.

"Zah, that ship is millions of kilometers away from us. We are a hole in space. No emissions. Maybe if they were coming right at us, painting us with radar and lidar, *maybe* they would see us. We are just so much space dust in the vacuum. Take a breath, calm down, and understand that Allah protects us."

Al-Zaheem visibly relaxed. "I'm sorry, sir, of course you're right," he said loud enough for the bridge to hear.

Good Job, Zah. Reassure them. Let them know we have the upper hand.

Not for the first time, Kareem cursed the Alliance for

destroying their FTLC capability. If only he could call his admiral and convey the precise moment for them to arrive. Instead, they had to use a pre-arranged time. If the battleship was in the right spot when his fleet entered the system, then they would overwhelm the single ship and destroy it. There was no question. Nothing the Alliance had could withstand the might of the dreadnaught.

But even if that did not happen... he might be able to maneuver his ship in behind the battleship without detection and do serious damage with his main gun. But it would cost him and his crew... everything.

Kareem pulled his tasbih out and silently recited the verse they were meant to remind him of. *Allah has purchased from the believers their lives and properties in exchange for paradise...*

He had a duty to his Caliph, a devotion to his God, and a requirement from his faith.

"Helm, once the contact has passed and we're in their wake, bring us about. I want to come in behind them where they can't see us."

"Yes, my Captain!"

"Comms, make sure the latest information is uploaded. I want to drop a burst buoy for the fleet... just in case."

"Yes, sir. Burst buoy ready."

If he did make the great sacrifice this day, he would have fulfilled his duty and maintained his honor. When the fleet arrived, the buoy would detect their signal and send all the information they had collected from their rigged scanning array... along with *Al-Hikma*'s final moments, if need be.

Kareem closed his eyes and prayed for the courage to do what was required, and the wisdom to do it right.

CHAPTER THIRTY-ONE

Lights on the bridge illuminated every station with pools of light making them stand out like little islands in the otherwise dim light. Bells rang out 2200 hours as Jacob eased himself into the chair. His back hurt and his knees ached.

He rubbed his eyes, trying to shed the sleep from them. He'd gone days with minimal sleep before—why was it bothering him this time?

Maybe because you're closer to forty than thirty. He thought about what Devi had done for rejuvenation, and why, no matter what, the Navy wouldn't risk her experience much longer, but at least she could fly a bit more. Passing on knowledge and experience to the next generation was a core tenet of the Navy.

For him, it was more a matter of staying sharp and focused. He would have to wait, though. A while, maybe another decade or two. As the technology stood, you could only rejuve once. Doing it before sixty seemed a waste. Meanwhile, Jacob would just need to rely on discipline... and the Navy's orange drink.

As if reading his mind, PO Mendez appeared with a tray of sealed drinks for the bridge. It wasn't technically his job, but

Josh had looked out for Jacob since the day he'd first set foot on *Interceptor*.

"You know, Josh, you keep this up and I'll have no choice but to promote you."

Mendez grinned at his captain and handed him the drink. "No worries, Skipper, I have a plan for that. I'll just find some unassuming Marine officer and smack him in the face."

Jacob chuckled along with his cook. *Wait, was he joking?* So far, luck and the admiral were on his side. He managed to serve with the same fine officers and NCOs longer than anyone. And his favorite people also brought along *their* favorite people. His command was like a human chain. Everyone attached to him was promoted and given more and more responsibility.

But it was about to come to an end. He could feel it. Ever since they promoted him to captain JG and decommissioned *Interceptor,* he knew the end was nigh. His next assignment would have to be at the academy or some other school on Blackrock.

He would command a ship again... just not for a while.

"Skipper?" Tefiti said.

Jacob spun his chair to face the Ohana native. "Give it to me, Tefiti."

"Our sporadic contact is behind us. I-I almost feel bad about this. They've worked hard to stay undetected."

"Don't feel too bad, PO. They *are* trying to kill us."

Tefiti coughed, clearing his throat. "I know, sir. I admire their ship handling, is all."

"Understood. Where are they?"

Tefiti sent the updated plot showing the enemy ship's path to Jacob's MFD. Dotted lines displayed where it disappeared into their grav wake.

Jacob did some quick math. If it were him, he would immediately accelerate to catch up. Running inside the enemy ship's wake would make them all but undetectable.

"Check my math, Tefiti."

"Looks good, sir," he replied a moment later.

"Two hours, then. They'll be inside one million klicks in two hours. Do you have an idea of tonnage?"

"No, sir. Could be anything from a destroyer to a heavy cruiser. Though I doubt it's a heavy."

Jacob nodded his agreement. Heavy Cruisers weren't sent on scouting missions—too much mass to hide efficiently. It was either a light cruiser or a specialized cruiser—like the one they fought near the black hole.

He needed a plan. If he could force them to surrender, the intelligence gain would be astronomical. Of course, if they were here and maneuvering to attack him... that could only mean one thing.

"PO Oliv, what's around us?"

Oliv overrode the main display to show Jacob a two-dimensional map of the area, zoomed out to fifty million kilometers. The gas giant Aether, and its many moons, were four hours away toward the outer system. Multiple smaller freighters appeared as glowing blue icons. Dotted lines showed their presumed destinations, and solid lines their past course. The closest friendly ship was more than fifteen million klicks away.

"It has to be Aether, then..." Jacob muttered.

"Sir?" Oliv asked.

"Where's the starlane at, roughly speaking."

Starlanes didn't move... sort of. Jacob always had a hard time wrapping his mind around how they worked. Alexandria's G-type star reached out to multiple stars around her. The starlane had an anchor point that didn't move. However, star systems orbited the galaxy, and planets orbited stars; the starlanes were a fixed point in a universe where everything else moved.

"None near us, Skipper." Oliv said. "If we set out for Cordoba, it would take us eighteen hours to reach the correct departure point."

"What if we laid a course for Zuckabar?"

"One moment, Skip," Oliv said. "Fourteen hours, thirty-seven minutes, best speed."

That's what he thought. Could it be a coincidence? Not likely.

"We're pretty much as far from any starlane in the system as we can be. The traffic out here is light, no reason at all to even have a presence." And they wouldn't if Tefiti hadn't picked up the faintest echo of a grav wake that didn't belong. If the Caliphate had a ship in system, and they were willing to attack him, then it could only mean they were bringing a fleet in to attack Alexandria.

PO Felix Gouger manned the comms station. "Felix, I need a tight beam to the Imperial Fleet's last location. I don't think they've moved. Text only."

"Aye, aye, sir. Tight beam one-eight-zero. Ready."

Jacob typed out a quick message. *Come to Aether, best speed. Be loud. Please.*

"Ready," he said.

"On the chip," Gouger replied.

"Send it."

"Sent."

Even if they departed the moment they received the message. It would be too late, Jacob knew. Well... maybe not too late to save the system.

"One more, Felix. Naval Space Command." Jacob typed it up and sent it over.

PO Felix Gouger, who had been in more than one combat

encounter while serving with Jacob, froze stiff upon seeing the message. He looked at his CO.

"Send it, Felix."

"A—aye, aye, sir. On the chip... sent."

Jacob closed his eyes and envisioned the time it would take for Naval Command to receive the message. The entire point of his current command was to prevent the enemy from wanting to attempt what they were about to do. No one could have known they had already put the plan in motion.

Enemy contact. If no follow-up in twenty-four hours, sound the alarm. Was all his message said. It was all it needed to say.

"Do they see us?" Kareem asked, his voice barely above a whisper.

"I don't see how," Al-Zaheem said. "We're in their wake. They've not made a course change. No radar or lidar sweeps. We have our emissions buttoned down—"

Kareem raised his hand in surrender. "Okay, Zah, I get it. We're sneaky. Distance?"

His bridge moved with a quiet calm as they approached the behemoth, unaware of their approach. He felt like a house cat attempting to bring down a bear. If they continued in such ignorance, he would be Dawud to their Jalut. Though he knew it would take more than a single blow.

"Torpedo rooms, load the weapons. Charge the turrets and power up the main gun," he ordered.

"Yes, sir," Lieutenant Vizer said. "Five minutes to readiness."

"Captain Kareem, the range is six-zero-zero thousand kilometers and closing."

He could fire now. He should fire. If they were just another three hundred thousand closer, there was a chance he could destroy the big ship. A small chance. Allah willing, though, he would.

"Maintain course and speed. Keep an eye out for any change in their course. If they do, fire. Don't wait for my order."

"Mark, helmet's on," Jacob ordered. He was risking much, waiting this long, but he hadn't wanted his crew sitting around inside their suits for hours. He doubted the captain of the enemy ship would fire before a million klicks, and even if Tefiti was off by twenty percent, the ship would only be at eight hundred thousand by then. If it was a cruiser, and Jacob was sure it was, then firing before five hundred thousand would be suicide.

"All hands, helmets on, helmets on, helmets on." The pre-battle cry sounded in every corner of the ship. On every comm. On every screen. Since the crew wore the ELS suits under their regular uniforms as opposed to having to change out, it was much easier to go from zero to battle stations, with helmets stored at stations and in compartments throughout the ship.

Jacob waited for his crew on the bridge to don theirs first, then slipped his on. He turned the seal and waited for the telltale hiss of canned air... *there it is.*

"Skipper, all departments report one hundred percent."

"Drain the can."

"Aye, aye, sir. Draining the can."

Air hissed out of the ship, pulled into compressed canisters. If needed, they could fill the whole ship, or parts of it—like sickbay—with inert nitrogen, but in any case there wouldn't be any atmosphere to vent—so no chance of explosive decompression. Even if there was some slight efficiency lost from using the suits.

"Can drained, Skipper," Mark said.

"Good job. Tefiti, any sign of them?"

"No, sir. Not since they snuck in behind us. Best guess is they're closing on six hundred thousand klicks."

Jacob swiveled his chair to face weapons. "Misha, status?"

The very young lieutenant stopped to clear his throat, then continued. "Sir. All turrets are online and ready to fire. All torpedo tubes are loaded."

"Good man. I'm going to give them the chance to surrender first, but if they refuse—or look like they're going to fire—then it's all over."

"Captain, DCS. All ZULU compartments are sealed. She's as ready as she'll ever be, Skip," Kim said, her face displayed on one of his MFDs.

It was now or never. He desperately wanted them to surrender. Not only to avoid the loss of life, but to gain the intel he would need to defeat the incoming enemy. He'd already said all the prayers he could. It was time to act.

"Devi, cut the engines. Hard to port, nine-zero degrees."

"Aye, aye, engine power to zero, hard to port nine-zero degrees."

The hum of the gravcoil died, followed by g-forces from the thrusters pushing them all to the side.

"Tefiti, full power on radar."

"Aye, sir—CONTACT. Bearing one-seven-five, mark, one-eight-eight relative. Range... four-zero-zero thousand klicks."

Damn, much closer than we thought.

"Comms, send it."

Kareem opened his mouth to give the order when his comms man interrupted him.

"Sir, message from the enemy ship."

They hadn't fired yet... he'd heard of the Alliance's squeamish desire to avoid killing.

"Play it."

"This is Captain Jacob T. Grimm, Alliance Battleship *Seventeen*. Surrender without delay and you and your men will be treated with respect. This is your only warning."

Kareem hesitated. *How did he know? We did everything right.* There could be only one answer. The Alliance had outmaneuvered him. He wouldn't accept they could lose, not with Allah on their side.

"Vizer, fire!"

"Energy build up!" Tefiti shouted.

"Weps, fire!"

The Caliphate light cruiser *Al-Hikma* fired its main gun, a terawatt-pulse plasma laser, eight plasma turrets, and her torpedoes for good measure. Her main gun reached out through space at the speed of light. Two meters wide at its focal, the laser beam sliced through armor, hull, and crew like a supernova. *Seventeen* shook from the transferred energy.

Three turrets—with three barrels each—returned fire. Nine shells, each as wide as Jacob's forearm was long, lashed out and struck the light cruiser. It only took one. *Al-Hikma* blew apart in a violent explosion of burning plasma and melting hull.

Jacob closed his eyes, saying a silent prayer for the enemy and for his own people.

"Kim," he said, "causalities?"

"Two dead, six wounded, sir. It could have been much

worse. The beam hit frame eight-thirty-two, compartment's nine and eleven. No systems offline."

If he'd fired instantly, there would be no dead. *Dammit.*

"Secure from battle stations. Ops, send out search and rescue. I doubt they'll find anything but..."

"Aye, aye, sir. Secure from battle stations and initiate search and rescue," Mark replied. His voice had a hollow sound to it; the Ops officer clearly felt what Jacob felt. The raw power of the ship was nigh on incalculable. Three of those light cruisers had nearly destroyed *Interceptor*... and he'd just vaporized one with ease.

My God in heaven.

CHAPTER THIRTY-TWO

Nadia sipped her piping hot tea, crinkling her nose in disgust. "How in the hell does he enjoy this," she muttered to herself. Elsa slept on the pullout couch. Her long legs were draped over one end and a blanket pulled up to her chin.

Spread out on the table for Nadia to examine were all their notes on what had happened. Everything she could remember without her NavPad, which was destroyed in the hospital basement.

Images of the assassins who attacked the president were publicly available, as were those for the Capitol police officer who let them in. It got trickier from there. There was no news story about the hospital attack. No obituary for the murdered nurse or the dead men who had attacked them in the mortuary. From there, she added a few unknowns, including the saboteur aboard Jacob's ship.

All of it pointed to the Republic Security Services attempting to either disrupt the growing friendship between the Alliance and the Empire, or start an outright war. She only had one problem... proof. With her NavPad destroyed, all she had was conjecture. Yes, she could contact DNI, lead them to the corpses, tell them what to look for, and hope they weren't in on it... but she knew that ship had sailed. If the firefight in the hospital were all over the news, she might believe there was a chance of making it happen. They had covered up three—no, four—bodies in a hospital morgue. It wasn't like they could claim it was an accident either.

Three foreign agents and an innocent nurse. Nadia closed her eyes—Hensley's face was going to haunt her for a long time. Maybe forever.

Dammit. Why did they kill her?

She understood them coming in hot on her, but killing the nurse was like declaring war. They did it to prevent any witnesses, but had they waited, they wouldn't have overplayed their hand... unless...

They had arrived incredibly fast. As if they were simply waiting for her in the hospital or close by. Or... or they were tipped off to her arrival. It could be RSS felt like the hospital was the only place for Nadia to really go. Keeping an eye on it made sense. That didn't track as well, though. There were a lot of risk factors involved in staking out the hospital.

There's no way Wit would ever try to kill me, so that leaves one thing. His office is bugged.

She found it hard to believe that anyone could bug Wit's office without him knowing, but the facts were hard to ignore. Proving it would be easy enough, and it wouldn't even take that long.

Using the cabin's built-in terminal, the one secure from any trace and hidden beneath his kitchen counter, Nadia called her former mentor.

"Office of the SECNAV," Wit's assistant answered.

"I'd like to speak to Wit," she said.

"I'm afraid he's in meetings all day. Is this urgent?"

"No. I can leave a message for him. Please put me through."

"Are you sure, ma'am? I can always have him call you as soon as he's—"

"I'm sure. Just put me through."

A moment later, she heard Wits perpetually aggravated voice ask for the pertinent information at the beep.

"Wit, it's me. I'm staying at your place up in the mountains. I know who's behind everything. As soon as it's safe, I'll let you know."

Just enough info that it sounded legit, but without too much bait. If she told them where in the mountains, or how long she would be there, it would seem too obvious. However, Wit's cabin home location was already compromised. They couldn't trace the call, couldn't use satellite surveillance to find her, the information would have to come from them having tapped Wit's office.

She just needed to make sure there were survivors for her to question. It wouldn't do any good for her to rack up a bunch of bodies.

"Elsa, wake up," she said.

The statuesque blonde woman was instantly alert. "What?"

"Either nothing or we're going to have an RSS hit squad here in a half hour. Come with me."

Nadia didn't wait for Elsa to follow, trusting that the girl would. Wit's cabin had been completely remodeled since her last visit—when the mercs tried to kill them. She assumed the cabin had all the same bells and whistles as before, and found the hidden mechanism beside the fridge. The fridge lifted silently, sliding into the ceiling, revealing the stairs into the bunker.

"What's this?" Elsa asked.

"The owner had a healthy paranoid streak. Turns out he was right. A couple of years ago a hit team came here to kill us.

We got lucky and were down here doing research when they arrived. You and I going to hide here and see who comes looking for us."

When she closed the secret door, dim lights illuminated the small room, revealing only a holo table, four chairs, and a bank of lockers.

"I don't know what weapons they're going to have, or if they will have any, but..." Nadia opened the first locker. Inside were six CP-9 pistols. The next locker contained the SMG version of the coil pistol, which she loaded with a hundred-round magazine and slung over her good shoulder.

"Can I?" Elsa asked.

"Of course. Don't forget the goggles." Inside the lockers hung several pairs.

"What do they do?" Elsa asked as she slid a set on. Nadia didn't answer, knowing she would figure it out when she gripped the pistol. "Oh, never mind," Elsa said.

Nadia grabbed another pair and worked them over her eyes. Everything was far more difficult with one arm. Part of her wanted to just go home to the ranch, collapse on Jacob's bed, and wait for him to come home. She chuckled to herself.

"What's so funny?" Elsa asked.

"Oh, something I just realized," she said. "I thought I was this strong, independent woman... and I am... but now... honestly, if Jacob were here, I'd turn this whole mess over to him and go home."

Elsa lifted the goggles to her forehead. "Really?"

"Look at me, Elsa." Nadia gestured to her missing arm. "Look what I've already given. I don't have much more left. I want a normal life. I want kids. I want a lot of things. Most of all, I don't want my entire civilization to hinge on my actions."

Until she said them, she hadn't realized how much she felt those words. A deep well of sadness bubbled up in her. She'd seen so much, done so much, suffered so much. What more did she have to do to earn a rest?

The cabin shook as something big roared overhead.

"You're not done yet," Elsa said.

"Don't I know it." Pushing her thoughts away, Nadia focused on the present. What needed to be done, not what she wished she could do. The monitors flared to life; a Corsair hovered a dozen meters up. The side door opened, and ropes descended.

"That looks military—" Elsa said.

Nadia didn't respond. She focused hard on the image, willing the next thing she saw not to be camouflaged uniforms. Eight soldiers, all in camo and military gear, rappelled out the side. They hit the ground and spread out with precision.

"Who?" Nadia asked, more to herself than Elsa. Elsa couldn't know. But there were only so many people who could order the military around. It wasn't like they could make their own missions, nor could a civilian tell the army to send a platoon after her. It had to come from somebody in the chain of command.

"What do we do?" Elsa asked.

"Nothing. I'm not shooting Alliance soldiers. They probably don't even know why they're here. Somebody wants us to, though. They want us to get in a firefight and die, so all of this goes away."

The men approached the cabin with caution. With a Corsair providing air support, they were relatively safe. No one was stupid enough to face the nose gun. Something felt off to her.

They're Alliance Army regulars, girl. Of course it's off. They shouldn't be here at all. The Alliance had recently expanded the Army's mission. With Caliph planets to hold, they needed the Marines on the frontline. Up until a few years before, the

Army's main operations had involved military prisons and logistics on the home worlds.

Everything about their gear seemed right, though. They carried M-21 coil rifles, the right camo, right helmets, but... She manipulated the camera to zoom in, thanking Wit for his paranoia that covered the entire area in micro cams.

"No unit badges," she whispered.

"What?" Elsa asked.

"They're not wearing unit badges. Look." She zoomed the image in on a shoulder. "No name badges on the chest, no shoulder badge, no rank insignia."

"They aren't your army, then?"

"Either they're very far off book, or they're just trying to look like my Army. And I know how to find out."

Jai hated this plan. It was a terrible plan. He wanted to shoot his superiors for coming up with it. They'd already lost three agents to these women at the morgue. If they ignored them, let them run their investigation—*maybe*—they would come up with something they could use, but it seemed unlikely. Throwing more bodies at the problem meant more messes to clean up. Especially since they decided they wanted her alive.

It was a miracle they were able to cover up the hospital mess. The only saving grace to this mission was that they were high in the Horseback Mountains. No one would know.

Nadia Dagher was still dangerous, though. Which was why he and six of his men were dressed as Alliance Army, with a stolen Corsair hovering above. Anything to put her at ease and give him the edge.

"Alliance Army, you're trespassing on private property.

Return to your vehicle and depart," a computerized voice said from everywhere.

Jai froze. Could she see them? This was supposed to be a hunting lodge, not some hi-tech safe house.

He had to think fast. "I'm Lieutenant Jai"—lies were always best when mixed with the truth—"I'm here to escort Ms. Dagher to safety."

He lowered his rifle to point at forty-five degrees, and with his offhand, he motioned for his hit team to do the same. They were all just one big, happy family. If this didn't work, they would retreat to the Corsair and blow the cabin to pieces instead of taking her alive. Something he advocated from the beginning.

"Who sent you?"

"The orders came through the DNI, ma'am. I'm just here to execute them."

Come on, woman, buy it. Once she showed herself, they could overpower her.

"I'll be out in a moment."

"Stand down," he said to his men. They relaxed but only slightly.

A minute later, the front door opened and a slim woman with long brown hair stepped out. Jai almost felt bad for her. If she knew what waited for her back at the base, she would die before coming out. He turned and signaled for the Corsair to land.

"Anyone else here?" Jai asked. He looked her up and down. Modest boots, slacks, a dark shirt, and leather jacket with one arm pinned behind her. Intel said she was missing an arm.

She shook her head in response. Jai waved his rifle to the cabin. Two of his men charged past her.

"This way, ma'am," he said. He walked her back to the

Corsair. Air blew debris all around as the powerful craft settled on the uneven ground.

"Can you help me in?" she asked.

"Of course. Sorry." Jai climbed in first before extending his arm. She took it, and he easily pulled her up. *And I thought this was going to be hard.*

As she entered the ship, he slipped a hypo out of his pocket and pressed it to her back. Compressed air hissed, and the drug rushed into her system. She didn't even have time to respond before she collapsed. He caught her, dragged her over to the chair and strapped her in.

"Zix? Is the cabin clear?"

"Yes. No one else is here. Are you sure the Imperial princess was supposed to be with the target?"

Strapped to the chair, Nadia Dagher didn't move. She was completely out. She'd come on board so easily... No, if the princess was there, she would have told them. She'd obviously trusted him. Her mistake.

"Our agents must have missed her departure. Set the decoy body and firebomb, and let's get out of here."

Fifteen minutes later, the stolen Corsair lifted off the ground, engines thundering, drowning out the sound of the crackling fire consuming the cabin.

CHAPTER THIRTY-THREE

Seventeen's CIC was a wonder of technology. A massive holographic table dominated the center of the room. From it sprang to life the planet Aether and her many, many moons. The display zoomed out to show the local system up to ten million klicks around the planet. No ships, civilian or otherwise, were on the scope. On the very edge of the screen floated numbers and codes, identifying civilian shipping based on IFF—not real-time sensor readings.

"Impressive, Mark," Jacob said to his second officer.

"This is Lieutenant Owusu's shop, Skip." Mark clapped the Black man on the back. "I just work here."

"Well done, Owusu," Jacob said.

"Thank you, sir. As you can see, we have detailed readings of the area since we dragged our towed array along with us for the last two days."

The holograph covered an area three-by-three wide and two meters tall. The image stretched all the way to the overhead. Jacob gestured to three tiny icons, a million klicks apart but in a line.

"Yes, sir, good eye. That's why I wanted to bring you down here. I think the Caliphate deployed sensor probes."

Jacob took off his watch cap and ran his hand over his short hair. They were getting close to dropping the heat sinks; the ship had warmed considerably as the time approached.

"Mark, what do we know about Caliph sensor probes?"

"Precious little, sir. I would say let's go and get them, but they're probably rigged to self-destruct without the right codes to disarm upon approach."

Jacob let out a little chuckle. "That does sound like a Cali thing to do. Why leave probes here, though?" Jacob pointed at the three blinking icons, then to Aether.

Owusu adjusted the controls to show just Aether. "While Alexandria is heavily exploited, she's rich with gas giants. Due to its heavy gravity, unstable moon orbits, and wide electromagnetic presence, Aether is ignored. I don't think there are any gas mining operations on her, and if there are, they're hidden."

Which brought Jacob back to his original question: *Why here?*

"Owusu, any starlanes, even ones we don't use, near here?"

Lieutenant Owusu displayed the navigational charts of the area. Blue Beetle's starlane was on the other side of the system. The other lanes were spread out. The number of lanes leading to Alexandria was what made her the trade capital of the Alliance—but it could also make her vulnerable.

"None, sir. In fact, we're about as far from a starlane as possible and still be in-system."

"I'm sure you checked, but this includes the Guild navigational data, correct?" Mark asked.

"Aye, sir. It does."

Jacob walked around the table, examining the image from different angles. There simply wasn't anything of note out here. When Tefiti picked up the gravity wake from the Caliphate ship,

Jacob had expected to find an invasion fleet nearby. Perhaps hiding in the gravity shadow of Aether, not a single scout... a scout.

"Mark, Owusu... I was acting under the impression that the Caliphate were already here in force. What if they're not?"

"Sir?" Mark said. "You mean, not at all? Or just not here yet?"

"Gas giants pose navigational hazards," Owusu said. "Aether has an unusual number of moons, more than thirty at last count. As one of the planets farthest out, she doesn't get the study and attention of the closer ones. In reality, Skip, you could hide a fleet behind her and never know they were there."

That's what worried Jacob.

"It wouldn't do them any good," Mark said.

"I don't know, Mark. Suprise attacks work pretty well," Jacob said.

"I get that, sir, but look at the distance. We're talking thirty hours to Alexandria, and that's if you're *Interceptor*. Much longer if you have a bunch of slow logistics ships... which... if they're invading, they have to bring. Any—literally any—of the other starlanes would serve the Caliphate Navy better, even if it wasn't a sneak attack. A full-frontal assault through Zuckabar would stand a better chance."

"Owusu," Jacob said, "can you bring up the whole system?"

"One moment, Skipper."

The computers in CIC rivaled most planetary installations. However, there was a cost associated with using their power. For now, though, Jacob had the currency.

"Captain, Bridge. Permission to dump the heat sinks, sir?"

Jacob sauntered over to the bulkhead and pressed the button flat.

"Bridge, Captain. Permission granted."

"Aye, aye, sir. Dumping the sinks."

A chime alerted the ship to what was about to happen. "All hands, heat sink dump in five seconds."

Sure enough, the ship shook slightly as, one by one starting with the bow, the sinks were ejected. Cold air instantly flowed through the ship. It was Naval policy to try to limit the temperature disparity, but sometimes ships had to run the sinks longer than others. It wasn't always convenient or safe to dump them.

As the Celsius dropped, Jacob replaced his watch cap, making sure to cover his ears.

"I hate that," Mark muttered. Where Jacob had, as he put it, "insulation" on his frame, Mark was much leaner. More of a runner than Jacob would ever be.

"Here you go," Owusu said. The entire solar system appeared in relative real time. With the vast distances involved, it was part model, part sensor scans. However, as well tracked as Alexandria was, all they needed to know was the location of a few celestial bodies, and they could accurately calculate the rest. "Eight starlanes. Four of which can lead to Cali space, though some would be roundabout. Two can take us to Rōnin, and the remaining two lead to the Terran Republic and Iron Empire."

Owusu highlighted the starlanes and the systems they connected to. Starlanes didn't move, or rather, the system they were in moved, but the lanes remained a constant distance—the shortest distance—from the star they led to.

"Very good, Owusu," Jacob said. "What do you gentlemen see?"

The junior officers examined the map in earnest, trying to figure out what Jacob saw that they didn't, or if there was something he was trying to find out.

"Dam—" Mark caught himself with a cough. "I mean, I wish I saw something, sir."

"Aye, sir. Me too. Nothing."

Jacob leaned over the holographic display, activating the controls for himself, using the filter to remove everything but the planets and asteroid belts. Then he changed their perspective to a top down, with rotational lines and gravity wells added. "See it now?"

Owusu grinned like a fool. Mark looked on, slack-jawed. "How in the hell did you see that, Skipper?"

"That's why they pay me the big bucks. From Aether to Alexandria, there's nothing in the way. All of our outer system defenses will be out of range. Even the long-range torpedo batteries in the asteroid belts won't be able to hit them. How they know our orbital mechanics well enough to figure this out is beyond me, but they do. They're either hiding behind Aether right now—"

"Or they're not here yet," Mark finished.

Jacob took a moment to think through his options. They were coming. None of the system's static defenses could even slow the attack. Alexandria had formidable orbital defenses, plus some ships in reserve. Enough. Maybe.

Unless the Caliphate sent a battle group.

But how? There was no way to get through the starlane and still... "Mark, have the XO meet me on the bridge. Owusu, plot a least-time course for Aether. I want to do a full orbit. I don't think they're there, but I want to know."

Both men snapped to attention, "Aye, aye, sir."

"Good men."

From CIC, Jacob walked the corridor. He could go directly to the nearest lift, but he wanted another minute to collect his thoughts. The last few weeks had been a roller coaster—from the assassination attempt to spies on his ship. He'd barely had time to bring it all together in his head.

He'd been operating under the premise that the Caliphate had snuck a small force through one of the starlanes, and that they would raid the system, blasting away at whatever defenses they could find. That wasn't the case. No. If he had to guess—and he did—they were sending a full battle group, maybe even a fleet. Enough ships to destroy the home guard, which was normally much larger. Enough ships to obliterate every man, woman, and child in the system.

Jacob let out a chuckle at his own misfortune. Or was it? He stopped to watch a pair of maintenance crew cleaning out the ducts. Was it misfortune? Surely there were other officers who, when put in the same situations he had encountered, would have persevered.

Was it providence, or serendipity?

A matter of perspective, I suppose. His mother believed God wouldn't give challenges he wasn't prepared to overcome. She'd told him that on a number of occasions. Maybe that was it. Maybe the Big Guy was putting him in the right place at the right time.

"Or you seriously pissed him off," Jacob said aloud. He chuckled at his own joke. It was time. He headed for the bridge. Resolve turned his spine to steel. If they came for his home, they would pay for every meter.

"We're in orbit, Skipper," Chief Suresh announced.

"Thank you, Chief. Owusu, status?"

"All clear so far, Skipper."

He decided against draining the can for the moment. Something told him they weren't in system—yet. Combat would come all too soon, and when it did, he wanted them fresh and in fighting form.

Seventeen shook, jostling the crew as the secondary gravcoil struggled.

"Gravity buffeting, Skipper," Devi said. "I see why no one wants to build here."

"Owusu, anything for us to worry about?" Jacob asked.

"No, sir. I wouldn't want to fly too close, though."

Jacob keyed the comms to the boat bay. "You ready down there, Viv?"

"As I'll ever be sir."

"Depart at your leisure."

Lieutenant Boudreaux sealed her helmet. Air hissed when she connected her suit to the Corsair's internal atmosphere. "You ready to go, Rupert?"

Behind her in the second seat, or weapons seat, Petty Officer First Class Rupert Stawarski went over the startup procedure. "As always, ma'am."

She leaned over to look down the ladder leading to the EW station. "Spacer Fott, you good to go?"

"Yes, ma'am. All her systems are purring like a kitten." Fott's New Austin accent was the thickest cowboy drawl she'd ever heard, and that was saying something. She almost thought he'd done it on purpose, but the kid was so dang earnest otherwise...

Green lights flashed across her controls. Corsair Sierra-One-Five was powered up. She tested the pedals, the throttle, and the stick, making sure all her flight controls moved freely, and the corresponding systems responded correctly. Ninety percent of her day was spent administering the boat bay. Actually flying? She would never pass up the opportunity.

"Bridge, this is Sierra-One-Five, all systems are go. We're launching. Boat bay, open the doors."

Beneath the sleek dropship, massive, armored doors swung open like a clamshell. Blue light illuminated the edges where the Richman field emitters prevented the atmosphere from leaving.

"Doors are fully open," Stawarski said.

"Applying thrust." Viv was an exceptional pilot. One of the reasons was her ability to think in three dimensions. Using the hat switch controls on her joystick, she engaged the vertical thrusters, pushing the ship "down" and out of the boat bay.

"Clear of the ship," Stawarski said.

She rolled the Corsair, pointed the nose at the planet, and engaged the gravcoil. Three gs smashed her into the chair as the ship shot forward. Thrusters controlled her direction, but the gravcoil was the Corsair's only engine in space.

"Coming up on course change in three..."

When Stawarski hit one, she pulled up, aligning the nose with the yellow nav points superimposed on her HUD. She needed to be quick. The longer she hung out in space with her bird, the more likely she would be detected.

The Corsair bucked hard as a gravity buffeting hit them. The planet was unstable, at least on an astrophysical level; its gravity fluctuated unpredictably. Not enough to worry a ship like *Seventeen*, or even *Interceptor*, but a Corsair was infinitely more fragile than either of those.

More buffeting jerked the ship around, slamming Boudreaux into the restraints. Alarms wailed, which she immediately silenced. The bottom of the ship skipped on the surface of Aether's atmosphere. More warnings flared to life, alerting her to heat buildup.

"Lieutenant," Spacer Fott yelled. "I'm getting a lot of interference."

"Hang in there," she replied. While the computer outlined her course, there was a level of *feel* that came into play. The sixth sense great pilots had for maneuvers. She pulled up on the stick, edging the ship up a few meters; the rampage of shaking slowed considerably.

"How about now, Fott?" Stawarski asked.

"Good, PO. I've got a clean signal."

Boudreaux eyed their vector every few seconds, keeping the ship surging forward at hundreds of KPS but tethered to the planet's gravity. Her arm ached from the exertion.

"Coming up on the line," Stawarski said.

The line was where they would have full visibility of the space on the other side of the planet from *Seventeen*. She didn't have time to spare to look at the radar. "Anything?" she said.

"Nothing on the scope," Fott said. "Wait... maybe..."

Seconds ticked by.

"Lieutenant, I'm getting a hit on the RWR. Faint, but it's there," Stawarski said.

"Contact. Unknown number of contacts at unknown range, but they're there, ma'am. Dozens of them. The screen is too muddled to make out. Maybe a million klicks; it's hard to say with all the interference."

Boudreaux pulled the throttle back, powering down the gravcoil. The ship went silent as her main thrust vanished.

"Power everything down. We have enough momentum to get us to the other side. If they see us, it's all for nothing."

CHAPTER THIRTY-FOUR

Jacob had never seen the briefing room so full. Every officer aboard ship, every department head, every senior NCO. At that moment, the ship was being run by junior NCOs and spacers. Everyone else needed to be present for what he was about to tell them. With standing room only, he had all the chairs removed, even his.

"Thanks to Lieutenant Boudreaux, PO Stawarski, and Spacer Fott, we have these images. It's not pretty." Jacob nodded to Lieutenant Brennan to start.

The first image was a mass of white blobs on a black background. There wasn't anything to make out until the second image was overlaid, then the third, the fourth, and so on. Every new image was cleaner, more detailed. The longer the Corsairs EW suite saw the targets, the better the image resolved. By the time the bird had swung back around to *Seventeen*'s side of the planet, the images were highly detailed.

"What in God's name is that?" Lieutenant Sanchez said.

Jacob could only agree. "That is why I have everyone here. Not only does the computer not recognize it, but I have no idea what it is either."

The Caliphate fleet had many small ships in a globe formation. This in itself wasn't unusual, especially if the goal was to protect a larger capital ship; however, the battleship he expected to find wasn't there.

What actually was there was monstrous.

It wasn't a ship so much as a platform, wider than any man-made structure he'd ever seen in space—like two mountains tied together by a valley.

"Is that a ship, or are they towing a space station?" Gabriel asked.

"Can't be a station," Chief Redfern said. "It wouldn't be able to go through a starlane looking like... that."

"Why not?" Jacob asked.

"You need a single point of gravity to lock on to. The line passes through the center of the gravcoil. That thing is too wide. It would be torn apart by shearing forces. It's the entire reason our ships are tall, but not wide," he said, using his hands to demonstrate.

"Yes, Chief... yet here it is," Kim said. "The fact is they have it. They're going to Alexandria, and there are too many of them for us to stop."

"I get that, ma'am. I'm not saying we're imagining it. I'm saying whatever it is, it isn't a space station, and it doesn't look like any ship I've ever seen or heard of."

Beech cleared his throat.

"You have something to add, Lieutenant Beech?" Kim asked.

"Yes. May I?" He gestured at the controls.

"By all means," Jacob said.

Beech stepped forward, not appearing nervous to be in front of the entire ship's officers. "I think what we're missing is a matter of"—he fiddled with the knob, and the image rotated ninety degrees—"perspective."

"Holy crap," Chief Redfern said.

"What the hell?" Kim said.

"Maybe I should make you the captain, Beech," Jacob said.

"No, sir. It's just a design I've played around with myself."

It was a ship. What he'd mistaken as a gap in the middle of the ship was a gravcoil: a single, massive gravcoil. And instead of having only one superstructure built on the coil, there were two.

"It's a dreadnaught," PO Oliv said. "The Alliance built one... maybe a hundred years ago? It's not practical. Slow. Very slow."

Based on the readings from Boudreaux's recon flight, Oliv was correct. Navigation estimated the ship would be capable of accelerating at no more than one hundred gravities. And with a structure that large, their top velocity wouldn't be high either. It would be fourteen hours before they passed by the planet.

Kim let out a whistle. "A dreadnaught. Why?"

Conversation broke out amongst the collected crew. Jacob tuned it out, knowing Kim would handle it if it became disruptive. At least they knew what the big ship was, but what were the smaller ones? They would have to be a lot closer before the computer could positively identify it.

"Chief Redfern," Jacob said. "Is that a Mussafah-class destroyer?" Jacob had only ever seen one in old vids.

"Yes, sir, I think it is. That doesn't make any sense."

"Does someone want to enlighten the rest of us?" Kim said.

"Yes, ma'am. It's the Caliphate equivalent of a Hellcat. They used them a lot during the Great War but retired all of them after. I don't think I've seen one in service since I was a spacer," Redfern said.

"These other ones," Beech said. "Are also pretty old. Light cruisers, heavy... and there's a couple I don't recognize. All of them are Great War era or older... this doesn't make any sense."

"If all those ships are that old, Skipper, it stands to reason the dreadnaught is too," Oliv said. "I know we put a hurting on them in Medial with the Enterprise battle group. What if..." She frowned for a second. "No, not what if. It's certain. This is a last-ditch suicide run, Skip. Whoever's in charge of that fleet is meant to fail."

Redfern let out a long chuckle, silencing the room. "That totally fits. About the time the war began was when the designs and interest in making a super battleship, or dreadnaught, came to an end. This is their prototype, probably as old as I am, and never used in battle."

If his crew was right—these were old ships and not just ones they didn't recognize—then where were the new ships? Where was their cutting-edge fleet?

The entire reason he was in system was that the Alliance fleet was massing at the wormhole to attack the Caliphate. What had he thought when she told him about it? *Endgame.* This was the Caliphate's endgame. Which meant...

"Damn."

Jacob's one word silenced the briefing room. All eyes turned to him. *There's nothing we can do about it, you shouldn't have said anything.*

"Sir?" Kim asked.

"I was just thinking. If the Caliphate wanted to divert our forces from a real attack, this is exactly the kind of thing they would do. This... fleet... is like you said. It's a Hail Mary. They're going to die. They know it, we know it. But once we notify command, the word is going to go out, and our fleets at the wormhole are going to rush home."

They were on their own. He was on his own. He had to be. If the fleet departed from Zuck or Praetor and returned to Alexandria, no matter the reason, then the Cali would attack the wormhole in force.

If the fleet in Alexandria succeeded, Nadia would die and his home with her. If the attack at the Bella Wormhole succeeded,

Nadia would die and his home with her. Both had to fail. The only way for that to happen was for him to defeat the Caliphate here and pray—beg—for the Admiral to win in Praetor.

"Kim, get a message to Prince Faust. See if we can't get them out here. We've got—" He looked to Owusu for the answer.

"Fifteen hours until they pass Aether orbit, sir. Assuming they don't change course."

"That's our time frame. Make it happen."

"Aye, aye, Skipper." Kim darted out.

"The rest of you, make sure your departments are ready. I want every member of this crew well fed and well rested before the battle begins. When it happens, it's going to be sudden and violent. And we will prevail."

"Sir? How? They have twenty-plus ships. The number of barrels alone will destroy us in a single volley. We can't beat those odds."

Jacob was glad Gabriel said it, even if the young man looked aghast that he'd spoken to his CO with such candor. There were people in the compartment he didn't need to convince: Redfern, Oliv, Owusu, West, and more. Men and women who'd served with him over the years and seen what a crew working together toward a common goal could accomplish.

There were others, faces he didn't know as well, who would look at the coming fight and think exactly what Misha just said. They would believe the best thing to do would be to turn and run. Alert high command. Call in the reinforcements for help. Jacob knew it would be a mistake. As sure as the sun rose over his ranch in the east. Maybe at that very moment, maybe in a few days, Admiral Villanueva would find herself under massive attack. She would need every ship.

"Three-hundred-some-odd years ago, men and women from Alexandria and Seabring banded together to defend Alexandria. They understood how important it was to hold the planet. They had a vision, a goal. To stabilize the region and make something that lasted. Something great.

"They fought for what we now have—freedom. Through courage and conviction, welding scrap onto the bows of their ships as armor, turning their magnetic cargo launchers into the first crude coil guns, they turned their merchant ships into navy frigates of war. It must have seemed impossible. Defending an entire planet with... how many ships?"

"Sixteen, sir," Redfern said with solemnity.

"Sixteen. Against an entire fleet. A fleet of pirates who wanted to plunder the planets of the Alliance. Here we are, facing down a fleet looking to plunder Alexandria, enslave her people, and take our freedom.

"Freedom is why we're here. Freedom is why you joined the Navy and Marines in the first place. You weren't forced. You weren't drafted. You chose.

"When those first shots were fired, the crews of the merchant ships had to be terrified. Fear is a useful emotion. It keeps us safe. *Don't jump off that cliff. Don't speed in the aircar. Don't pick a fight with a champion boxer.*"

Jacob paused for a moment, looking up at the overhead as he remembered the dumb crap he had done as a teen.

"Fear, though, can be defeated with courage. Courage is gained when your heart tells you this is right. When you know what you should do, even if you also know it could lead to your death. Courage is freedom in its truest form.

"Through courage and training, we can prevail. We can defeat the enemy fleet, hurt them badly enough they're either forced to withdraw, or they crash in vain against our defenses, to fail in their goal because of our commitment.

"You were all handpicked for this boat. Chosen by Admiral Villanueva herself. She knew we had a hard job ahead of us and wanted the best on *Seventeen*. Well, she got the best. From the lowest spacer's apprentice to the XO. The very best.

"I need you all working hard. To lead your departments. I can only command, only set an example from the bridge. You must lead the crew."

Jacob let his gaze sweep the room for a moment, making sure to catch and hold each person's attention.

"I'm the captain. I give orders and you follow. You, though, must believe in your heart that what we're doing—fighting for freedom of the Alliance—is worth the cost. I accepted long ago that I would pay any price for my nation. Now it's time for you to do the same."

Jacob hoped his words would ease the rampant fear in the junior officers, hoped they would be inspired to go above and beyond for their duty.

In the end, though, hope was all he had.

CHAPTER THIRTY-FIVE

Fleet Admiral Villanueva strode her flag bridge like a knight on patrol in an ancient castle. Twenty stations crowded the bridge, each one with information she might need. Links to the other ships in the fleet. Munitions levels. Damage reports. Casualties. Her flag captain, Ganesh Hatwal, was the master of the ship. All the maneuvering and actual ship handling was his.

And she was in charge of the fleet. USS *Alexandria*, USS *Enterprise*, and USS *Whirlwind* made up Task Force 11. Her sole mandate was to charge down the starlanes, lay waste to every piece of infrastructure they encountered, then finally choke the life out of the Caliphate capitol world.

Thanks to the Guild, they knew exactly where it was. Eighteen starlanes between her and the end of the war. Three battleships, forty heavy cruisers, sixty light, and almost every destroyer the Alliance had. Not to mention several Marine transport ships and the new Army transports that would be coming in behind them. They needed all the destroyers. They would make up the bulk of the forces they left behind in each system to protect the army soldiers whose job it was to take and hold the planets.

Noele sagged at the enormity of the risk: the lives of over a hundred thousand Marines and Army soldiers in those transports and on her ships. Another hundred thousand spacers manning the fleet. The best and the brightest. Her worst-case scenario was to lose everything.

She couldn't do that.

No. The three battleships would scoop up *Ticonderoga* and half her ships in Medial and head for Caliphate Prime, the home world of the enemy.

If only—if only they could have convinced the Consortium to help. Admiral Endo had more than rolled out the welcome mat for them. Providing everything logistically he could afford. At the end of the day, though, he was under orders.

"We are all under orders," she muttered to herself.

"Ma'am?" Commander Sichi said from the comms station. "All ships are reporting ready."

"Good. One moment, Ria."

Noele closed her eyes and tried to imagine what victory looked like. "Order the formation to train tracks. Send the scouts ahead. Set Condition Yankee."

Commands rolled out from her subordinates, klaxons alerted the crew, and the entire ship took on a tone of seriousness.

"Time to see if we're the victor or the vanquished," she whispered to herself.

CHAPTER THIRTY-SIX

Nadia awoke in a dark room. Years of training allowed her to maintain her breathing and heart rate to mimic sleep—at least for a few minutes. Carefully, so as not to alert her captors, she tested her muscles. Inflexible metal straps bound her ankles. Something, probably a rope, was wrapped around her waist. Inwardly, she smiled. They must have struggled with how to tie down her single arm. That arm was somehow secured behind her back. She could lean forward a tiny amount. Other than that, she was held fast.

Based on the lack of light through her eyelids, she guessed the room was dark. Straining her hearing to the limit proved fruitless: Either there was no one in the room, or they masked their noise.

If they were amateurs, they would announce themselves. If they were pros, they would wait for her to wake—

"We know you're awake," an electronic voice said.

Nadia suppressed her grin. Amateurs, then. Of course, even they could hurt her. Hopefully not before her backup plan arrived. She needed to buy time.

"Wha... where am I?"

"Someplace no one will ever find you."

"What do you want with me? Why are you doing this? Let me go!"

The voice laughed. "We know exactly who you are, Nadia Dagher. Former chief petty officer in the United Systems Alliance. You served with ONI for most of your ten years. You still serve them now."

"You're confusing me with someone else. I'm retired... and my name isn't Nadia Dagher."

No response. No doors opened. Still no light in the room. As her hearing adjusted, she picked up the distant hum of air circulation. She panicked for a moment before realizing she wasn't on a ship. No gravcoil hum, and she didn't have that slight vibration tingling up through her feet. Which meant she was most likely still on Alexandria.

They were probably double-checking her face against a public database. Making sure they'd grabbed the right person.

"Don't play games with us, Dagher." A jolt of electricity passed through the chair. Not enough to hurt, but more than enough to promise future pain.

"Fine, you've got me. I confess. I slept with your wife. What can I say. You're just not man eno—" Her mouth clamped shut from a much more painful jolt.

"Stop. We will ask you questions, and you will answer them—or you will feel more pain than you've ever felt in your life."

"You're going to have a hard time topping listening to you. That's pain."

"Your name is Nadia Dagher. You spent ten years in the Navy and served ONI. True or False?"

She mentally braced herself for the pain that was about to come her way.

"False."

Nothing. If she had to guess, they were running diagnostics

on their equipment, trying to figure out how she was beating their lie detector.

Pain. Lots of pain. Her vision went red from the electricity jolting through her, causing her entire body to convulse.

When it passed, she breathed hard, chest heaving. One of the things no one realized when using electricity was the subject's inability to breathe when zapped. She had to oxygenate her blood as much as she could before they hit her again.

"You will tell us the truth." More pain. Nadia struggled not to scream as her muscles clenched. When it stopped, she let out an involuntary sob. The pain was awful, but it wouldn't break her. There was no pain, no threat they could give that would make her break.

"Now. Your name is Nadia Dagher—"

She shook her head violently. "No."

That time, she screamed.

Elsa marched through the embassy. Every door she approached opened to her identification. Even if she wasn't in line for the throne, she had her clearance as a member of Imperial Intelligence. What she was about to do, though, had nothing to do with the ImpInt.

The final door slid open to reveal a young man with a razor-short haircut and smart black uniform. He was speaking with a young woman whose hair was as black as her uniform.

"Who's in charge of the Fallschirmjäger platoon?"

"My lady, I am. Leutnant Hans Weber."

"And you?"

"Leutnant Klara Müller, ma'am. Second-in-command of Eagle Assault Platoon."

Elsa walked behind the desk and palmed the computer, which immediately spat out her clearance and identification. Weber gulped and leaped to attention.

"Esteemed Princess, how may we serve?"

"How many Fallschirmjägers can you outfit in power armor and have ready to go in thirty minutes?"

A proud smile spread across Weber's face. "For our princess? All of them. Forty in total, myself and Klara included."

"Leutnant, what I'm about to ask you to do might cost you your career. It could start a war. I can't order you to do this; all I can do is ask you to trust me."

Weber's smile became infectious. "I swore an oath, Princess. My duty to your family is the same as my duty to the uniform. Eagle Assault Platoon stands ready."

One look at Klara told Elsa the woman felt the same way. "Collect your men, Leutnant. We have to rescue a target from a hostile bunker in the city, and we don't have long before they kill her."

"Jawohl!"

―――――

They finally entered the room. Two men wearing black, long-sleeve turtlenecks, and generic khaki pants with military-style boots. They weren't particularly tall. Maybe her height.

"We grow tired of your games. Who knows about the origin of the bodies in the morgue?"

"Your wife. I told her last night while we—"

The hand hit her with jarring force. Her eyes crossed and blood filled her mouth. It was no flesh hand. The man had cybernetics.

Nadia spat the blood onto their boots. "Tell me, are you RSS or something else?"

The second man tensed, perhaps surprised she knew?

"We ask the questions. Where is Princess Faust?"

Nadia relaxed her neck muscles. What was next would hurt even more. "Probably with your wife—"

She wasn't wrong. He slapped her across the cheek. Waves of fiery hot pain radiated out from her face. It took her even longer to come back. Shaking her head, she didn't even have the energy to spit out the blood, just let it dribble from her split lip.

"Listen, tell your master's back on Earth their operation is blown. Both here and Cordoba. You blew it. Not only did you fail to sow division between us and the Empire, you, in fact, made us even closer allies. How does Terra execute her traitors these days? Firing squad, hanging, or a good old-fashion spacing?"

The first man barked an order to the second in a language Nadia didn't speak, but knew it was from Earth. The second man exited the room for a minute and returned with a case.

"Are you going to try and bribe me now?" she asked.

"No, Nadia. I'm going to inject you with nanites that will rewrite your brain and make you our most willing operative in the Alliance."

Cold shot through Nadia like she'd fallen in Anchorage Bay during the winter. She jerked at her bonds, cursing not having her cybernetic arm.

Anytime now, Elsa.

———

Elsa hadn't used the Imperial power armor since she'd taken the classes, but she'd be damned if she'd sit the operation out. For the most part, user biofeedback ran the suit. Nothing special was required of her to run, jump, and punch. Most of the other functions she needed ran off the neurolink tapped into the base of her neck.

The ship shuddered as it flew low and fast over the city.

"You know, Princess, there's going to be hell to pay when the Alliance finds out we flew a gunship over their city."

She simply nodded. There would be hell to pay, but she wouldn't be the one paying it. The Terran Republic attempting to incite a war between the Empire and the Alliance was more than enough for her to justify attacking a Terran Republic Embassy—even if she didn't technically have her father's permission. Her friend was inside enduring who knew what and relying on Elsa to rescue her. She wasn't about to let Nadia down. She owed her too much.

"ETA, two minutes," the pilot said over comms.

"You better turn on all your EW as soon as we hover," Elsa said.

Hopefully, they would take the embassy by surprise and no one would be the wiser until it was too late.

"Thirty seconds. We're being hailed."

"Ignore them," Leutnant Weber said.

Elsa did a last-second check. Everything was green.

"Leutnant, you're in charge. I'll follow you and stay out of the way."

"Fair enough. Fallschirmjägers, prepare to drop. Avoid casualties where you can. Our target is located in the subbasement, west side. Your computer has the data."

Elsa admired their steely-eyed professionalism. None of them had hesitated to suit up and follow her to the Terran Embassy. This was an act of war. She knew that. Stopping the Terrans from helping destroy the Alliance was important. Even if the Empire and Alliance didn't have a formal treaty, she knew in her heart they were more alike than different. One day, her brother would be emperor. When that day came, the Alliance would be a strong ally.

"Drop!"

Kai frowned at the readings on his screen. As a thirteen-year security man for the Terran Republic he'd spent three on Alexandria enjoying her majestic vistas and excellent skiing. When he first arrived, they'd assigned him to ambassador security. He had enjoyed traveling with the ambassador. Whoever it was—it seemed to change more often than not. For the last six months, he had headed internal security for the campus.

Kai had overseen the upgrade to state-of-the-art three-vee cameras, capable of seeing in every spectrum and recording with perfect visual fidelity. The recordings were encoded onto polymolecular chips and stored in the basement. Even after the planet was nuked from orbit by the Caliphate—or Guild, he wasn't sure which—the embassy had survived with her computers intact.

A mini fort on the outskirts of Anchorage Bay, the only thing the embassy didn't have was emplaced cannons to fire on ships in orbit.

He tapped the screen out of habit. The energy readings showing an approaching high-powered ship of some kind didn't change.

"Anything on radio?" he asked.

"No, sir. No response."

"Transponder?"

Every legal ship had to have a transponder in order to fly—otherwise Anchorage Bay ATC couldn't see them.

"It's either off, or they don't have one."

Kai didn't hesitate. He slammed his palm down on the

emergency alert button. Alarms wailed and klaxons sounded as every person in the embassy was notified of the attack.

Nadia tried to stay calm when the man approached her with the syringe. She'd had her DNA overwritten once, had her mind nearly broken by the damned Caliph collar, and had lost her arm in the process. Having nanites change who she was? That was enough.

He knelt over her, grabbing her head and forcing it to one side. "In an hour you will tell me whatever I want, and do so gladly."

"You know this works? How? Who do you already have?"

"The best part about this procedure is that when it's over, you won't even remember your loyalty to the Alliance. You will be the perfect sleeper agent."

She closed her eyes and tensed her muscles for one desperate move. Cold steel pressed against her neck, and she lunged with all her might. The hypo jammed into his hand, causing him to fumble it.

An alarm bell rang, startling everyone in the room. *Oh... thank you, Princess.*

Explosions rocked the compound. Dust rained down from the ceracrete ceiling. The high-pitched whine of discharging energy weapons sounded over the din. The alarm silenced.

"You better run if you know what's good for you," Nadia said.

The agent looked to the broken hypo and back to Nadia. "You got lucky."

"Better lucky than good."

Whatever he opened his mouth to say was lost when the

wall exploded inward. Chunks of ceracrete and steel showered the room in a cloud.

A black-armored figure strode in, raising its arm to point at the agent. The RSS agent drew a sidearm Nadia hadn't seen him carry. He pressed the weapon hard against her head.

"Move and she's—"

A plasma pellet burning at 3,000 degrees seared a ten-centimeter hole through the man's shoulder, severing his arm. He screamed in agony, wallowing in a circle, unable to process the pain. A black-armored fist put him out of his misery.

"When you told me your plan, I thought it was insane. No possible way was the RSS going to bring you to their embassy," Elsa's electronically enhanced voice said.

"Never underestimate a spy's arrogance."

"But you're a spy..."

"I'm the exception. Now get me out of here."

CHAPTER THIRTY-SEVEN

Jacob was alone in the briefing room. He could have used his quarters, but his rack was too out of the way for him to hear anything but the hum of the gravcoil. He preferred the hustle and bustle of the crew moving down the passageway outside the hatch.

A holographic projection of Aether, along with the enemy fleet, floated before him. Aether had enough moons that he could hide *Seventeen* and let the enemy fleet sail on by.

Which wasn't the decision he intended to make. Under no circumstances could he allow them to pass Aether without resistance. Once they were in the system, they could split up and do untold damage to the infrastructure. Worse, they could head straight for Alexander, launching nukes the entire way in the hopes the long-range bombardment would get lucky and land some blows.

No, his issue was how to stop them. Twenty-three ships: destroyers, cruisers, and a dreadnaught. Regardless of how old they were, the weapons technology for the Caliphate hadn't changed all that much in the last hundred years. Plasma turrets and torpedoes were still going to do damage.

Jacob manipulated the controls of the holo, allowing him to see different options. He could run *Seventeen* directly at them, firing the entire way, but his ship would be destroyed. If he hid the ship, lay doggo, and came up behind them... well, he would be making the tactical mistake of his career. Chasing a fleeing ship was the last option—they always had the advantage.

Despite their hidden entrance into the system, they altered course every few minutes—enough to avoid anything fired from beyond their sensor range. He couldn't use the trick he'd suckered the Guild with time and time again.

He had one ship. One. Somehow, he had to get in range, fire at least three salvos, and survive long enough to get out of range. Battleships weren't known for their hit-and-run tactics, but if he was going to bring his crew out of this alive, he was going to have to adapt.

The question was, how?

"Skipper?" Kim said from the open hatch.

"Come in."

"Everyone's ready. We just need to know what we're doing."

Jacob leaned back from the screen and sipped the orange drink Josh had brought him, enjoying the tangy flavor. "What do you think?" He gestured to the holo.

"Guile and subterfuge, Skipper. Just like we always do."

Jacob let out a long breath, willing his frustration to go with it. "There's not enough guile and subterfuge to turn our one ship into twenty. They may hesitate when they see us, but as soon as they engage with all their weapons... you know what happens."

Zooming the map out until Aether was a dot amongst other dots, he pointed to three different places.

"A hundred thousand people live and work on those asteroids. Once the Calis are past Aether, they can destroy them with impunity. Another million lay beyond them in the stations, a hundred million on the inner worlds... everyone on Alexandria."

Kim, whose optimism didn't falter, pointed at Aether. "That's why they're here, right? Hide behind Aether until it's too late? And that's why they sent a scout—they can't see beyond it any more than we can. Our advantage is they don't know we're here."

"They're expecting a battle group to be in the system. They came prepared. Maybe if we had all the ships we're supposed to, and maybe if the Iron Empire ships joined the fray— it's a lot of ifs and maybes."

"If Beech is right," Kim said, "they didn't exactly send their best."

Jacob thought back to the first time they had faced impossible odds together. It was both comforting and somehow unfair that she was asked to do it again. "How's the crew?" he asked as a way of changing the subject.

"Morale is high. After the speech you gave, I suspect the officers and enlisted would leap off a building if you told them it would save the Alliance."

Jacob couldn't help but chuckle. "Not quite what I intended. They're good kids, though."

"Hardly kids, sir. You forget, we're not on *Interceptor*. The captain is about to turn forty if I recall..."

Jacob let out a dramatic groan. "Don't remind me."

"Forty is not that big of a deal. Besides, it's not like you can't get the treatment done..."

Jacob thought of poor Devi, who looked and sounded like she was eighteen. "I'll pass. They still have problems with that. I doubt the Navy would let me continue being a ship's commander if they screwed it up and I came out on the other end like—" He gave a silent shrug toward the bridge.

Kim winced. "It's not the worst thing, but yeah, at least she can still fly."

Commanding a starship took gravitas that only age brought. Despite the genetic de-aging that the rejuve treatment allowed, no one would follow the command of someone who looked like a kid.

It's not like he would blend... in... as... "Oh boy," Jacob said.

Kim sat up straight. "I know that look," she said. "You just came up with something crazy."

"You know, the downside of serving with a crew that thinks they know me so well is the damn looks you think I have." He paused for a second. "Yes, it's crazy. Go get Chief Suresh. If this might work, she's the only one who can pull it off."

A minute later, Chief Suresh arrived, looking sharp in her day uniform.

"Skipper?"

"Devi, how deep into the atmo of Aether can you take the ship?"

Suresh gestured to a seat. When Jacob gave her the okay, she sat and brought up the navigation screen on her NavPad, displaying Aether over the conference table. A glowing point represented *Seventeen* orbiting the planet.

"Aether's not a planet in the conventional sense. Just a ball of hydrogen and trace amounts of other chemicals, it has no real 'surface.' If it weren't for her shifting gravity and strong magnetic interference, the Alliance would probably have stations orbiting her, siphoning metallic hydrogen from the core. If you're asking how close we can *safely* get, Skip, the answer is not close at all. Maybe 1,200 klicks above the deck."

Jacob's shoulders sagged from her revelation. He'd thought maybe they could hide in the upper atmosphere of Aether and sneak up on the fleet, giving them a shot at crippling or destroying most of the ships.

"Thank you, Devi. I—"

She raised her hand. "I said safely, sir. By *The Book*, 1,200 is as close you can go."

"Are you saying we can get closer?" Kim said.

"Ma'am, I can put this rig down in the clouds if you want. Her hull will heat up, the pressure will likely cause some problems, but her thrusters can pull us out. Hell, they're designed to push this hunk of pig iron in orbit and change her headings. They can push her out of a little atmospheric chop."

"If we can make it into the thermosphere," Jacob said, "we might be able to hide from there."

Chief Suresh shook her hand. "Sorry, Skip, that won't work." She raised her hand to forestall complaint. "You can get Beech in here if you don't believe me."

"It worked in Wonderland. We hid *Interceptor* from the Guild while we did repairs," Kim asked.

"Yes, ma'am, we did," Suresh replied.

"Then why not here?" Kim asked.

Devi, ever patient to explain things to officers and spacers alike, changed the image to superimpose Wonderland over Aether.

"Wonderland had a distinct ionosphere and separate thermosphere. Along with the dark star's unusual gravity, it allowed us to conceal the ship. Here, the thermosphere and ionosphere overlap—we can't hide where the two clash. Of course, that's assuming they are using their radar and it's in the usual frequency range."

Kim stared at Suresh in open-mouthed amazement. "How do you know all this?" she asked.

"You pick up things here and there. Planetary dynamics and stars interest me, so I read about them," she said. "Also, the Skipper here likes to do crazy things. It pays to stay informed."

Jacob would object; he couldn't since she spoke only the truth.

"Devi, from the way you're telling us this, I'm inclined to think you have a solution?"

"The captain is always observant. Yes. We take *Seventeen* into the polar region—here." She adjusted the map to show the north pole and placed the ship in orbit there. "From there we have a better view of the oncoming fleet, and the plasma from Aether's auroral zone will cover us. Unless they plan on using millimeter wave detection... but they won't."

It was a lot to go over. They could probably hide as long as the enemy didn't look too hard. Could he risk the ship on a "probably?"

"We don't, Skipper," Kim said. "Use microwave radar that is. I can't think of a reason they would. Other than scientific curiosity, there's no reason to use radar at all to look at a planet you're orbiting. But this might all be for naught. We could just dip down into the thermosphere around the equator, wait for them to pass, then come up behind them and shoot," Kim said.

"That's my plan. It's not enough to shoot at them, though. It's not even enough to engage with them. Unless we can reduce their effectiveness to twenty percent or less, we lose. The system defenses can only repel attacks from someone who wants to take the planets and stations intact. Once they have radar returns on an installation, they can bombard it from range with kinetic strikes. They don't need nukes or even live warheads. When they've cleared the way, Alexandria will get the nukes. And this time they won't settle for just the capitol— it will be the whole planet. We stop them all, or we lose."

Kim, ashen faced, audibly swallowed. "What about treaty of Okinawa-Deruta? The Caliphate signed it just like we did. The Guild didn't, but—"

"I'm not going to bet Nadia's life on a treaty the Caliphate signed," Jacob said. "They only keep their word when it benefits them. We wait for them to pass close by, pop up behind them, and fire everything. We should get two, maybe three salvos off before they even know they're under attack. Once the battle is engaged, we'll send word to the system and to Prince Henry's ships."

A notification from the bridge interrupted him. "Skipper, we've received a reply from the Imperial fleet. They're heading this direction. ETA fourteen hours," Mac said.

"Understood. Thank you for the update, Mac."

"You're going to lead them into a trap? Prince Henry likes you, sir, but I don't think he likes you that much."

Jacob feigned surprise. "I'm just as shocked as you that there are Caliphate ships in Alexandria, XO. I would never have dreamed it possible when I invited the Iron Navy to do a joint training exercise in the outer systems. If we engage the fleet just after they pass Aether, and if we can survive long enough to run in system, they will follow. If they run into an Imperial squadron, that's not my fault."

Kim shook her head in disbelief. "Right. You know we could alert the system to the incursion. I know you're concerned they'll pull the fleet back but..." She let the "but" hang there.

"I know, and I'm on record that these are my orders. If we go *By the Book*"—he nodded to Devi—"then we are technically in violation of standing orders. I'll deal with that after we stop the enemy fleet. If I'm right, though, and this is nothing more than a suicidal distraction designed to make us panic and withdraw the fleet from Zuck... then the Caliph Navy may never attack the wormhole. If I had to guess, they have scouts in Praetor waiting for the fleet to withdraw. When that doesn't happen they'll either be forced to attack a fortified position or withdraw. Either way, we win."

"If you're wrong, they'll court-martial you, Skipper."

"If I'm alive for them to do so, then we'll have won. To be honest, they may do that anyway," he said. "Wouldn't be the first time I was on the Navy's 'do not promote' list. At least this time everyone will know the reason why... if it happens. Let's focus on the immediate future. Devi, thank you. Do what you need to do. Prepare the ship to go into the auroral zone. As soon as you're ready, we're heading in."

CHAPTER THIRTY-EIGHT

How was she in the hospital again? Nadia shook her head at the sheer amount of bad luck she'd had in the last month. Lost her arm? Ended up in a hospital. Looking for clues? Firefight in a hospital. Kidnapped by Republic Security Services? Torture and hospital. A psychotic laugh echoed around her before she realized it was her.

Better clamp that down. How much did one person have to go through to keep her damn home free? Jacob was out there facing death every other day, and she couldn't even stay at home and keep his tea warm. No, she had to go out and uncover multiple conspiracies against her government.

How did they thank her?

Nadia shook the magnetic cuff holding her only arm to the bedframe. The two plain-clothed agents who stood guard watched her through the transparent door. She smiled and waved her fingers at them as best she could.

They wouldn't even let her watch the news. *Does Wit know they've arrested me?* The two men had civilian security written all over them. Not ex-Marines, or Army, but civvies.

DNI.

Nadia leaned her head back and closed her eyes. After Elsa had rescued her from the Terran Republic embassy, she'd had to take her to the hospital. A platoon of armored Fallschirmjägers dropping her off made an impression. Not a good impression. After hours of electrocution and the savage beating they'd given her, medical attention couldn't be avoided. And without their ships, the Imperials didn't have the facilities to help her.

Her door swung open, and two more agents entered. They took up positions beside the door. A moment later, DNI Charles Gradford walked in. The heavyset man looked tired, overworked.

"Mrs. Grimm," he said before coming to a stop at the foot of her bed.

"Finally, someone remembers," she said with an exhausted smile.

"Quite. Wit has reminded me on multiple occasions. I'm sure you want to know why you're under arrest?"

Nadia let out a long, slow laugh. "No. I know why."

That seemed to disturb him. "You can't possibly know why."

Nadia re-examined the man. He was tired, overworked, certainly overfed. "Yes, I can. I know the crimes I've committed in the last few days to find out who was behind the assassination attempt. I know why they were doing it, and I know who they were. Do you?"

He harrumphed, fidgeting with his Pad. Light flashed above it, showing the Terran Republic Embassy. "At 0439 this morning, Imperial Infantry in powered armor violated Anchorage Bay's airspace and attacked a sovereign embassy—an act of war I might add. Normally, such a violation would result in the Imperials finding their diplomatic status revoked and being asked to leave."

The way he said that made it sound like it wasn't happening. Gradford had said, "normally." Nadia was sure Elsa knew what she was doing. Finding out the truth of who was behind the assassination was worth losing an embassy if it helped their two people come closer together.

"For some reason he hasn't chosen to share with me, President Axwell is overlooking the matter. Tell me, Mrs. Grimm, who do you think was behind the assassination?" Nadia looked hard at him, not blinking until he looked down.

"My agents determined that while the Caliphate were made to look like they were behind the attack, it was actually the Terran Republic..."

"Your... agents. Right," Nadia said. Her deadpan voice and expression held no give. "What agents were those? Were they hiding in the basement of the embassy? Were you even looking into the assassination?"

"Yes. If you must know, DNI relies less on HUMINT than SIGINT. While you represent a significant human intelligence asset, you aren't all knowing, Mrs. Grimm. We intercepted multiple messages from the embassy about agents here on Alexandria. We also traced those messages to people inside the cabinet. What we didn't have the authority to do was track it all down."

Realization dawned on Nadia. She almost laughed. Almost. "You knew I would go after this. Let me guess... Did you go to Wit and warn him to put me on a leash? News flash, I don't work for Wit anymore. I don't work for anyone. I did this because they tried to kill the president, and you all didn't appear to be doing anything about it." Not to mention they almost killed Jacob in the process. She wouldn't tell him that, even if it would be easy to guess.

"You're either going to prison," Gradford said, "a maximum-security prison like Fort Icarus, or—"

Nadia's eyes narrowed. *Was this a job offer?* "Come work for you?" she asked. In her mind she reeled in disbelief. None of it showed on her face.

"You quit ONI. You won't work for Wit. You clearly can't stay out of the spy business. Come work for DNI. We have more resources than you ever had."

Nadia held her poker face, not wanting to give away her true feelings. Which were complicated. "Can I have a few days to decide?" she asked.

"Of course. Until you do, though, you're a guest of the state in preparation for trial. Enjoy."

Gradford's self-congratulatory tone told Nadia she'd hate working for the man. Of course, she'd hate prison even more. "If I do say yes, how long?" she asked as he was about to close the door.

"Until I say otherwise."

Nadia knew full well that would be never. Not only would it be never, but she would also give DNI the power to force her to do whatever he wanted. Infiltrate, assassinate, interrogate—all things she had refused to do at ONI.

How could she escape, though? He had legitimate charges against her. She *had* shot up a hospital, infiltrated an embassy, and assisted in combat actions against the embassy. Even if some of the charges wouldn't stick, he was DNI; he could make up new ones.

She was, in a word, screwed. Nadia dropped her head back onto the hard pillow and blew out an exasperated breath. If she could get out of the hospital, she could put one final exit plan into place. It was... drastic... but under no circumstances would she be drawn back into the intel world, working for a despicable man who was blackmailing her to do so. If she was going to make it out of this without spending the rest of her life in prison or having some device implanted in her to force her loyalty, she was going to have to be quick and dramatic.

CHAPTER THIRTY-NINE

While he couldn't walk the ship in the traditional sense, at least not the way he had *Interceptor,* there were parts he could. Turrets #1 and #2 were three decks tall, with the loading mechanism bringing up rounds from the armored core of the ship. The final loading was up to the thirty crew who occupied the different decks inside the massive machine. The actual coils and loading happened in the exposed turret.

Jacob ducked his head in through the hatch and waved for the PO to carry on, stopping him before he could call officer on deck. They were sharp as a knife, readying the turret for action and Jacob didn't want to interrupt them.. From #1 he walked to #2.

"PO Ignatius," Jacob said, stopping him in the same way.

"Skipper, what brings you down here?"

Jacob smiled at the spacer who'd quietly served with him for so long. "Walking the deck, PO."

"We're getting close, then, Skipper?" he asked quietly.

His people knew him well. If Jacob had the luxury of time, he would always walk his ship before battle. Time wasn't always available, though. "I'm afraid so. Maybe six more hours at most."

"Understood, sir. Number two won't let you down."

Jacob clapped the PO on the shoulder. "Never a doubt in my mind. Carry on."

"Yes, Skipper."

Everything was in order. It was like the times before when he'd commanded spacers, except this time, he did it with a behemoth beneath him and his home on the line. Half the crew were from Alexandria. They had everything to fight for. As did he.

Last but not least, he found himself in the small galley outside his quarters where PO Mendez and his crew of misfits worked. The lights were off, and no one moved inside. He leaned against the inside of the hatch, taking a moment to absorb it all. His crew worked their butts off.

"Captain to the bridge," PO Collins said over the ship wide.

"Bridge, Captain. On my way," he replied at the nearest intercom. Jacob closed the hatch to his private mess, never noticing the two shadows in the back, hidden and motionless.

"Is he gone?" Fionna whispered.

"Yes, and the hatch is closed," Josh replied.

She quickly adjusted her mussed uniform and straightened her hair. When it didn't want to go back into the bun, she pulled it out and started fighting with it.

"This was a mistake, Josh. We can't do this again."

The PO deflated somewhat. Their impromptu date had turned into an impromptu make-out session and had almost... almost gone much further than she was ready for. Neither one of them had their own quarters—she shared with other officers, and he shared with POs. There wasn't a single place on the entire ship they could go to be alone... except the captain's mess, which was only used for official dinners. The captain liked to dine with the crew.

Josh had brought her there, having laid out a blanket on the cold deck, along with candles, pillows, and a homemade meal. Clearly, she realized as the endorphins faded, he'd intended to take it further. Her cheeks heated in shame at what she had done, had let him do. *Idiot.*

"Fi, I get the feeling you're mad at me?" he said.

"Don't," she snapped, her Irish lilt clipped and hard. "Don't even say a bloody word, Josh. I'm not in the mood."

Josh, still breathing hard, ran a hand through his dark hair and stepped closer, his navy boots scuffing the deck.

"Fionna, come on. We need to talk about this—"

"No, we don't." She whirled on him, her voice low but fierce. "I'm not some eejit you can drag into a corner and have your way with. I should've known better than to trust you'd keep your hands to yourself."

His brown eyes widened, either feigning disbelief or... Did he really not know?

"What? Fionna, that's not—I didn't bring you here for that!"

"Oh, don't give me that," she shot back, crossing her arms tightly over her chest. "You think I'm daft? Dragging me into an empty mess. All that kissing, your hands everywhere—don't tell me it wasn't leading somewhere, Josh. I'm not one of your portside flings."

Josh's jaw tightened, and he took another step toward her, his voice rising.

"I don't have portside flings, Fi. For heaven's sake, I never even had a girlfriend before you. Dios mío, Fionna, I love you! I'd never—"

"Love?" She laughed, bitter and sharp, cutting him off. "You've a funny way of showing it, then. Sneaking around, pawing at me like some randy teenager. I thought you were different, Josh. I thought—" Her voice cracked, and she turned away again, blinking hard. "I thought you cared about me, not just what you could get from me." She was angry. Fueled by shame, the anger burned through her, igniting her Irish heritage. She turned away from him; easier to be mad when she didn't have to look at his handsome face.

"I do care!" he insisted, his accent thickening with frustration. "Fionna, listen to me, por favor. It got out of hand, sí, I'll own that. I couldn't help it—you're—you're everything to me. But that's not why I brought you here."

She snorted, still facing away, hurriedly fixing her undershirt that hung loose from her trousers.

"Oh, aye? Then why, pray tell, did you lure me into this godforsaken mess hall if not to—to—" She couldn't finish, her cheeks flushing red with a mix of anger and shame.

"Fine," he said, his voice steady now. "You want the truth? You're gonna get it."

She didn't turn, but her posture stiffened, waiting.

"I brought you here because I wanted it to be special," he said, stepping closer. "Not some crowded deck or a noisy bar in port. Just us. I didn't plan on—on all that kissing. Believe me. I got lost in you, Fionna. But that's not why we're here."

She half turned. "What are you on about?"

He took a deep breath, then dropped to one knee, the metal deck cold against his trouser leg. Fionna's breath hitched as he pulled the small velvet box from his pocket and flipped it open, revealing a simple silver ring with a tiny emerald glinting in the dim light.

"Fionna Brennan," he said, his voice soft but sure, "I brought you here to ask you to marry me. I love you—more than my life, more than anything. I want to honor you, in God's eyes and everyone else's. Will you—will you do me the honor of becoming my wife?"

Her hands flew to her mouth, her anger dissolving into shock. The ring sparkled between them, a quiet promise cutting through the storm of their argument. For a moment, the only sound was the hum of the ship's engines far below. Then her eyes softened, and the fight drained out of her, leaving something fragile and real in its place.

"But..."

"But nothing, Fi. I love you with all my heart. I looked into it, actually. I checked with NAVPER. We can put in for Joint Spouse assignment. Assuming the needs of the Navy—"

She cut him off with a fierce hug, wrapping her arms around him and showering him with kisses. "Yes," she said. "Yes. I will."

Jacob entered the bridge, waving for the Marine guarding the hatch to hold off announcing him. He was there to see Mark West and commence the operation. "Mark, what's going on?"

"Skip, Beech had a great idea. I went ahead and implemented it, just so you know."

"Great—" *Seventeen* shuddered as a torpedo launched toward the distant Alexandrian sun. "Is that the idea?"

"Yes, sir. See, since we think the LC was in system spying on us, we wanted to make sure any probes that remain behind don't see *Seventeen* as orbiting Aether. If the incoming fleet gets an update, they'll see us shoot off toward the system center at 300 g's, just as expected. They will be none the wiser."

"Well done, Mark. Pass my compliments to Beech."

The Caliph ships were another three hours from passing

Aether. They wouldn't be able to hide their gravity signature in her shadow much longer. At the same time, every minute *Seventeen* spent in high orbit increased the chances of detection.

It's time. "I have the conn."

"Captain has the conn," Mark relayed sharply to the bridge.

"Ops, set condition Zulu, battle stations."

PO Collins confirmed his orders. Within seconds, alarms wailed throughout the ship. "All hands to battle stations, set condition Zulu," repeated several times.

Jacob eased himself into the center seat. His many MFDs were preset how he liked them, showing weapons status, heat, gravcoil, etcetera. Everything he needed at a glance. During combat, he liked the main viewer to act as his tactical display. All his screens were mirrored in CIC where the XO was stationed. If anything happened to him, Kim could take over without missing a beat.

He said a silent prayer, asking for protection to his crew, praying they would make it.

Crew shuffled onto the bridge, replacing the current watch. Normally, whoever was on station stayed on station when they went into combat. He needed his A-team, though, and had called them up.

Devi climbed into the Pit. She gave him a thumbs-up when she was ready.

"Owusu, get the course we discussed to the COB," Jacob ordered.

"Aye, aye, Skipper. Helm, steer thirty down bubble, ahead full thrusters."

It was an unusual course, for sure. No gravcoil. Thrusters only.

"All turrets report crewed and ready, sir," Lieutenant Gabriel said.

"Thirty degrees down bubble, thrusters ahead full," Devi

said. She pushed the throttle forward. *Seventeen* shook as her immense bulk dove deeper into the gas giant.

Lights flashed on Jacob's MFD. Just as Devi predicted, the hull began to heat, and pressure built up. All within tolerance, but it was there.

"Bridge, engineering, Lieutenant Beech."

"Go ahead, Beech," Jacob said.

"Something I didn't think about, sir. The thruster nozzles are exterior to the ship. We might see some failure in them. I don't think it's anything to worry about, but I wanted to let you know."

"Anything else you want me to worry about by not worrying about it?" Jacob asked, though the smile robbed his voice of any sting.

"Uh, no, sir. That's it."

"Bridge out," Jacob said. Thruster nozzle failure could be a large problem, but the ship had hundreds of them. Enough to sustain serious hull damage and still maneuver.

"Velocity is picking up," Owusu said, eyes glued to his screens.

Seventeen creaked. A sound Jacob had never heard on a starship before. "Devi?" he said while looking at the overhead.

"Pressure, sir. We're essentially diving into a pool. The deeper we go, the more we will have."

Seventeen wasn't designed to land, but she should be able to handle pressure. *Should,* he thought.

Another rumble rolled through the ship.

"Coming up on course change," Owusu said. "Set bubble to zero, ahead zero on my mark."

"Aye, set bubble to zero ahead zero on your mark," Devi replied.

Owusu raised his hand, counting down with the computer. "Mark," he said, slashing his hand down.

Devi pulled smoothly on the stick, dragging *Seventeen*'s nose up from pointing at the cloud cover to just above it. As soon as the ship ran true, she eased the throttle back.

"We're coasting, Skipper. In twenty minutes, we fire the thrusters and come to a halt above the magnetic north," Owusu said.

"Fionna, what's our passive sensors looking like?" Jacob asked.

"Not good, sir. I can't see anything beyond a few hundred klicks. The same interference that's hiding us is hiding them as well."

Jacob would just have to rely on the math. They knew the speed and course of the Caliph fleet; that they would pass close enough to the gas giant to almost touch it. Once they did, he would rise up behind them like a sea serpent and destroy as much of their fleet as he could.

That was the plan. What could go wrong?

CHAPTER FORTY

Admiral Hamza enjoyed the feel of the dreadnaught beneath him. The ship was indeed massive and power flared through the hull.

"Any word yet?" he asked again.

"No, sir. Nothing to report."

The light cruiser, *Al-Hikma*, was supposed to meet them in orbit around the largest outer planet, Aether. Not one of his twenty-three ships had picked up any signal from the light cruiser. That bothered him. They weren't supposed to go in-system, just observe and report.

"How long until orbit?"

"Fifteen minutes, sir."

Hamza nodded. Did his crew trust him? Was having the blessing of the Caliph enough? The crew, he could trust. The other captains in the fleet? Not so much. Long had the Caliphate suffered fools who would, at any opportunity, seek to increase their status at the cost of leadership. They had to know, though, they couldn't possibly hurt his ship. No. They were there to absorb damage and give the *Al-Baraq* time to destroy whatever threat emerged. With her hundreds of plasma cannons and torpedo launchers, even if she were on the older side, nothing could stand up against her. Nothing.

"Should we enter orbit, sir?"

"Yes. Send one destroyer to the other side. Make sure we're not missing *Hikma* in the planet's blind spot."

"Yes, sir."

In the month they had taken to arrive, slowing well short of the system and using the gravcoil on low power to slowly approach and avoid detection, his crew had trained. They knew their ship and weapons. He was confident, when the moment arrived, they would all make Allah proud.

"*Alulu* is responding, sir. They will do one orbit and report back what they see."

"Good. Let's be safe, though. Low orbit. Our intelligence tells us Aether is unstable, with much electromagnetic interference. The last thing I want is for someone to spot us before we're ready."

CHAPTER FORTY-ONE

Angry, swirling clouds moved below... so close Jacob felt he could reach out and touch them. The ship shook, swayed, and creaked every few seconds. Alarmingly so. A shudder ran through her, shaking the chairs and forcing the crew to hold tight.

"Devi... is that normal?" Jacob asked.

"Sir, we're sitting at thirty kilometers per second escape velocity now. I've got the thrusters running at ninety percent just to keep us from plummeting to our deaths. There is no normal."

Jacob, ever needing to show a brave face to his crew, simply smiled and nodded. When she said she could put them down in the plasmasphere but "it wasn't going to be by *The Book*," she wasn't kidding.

"Owusu, anything?"

"Nothing, sir. The electrons charging the atmosphere are blocking all signals. It's like we're in a Faraday cage for the ship. The gravitic pull of the planet is enough we couldn't hear a gravcoil if they were on top of us. And forget about radar and lidar. We're as invisible as a kilometer long battleship can be."

Jacob's plan eliminated many of the variables. There were still a few things the enemy could do, though. A thermal scan of the planet might show their thrusters. Millimeter wave radar would likely pick them up. Neither one of those were standard practices. *Seventeen* didn't even have millimeter wave radar capability.

"Aren't you worried they'll see us?" Lieutenant Gabriel asked.

"No, Lieutenant," Owusu said. "Aether is 1,400 times the size of Alexandria. She's far too big to visually search. And even if they wanted to, where would they start looking?"

"Time?" Jacob asked.

"Fifteen minutes, twelve seconds until they're past us, sir," Tefiti said.

Seventeen dropped. Her secondary gravcoil fought to keep everyone in place, but if it weren't for their harnesses, they would have smashed into the overhead.

"Thruster 14-foxtrot just went offline, sir," Devi said, her lips tight as she fought the controls.

"Bridge, engineering," Beech said over the radio. "I've got three thrusters overheating. They weren't really designed for this."

"Do your best, Beech. Bridge out," Jacob said. He swiveled his chair to face ops. "Mark, get with engineering, find out where those thrusters are and let's do a heatsink swap on the affected ones. It might buy us a little time."

"On it, sir," Mark replied.

Another series of alarms rang from the weapons console. "Sir, turret #1 is reporting hull discoloration on the external feed mechanism."

"Devi, I think we're nearing the limit of time we can be down here. Mark, helmets on, drain the can."

"Aye, sir. Draining the can," Mark replied.

Jacob grabbed his helmet and rested it in his lap until Mark reported the crew had theirs on.

"All departments show green, Skipper," Mark informed him.

Jacob slid the helmet on until he heard the click and a hiss. His HUD booted up, showing him a good seal.

"COB, get us out of here. Nice and slow."

"Aye, aye, sir. Nice and slow."

Seventeen rumbled and groaned as she applied more power to the thrusters.

"Weapons, everything forward. If we did this right, they'll be showing us their aft ends. We'll get maybe a minute for a firing solution before they detect us."

"Aye, sir," Lieutenant Gabriel said. "All weapons ready for targeting lock."

On the front bulkhead, the big screen showed the tactical readout. *Seventeen* was in the center. When more ships were detected, they would start to appear on the screen.

"Exiting the plasmasphere," Devi said.

"Tefiti?"

"Nothing yet, sir."

That was odd. At least they were using thrusters, and not the gravcoil, to rise up out of the atmo. It would make them all but undetectable.

"Conn—ALL STOP," Owusu shouted.

"All stop," Jacob echoed to Devi.

"Aye, all stop," Devi said. The ship shuddered as she killed the thrusters.

Jacob waited for Owusu to explain his orders. He trusted his crew enough to give them the leeway they needed to make decisions without him riding their backsides.

"Skipper, I don't think they passed the planet—" Owusu switched the main viewer from the tactical readout to the cameras. Aether flared to life like a jewel in the black. White and brown clouds swirled beneath them, showing the gas giant's erratic, atmospheric nature. Owusu panned the camera up—Jacob caught his breath.

"How close?" he whispered.

"Ten klicks, sir. No more. They don't see us."

"Then the rest of them must be nearby," Mark added.

Jacob took a breath. Floating above them was a Caliphate ship. Old, yes, but still deadly. He could just make out the glint of the gravcoil.

"How did you see them?" Jacob asked.

"Thermal radiation, Skipper. I've got the passive sensors turned up to max. They must not be running silent—or they're just not good at shielding any of their heat sig."

"Why would they run silent, sir?" Chief Suresh added from the Pit. "It's not like there's anyone to hide from out here. Keeping their acceleration low would be more than enough."

Jacob leaned back, his fingers tapping away on his chair. "Okay, we see them, they can't see us. That's one ship, Owusu. I need your people to find the rest of them."

"Aye, aye, sir, we're on it."

Jacob's heart raced in his chest. It took all his control to keep the panic out of his voice. "Misha, work up a firing solution on the enemy ship," Jacob ordered.

"Aye, sir. Firing solution coming up."

Anything they planned for would be useless if the target ship, or *Seventeen*, moved. Without a solid radar/lidar/gravity return, they couldn't score a hit unless everything sat still.

Seconds ticked by. His suit worked overtime, keeping him cool as the tension poured on. *Seventeen*'s passive sensors were good. Very good. State-of-the-art, in fact. The people manning them were well trained. Caliphate ships used plasma weapons, which almost always required massive amounts of energy—energy that they could detect passively. If the enemy ships were about to shoot at him, he would have a warning. Not much of one, but some.

"Six, so far," Owusu updated him. "They're orbiting in a pattern—"

"Got it," Tefiti said. "Here, sir." The PO from Ohana reached over and adjusted something on Owusu's console.

"Excellent. All of them, we can see all of them, sir."

"Well done!" Jacob said over the bridge wide. "Everyone stay calm. They can't see us while we're underneath them. If they could, we would already be dead. Owusu, on screen."

Jacob unbuckled, showing his crew how unworried he was, and approached the giant screen. Almost two dozen ships appeared. *Seventeen* was at the very edge of their formation. They appeared to be in a layered defense, with the dreadnaught in the middle. All of them were within a hundred meters of the same plane.

There had to be a way to use this to his advantage. Here they were, floating all but helpless in orbit around Aether. He could shoot, just like they had planned, and probably get more than he bargained for on his original plan. However, he still wouldn't get them all. They circled the dreadnaught like a shield. Clearly, their leader was on that ship. No admiral would want to be on a smaller vessel. Not with that behemoth in the fleet.

Jacob searched his memory for something that would help him defeat them. Some weakness he could exploit. "Captain to Redfern," he said. There was one other person aboard who knew as much about history as he did.

"Chief Redfern here, Skipper."

"Chief, the coup d'état that Hamid pulled on his father... was he assisted by the Navy?"

"Yes, sir. Of course, he had all his admirals shot soon after. Their captains too. One of the advantages we have over them is we don't execute popular officers because we're afraid they'll lead a coup against us."

"Thanks, Chief. Captain out."

Redfern had said it as a joke, but that was it. Their entire society was built on fear of losing power. Fear of the guy under you taking your place. A fear that made men like Captain Ali, of the *Glimmer of Dawn*, request asylum rather than return to the Caliphate and face a firing squad... if he was lucky. If he wasn't, his whole family would be slaughtered or enslaved. And yet, somehow, these people persevered. Part of him admired the average Caliph citizen for surviving such an environment. Mostly, he just pitied them. "Fear," Jacob muttered.

"What was that, sir?" Devi asked.

Jacob returned to his seat. "Fear, Chief Suresh. Their entire political structure is built around holding power. Anyone handed this fleet would be politically connected. We're going to play on that." Jacob strapped himself in, making sure they were nice and tight.

"Mark, rig for silent running."

"Aye, sir, silent running." The ship wide sprang to life. "Now hear this, rig for silent running." The message repeated. The lights switched to dark red, and the illumination on the panels faded. While running silent, the ship used thirty percent less power, all heat was transferred to the sinks, and EM was locked down.

"Chief, Z+ 9,000 meters, nice and slow. Five percent power."

"Aye, sir. Z+9,000 meters at five percent power."

Jacob would need every ounce of his tactical acumen to pull this off.

"You want to share what you're up to with the rest of the class, Skipper?" Kim asked.

"Tefiti, what is the dreadnaught's designation?"

"Delta-Tango-One, Skip."

Jacob quickly pulled up the ship's library on how the Caliphate Navy was organized. He wanted to be right... needed to be right... But was he?

"Okay, Misha. Give me a target lock with just the 120s on Delta-Tango-One."

"Just the 120s, sir? Not the 400 mike-mikes?"

"Correct, Lieutenant. Just the 120s."

"Aye, aye, sir."

"When we fire, we're only shooting once. I don't want any other weapons firing. It's going to take some luck, but we can pull this off if we do it right."

"Pull what off, Skipper?" Kim asked from CIC.

"The admiral over there," he waved at Delta-Tango-One on the plot, "is about to experience a coup d'état. When this happens, everyone is going to be moving at once, so keep us clear of their traffic, Chief. We don't need to ram anyone by accident."

"Yes, sir. Keep us clear. Not crazy at all."

Jacob eyed her through the mirror. She nodded, knowing his plan was crazy at best, but also their best chance of success.

The plot showed no sign that the Caliph fleet had detected them. If they did, they would charge their weapons—which would generate an enormous amount of heat the ships sensors could pick up.

"Come on," he whispered. "Just stay put; we're all one big happy fleet."

The moments before a battle, at least the battles they saw coming, were always the hardest for PO Josh Mendez. His secondary job as weapons controller came into play whenever they went to battle stations. There wasn't much call for a cook when the tungsten penetrators were flying.

Manning the 120mm turret wasn't much different from the Long 9 back on *Interceptor*. The interface was newer, as was the software. He could also fire five rounds a minute. However, all the ammo loading was automated, with two loaders as backup. They would clear any jams, make repairs, or fetch ammo as needed.

Which meant he had Zach and Perch in the turret with him. As usual, the two men bantered about the fleet, about entertainment, about almost anything to take their minds off what was ahead. Josh couldn't blame them one bit.

"Zach," Josh said, "did you ask Nika out?"

That stopped the two men's discussion about the virtues of railguns versus coil guns dead in their tracks.

"Uh, yes I did," he said and looked away.

Perch chuckled. "Oh, he asked her out all right. We were at Frosty's, and Zach here had a little too much to drink. You know... to drum up the courage."

Josh grinned ear to ear. There were few things spacers loved more than drinking. Something Josh tried hard not to do. Since the captain didn't drink, there had to be merit to it. Made it hard, though, when he was out on leave with his friends.

"Don't keep me in suspense, amigo. What happened?" Josh asked.

"She said yes," Zach said. "Just... you know, after I spilled my drink on her... but she said yes."

Perch was quick to clarify. "My boy Zach was so nervous, even after two shots of tequila to help. He took her a glass of wine and tripped right in front of her. The wine went all over her *white* dress."

"Tell me it wasn't a red," Josh said.

"Oh, it was, PO. It was. He thought red was romantic."

"And she still said yes?"

Zach looked back, smiling now, though bright red from blushing. "Yes, she did. She found me endearing and earnest. I also bought her a new dress."

Orders appeared on Josh's terminal. From their perspective, the room didn't move, even though Josh knew it had. The hatch, though, twisted at an angle as the turret shifted to its new target.

"Get ready, boys. It's go time."

CHAPTER FORTY-TWO

What he was about to do was possibly the most insane move Jacob T. Grimm had ever pulled. If it worked, he'd stop the Cali fleet at Aether. Even if it failed, he would seriously hurt them.

Either way, though, he knew this was the end for him and his crew. Twenty-two ships in total. A dreadnaught, six heavy cruisers, and fifteen screening units was more than enough to turn *Seventeen* into its component atoms. His crew, likely all of them, were going to die.

How many could they take with them was the only question left to answer.

"Mac, ship wide."

Jacob closed his eyes and said a silent prayer for his crew.

"Aye, aye, sir. You're on."

"Crew of *Int*—" Jacob coughed, almost saying the name of his old ship. The next words came out with a sheepish smile on his face. "Crew of *Seventeen,* this is your captain speaking. We stand here on the edge of a precipice. *Seventeen*, with all her firepower and armor, is the *only* ship between a Caliph fleet and our home. A fleet we can't beat in a straight fight."

Jacob paused for a second, his mind working to find the words that would rouse and inspire.

"This is no skirmish. No fight among symmetrical opponents. The enemy has many ships to our one. But one ship defending her home is worth a hundred enemy ships. Caliph Hamid has sent a fleet to smash Alexandria and force our brothers and sisters defending the wormhole to retreat. I have no doubt there is a similar fleet poised to strike at Praetor this very moment. They're waiting for our ships to fall back, and when they do, they will destroy Praetor, then Zuckabar. They won't stop until they plant a Caliphate flag on every Alliance planet. Until every man, woman, and child is under their yoke, wearing one of their damned collars."

Jacob's voice broke on the last word. His thoughts turned to Nadia and what she had gone through. Where was she at that moment? Would she know he thought of her to the very last?

"We cannot let that happen. We could run, alert the static defenses of Alexandria, work with what few ships there are in-system to fight back. If we do that, though, a message will go out to the fleet guarding the wormhole, and they will return. We cannot let that happen. We stop the Caliphate here and now. We obliterate so much of this fleet that their descendants will feel the sting of loss."

Jacob stood up, feeling the need to move as he spoke.

"We are in the most advanced ship the Alliance has ever built. Look to your crewmates. We're the best crew in the Alliance. You have my complete faith.

"The Caliphate have asked the question: 'Does the Alliance deserve to survive?' Let us answer with our cannons and our hearts. This is our home. This is our family. This is our legacy. We will never stop fighting. To our very last breath. Trust your training, listen to you POs, we will fight to the very gates of hell themselves. Good luck. Captain out."

Jacob returned to his center seat and strapped back in. Things were about to get rough.

"Listen up, people," he said on the bridge wide. "Things are about to get interesting and not in the fun way. Comms, download all logs, records, and final mail to the buoy, and eject the moment the shooting starts. Ops, the second we take fire, eject the heat sinks and don't hesitate to do so again if needed. Weps, activate the giga-pulse laser defense system first thing, understood?"

A chorus of "aye, aye" returned. Jacob smiled at the bravery of his crew in the face of overwhelming odds.

"This isn't the first time we've been outnumbered. God willing, it won't be the last."

Admiral Hamza hated the waiting. They'd spent over a month under gravcoil to arrive in Alexandria undetected. He desperately wanted to fly straight to the cursed home of his enemy and burn it down to the bedrock. If he could literally destroy the planet, he would. His uncle, the Caliph, gave him this mission because of his loyalty; he would not reward that with failure.

Especially not after seeing firsthand what his uncle would do to those who failed—or those he thought might betray him. Something all too common in the Caliphate. Betrayal by inferiors.

The light cruiser he'd sent ahead to recon the system for intel wasn't where it was supposed to be. Nor had they left any message as to their whereabouts. Not wanting to fail meant moving carefully. There was a time for aggression; this wasn't it.

"Bakir, any word?" he asked his chief communications officer.

"Nothing yet, sir. We're on the wrong side of the planet to pick up any signals, not to mention this gas giant has dozens or more moons that block line of sight. It could be a few more hours before we hear back from *Hikma*, or the destroyer *Halal*."

"Understood, keep me posted." Hamza stretched his memory for the name of his sensor officer. "Rai'is," he said more cheerfully than he intended, simply happy to have remembered the lieutenant's name. "Anything on Passive?"

Rai'is was a young man, on only his second or third tour with the Caliph Navy. Hamza grinned as the lieutenant struggled to speak to his admiral.

"Sir, uh, well, with the interference, our gravity receivers are all but useless. With the electron noise coming from the planet, our passive EMI isn't working either. R/LWR is unaffected, but there's no one out here using radar or lidar. If they were, we would see them."

"Very good. Keep an eye out. The Alliance are a bunch of sneaky bastards. I wouldn't put it past them to have a cloaked and hidden satellite or station out here as an early warning. They would think nothing of wasting billions on such frivolity." The irony of him calling "frivolous" an early warning system that would in fact help them, was lost on Hamza.

"Sir," Rai'is said. "Uh, I am picking up something odd. It might be nothing."

"What is it?"

Rai'is played with his console, running a diagnostic as he spoke. "Well, for a moment, I thought I saw a heat bloom under the heavy cruiser, *Saladin*. It only lasted a few seconds, but it was odd."

Hamza debated breaking their stealth for a minute to go active on radar, if for no other reason than to confirm there was nothing there other than the heavy cruiser. Was the captain of the *Saladin* planning a coup against him? This would be the perfect time to do so.

"Bakir, what's the closest ship to *Saladin*?"

His comms man pulled up the screen, showing each of his ships and their corresponding call codes. "Destroyer *Saif*, sir. They are one hundred kilometers off the port side."

"Contact them and have them scan *Saladin* with their radar. It may be nothing, but the weak radar of a destroyer is less likely to be detected than our own."

"Okay, Misha. This is what we're going to do," Jacob said over his direct channel to the weapons officer.

"Ready, Skipper," Lieutenant Gabriel replied.

Jacob didn't miss the weapon's officer using the honorific for the first time. It brought a smile to his face. Misha was one of the best, no doubt. When the kid had a little more experience, he would... be... a fantastic officer. That thought killed his smile. No one was going to have more time.

In the words of an ancient seafarer, the navy is the shield of the republic, and I will wield it with all my strength. Jacob hated the idea of a scenario in which he could not bring his crew home alive. Alive or dead, though, *Seventeen* would win the day and act as a shield to Alexandria.

"Are the 120s ready?"

"Aye, sir. One volley only against the dreadnaught."

"If this works, they'll start shooting at one another. If it doesn't, fire everything at the dreadnaught. Launch a pair of MK XIVs, one fore and aft. Two battleship signatures heading in opposite directions will buy us some time."

"Aye, sir. After the dreadnaught is destroyed, who do we fire on next?"

Jacob's heart swelled with pride at the man's optimism. The idea that they would live to continue firing was bold and refreshing. "Go by weight, largest to smallest."

"Aye, aye, Skipper."

They were out of time. They could probably stay longer, but Jacob didn't want to risk his maneuver. Sowing distrust among the enemy fleet would only work if they thought they were out here alone.

Jacob took a deep breath to steady his nerves and let it out slowly. "Lieutenant Gabriel... fire."

―――

"Sir?" Lieutenant Rai'is said.

"Yes, Lieutenant?"

"I'm picking up an energy surge on passive. It's coming from the direction of *Saladin*."

"What? Another one? Bakir, get me Captain Enami on comms," he ordered. They wouldn't come all the way to Alexandria just to betray him, would they? It would be the perfect time. Enami could make up any story he wanted, take credit for the operation, and end up Caliph Hamid's new fleet admiral.

Wasn't Enami related to one of the former admirals the Caliph had executed? Revenge and promotion. That had to be it.

―――

Captain Enami frowned when his comms man said the admiral was calling. They were supposed to be on radio silence. If the "admiral" wanted to chat, he should have done it with someone on his own crew.

Not that Enami thought of Hamza as a real admiral. More of a spoiled brat who happened to be the nephew of the Caliph.

"Admiral Hamza, are we moving out? Is this why we're breaking radio silence?"

Hamza looked genuinely angry. "Why are you charging your weapons?"

Captain Enami's guts wrenched. He stood. Was this a ruse to destroy him? "We're not charging our weapons, sir. How dare you think I would—"

"Sir, destroyer *Saif* is painting us with radar."

"Everyone calm down," Enami said. "We're not charging our weapons or planning to, Admiral. This is clearly a mistake."

Hamza's face softened the tiniest amount on the screen. "Perhaps you're right and—"

Alarms blared across *Saladin*'s tight bridge. "Weapons fire!"

Enami watched in horror as explosions rippled across *Al-Baraq* port side. Hamza's face vanished in static for a moment.

"Cease fire," Enami yelled.

"We didn't fire—"

The static cleared. Behind Hamza smoke filled the bridge. "You missed, Captain. My turn. Weapons, turn that ship to dust."

"Wait, no!" Enami yelled. The transmission vanished.

"Helm, get us out of here. Battle alert, all hands—"

Jacob let out a whistle at the sudden ferocity of weapons fire. The dreadnaught opened up on the heavy cruiser with enough plasma guns to melt a small moon.

"Sir," Tefiti said. "RWR. We're getting painted by one of the destroyers."

Here we go. "Weps, execute."

"Aye, aye, sir. Firing MK XIVs, commencing barrage on dreadnaught."

Saladin vanished in a blossom of fusion fire as the ship exploded. Radiation flooded the upper atmosphere of Aether, which was promptly ignored by the planet's ferocious storms.

For a brief instant, the destroyer *Saif* detected *Seventeen*, then *Saladin*'s death interfered with the signal. As the radiation cleared, two Alliance battleships appeared, speeding out of the formation at full throttle. None of the Caliph ships knew what to do. On the one hand, the enemy had appeared; on the other, the nephew of their Caliph had just opened fire and obliterated his second-in-command.

The commanders of the destroyers and light cruisers hesitated, not wanting to draw the ire of ships that could turn them to dust in a matter of seconds. Enami, the captain of the *Saladin*, wasn't only the fleet's second-in-command; he was the group commander for the heavy cruisers.

Heavy cruisers who now thought they were under attack by Hamza himself.

CHAPTER FORTY-THREE

Heat sinks ejected from the bottom of *Seventeen* like bombs. Ten carbon fiber thermal stars bloomed to life, then exploded as they hit the ship's burgeoning grav wake.

Seventeen shook as her 400mm turrets blasted massive nano-steel-coated tungsten rounds at the dreadnaught. The 120mms, while not nearly as impressive, fired twice as fast.

Nine rounds in total impacted the dreadnaught; three penetrated her armor. The overly thick armor exploded out, deflecting some of the kinetic energy but leaving an enormous rent in the hull. The second one smashed through the weakened armor, exploding into the interior of this ship, vaporizing metal and flesh alike, killing a hundred crew. Tungsten darts as wide as a large dog tore through nano-hardened armor plating. Molten steel followed the darts in as gases exploded out. The other six rounds all hit but failed to penetrate the ship's heavily armored frame.

Imparting their kinetic energy and heat into the ship, 120s rocked the dreadnaught further. All but one spent their energy against the armor.

Josh's round smashed into the delicate superstructure holding the gravcoil in place. Tungsten blasted through light armor, deflecting off the hyperdense gravcoil to fragment and explode like a grenade in the relatively unarmored keep. Chunks of tungsten as thick as a finger shredded lifeboats, the living quarters, and two dozen crew unfortunate enough to be in their path.

Alarms wailed, smoke filled the bridge, and someone screamed in agony. Hamza shook his head, trying to clear the noise and confusion. "Who's firing at us?"

"*Saladin* is destroyed, Admiral, but the shots came from her —or *Saif*?"

Hamza frowned at the ludicrous idea. A destroyer's weapons couldn't hope to hurt him.

"Deck nineteen is open to space. The gravcoil housing is reporting severe damage. There are—"

"Who's shooting at us? And don't tell me *Saif*," Hamza bellowed, shutting Bakir down mid-sentence

"New contact. Alliance battleship... no, two Alliance battleships. They're going in opposite directions, Admiral!"

Something was terribly wrong. This was all wrong. Alliance ships, here?

"Battle alert. Go active on all sensors. Get us moving."

"Damn, that's one tough ship," Jacob said. The dreadnaught shrugged off the first volley from the 400s. It took some damage, but not nearly enough.

"She's moving, Skipper," Tefiti said. "Grav wake surging... two-five-zero gravities."

"Helm, pace her. Weapons, keep firing."

While the 20s and 120s could fire multiple times a minute, the 400s took almost a full minute to reload, charge the coils, and dissipate the heat. It was like having three Long 9s at his disposal, but the turrets let them shoot in almost any direction. At their current range from the dreadnaught, they almost couldn't miss.

"I don't believe it, sir," Mark West said. "Only a few of the rounds penetrated her. That ship must be thirty percent armor."

Jacob agreed. He'd shot battleships with smaller guns and done more damage.

"Captain!" Owusu said, his voice overly excited. "One of the light cruisers opened fire on a heavy. The rest of the fleet is shooting at each other and the decoys. They must have thought the dreadnaughts departure was a sign of aggression."

"Misha, how long until the 400s can fire again?"

"Fifteen seconds, Skipper."

"What's that?" Hamza asked, pointing at the plot. A grav wake nearly as strong as his had appeared the moment they accelerated. Interference from Aether and the two decoys made it indistinct and hazy. It was so close... was it a sensor echo?

"New contact, sir," Rai'is shouted. "Alliance battleship, range one hundred kilometers, two-five zero gravities, on our same heading."

"That's not possible. You're reading it wrong," Bakir snapped.

"I'm reading it right, sir. That's who's shooting at us," Rai'is retorted.

"Return fire," Hamza yelled. "All turrets, target that ship and—"

Al-Baraq lurched to the side as hundreds of kilograms of nano-steel-reinforced tungsten slammed into her armored hull. More alarms blared, lights flashed, and whole sections of his bridge blinked on and off as power was interrupted.

"Somebody fire at that ship!"

Despite Chief Petty Officer Deviyanee Suresh's decades of experience as a coxswain, there was no evading the shots fired at such close range. Weapons designed to hit targets from hundreds of thousands of kilometers away crossed the distance before a human could even register their existence.

What no one could have expected, though, was the giga-pulse laser defense system's radar picking up the incoming plasma rounds, registering them as threats, and firing.

High-intensity laser beams in Gatling-like emitters on top of turrets #1 and #3 spun to life, shooting hundreds of deadly laser beams per second. Coherent plasma held together by magnetic pellets at the centers exploded as the laser clusters found their targets.

Al-Baraq fired over three dozen plasma rounds, from low-powered megajoule to gigajoule; one hit.

Seventeen reeled as the plasma round smashed into her armored flank. Metal ran like water when the thermal energy that rivaled a sun washed over the portside.

"What the hell was that?" Jacob asked.

"Skipper, the GPLDS it... it activated against the plasma rounds, I think?" Lieutenant Gabriel said.

"Portside armor is severely reduced," Mark West said. "No casualties."

Jacob activated his comms. "Chief Redfern, Captain."

"Redfern here, Skipper."

"Chief, the GPLD just took out a few dozen plasma rounds... is that your doing?"

"That's amazing. And no, sir, not at all. The Calis use a launched magnetic pellet to keep their plasma stable over long distances. I suppose it's possible..."

"Captain out."

That changed the game.

"Weapons, keep hitting them. Helm, come one-zero degrees starboard. Maintain current acceleration." He didn't want to give them a chance to use their main guns; a running broadside would keep the fight in his favor.

"Aye, aye, sir," Misha said. "Helm turning starboard one-zero degrees; maintain current acceleration."

Turning would increase the distance from the enemy and allow more time to intercept enemy weapons. Jacob's mind reeled at the possibilities of the GPLD system. If they could intercept Caliph plasma turrets, they would be all but immune to Cali weapons. *No wonder the Guild didn't fear them.*

With the distance opening and the angle of attack changing, the turrets aboard *Seventeen* shifted to stay on target. Even with their increasing separation, they would be able to target the enemy ship for at least an hour.

Josh's turret rotated, though only the shifting ammo feeder told him so. With the atmosphere drained and no sound, it was almost impossible to feel any movement other than the hum of the gravcoil and the vibrations from the turret.

Zach and Perch watched over the loader, ready to step in if the mechanism jammed or if there was a problem. Josh sat in the firing chair, his right hand wrapped around the joystick with the single trigger. His screen showed a three-dimensional representation of the dreadnaught. He could try to aim for specific spots, but it was almost impossible to hit a small target with both ships traveling at high speed and maneuvering. The computer could account for a lot, but not that much. The best they could hope to do was lead the target and try for a hit at all.

He could override the computer firing if he needed to, but mostly he was there as a backup in case the bridge was cut off or the computer firing controls were damaged.

Josh slammed to the port in his chair, his harness biting painfully into his body. Zach yelled from the sudden shift in gravity.

Alarms wailed on his suit at the sudden increase in temperature. Sweat broke out on his brow before the suit flushed him with cool air.

"What the hell was that?" Perch asked.

"Plasma hit. Probably close," Josh replied. "Hang in there."

"Where are we going to go, PO? The head?"

"Hang on, they're firing again," Owusu said.

Jacob didn't want to distract Misha, who hunched over his console, overseeing the weapons fire from *Seventeen*.

"Owusu, is the GPLD activating?"

"Aye, Skipper, and—"

Seventeen wrenched to the side; only the gravity harness kept his crew from smashing into the bulkhead. Still, it was enough to rattle his brain and blur his vision.

The dreadnaught's main guns fired gigajoule plasma rounds buoyed by a magnetic pellet. Launched at near light speed, the plasma crossed the distance to *Seventeen* in the one-third of a second—almost too fast for the computer to fire lasers in defense. Thirty-six turrets from *Al-Boraq* fired. Two hit.

Seventeen's armor melted like fat hit by hot water. Just aft of frame 516 on deck seven, it ran in rivulets away from the center of the ship. Forty-three men and women manning the fabricator, repair workshop, and portside damage control burned to a crisp before their brains knew they were dead. Metal hardened instantly in the cold of space, leaving a smooth hole twenty-five meters long and two decks tall at its highest point.

The second round impacted boat bay three. Heavily armored bay doors warped and disfigured under the intense release of thermal and kinetic energy. They gave, exploding inward. Two Corsairs and a Mudcat shielded the internal deck and the other three boat bays from the worst of the hyper-accelerated shrapnel. Three crew went down in a gout of black blood as their suits desperately fought to save them.

"Medical personnel to boat bay three," Boudreaux called over the emergency channel.

"That one hit us hard, Skip," Mark said.

"Weps, are we hitting them?"

"Aye, sir, we are. But it's so damn big. Half the time the 400s aren't even penetrating the armor. I've never seen or heard of anything like it."

Jacob hadn't either. The 400s were as wide as his forearm was long. They should drill through that ship like wolf moles back home. "Rapid fire on all batteries. Rain down hell on them."

"Aye, sir. Rapid fire all batteries."

Within seconds of the order going out, the 20s and 120s doubled their volume of fire. The radar return on the enemy ship showed metallic debris raining from its stern as armor flaked off the hull.

"Devi, roll the ship, protect the portside."

"Aye, sir. Rolling the ship."

Seventeen's dozens of thrusters fired, rolling the ship until her untouched starboard side faced the dreadnaught.

Turrets #1 and #2 fired in tandem, sending six rounds at the bow of the dreadnaught. At the last second, the dreadnaught changed course, turning into the trajectory of the rounds. Four missed; the fifth deflected off the apex of the pointed bow, digging a furrow fifty meters long into the armor.

Lucky number six hit at a ninety-degree angle, right below the horizontal clipper stem. Four hundred and twenty-eight kilograms, accelerated to ten percent the speed of light and shaped like an arrow, blasted through the weakest point of the dreadnaught's upper bow.

The tungsten penetrator continued on, smashing through the lighter interior hull where they hadn't used as much armor, then out the portside amidship. Two hundred and twenty-three Caliph naval personnel died instantly. Three turrets lost their supercapacitors, and half the ship's food stores went with it.

Hamza's head pounded and his shoulders ached from the beating his ship took. The last hit damn near killed him with the sudden jerking forward in his harness.

"Helm, close with that ship. Whatever they're doing to intercept our weapons won't work if we're close enough."

"Sir, we could try turning using the main gun," Bakir said.

Al-Baraq had eight pulse plasma lasers that would turn the enemy ship to ash. However, the power drain was enormous. If he fired, the other turrets would be offline for a few minutes while they charged. They were hitting the ship, despite their wizardry. It would only take a few more blows, and the Alliance vessel would fall.

"Helm, if you think you have a shot at the main gun, take it."

CHAPTER FORTY-FOUR

Captain Yazeed, of the Caliphate Naval light cruiser *Salam,* gripped his chair tightly. A dull ache in his hands warned him to let go, but he just couldn't.

"Keep firing. I don't care who you shoot, just don't get shot," he said.

His first officer, Lieutenant Ammar, acknowledged.

How had this happened? Ten minutes before, everything was fine. Then, without warning, *Saif* turned on its radar, illuminated *Saladin*, and the admiral erased it—without so much as a warning to the rest of the fleet. Before Yazeed could get clarification, the dreadnaught accelerated out of orbit.

If it weren't for the jamming that followed, he would have sent a message asking for clarification as the fleet's next senior officer *after* Captain Enami... of the *Saladin*. Who was now dead.

Before he could even begin to pull the fleet together, the heavy cruisers *Mansurr* and *Haqq* lit *Saif* up like a funeral pyre. The destroyer didn't stand a chance.

A ship under his command, along with her crew, killed by an obvious act of rebellion. As the acting fleet commander, he had a clear duty. His four light cruisers and five remaining destroyers opened fire on *Mansurr* and *Haqq*. Then the other three heavy cruisers returned fire.

We're all going to die.

———

Seventeen faltered, her gravcoil losing power.

"Skipper, we're down to two-three-zero g's. The last hit clipped the gravcoil," Chief Suresh said. "They've turned into us. With their higher acceleration, they're going to close the gap in a hurry."

"Roger, Chief. Do your best."

Damage reports flowed in from Ops nearly nonstop. The GPLDs stopped most of the plasma hits, but not all of them. The dreadnaught had at least twice the mass to absorb blows, and Jacob was running out of time and ship to stop them. At some point, one of their plasma blasts would hit something critical or do more damage than his ship could absorb, and that would be that.

"No sign the rest of their fleet is pursuing us, Skipper. The last we saw, before Aether blocked our view, they were shooting at each other," Owusu said.

That was something. No matter what, then, he'd stopped them. Their fleet was in disarray, and the dreadnaught was badly damaged. They weren't going to be bombing Alexandria any time soon.

"They're trying to close with us, Skip. I think they're lining up for a main gun shot."

That would put an end to *Seventeen* pretty quick. "Distance?"

"One-zero-five thousand kilometers."

There just wasn't much precedence for a close in battle between two ships of their size. Normally, you would stay at mid-range and duke it out. The fact that the Caliph battlewagon had survived this long was a miracle of engineering.

Engineering...

"Lieutenant Beech, Captain," Jacob called.

"Beech, here sir."

"Why didn't they use this beast more? We're dumping fire into her, and she just won't stop. Why didn't your plans work?"

"It's pretty simple, sir. The inherent instability of the gravcoil pulling two opposite masses through space. If the mass of the ship becomes unbalanced, or if the gravcoils take any serious damage, it won't just slow acceleration, the ship will tear itself apart."

"Good man, Beech." Jacob killed the line. "Misha, I know it's asking a lot, but we're close enough that this could work. Redirect all weapons fire to the enemy coil."

Misha actually looked up from his panel and turned to the captain. "Sir? Are you saying called shots?"

"Yes, I am. If we can hit the coil, even once, it will end the fight."

"Aye, sir. I'll do my best."

Jacob prayed his best was good enough. They were so close; they had to take the chance.

"Energy surge," Tefiti said.

Devi reacted instantly: *Seventeen* rolled on her side and slid sideways several hundred meters. Three of the dreadnaught's pulse plasma lasers blasted through space where *Seventeen* had been a moment before. Radiation alarms wailed from the near miss.

"You keep that up, PO," Devi said to PO Tefiti.

"Aye, Chief," Tefiti replied.

"All turrets, hold fire—" Misha went to work on his console, numbers flying by while Jacob waited.

Lights dimmed as the GPDL rapidly intercepted more plasma rounds; this time none made it through.

"You've got the math, Misha?" Jacob asked. "We're kind of in a hurry."

"One second, Skipper, almost there... got it. Sir, if we flip the ship presenting our top deck to them, I can fire every turret. Even if only one hits, it might be enough."

Jacob liked the audacity of the plan. At the same time, it would open his ship up to the most possible damage.

"Keep that move in your back pocket, Misha. We might need it. Fire when ready."

———

"Pulse plasma lasers need five minutes to recharge, sir."

"Sir, the enemy ship has ceased firing—"

Admiral Hamza fought to keep it all together. Was it a trap? Hamza couldn't take his eyes off the radar return showing the fleeing vessel. For fifteen minutes, they had fired volley after volley. He'd fully expected the first volley to be the last. Then they fired the main gun, and *somehow* the enemy anticipated the shot and dodged it.

If he ordered them to close with the enemy... In five minutes they would be so close, there would be no evading the main gun. He'd scored several good hits. The ship's acceleration had lagged, and they were closing on them again. Had the last volley done some critical—

"They're firing again. Helm, right zero—"

A wall of metal from half of the Alliance turrets bore down on the dreadnaught. Despite their relatively short distance, the slower rounds from the coil weapons still took up to three seconds to traverse the gap. *Al-Baraq* shook like a rag doll as dozens of rounds smashed into the lower decks, flanks, and armor.

"Portside-upper hull, three turrets down, multiple hull breaches," Bakir reported. "I think they're trying to hit our gravcoil, Admiral."

"Evade. But dammit, I don't care what you have to do. Close with that ship and destroy it!"

Jacob frowned at the reports coming in from CIC. He checked the radar returns; what he saw made his heart sink. They were closing with him. With the damage to *Seventeen*'s gravcoil, she could no longer force them to keep pace. If that ship survived, even if the rest of the fleet died, Alexandria would burn. If the dreadnaught died, and the rest of their fleet lived... Alexandria would make it. In a career full of impossible odds, Jacob T. Grimm was no stranger to beating no-win scenarios. He couldn't beat this. Not with *Seventeen*. Not with any ship.

There was only one option left. Decision made, he found himself far calmer than he ought to be. "Good hits, Misha. Not what we wanted, but good hits all the same."

"Sorry, sir. The delay is just too long. The 400s take three point two seconds to traverse the distance."

"Understood, keep trying. Closing velocity?" Jacob asked.

"Three-four-seven KPS, Skipper," Owusu said. "I estimate nine minutes to zero."

That wasn't long.

"They're on to us, sir," Misha said. "They're rotating around their gravcoil, hitting it will be that much harder."

Why hadn't they continued to fire their main gun? "Understood. Weps, do your best."

Stopping the enemy ship was the single most important

goal. Not survival. Not making sure his crew survived. The dreadnaught had to die. Jacob had already accepted in his heart that they weren't going to survive the engagement. Not against twenty-two ships. When they managed to peel the dreadnaught off and trick the rest of the fleet into shooting at each other, he had allowed himself to hope they would escape. That hope was gone.

Jacob switched his channel to private with Chief Suresh. "Devi, I want to close with them as fast as possible. Can you do it?"

Devi turned to look in the mirror they shared, her eyes meeting his. "Skip, you asking me to ram them?"

Jacob thought about it for a moment. By *The Book* it wasn't possible, but he'd done a lot of things that were forbidden by *The Book*. This would likely be the last one, though. Would it work? Audacity wasn't useful if they couldn't pull the maneuver off.

"Yes, I think I am. Can you?"

Devi met his gaze with the steel of her spine. Despite her youthful appearance, in that moment, she was every bit the chief petty officer he knew and needed.

"Skip, I could fly this thing through Utopia shipyard blindfolded while brushing my hair."

Jacob couldn't help but grin. "Good to know. Make yourself ready."

"Hell, Skipper, I knew from the moment I met you I was going out in a blaze of glory. This is what I signed up for."

Jacob flipped his channel to proximity so everyone on the bridge could hear him. "You all have served with impeccable skill and immeasurable courage. The next few minutes will decide the outcome of the battle and the fate of Alexandria. Whatever happens, it's been the honor of my life to serve with you."

"Skipper, what are you planning?" Kim asked.

"We're going to rapidly close with them while firing everything we have. If we close the distance quick enough, Lieutenant Gabriel might be able to score a hit on their gravcoil. If he does, and it cracks... the fight is over."

"Skipper... Jacob... as your XO, I'm behind you 110 percent. But sir... you know we're not going to survive."

Jacob clenched his jaw. He knew it. He'd thought it. Hearing it out loud made him feel it. "I know. Good luck, Kim."

"It's been an honor, Skipper."

Jacob turned his attention back to his MFDs. There wasn't time to say all the things he wanted to say. There wasn't time to send a last message or even think about who he wanted to think about.

"Misha, we're going to change course and head straight for them. I want you to time your turrets to fire all at once. You'll get four, maybe five volleys with the 400s. Don't waste them."

Lieutenant Misha Gabriel turned to the CO he had once not trusted. "Skipper, I... I won't let you down, sir."

"Good man." Jacob tapped numbers into his keypad, verifying that what he wanted to do could work. He switched his comms to helm only. "Devi, I'm sending you the course. Ready?"

"Aye, aye, Skipper," she replied.

Jacob took a deep breath in preparation to utter words he never thought he would say. "Conn, change course two-seven-zero mark three-four-zero... ramming speed."

"Aye, sir. Changing course two-seven-zero mark three-four-zero, ramming speed."

The bridge went deathly still. There was nothing to say. The captain had made his decision. It was up to them to carry it out.

"Admiral, the infidel ship is changing course."

Hamza took his eyes off the fire control board for a moment to look. "What are they doing?"

Al-Baraq's full acceleration propelled the dreadnaught sidelong into the battleship. His helm kept the ship rotating, keeping the enemy from targeting their gravcoil. Every roll of his ship brought new turrets online, allowing for a near-continuous barrage of plasma fire. Yet, somehow, the Alliance had a weapon that intercepted his plasma rounds.

They couldn't stop the pulse plasma laser, though. With the fools altering course and closing with him, they would meet their end soon enough.

"How long until we can fire the main gun?"

"Two minutes, three zero seconds."

Jacob double-checked his harness, making sure it was as tight as possible.

"GPLD continues to stop ninety percent of their weapons, Skipper," Owusu informed him.

"Good to know. Mac?"

"Yes, sir," PO McCall said.

"Load up the distress buoy. Put all our combat data and logs into it."

"Aye, sir," Mac said. He gulped audibly as he set about his duty. "Buoy ready to launch."

"Send it," Jacob ordered.

The launch of the buoy was lost in the mix of coil turrets firing near nonstop. It ensured that, no matter what, the Alliance would know of his crew's sacrifice and what they had accomplished so far away from Alexandria that it took light six hours to reach her from the sun.

Second by second, he watched the radar returns closing. At the one-minute mark, he had to zoom the screen in as the two blinking lights merged.

"One minute," Owusu said.

Please God, let this work. Let me stop them. Let me save her. "Misha, at the ten-second mark, I'm going to have Devi roll the ship and give every turret a single salvo, just like you suggested."

"Aye, sir. I'll be ready."

"Sir!" Bakir shouted. "They're not changing course. We won't have the main guns charged before our courses merge."

Courses merge? Hamza watched the plot as well. He knew the enemy ship closed with them, but what was he planning? Probably an effort to score more hits before they were destroyed. The Alliance had no idea how powerful the dreadnaught was. It was a flying fortress.

"What are you saying, Bakir?"

"I think they're meaning to ram us—"

That was foolish. For one, at their velocity, it would be near impossible. They would have to match and—"

He glanced at the *absolute* velocity of his ship, which was astronomical. They couldn't hope to hit *Al-Baraq*. Then why try? So far, the commander of the enemy ship had acted with guile and subterfuge. Assuming he wasn't stupid...

"Thirty seconds. Sir, I think we need to change course," Bakir said.

"Nonsense. We're going over three thousand KPS, they can't hope to hit us..."

"That's not our closing velocity, sir."

Hamza realized his mistake. Everything in space was relative, every course change, every roll of the ship, changed its velocity relative to the other ships around them. It was almost too much for anyone to keep track of.

"Reverse, reverse!" he yelled.

Ten seconds before the impact, *Al-Baraq* swiveled on her axis and went to maximum power. It bought them all of point seven-seven seconds.

It did, however, expose their full gravcoil to Lieutenant Misha Gabriel's guns as Chief Suresh rolled the ship, giving every turret a clear shot.

Nine coils charged and fired 400mm reinforced nano-steel-wrapped tungsten rounds. Twelve coils blasted 120s, and all the 20s fired.

The 400s did the most damage, shredding armor in the less protected flank, blasting through the decks, vaporizing armor, hull, and flesh. Thousands of tons of steel exploded inward, maiming, killing, and shredding flesh and steel. Crew died by the hundreds in a blender of shrapnel.

For all that damage, though, it was the 120s that killed her.

Four hit the armor around the gravcoil deflecting the projectiles off into space as the ship's designers intended. Six missed entirely. Two, though, including one fired by PO Josh Mendez, struck the hyperdense alloy of the gravcoil itself. Five-kilogram tungsten darts barely separated from their housing when they impacted with a petajoule of energy—far more than the gravcoil could absorb.

The coil cracked.

A millisecond later, the energy flow of eight fusion reactors accelerated the ship in two directions. The ship's superstructure could not withstand the shearing gravity forces without her gravcoil.

Al-Baraq, the jewel of the Caliphate, shattered like glass struck by a hammer. One point three seven seconds later, all her fusion reactors unleashed their energy in a blast of incalculable power. Thermal ferocity of a sun brightened to a point, followed by a wave of deadly radiation.

Unfortunately for *Seventeen*, it was too late to change course. Thermal and hard radiation enveloped the battleship, melting armor, burning the hull, and killing crew by the hundreds.

Turrets one and two, along with Lieutenant Sanchez, PO Ignatius, and forty spacers, vanished. Six of the twelve exposed 120s melted into the hull, killing and maiming their crews. Including Spacers Zach and Perch, who died when radiation burst through their turret and vaporized them.

Josh didn't have time to scream as thermal radiation burned through the hull, killing his friends and melting the steel at his feet. The ELS suit burned. The reactive material flooded his system with pain killers while the ship's fire control systems vomited foam into the burning compartment, cooling it instantly and limiting the damage.

The price of *Seventeen*'s victory was high. No quarter of the ship was spared, not even the bridge.

Jacob held the chair tightly at the first sign of the explosion, but it all happened faster than his mind could keep track of. The overhead burned bright red as the ship's hull absorbed more thermal radiation than any ship was designed for. Consoles exploded, crew screamed, and death called. Once again, though, the Alliance protocol for draining the atmosphere from the ship saved more lives than were taken, as no fires erupted and no one was sucked out into space.

The starboard side crumpled in surrender, killing Spacer

First Class Felix Gouger sitting next to PO McCall. Lieutenant Owusu, his console, and his spacer assistant were crushed under the wreckage. PO Tefiti survived by the grace of God; as he regularly leaned over his console, his suit took the worst of the heat, burning black but holding. The overhead wreckage crashed into the console, trapping him.

Mark West didn't see the hull fragment that severed his legs, nor did he feel it. His suit instantly sealed the breaches and pumped him full of pain killers, knocking him unconscious.

While the port side was spared the collapsing superstructure, they were still hurt. Lieutenant Gabriel's chair broke free, slamming him into the overhead before he crashed against the deck, over half the bones in his body broken.

As *Seventeen* passed through the ferocious reactor detonation, the only two crew on the bridge unharmed were Captain Grimm and Chief Suresh.

———

Prince Henry marveled in awe at the destruction Captain Grimm had wrought on the enemy. A field of wreckage was all that remained around Aether. Any ship not destroyed when they turned on each other must have sustained enough damage and either fled or was pulled to the planet below and crushed in its gravitic depths.

"Comms, let them know we're coming to render aid as fast as possible."

Seventeen was still two hours away, and he cursed himself for not being able to arrive sooner.

CHAPTER FORTY-FIVE

ONE MONTH LATER.

J acob said goodbye to Lieutenant Gabriel, the last of the surviving crew he'd come to see at Naval Hospital Anchorage Bay located on Melinda Grimm Naval Base. He'd wanted to see PO Mendez, but the young man was in a medically induced coma and would be for at least another month. Lieutenant Brennan was there with him. She showed Jacob the ring; he was proud of the two for the way they conducted themselves. Josh's prognosis was good; he just needed much of his soft tissue regrown. A long and painful process.

Of the 1,052 crew that boarded *Seventeen*, only 607 had survived. Directly after the battle, his damage control did what they could, but *Seventeen* was ruined. All they could do was save as many lives as they could and wait for rescue. When the Iron Empire fleet had arrived, Jacob and the remaining crew had cheered.

Lieutenant Boudreaux, in her quick-thinking fashion, had launched the remaining Corsairs. Instead of searching for

First Class Felix Gouger sitting next to PO McCall. Lieutenant Owusu, his console, and his spacer assistant were crushed under the wreckage. PO Tefiti survived by the grace of God; as he regularly leaned over his console, his suit took the worst of the heat, burning black but holding. The overhead wreckage crashed into the console, trapping him.

Mark West didn't see the hull fragment that severed his legs, nor did he feel it. His suit instantly sealed the breaches and pumped him full of pain killers, knocking him unconscious.

While the port side was spared the collapsing superstructure, they were still hurt. Lieutenant Gabriel's chair broke free, slamming him into the overhead before he crashed against the deck, over half the bones in his body broken.

As *Seventeen* passed through the ferocious reactor detonation, the only two crew on the bridge unharmed were Captain Grimm and Chief Suresh.

―――――

Prince Henry marveled in awe at the destruction Captain Grimm had wrought on the enemy. A field of wreckage was all that remained around Aether. Any ship not destroyed when they turned on each other must have sustained enough damage and either fled or was pulled to the planet below and crushed in its gravitic depths.

"Comms, let them know we're coming to render aid as fast as possible."

Seventeen was still two hours away, and he cursed himself for not being able to arrive sooner.

CHAPTER FORTY-FIVE

ONE MONTH LATER.

Jacob said goodbye to Lieutenant Gabriel, the last of the surviving crew he'd come to see at Naval Hospital Anchorage Bay located on Melinda Grimm Naval Base. He'd wanted to see PO Mendez, but the young man was in a medically induced coma and would be for at least another month. Lieutenant Brennan was there with him. She showed Jacob the ring; he was proud of the two for the way they conducted themselves. Josh's prognosis was good; he just needed much of his soft tissue regrown. A long and painful process.

Of the 1,052 crew that boarded *Seventeen*, only 607 had survived. Directly after the battle, his damage control did what they could, but *Seventeen* was ruined. All they could do was save as many lives as they could and wait for rescue. When the Iron Empire fleet had arrived, Jacob and the remaining crew had cheered.

Lieutenant Boudreaux, in her quick-thinking fashion, had launched the remaining Corsairs. Instead of searching for spacers overboard, they used the dropships to scan the hull, looking for casualties that were easier to rescue from the outside.

Engineering fought the good fight for twenty-six hours, keeping the three reactors from going critical. More awards he needed to make sure happened. He'd written his after-action report and used painfully clear language in citing his decisions—why he made them, and how he alone was to blame for their failure.

When they finally returned to Alexandria, he'd spent the first week writing letters to family who'd lost their sons and daughters. Then the funerals started, so many they blurred into each other. No matter how exhausted he was, he'd gone to each one performed on Alexandria. The others, beyond the letters, he sent vids to the family with his deepest condolences.

No captain lost a battleship and was rewarded, especially not one who violated regulations by failing to alert fleet command of an enemy battle group in the system.

His ploy had worked, though, and Jacob couldn't help but feel a sense of career satisfaction at that. If *Seventeen* were to be his last command, he'd made her and his crew proud. Those that died would forever be remembered by those that survived. He would make sure of it.

Most of the more severely wounded were in orbit above in the hospital ship, *Hope*. The spies Jennings had captured had miraculously survived the engagement and were turned over to ONI the moment they'd made it back to Alexandria.

"Skipper, you ready to go?" Boudreaux asked.

"Viv, you don't have to call me skipper. I'm not a ship's captain anymore." He wasn't. His white uniform bore the emblem of naval fleet command, but not with a specific ship. Nor did he have the red cap of an active commander.

"Right, sir. I'm ready to go when you are."

Jacob climbed into the aircar, happy to have someone else drive. It was odd, having a lieutenant as his chauffeur, but she'd volunteered for the duty.

"Where to, Skipper?" she asked in her delightful accent.

"Until Admiral Villanueva returns from Zuckabar, I'm on—" he used his fingers to make air quotes—"leave. Not that I wanted to go on leave, mind you. Admiral McGregor of NAVPER made it clear he wouldn't allow me near a ship until the matter of the court-martial was cleared."

"I'm sorry about that, Skip. It's not fair. We won the battle, but you lost... more than most." Boudreaux gave him a sympathetic smile as she tiptoed around the topic.

"It's okay, Viv. Take me home."

"Aye, aye, sir. Buckle up."

Jacob did just that. He opened his NavPad to look at the letter he'd received upon arriving home. He'd read it, and reread it a dozen times.

Anchorage Bay Police Department
127 Harbor Lane

Dear Captain Jacob T. Grimm,

It is with the heaviest of hearts that I write to you today on behalf of the Anchorage Bay Police Department. I regret to inform you that your wife, Nadia Grimm, was involved in a tragic aircar accident on the evening of April 5th, along Coastal Route 17. The collision resulted in a fire that, tragically, burned her remains beyond recognition. However, through DNA analysis conducted by our forensic team, we have confirmed her identity with certainty.

In accordance with standard protocol and her known wishes, her remains have been respectfully transported to the Anchorage Bay Memorial Facility. We have ensured that every measure was taken to handle this process with the dignity and care she deserved.

I cannot begin to express how deeply sorry we are for your loss. Please know that our department stands ready to support you in any way we can during this unimaginable time. If there is anything you need—whether it be assistance with arrangements, a listening ear, or simply time to process —do not hesitate to reach out.

You have our sincerest condolences, Captain Grimm. May you find strength in the days ahead.

With deepest sympathy,
Captain Daniel R. Kessler
Anchorage Bay Police Department

He would be lying if he told anyone the letter hadn't crushed his heart.

Right up until Admiral DeBeck also offered his condolences but refused to talk about what Nadia had worked on while Jacob was away. He had very carefully *not* said she wasn't working for him.

Along with the news of his wife's death came the headlines that were on every station. The Terran Republic, the oldest government in the galaxy, one that spanned back to the exodus from Earth, had collapsed. Its economy was in shambles, and unable to maintain its bloated budget, it collapsed. In the five months since the first sign of trouble, a dozen coups had taken place. Worlds on the edge of Terran space were pleading with the Alliance for entry, or at least protectorate status.

A minor headline, and one Jacob instinctively knew involved Nadia, was the news that an Imperial military unit had attacked the Terran embassy on Alexandra—a clear violation of the treaty all three nations held. However, there was no more Terran Republic. Perhaps, thought Jacob, that was why the Imperial Navy had departed the system ahead of schedule. He doubted it, though. More likely they were concerned about more radical forces taking hold of old Earth and starting a war with the empire. The Terrans hated the Iron Empire. They'd started more than one war against them, and it didn't take a fortune teller to know they would start another.

Regardless, he wouldn't be involved in anything for at least a month. Possibly more. If NAVCOM wanted to go through with his court-martial for losing his ship, they would have to wait for Admiral Villanueva to return. It would still be another week before they received word, if any, of how the invasion she led had gone. Jacob could only hope and pray his navy would persevere.

For him, though, for the moment, the war was over and his duty on hold.

"We're here, Skip," Viv said.

"Seriously, Viv. I might be in uniform, but the moment I met with Admiral McGregor, I was relieved of duty. You can call me Jacob."

"That seems odd, Skipper."

Jacob shook his head. In her own way, she was as stubborn as Jennings. At least his Marines survived the battle. Even if they were scattered and reassigned.

"It's okay, Viv. Really. Thanks for the ride around town. I hope your next CO lets you fly."

"Sir, I can always find a way to fly. I just don't want to get saddled with a paper pusher."

The aircar settled down outside the ranch house. The barn

had a fresh coat of paint on it. A hover tractor was up on supports; the right-side engine panel was open, and his father was buried inside it, doing repairs.

"You take care." Jacob hefted his blue navy duffel from the backseat.

"You too... Skipper."

Jacob exited the car with a rueful grin. At least he was the only one the Navy would blame for the loss of the ship.

"Son," his father said without pulling his head out of the engine compartment.

Jacob dropped his head, almost laughing. His father's casual tone was as if he'd just seen him the day before.

"Dad," Jacob replied. He walked by, heading for the house.

"Jacob." His dad's head actually came out of the tractor.

He turned around to look at his dad.

"Maybe put your bags in your room."

"Okay..."

Jacob headed into the house, half sure of what he would find, fully terrified he was wrong. He tossed his bag on the floor and headed for his room, carrying his guitar in one hand while he discarded his cover and coat.

He opened his door—his heart pounded in relief.

She was lying on her side, her only arm supporting her head, wearing something Jacob was sure wouldn't be on her for much longer.

"Heya, stranger. You play that thing, or is it just to excite freighter skippers?"

CAPTAIN JACOB T. GRIMM will return in... THE LONGEST BATTLE

THANK YOU FOR READING GRIMM'S LEGACY

We hope you enjoyed it as much as we enjoyed bringing it to you. We just wanted to take a moment to encourage you to review the book. Follow this link: Grimm's Legacy to be directed to the book's Amazon product page to leave your review.

Every review helps further the author's reach and, ultimately, helps them continue writing fantastic books for us all to enjoy.

―――――

ALSO IN SERIES
AGAINST ALL ODDS
WITH GRIMM RESOLVE
ONE DECISIVE VICTORY
A GRIMM SACRIFICE
KNOW THY ENEMY
A GRIMM DECISION
TRADITIONS OF COURAGE
GRIMM'S LEGACY
THE LONGEST BATTLE

Calling all SciFi fans: be the first to discover groundbreaking new releases, access incredible deals, and participate in thrilling giveaways by subscribing to our exclusive SciFi Newsletter.
https://aethonbooks.com/scifi-newsletter/

Want to discuss our books with other readers and even the authors?

JOIN THE AETHON DISCORD!

Looking for more great Science Fiction and Fantasy?

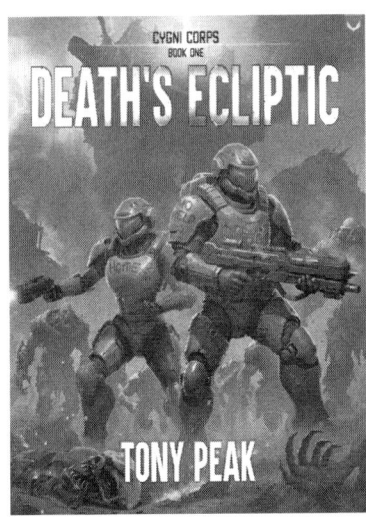

The fate of the colonies rests on the shoulders of this elite squad of outcasts. *Marco Morelli, a rookie marine private, botches his first op and gets transferred to the most rough-and-tumble outfit in the Merged Earth Colonies: Cygni Corps. Though the Corps is filled with the military's rejects, Marco soon learns it's also the testing ground for a new serum that will make him and his comrades the finest soldiers in the galaxy. He'll need it. Rebel groups have begun unleashing vicious mutants on defenseless worlds. And a more sinister force looms behind the attacks. As the conflict escalates, it's time to power up and roll out for the Cygni Corps.*

Get Death's Ecliptic Now!

War Is Coming... *A conflict of unimaginable scale threatens to end ten thousand years of Realm primacy. But not if the empire's top spymaster can prevent it. Jeryn Lorsi, the spymaster's young apprentice, is hardly ready for an operation of this importance. An ex-black marketeer turned spy, Jeryn's no hero. But when tragedy strikes the mission, that's exactly what he'll have to become.* ***The explosive first entry in a galaxy-spanning science fiction thrill ride by bestselling author D.L. Young! Grab your copy today!***

Get Jeryn's Dagger Now!

A new action-packed military science fiction series from award-winning author John J. Spearman. *A disgraced officer may be the key to winning the war.* Bad luck seems to follow Archer Devereaux like toilet paper stuck to his shoe. Even when he tries to do the right thing, he ends up in hot water—or behind bars. Hemmed in by circumstances beyond his control, his reputation, particularly among graduates of the Phlegraean Naval Academy, has become a mess. Fortunately, one of his superior officers knows that Devereaux is more than his mishaps. She sees that he's a clever young officer. Cool under fire. He also demonstrates remarkable resilience, looking for—and finding— ways to overcome adversity. It's a good thing too. As war has just broken out, and it'll take the Navy's finest to turn the tide. **Don't miss this new military sci-fi thrill ride from #1 Amazon bestselling author John J. Spearman. It's perfect for fans of Rick Partlow, David Weber, and Jeffery H. Haskell!**

Get Misfortune's Favorite Now!

For all our science fiction books, visit our website.

GRIMM'S LEGACY

AUTHOR'S NOTES

I'm getting a new website! www.jefferyhhaskell.com is still the address, but it will be updated with new information and new options, including the ability to order signed books, paperback and hardback. I also started a podcast with Rick Partlow, James Aaron, and Josh Hayes. It's the Military Science Fiction Podcast on Youtube and other podcast places.

If you like Grimm's War, please share it with a friend or family member. There are a lot of options for reading and listening to it. Your local library can order audio books and even a paperback if you ask them too. As always, thank you for spending your hard-earned money, and precious time, reading my flights of fancy. You're what makes Grimm's War the success it is.

All the best,

GLOSSARY

ATG – Air to Ground. Usually refers to ordnances like missiles, bombs, and rockets.

DesRon – Destroyer Squadron. Usually comprising 3-5 destroyers. Multiple DesRons could be combined to form a flotilla.

SECNAV – Secretary of the Navy. The civilian leadership of the Navy.

ONI – Office of Naval Intelligence. The primary intelligence resource for the navy. They engage in espionage and counterespionage.

OpSec – Operational Security. It refers to keeping operations private. Loose lips sink ships.

DNI – Department of National Intelligence. The agency responsible for domestic defense against espionage.

ASAP or ASAFP – Military acronym meaning As Soon As Possible. You can guess what the F stands for.

CP – Command Post

MarPad – The Marine equivalent of the NavPad. Each one is keyed to a specific user and has all the functionality a device could possibly need.

NavPad – The Navy's all-purpose digital device for E-4's and above.

MP-17 – standard sidearm aboard Navy ships. The Marine variant comes equipped with an extended nanite reserve, allowing multiple functionalities.

XO – Executive or First officer.

MK XII Torpedo – (Pronounced Mark Twelve) Standard Alliance munitions. Armed with tungsten balls that are super accelerated with explosive force.

MK XIV Torpedo – State-of-the-art ECM torpedo capable of blinding or fooling an enemy ship for a few minutes.

ECM – Electronic Counter Measures

EW – Electronic Warfare

IFF – Identify Friend or Foe. Ships (and vehicles) generally carry a transponder (if they're not pirates) that is switched on to prevent friendly fire.

ELS – Emergency Life Support

LRRP – Long-Range Reconnaissance Patrol

BDA – Battle Damage Assessment

FOB – Forward Operating Base

M-21A2 – Coil rifle for ground-based infantry

RWR – Radar Warning Receiver

R/LWR – Radar/Lidar Warning Receiver

RP – Romeo Papa or Rally Point

QRF - Quick Reaction Force

SOTA – State-of-the-Art

FUBAR – Fouled up beyond all repair

C&C – Command and Control

Triple A or AAA – Anti-Aircraft Artillery

MAR – Minimum Abort Range

GPLD – Giga Pulse Laser Defense

ABOUT THE AUTHOR

Join Jeffery on his mailing list to receive the latest information about his writing. Find his other books on Amazon.com under Jeffery H. Haskell.

He occasionally sends out free stories, art, and other updates.

https://goo.gl/LJdYDn

Or via his website @ Jefferyhhaskell.com

https://x.com/jeffery_haskellJeffery.haskell@gmail.com

Join other fans...

Haskell's Heroes | Facebook